Other Books by
Linda Nagata

Mythic Island Press LLC
www.MythicIslandPress.com

THE LAST
GOOD MAN

LINDA NAGATA

Mythic Island Press LLC
Kula, HI

The Last Good Man

Copyright © 2017 by Linda Nagata

First edition: June 2017

ISBN 978-1-937197-22-3

Cover art copyright © 2017 by Philippe McNally

Mythic Island Press LLC
P.O. Box 1293
Kula, HI 96790-1293
MythicIslandPress.com

THE LAST GOOD MAN

THE BUSINESS OF WAR

"WE TOLD HER not to go. It was too dangerous. She told us it would be all right. There would be security."

The gray-haired gentleman speaks in quiet syllables, each chiseled by the emotions he holds in check as he explains the circumstances that have brought him to Requisite Operations Incorporated, a private military company headquartered in Thurston County, south of Seattle. In a conference room elegantly appointed in dark-brown fabrics and hardwood surfaces, he recounts all that has gone wrong.

"The so-called security was a joke. Only six armed guards, none with adequate training, all murdered in minutes and now she's their captive. They've made her speak their propaganda. They've put her under the veil, but it's her. They don't reveal her name, but it's her voice, her eyes on the videos. My daughter, my precious Fatima. My only daughter."

True Brighton, ReqOps' forty-nine-year-old Director of Operations, sits at the end of the conference room's oval table, an observer, positioned on the periphery of this conversation, there to evaluate the suitability of the proposed project and of Mr. Yusri Atwan as a potential client.

She is struck by Yusri's calm, reserved manner. He is striving mightily to present himself as a rational man, a man Requisite Operations can work with. A determined man who understands the realities of the world. For all that, he cannot hide the fact that he is also a desperate man.

True notes the slight tremor in his hands as he opens a folder he earlier placed on the table. He turns the folder around, slides it across the table's short axis to Lincoln Han. "This is my daughter," he says quietly.

Lincoln is the principal owner and Chief Executive Officer of Requisite Operations. He is conducting this interview. He reaches for the folder with his prosthetic left hand, articulated fingers curling as he drags the folder closer. The hand does not try to hide its technological nature. No flesh tones. It's made instead of a semi-translucent, smoky gray plastic that reveals the embedded electronics as glints and shadows. Soft pads at the fingertips allow him to grip the corner of the folder, lift it. True sees a printed photo inside—a smiling dark-haired young woman. Lincoln studies her image while Yusri continues.

"I've been to the State Department," he says. "I've seen my congressional representative, my senator. They all tell me they're doing what they can, but they're doing *nothing*. It's been four months. I would pay a ransom if I could. If I knew how."

Lincoln uses his artificial fingers to slide the photograph over to True. He is forty years old. An army veteran, he lost his hand in a helicopter crash that ended his career and nearly took his life. That was five years ago.

True still wonders: If she'd been his pilot that day, would things have been different?

She flew for him for years on clandestine missions, but she was home, working as an army flight instructor, when his helicopter went down. The ensuing fire left his face a scarred, immobile mask, worse on the left side. His nose and his left ear are prosthetics. His left eye is a bionic device that translates gray-scale visual input to his brain, extending his peripheral vision and improving his depth perception. The eye has a black iris darker and larger than his natural eye. The imbalance, combined with his scars, a flattop haircut, and arms sheathed in colorful tattoos, gives him a slightly maniacal aura despite the counterbalance of his casual civilian clothing—a tan ReqOps polo shirt and brown slacks.

Lincoln returns his gaze to Yusri and says in a soft rasp, the result of more scarring in his larynx, "The United States government does not pay ransoms, Mr. Atwan. Ransoms only encourage more kidnappings. As a military contractor licensed to work with the federal government, Requisite Operations is required to abide by that policy. So we cannot help you pay a ransom."

Yusri's voice grows plaintive. "She is not political. She only wanted to help people, to do some good in the world."

"I understand that, sir."

True confronts the photo of Fatima Atwan. A bright-eyed young woman, the prime years of her life still ahead.

Yusri's reserve slips. "She doesn't deserve this!"

True looks up to see tears shining in his eyes.

Yusri Atwan is a Seattle native. He owns a small but prosperous company that manufactures chemical sensors. His daughter, Fatima, is a young medical doctor and an idealist, dedicated to helping those less fortunate than herself. She committed to a year of overseas service with a charitable foundation. And her father is right: She doesn't deserve what happened to her. But then, most people overrun by the firestorms of chaos and anarchy don't deserve their fates.

It takes Yusri only seconds to recover his composure, and when he speaks again to Lincoln, it's in a hard, determined voice. "I've talked to people, Mr. Han. They say you, your company, can help when no one else can. I understand it costs money. I can pay. I can get six hundred thousand dollars in cash within two business days. It's all I have and I know it's not enough, but she's with El-Hashem."

As these words pass his lips, Yusri's face flushes dark. He looks away; he looks at the wall. True watches him intently, sure that he is contemplating what that fact means for his daughter. Is there anything worse than knowing the brutality your child endures and being helpless to affect it? *No*, she thinks. *There is not.* Breathing softly, shallowly, she schools herself to stay focused.

Hussam El-Hashem has styled himself a holy warrior, head of the Al-Furat Coalition, but in truth he is nothing more than a gangster grown wealthy on protection money and kidnapping-and-ransom schemes. There are men like him all over the world, bereft of conscience and willing to commit atrocities in the name of any convenient cause.

There is no shame but only lethal anger in Yusri's voice when he speaks aloud the blunt truth of his daughter's plight: "El-Hashem beats her, he rapes her, he calls her his wife."

The ceiling light sparks in Lincoln's artificial eye as he leans forward. He knows the sort of information this frustrated father should have access to, because prior to this interview he commissioned a preliminary report on Fatima Atwan. Nothing in that report indicated Hussam regarded her as a wife. "How do you know this, Mr. Atwan?"

Yusri's gaze settles again on Lincoln's scarred face. He does not flinch from it. "Another hostage, an Italian. She was ransomed a few days ago. She called me. She begged me to act, to do all that I could." His passion is easily read in the set of his jaw, in the tension of his brow, but despite it, his voice holds only the slightest tremor as he plays what he must consider to be his strongest card: "The United States government and the Iraqi government together have offered a two-million-dollar bounty for Hussam El-Hashem. I will pay you six hundred thousand dollars now. And when you go to rescue my Fatima, you will also kill El-Hashem and take his head and earn two million dollars more. I am begging you, Mr. Han. I am begging you to do this. For Fatima. For her mother. For me. She is my pride and joy and I am begging you to bring her home."

True remains in the conference room, contemplating the portrait of Fatima, while Lincoln escorts Yusri across the hall. She listens for the click and soft buzz of the electronic locks on the security door that opens onto the lobby. When the locks buzz a second time, she knows the door has closed again and that Yusri is on the other side.

She stands to her full five-eight height, stretching lean muscles stiff from yesterday's workout. Despite her age, she maintains an athletic figure—and dresses to emphasize the fact. Being the oldest among a staff of physically fit veterans, she knows it's not just a matter of maintaining her strength and conditioning, but also of preserving their confidence in her abilities. Today she wears a scoop-necked, cinnamon-brown microfiber T-shirt that shows off the muscle definition in her shoulders, her neck, and her arms, along with form-fitting slacks in a lighter shade.

At the same time, she doesn't deny her age. She has never bothered with cosmetic surgery, and so far, she is letting her thick hair follow its natural transformation so that its dark brown has become mixed with lines and highlights of silver and gray. She wears her hair confined in a short French braid.

"Hello, Friday," she says, addressing the house AI. "Let me see Mr. Yusri Atwan."

A wall monitor at the opposite end of the room wakes up with high-definition video from a lobby security camera. It shows Lincoln, still fit and strong despite his injuries, escorting the taller Yusri past the glass exhibit cases in the lobby. Lincoln is saying, "We'll be in touch, sir. We'll let you know our decision."

Yusri nods. "Whatever you need me to do," he says, "I will do."

They shake hands. Then Yusri exits past glass doors, crossing the front terrace with a determined, almost angry gait. But at the parking lot's edge he hesitates. He looks back, his expression quietly desperate. Weighing the value of returning, of pressing his case? But he goes to his car instead, a sleek silver Lumina Zus. He doesn't notice the glint of a tiny camera lens, part of a low-profile tracking and surveillance device tucked against the black glass and rubberized lining at the top of the windshield. Prior to his meeting with Lincoln, Yusri agreed to background checks, although ReqOps did not specify the nature of those inquiries.

True looks around as Chris Kobeck, ReqOps' Director of Military Operations and Training, comes into the conference room. Chris is thirty-nine—ten years younger than True—a former Special Forces operator who served under Lincoln's command in the clandestine unit known as Rogue Lightning. True's oldest son was once part of that unit too, eight years ago now.

Chris had been watching the meeting, evaluating the client. As True returns her gaze to the monitor, she asks him, "What'd you think?"

"Good people," he tells her.

On the other side of the half-full parking lot is a high masonry wall, with three tall maples standing sentinel beyond it. Their leaves, yellowed by autumn, flutter through the air and skitter on a breeze across the concrete as Yusri gets into his car, secures his seat belt, and drives slowly toward the automated security gate.

"Good people, but naïve," Chris amends as he claims a chair and sits. "I hope there's something left of her when we pull her out."

True turns a skeptical gaze on him. Threads of gray are starting to show in his thick black hair, and still, his fine-featured Caucasian face relies on heavy eyebrows and a neat goatee to bring it some maturity. "*When* we pull her out?" she asks.

"Give it up, True. I know you can't wait to do this, and Lincoln's not going to be able to say no."

She gives him a dark look. Never mind that he's right. "It has to pencil out," she insists, sitting down again. "It'll cost at least ten K, probably more, just to determine if an action is possible."

"Pittance," he scoffs. "Lincoln won't blink at that."

This draws a smile from her—and reluctant agreement. "Not in these circumstances, anyway."

Mostly, Lincoln is a hard-headed businessman. He founded Requisite Operations on the back of a $500,000 VA loan, and only four years later the company is valued at twenty-five million dollars. But despite his pragmatism, Lincoln possesses a penchant for dangerous idealism. It's a trait she admires. It keeps her job interesting.

She hears the electronic locks on the security door cycle, feels the slight change of pressure as it opens—and resists a rush of anticipation.

"Get ready for it," Chris says with an expectant smile.

Lincoln appears at the door. "I like it," he announces immediately in his growling voice. "I want to look further into it, confirm the situation, the current circumstances."

True assumes the role of devil's advocate: "The State Department might already be planning something. I'll check into that. We need to know we've got an open field before we commit too many resources."

"Do it," Lincoln agrees, returning to the seat he inhabited before. "But while we're waiting for confirmation, we move ahead with our investigation." He looks from Chris to True. "If it comes to it, are you both willing?"

Chris speaks first. "If the setup looks right."

"True?"

"Yes," she says without hesitation. "It would be a privilege to bring down Hussam El-Hashem."

"Good." Lincoln rests his elbows on the table. He weaves his fingers together, articulated machine digits and jointed flesh. "This is how we're going to handle it. We'll do an initial assessment on our own dime. No fee to Atwan. If the mission looks like a go, we bill him two hundred thousand. That way he's got skin in the game and doesn't feel like a charity case."

"You're okay with just two hundred?" Chris asks. "If we don't get Hussam—"

"Fuck Hussam. If we get him, we get a two-million-dollar bonus. Yay, hooray. But we're after Fatima Atwan. *She* is our mission goal. The way I see it? We make a hell of a profit from the business of war. We can afford to do the occasional pro bono. So get started on the intel. I want a go/no-go within three days."

MERCENARY

LINCOLN STARES INTO the cool blue eyes of his sparring partner as they commence another round. Renata Ballard is tall, fast, aggressive. She moves first, opening with a headshot that he blocks with his left forearm. He's careful to take the impact high on his forearm, but he still feels a stab of pain at the junction with his prosthetic hand. He ignores it and, using the same arm, he blocks a second strike, this one aimed at his solar plexus. He sweeps her arm away while stepping in, stepping close.

She tries to evade but he gets his arms around her in a bear hug. His right hand locks high on his left forearm to hold her. She locks her arms around him too, tries to take his foot out from under him, but this time he's faster. He leans back, lifts, lofts her off the ground. He twists at the same time. She holds on tight, not letting any space open up between them.

He drops to his knees, dropping her hard on the mat. She doesn't yield her grip at all—and he doesn't get his left arm clear in time. Her weight comes down on top of the junction between his flesh and his prosthetic hand.

"*Aw, fuck!*" he swears, grimacing as his arm ignites in white-hot wires of pain that shoot past his elbow to curl around his shoulder.

He pulls back, biting down against a howl that wants to escape the cage of his clenched teeth.

Renata rolls clear, coming up on her knees with an annoyed scowl. "Did you break it again?" she asks.

He's on his knees too, left wrist pressed against his belly. Sweat runs down his cheeks, his chest, gliding past his scars.

Focus.

Four deep calming breaths.

As the pain subsides, he's able to raise the hand. The bony mechanical fingers are trembling in response to his shocked nerves. He decides this is a good sign. At least they're still connected.

He experiments, moving each finger, tapping them against the thumb in a pattern he learned during physical therapy. "Not broken," he concludes.

Renata rises to her feet. "Come on, boss," she says in disgust. "This is why no one else will spar with you. You know you can't play that hard anymore."

"Yeah. Sorry."

His physical therapist had explained it bluntly: *You have fine motor control and even a limited sense of touch because, through its socket, the hand is wired into your truncated peripheral nerves. But if you stress the junction, it's going to hurt like hell. The pain's a signal to tell you to back off. To be careful. Because the prosthetic is not nearly as rugged as your natural hand.*

Truth.

He's broken the hand twice already.

He tells Renata, "Next time, I'll take the hand off. Cap the end to protect it."

"I've heard that before." She glares down at him, hands on her hips, pale cheeks flushed, eyes bright, blond hair escaping from her ponytail. Her gi is pulled open to reveal a flat belly and full breasts corralled by a lavender sports bra, white skin shining with sweat.

And it hits him again: *God, she is a beautiful woman.*

Early in her tenure as Director of Air Operations at ReqOps they'd twice spent the night together, curiosity on both sides, but she was a free spirit and he needed fidelity.

Just a brief liaison, but still a mistake.

He gets up. She straightens her gi and they bow to one another.

He asks, "You got time this afternoon to sit down and go over your flight schedule?"

"Fourteen hundred?" she suggests.

"That'll work." He tells her about Fatima Atwan and the bounty on Hussam El-Hashem.

This makes her smile. "Ooh, nice mission. I like everything about it. Action instead of flying another tedious escort job. And a damsel in distress. And *money*."

"Mercenary," he accuses.

A bold smile, a flash of white teeth. "All of us together," she agrees.

He offers no argument. ReqOps provides services that include intelligence acquisition and assessment, regional reports, personal security, equipment leasing, and specialized training of US military, foreign military, and law enforcement personnel—in security, assault, targeting, interrogation, evasion, surveillance, and negotiation. Offensive missions are the least of what they do, but as a PMC—a private military company—they are still mercenaries by most people's definition, no matter how carefully they select their jobs and vet their clients.

Lincoln doesn't like the term. It carries too much historical scar tissue. But Renata happily wears the label. She's a pirate at heart. A top fighter pilot, she's cool and efficient, but most of all, guilt doesn't stick to her.

Or maybe there's just nothing she'd undo.

Lincoln wishes he could make that claim, but during his clandestine service he was asked more than once to do dirty work—someone had to do it—and he's made some poor choices too. No setting things right after the fact. What you do, you own. What you witness, you get to live with.

As a counterbalance, he tries to run ReqOps on a philosophy of "right action"—a principle of ethical service that encompasses power and responsibility and an obligation to act at need, and to do so in the best manner possible.

Renata gives him a half-assed salute like she knows what he's thinking. "Make this happen, boss," she says. "I want to be in competition again, even if it's only virtual."

"I'll do what I can."

They part, heading for separate showers.

With hot water sluicing over him, he tests the hand again. It's amazingly dexterous. A biomechanical miracle of engineering, but it's weak. It's not good enough to get him back in the field. And for that, he hates the damn thing.

EMBRACING THE ENEMY

TRUE STANDS IN the middle of a great enclosed space within ReqOps' Robotics Center, her arms crossed, eyes narrowed in an impatient expression, watching—from a distance—the final preparations for a robot brawl.

The Robotics Center is housed in a two-story, dusky-green warehouse. A third of the building is subdivided into offices, lab space, and a 3-D printing facility, but the majority of the interior is open, uncluttered space, suitable for small-scale aerial battles or the testing of ground-to-air defenses. Curtains and inflatable barriers simulate more complex environments and to test navigational algorithms, but none are in use today.

Aside from True, the room contains a few pallets of supplies arranged in a neat line outside the printing facility, and two cluttered workbenches alongside the pallets. The engineering team is also present. It's made up of Tamara Thomas, Director of Software and Engineering, and her two young assistants, Michelle and Naomi. All three are busy loading lead weights into the ammunition rack of an experimental mini ARV—an armed robotic vehicle—to simulate the mass of live rounds.

"Just in time," Tamara declared when True first walked in. "You can be the enemy. Take a gun and go stand on the red X."

True had helped develop the specs for the new ARV—unofficially known as "Roach"—and she was eager to see the test. She wanted to know how fast and how smoothly it could deploy. But today she was here for a different purpose and time was short. She told Tamara, "It can wait. We've got a priority task. I need to set up multiple surveillance operations in the TEZ. A manhunt—"

She broke off when Naomi caught her eye. From behind Tamara, Naomi was holding up an open hand and mouthing the words *five minutes*.

True scowled at the request, but realistically, five minutes wasn't going to matter—and she really did want to see what Roach could do. So she took a battered Fortuna assault rifle from the workbench, one that had been rigged to shoot harmless laser pulses instead of bullets, and walked to the red X, where she now stands, waiting to learn if she will live or die in a mock battle involving allied helicopter drones, pitted against the mini ARV.

Tamara moves away from the workbench. She is a few years younger than True, but fitness is not her passion, and middle age has given a sturdy substance to her full figure. Freckles dot a dark-brown complexion that contrasts with the light hazel eyes peering over the frame of her reading glasses. Steel-gray coils are infiltrating the black of her tightly curled hair. Today, like most days, she's dressed in industrial colors: a simple charcoal blouse over gray slacks.

She watches as Michelle and Naomi—both young, not even thirty—lift the ARV, moving it to an empty pallet. Folded into transport mode, Roach is a rectangular gray lozenge, compact enough to be carried on a pack frame. Fully loaded with ammunition, it weighs around ninety pounds.

Chains attach the pallet to a winch, which begins to hum, lifting Roach into the air. The ARV is engineered for hard entry: tough enough to be heaved, pushed, or dropped inside an enemy compound, where it will deploy, autonomously distinguishing and removing threats before the entry of assault troops.

The pallet is hauled up twenty feet. The winch slides horizontally until the pallet is over the open floor. Michelle and Naomi walk out on the floor, bright-eyed and excited as they flank True, less than a meter away. Roach will need to distinguish them as unarmed civilians and leave them unharmed. Michelle says, "It's going to be a surprise attack."

She's right. With no word of warning, Tamara triggers the pallet to tip, dropping the folded ARV. It hits the concrete floor with a dull thud that True can feel through her boots.

At the same time, True's two mechanical allies drop from the ceiling. They're starburst helicopter drones, a meter in diameter, made of eight adjustable booms radiating from a central pod. The low-noise rotors at the end of each boom are powered by electric motors. Starburst copters are fast, and agile enough to compensate for recoil from the rifle barrel mounted at the base of the pod, but they can only carry about fifty rounds, so their best use is in facility defense where they can be kept ready to launch against individual intruders, or as the first wave of a stealth assault backed up by human soldiers.

Today, they're playing a defensive role. Under the autonomous control of an onboard AI, they swoop toward the intruder as it tumbles across the floor, firing bursts of green laser light to simulate bullets.

True joins in the defense. Bringing the rifle to her shoulder, she tracks the ARV's erratic motion and shoots, each trigger pull releasing a pulse of laser light. Sensors around the room score the hits. An artificial voice speed talks in a machine-gun burst of syllables as it reports damage on a one-to-ten scale: "*zero zero one one two one zero...*"

Every hit produces only minimal damage to Roach, while in actual combat, both ricochet and the kinetic force of the tumbling ARV are going to be serious hazards for civilian bystanders. This thought is evidently shared by Naomi, who backs rapidly away.

True holds her ground, and after Roach rolls over one more time, it unfolds. Six stout jointed legs snap out, abruptly arresting its motion. A 5.56 mm belt-fed machine gun rises on a swivel mount. A horizontal disc, smaller than True's palm, sits on top of the gun. True targets the tiny lenses glittering around the disc's periphery, glimpsing the reflected flash of green laser light—but the ARV's targeting system has already responded. Roach doesn't have to reposition itself; it doesn't even take a step. In less than a second, its gun snaps up, down, over—firing three times, targeting the starburst copters first and then True. She sees the red flash of the enemy's laser, and then Tamara calls out in triumph, "You're dead!"

The copters retreat to their ceiling lairs while Roach scuttles back to the workbench, moving with startling speed, in a manner disturbingly reminiscent of its namesake.

The entire battle has taken less than six seconds.

"Come on," True objects as she too, returns to the bench. "I hit Roach's targeting lenses. They should have been modeled as broken. How—"

Tamara waves a dismissive hand. "Multiple lenses. The damage was recorded but it didn't matter. You were killed, the copters were fatally disabled, and none of the civilians were hit."

True scowls at the ARV, watching as it folds up again into an innocuous gray lozenge. Roach worked well. That should be a cause for celebration, but still, it's annoying to be so easily beaten by a machine. "If I had a grenade launcher, the result would have been different."

"If you had a grenade launcher, you would have blown up your buddies in the compound, which, aside from the theoretical civilian losses, would have been an acceptable result too."

Robotics are an integral part of Requisite Operations' activities. Devices in inventory range in size from mosquito drones to jet-powered UAVs, and in cost from a few dollars to millions. Most are unarmed, used for surveillance, tracking, communications, or transportation—and many are off-the-shelf products, bought on the commercial market.

But ReqOps has a homegrown inventory too, one that True has contributed to. Like Tamara, she's interested in so-called "biomimetics"—devices designed for autonomous and semiautonomous operation, many of them small-scale, that mimic traits of biological life-forms. The insect-legged ARV is only the most recent, and one of the deadlier, examples. Several are based on insects or other arthropods, a few draw on traits of birds, one takes the form of a snake. Many are cheap to print and easy to assemble. True calls them the origami army; she carries a selection with her whenever she deploys, versatile tools that she can adapt to changing situations.

She thinks of it as embracing the enemy. Like most career military personnel, she's ambivalent about the rapid evolution and adaptation of robotic systems. Her decision to retire from the army was made as autonomous helicopters were steadily replacing piloted aircraft. And it wasn't just the helicopter pilots feeling the pressure. Ships, planes, tanks, missiles—all were being retrofitted to run under the control of remote pilots or of artificial intelligences.

It isn't hard for her to imagine a future in which programmers set up battles conducted between machine armies without immediate oversight, not a single soldier on the field—though vulnerable civilians will still be there. Or a future in which a narcissistic leader orders a machine invasion of a weaker nation, with no risk of creating grieving parents on the home front. Or one in which a military option in the form of a PMC powered by robotics is available to anyone with the money.

These are scenarios that offend her martial heritage. She imagines the consternation of bow masters when guns first appeared on battlefields. Like those bow masters, she has adapted.

Technology changes.

War is eternal.

Tamara pours coffee, hands a mug to True, then sits behind a desk cluttered with tiny sensors, wires, circuit boards, and insect limbs made of steel and plastic. She asks, "So what's the new task?"

"We want to find Hussam El-Hashem."

Tamara's eyebrows rise. "The Al-Furat Coalition, right?"

"That's our bad guy."

"Bold," Tamara says, nodding in approval.

True continues, "Our initial assumption is that he's somewhere in the ungoverned territories of the TEZ. It's possible the State Department already has him in their sights, so I've submitted an inquiry on current operations and potential closed areas. In the meantime, we initiate our own search. I've opened a research contract. The team will be looking at news, social media, curated databases, but that's a long shot. Our best hope's going to be on the ground, so I'm developing contracts for three freelance operators in the area, intelligence specialists. If we get any decent leads, I want to be able to supply them with printer files for data collection devices."

"You're assuming they'll have access to secure printer facilities," Tamara says. "My suggestion is we do the printing in Tel Aviv. Fly in the finished devices."

"That'll extend the time horizon significantly, and time's a factor."

Tamara sticks out her lower lip, considering. Then she says, "I'll investigate regional alternatives, but I do not want to send our manufacturing patterns to pirate facilities."

"Understood." True sips her coffee, then looks at Tamara with a wistful half smile. "We need to find him, Tamara. We need to make this work."

Tamara laughs. "Look at you. You can't wait, can you? Come on, True. Didn't anyone ever tell you this is serious work?"

True's smile fades. She finishes her coffee. "It's a hostage rescue," she explains. "El-Hashem is a secondary target."

"Ah, I see." Tamara is somber now. She takes a few seconds to reevaluate both True and the context of this mission. Then she promises, "We'll make it work."

True stands, ready to leave.

"Oh, hey," Tamara says, perking up again. "I saw Li Guiying copied you on that video she sent."

True feels a prickle of irritation. Li Guiying is a specialist in behavioral algorithms, with many positive contributions to robotics, from agricultural applications to search and rescue swarms. True met her by chance, several years ago at a seminar in London, and Guiying has striven ever since to maintain the connection. True isn't sure why and she isn't looking to be friends. She finds Guiying too cloying, too precious, too persistent. She's deliberately kept her distance. But Tamara likes her; they are colleagues.

"Did you look at it?" Tamara asks.

"I did. Flight algorithms." And then True adds, grudgingly, "It was nice work."

"Don't be stingy. It was *really* nice work."

"I'm sure you could do better if we didn't keep you busy blowing shit up."

Tamara laughs, and waves True out the door. "Go on. I'll do my research and I'll make sure we've got an inventory on hand."

Requisite Operations is situated on a thirty-acre campus hidden by a screen of trees and guarded by a tall chain-link fence. Besides the Robotics Center, it includes indoor and outdoor shooting ranges, running trails, climbing walls, a track, a gym, a weight room, an urban-combat training ground, and, of course, headquarters—a single-story building with a central lobby anchoring two long, curving wings.

True is returning to her office in the north wing, walking swiftly on a concrete path under lowering clouds, when her TINSL chimes an alert. Pronounced "tinsel," the acronym stands for Team Integrated Speech Link—a featherweight adaptive earpiece with a delicate boom microphone. TINSLs are designed to be worn nearly continuously and can integrate with a spectrum of registered devices, or conference in a team setting.

A synthesized feminine voice follows the chime. It's Ripley, True's digital assistant. "Connor Delgado is calling," Ripley says.

True smiles. "Take the call." Another chime sounds, a different note on a musical scale, this one to acknowledge her request. "Hey, love," she says.

Connor is twenty-one, in his last year of college, and living with his grandparents—True's parents—at their home outside Washington DC while he goes to school. Connor talks animatedly, amusing True with his description of a visit from his sister, two years older and now Second Lieutenant Treasure Delgado. "She's golden," Connor concludes. "Grandpa couldn't stop with the compliments and the good advice, and she couldn't stop rolling her eyes. By the time she left, Grandpa had mapped out her entire career for her."

True laughs. "He's just grateful to finally have another officer in the family. At least one of us did it right."

An army officer. In the opinion of True's father, Colonel Colton Brighton, retired, *that* is the proper occupation for a Brighton, or for the descendants of a Brighton, his grandchildren being technically Delgados. For Colt Brighton, these things matter. Brightons have served in the United States Army—officer or enlisted—every generation since the American Revolution. Served and sometimes died.

A sharp edge intrudes on Connor's voice as he says, "I don't get it, Mom. Diego's portrait is right up there on the wall when Grandpa tells his stories about the glory of combat."

Memories are physical things. It's been eight years since True's oldest son was killed in action, but she still feels Diego's absence as a powerful tide of shadow around her heart. "The old man remembers him, Connor. He remembers everyone he's lost. It's just how he handles it. He needs to know it means something."

"Does it?" Connor asks.

True lets this question slide, though she wonders what future generations will think of past sacrifice when soldiers are no longer present on the battlefield but instead are operating mechanical avatars from secure posts thousands of miles away.

For Treasure and Connor, Diego's death was a transformative event, though they responded in opposite ways. Treasure resolved to follow her older brother into military service, while Connor will always remain a civilian. "You've got your own path," True likes to remind him. "You're doing well, and we're all proud of you."

When Colt encouraged his grandson to attend college in the DC area, citing all the opportunities and offering him a place to stay, True knew—Connor knew—*everyone* knew the long-term goal was to persuade his grandson to take up the family profession.

But Connor has fended off the pressure with the calm determination of an old soul.

Let the old man try to break Connor's resolve. That's True's opinion. Colonel Colt Brighton will break himself first against that unyielding citadel—and he deserves it.

RUMORS

KHALID NAIM IS in Ramadi. It's 9 PM local time. He is leaning against his taxi cab, waiting with other drivers outside a crowded lecture hall where a political meeting is nearing its end, when his phone chimes in a tone that announces the arrival of a fading text.

Speaking in Arabic, he demands, "Meen?" *Who?*

The synthesized voice of his digital assistant answers through his TINSL. It's a private voice only he can hear, and it speaks in American-accented English: "Chris Kobeck, Director of Military Operations and Training, Requisite Operations."

Khalid's excitement spikes. "Iqra," he orders—*Read it.*

He is one of the few taxi drivers in the TEZ willing to transport passengers beyond Ramadi, through the ungoverned territories of the Tigris-Euphrates Zone. He is also a US Army veteran, working now as an independent intelligence contractor.

He listens eagerly as his digital assistant reads the content of the message: "I've got a short-term contract I want you to fill. Starts immediately. Stealth manhunt. We're looking for a bad guy. Call me when you can."

"*Shit*," Khalid whispers, disappointed and a little angry to learn this is just another small job. He's been talking with Chris about a permanent position, so he was hoping for more.

Still, it's an opportunity.

He looks at the lecture hall. The door is still closed. It'll probably be a few more minutes before the meeting ends. Time enough to talk to Chris, get more details on the assignment. He gets inside the cab, windows up for privacy, and puts a call through.

Chris picks up right away.

"Hey," Khalid says, "you know I want to come home."

"I know it, but we've got a task that we need to jump on right away. You ready to hear it?"

"Yeah, go ahead."

"We want to hire you on a contract basis for a minimum of five days. You run your fares between towns and villages in the ungoverned territories just like normal, but on the way I want you to listen for rumors and gossip about the movements of warlords: who they are, where they are, how long they've been in residence. I'll get you some stealthed data collection equipment. If you locate a potential target, you deploy it. No worries about picking it up again. It's just gone."

"Data goes direct to you?" Khalid asks.

"Correct. It'll verify identities, let us know if we've found our target."

Khalid will be one of three contractors searching the region. Chris will oversee their movements and do what he can to keep their paths from crossing.

He considers this and ponders the assignment's potential danger. "You don't want to tell me who you're after?" he asks, bothered that Chris hasn't entrusted him with a name.

"I can't tell you. Not yet. But if we find him, I'm going to need your organizational skills for phase two."

"Three of us are going to be out there looking. What if I'm not the one who finds him?"

"Doesn't matter. You've got the skills and the contacts we need."

Still, Khalid hesitates. Something feels off. He reviews in his mind the bounties presently on offer. He is sure none are large enough to tempt a thriving company like Requisite Operations to risk a mission in the volatile TEZ. There is more to this.

"You're not just going after a bounty, are you?" he asks. "Have you been hired to do a hostage rescue?"

Chris grunts. Not exactly a confirmation. "You in?" he asks.

Khalid is sure his performance on this assignment will have a direct impact on his employment prospects. He looks out at his fellow taxi drivers standing about, faces lit by phone screens or the embers of cigarettes. He's spent two years in their company and he's learned a hell of a lot, but it's time to move on.

He tells Chris: "I'm in."

A MATTER OF TIME

MILES DUSHANE SITS on a dusty floor rough with grit, his back to the outside wall of a little second-floor room walled and floored and roofed in concrete. The place must have been meant as a storeroom, but for the past few days it's served as his prison cell. The closed door is locked with a deadbolt and there is no real window, just a horizontal opening to the outside, tucked under the roofline. It's screened with a heavy mesh cemented in place to keep the rats out, and it's too narrow to squeeze through anyway. The mesh admits just enough dusty air to keep the room's four inhabitants alive.

His three companions might still make it home if ransoms can be arranged, but Americans don't ransom hostages, so Miles knows he won't be getting out that way. His value is as propaganda, and only then if his captor, Hussam El-Hashem, devises a particularly spectacular death for him, one aimed at enforcing the bloody reputation of his Al-Furat Coalition. It's been many years since a simple execution could command any media attention. So while no one's been crucified yet, Miles Dushane considers it only a matter of time.

Gray light seeps through the mesh along with a muezzin's amplified call to prayer. It's the start of another day in the TEZ—

the Tigris-Euphrates Zone. Though ostensibly Syrian or Iraqi, large regions within the TEZ are looked on as ungoverned territories. In these areas, warlords and gangsters rule, along with their appointed local councils.

Miles flinches at the rip-roar of an ancient gasoline-powered engine as a scooter shoots past on the street below. He is always on edge, always in a constant state of fear. Closing his eyes, he tells himself to go to sleep again. Sleep is his only respite, but sleep doesn't come.

He gives up and discovers that the gathering light has given shape to his companions.

They are all men, all bearded and filthy like Miles, clothed in loose drawstring trousers and shapeless tunics, dirty white.

Noël Poulin huddles closest to the door. He's a French Catholic missionary, called by God to render aid to the suffering children of Syria.

Dano Rodrigues sleeps on his side against the right-hand wall. A Brazilian doctor and avowed atheist, he came to the TEZ as part of a medical mission because he saw it as the right thing to do. He was taken hostage four months ago, along with another doctor, an American, Fatima Atwan. Miles has seen Dr. Atwan twice when they were ordered out to stand witness to executions. At least, Dano said it was her behind the veil.

The last inhabitant of their cell is Ryan Rogers, an American engineer with the good fortune to be employed by a British petroleum company, one with an insurance agency that *does* pay ransoms—although his is still under negotiation. Ryan lies on his back, the moist sheen of his open eyes just visible in the half light as he stares at the ceiling. That's how he spends most days.

Miles came to the TEZ to report on the war—a self-perpetuating conflict, mostly conducted among the warlords but with occasional interference from foreign governments convinced they can set things right by bombing civilian towns and highways. He is a freelance journalist. His reporting, informed by his background as a US Army Ranger, earned him a large and lively audience over the nine months he posted from the TEZ. His website fed stories to news outlets around the world. The last time he checked, his video reports had two hundred fifty thousand subscribers.

He suspects his subscriber count has ceased growing since he stopped posting updates.

The dawn light brightens, illuminating dust hazing the air, and defining pockmarks in the walls, surely made by bullets. The stains on the floor might be oil or old paint . . . though he doesn't believe that.

He and his fellow captives have been in this cell two nights. Every five or six nights they're moved to another house in another town. Some of the lockups have been better than this one. Most were worse. His captivity has gone on for weeks. Maybe a lifetime. It's hard to remember. He has to school himself not to give up. To wait, to watch for an opportunity. Any opportunity to get the fuck out of here—or to at least cause some damage before Hussam El-Hashem orders him killed.

He flinches as Ryan nudges his foot. The engineer, still lying on his back, is now pointing at the ceiling. Miles looks. Something moving up there. Tiny, glimmering wings that belong to a slowly flying insect with a glassy body the size of a rice grain. Miles watches it cruise toward the light leaking through the mesh. That light paints it with detail so that Miles gets a good look at it just before it escapes.

Holy fuck.

Ryan sits up. They stare at each other in the dim light, sharing the realization. Not an insect. A mechanical device, a mosquito drone, used to reconnoiter otherwise inaccessible targets.

Miles explains it to himself this way: Someone is planning to launch a rescue mission.

He fucking hopes he's right.

STATUS REPORT

"WE BELIEVE WE'VE located Fatima," True announces. "But we've got complications."

Forty-eight hours have passed since Yusri Atwan made his plea for help. In that time, a contracted investigator has monitored his activities as well as those of his wife. ReqOps has also purchased a report on the history and associations of the Atwan family. No red flags have turned up; nothing in Yusri's background or behavior suggests he is anything but sincere. This is the result True expected, but thoroughly vetting a potential client is always an essential step before engaging in a contract.

The news from the TEZ is equally encouraging. Khalid Naim, one of the independent contractors hired by Chris, followed up on a rumor that led him to a large foreign-owned home in the town of Tadmur. He was able to get surveillance devices undetected over a wall surrounding the home's compound while sitting in his taxi cab, ostensibly waiting for a fare.

Hour by hour, as the mission becomes closer to reality, True feels her emotional investment deepen.

It's been only a year since Requisite Operations moved into offensive operations, quietly establishing a QRF—a quick reaction force—a flexible, armed unit that could be activated on short notice to deal with acute situations. They ran an initial mission in Los Angeles, extracting a young boy from a hostage situation without a shot fired. They've run two operations since, one in Mexico and one in Turkey. Both succeeded in terms of the mission goal; neither showed a profit.

Going after Fatima Atwan is in line with their past endeavors. It's unarguably a white-hat operation, a "right action"—and given the bounty on Hussam El-Hashem, it could even boost ReqOps' bottom line.

But the mission could still be scrubbed.

True keeps this in mind, her expression neutral as she looks around the crowded conference table—at Lincoln, Tamara, Chris, Renata, and at the seven soldiers who are part of ReqOps' QRF.

All watch attentively as True presents what is known. "Our regional contractor identified a suspect house. Neighborhood gossip indicated a secretive group had recently arrived at the property, owned by a suspected associate of Hussam El-Hashem. A beetle, modified to carry a flock of mosquito drones, was able to infiltrate the compound."

Beetles are one of ReqOps' proprietary devices. Shaped like rectangles with rounded corners, they are an inch long—a little larger than True would like, but they're only three millimeters high. That low profile plus an adaptive, color-shifting skin lets them blend with their surroundings. They're most vulnerable to detection when in motion. They crawl and climb on four jointed legs equipped with tiny spikes, and they glide short distances on the stiff plastic fins that normally enclose their electronic core. A swiveling camera lens lets them monitor motion, and they are able to receive instructions and relay bursts of data over short distances, generally to a low-flying UAV.

True continues: "The beetle recorded an image of a figure in the courtyard that facial analysis identifies with eighty-nine percent certainty as Mr. El-Hashem. But Fatima Atwan was not observed. So we authorized DNA collection—"

"We got time to analyze that, Mama?" Marine Corps veteran Rohan Valeski wants to know. He's thirty-five, a lanky, ginger-haired mischief-maker with a scruffy beard who delights in questioning everything. "DNA takes hours to collect and process."

True's eyes narrow. When the desert wind subsided after midnight, Khalid signaled the modified beetle to set loose its cargo of off-the-shelf mosquito drones. The tiny devices went hunting for infrared heat signatures. Most were lost, but a few returned to the beetle with ghostly low-res images and, more importantly, with DNA samples collected from within the house.

"Don't worry, son," True tells Rohan. "Our contractor has spent the local day running the chip tests. The analysis is done."

He gives her a wink and a grin. "Good to know."

"Even better," True says, with satisfaction in her voice, "we've confirmed one of the collected samples belongs to Fatima Atwan. It's a perfect match for the DNA record provided by her parents."

Another soldier, Juliet Holliday, sounds impressed: "So we've got her." Juliet is sweet and neat, lean and dusky. Like True, she was an army warrant officer who flew for Special Forces. Also like True, she was pushed out of the army by the growing dominance of autonomous flight systems.

In contrast with Juliet, Jameson Adams is skeptical. He's a family man. Dark black skin, physically gifted. He was offered a football scholarship out of high school but became an Army Ranger instead. Like Lincoln and Chris, he's a Rogue Lightning veteran. "You mentioned complications, Mama. Let's hear them."

"That's right," True says. "Complication number one: We've got additional individuals in the residence known or suspected of having been kidnapped by Hussam El-Hashem."

"Ah, fuck," Felice Farr says. Like Rohan, she's a Marine, and intimidating as hell when she wants to be. She sums up the situation nicely when she says, "That makes it harder."

"It does," Lincoln agrees, speaking for the first time.

Both Lincoln and Chris have already seen the reports, and they've made their decision.

Lincoln says, "The additionals complicate our task. They also make the mission more expensive. We are being hired to extract one individual. But given multiple prisoners at the location, we are morally obligated to go after all of them. If we leave them behind, it's certain they'll be executed quickly and dramatically to discourage future recovery missions."

"How many additionals?" Jameson asks.

True tells him, "Four."

"*Damn*," Rohan says. "That's a lot of bodies to move."

"It is," True agrees. "And it brings us to the next complication—timing. It's night now in the TEZ. This is the fifth night Hussam will have been in residence. We've seen various reports speculating that his usual pattern is to remain in a given place for five or six nights, because that makes it more difficult to do what we want to do: stage a mission against him. Our target could be gone before we get there—and the cost of the mission will escalate if we have to track him down again. So from a financial perspective, we need to move quickly. We have to decide if we like the setup, if we can work with the current situation. If so, we deploy in the next few hours and finalize mission planning in transit. One point in our favor, since this is not a permanent residence: the security system is likely to be *ad hoc* and easy to penetrate."

Renata raises a hand, a gesture that instantly captures the attention of everyone at the table. True smiles to see it. Renata knows how to turn a knack for getting noticed to good advantage. "Aerial assets are in line," she reports, "for now. We've juggled schedules so the Hai-Lins will be available to provide air cover—but only during a narrow window. We've got contractual obligations coming up that have to take precedence."

"Our obligations don't end with the war birds," Chris says. "We've got a round of classes starting, students due in. That gives us a hard deadline to get the job done and get home. If we're not here when classes are scheduled to start, it's going to be a hit to our reputation, and we'll be digging ourselves a financial hole with the cancellation fees."

Lincoln nods. "Agreed. We need a quick go/no-go decision." He turns to True, a white reflection from the ceiling lights catching in his artificial eye. "You've heard from the State Department?"

"That's complication number three," she admits. "I'm in communication, but I haven't received confirmation one way or another."

Though it's a policy that will never be codified in law, the State
Department generally responds with a hands-off attitude whenever a US-licensed PMC engages in a white-hat mission within
any region lacking a functional or recognized political authority—
an ungoverned territory—assuming the mission doesn't interfere
with any official activity. By that standard, large regions of the
Tigris-Euphrates Zone are wide open for engagement.

Lincoln turns to the assembled soldiers. "If State has an imminent mission into the same area, our operation is no-go. Competing missions would endanger both teams *and* endanger our license
to operate as a US government contractor. So be ready, but know
that we are not going to move until we hear from State."

This draws a soft chorus of acknowledgments.

"In the meantime," True says, "I'm emailing a detailed intelligence report to each of you. Read it. Consider it. We'll meet again
in two hours."

THE VICISSITUDES OF WAR

ANOTHER NIGHT:

Sitting in darkness, Miles feels the concrete wall at his back tremble as fighter jets thunder overhead.

Dano mutters profanities in Portuguese.

Noël starts praying. Maybe his prayers work, because no bombs fall.

Twenty-two days ago they were locked up in an empty office in an abandoned cigarette factory when precision-guided bombs took out two adjacent buildings. But for some unfathomable reason to do with the vicissitudes of war, their location wasn't on the target list. Following the concussion of the bombs and the avalanche roar of collapsing buildings, there came screams and shouts and wails of grief, rage, and pain that went on and on in a slowly diminishing chorus until evening. Darkness brought silence. Only then did Hussam feel safe enough to move his entourage to a new hiding place.

Tonight maybe, the jets came only as a show of force . . . as if anyone on the ground still needed convincing of the deadly threat of aerial bombardment.

The retreat of the roaring engines reveals another, more ominous, sound: voices from beyond the door. They are male and oddly gentle, discussing soccer scores. Miles tenses as a key slides into the lock. The deadbolt retracts with a grinding click. The steel door opens, admitting a clean white electric light.

A fellow named Abu Khamani looks in. He's a skinny guy who has worn the same stained brown cargo cammies and loose muslin shirt every fucking day since Miles was placed under his custody. Abu Khamani smiles his usual friendly smile. "Aloha!" he exclaims. It's his standard greeting.

"Aloha, asshole," Miles mutters.

Noël whispers, "Salaam," and Dano replies with, "Ciao."

It doesn't matter what they say; Abu Khamani just insists that every man say something. Ryan sits up, inching backward on his ass to put himself a little farther from the door.

"Fuckin' lovely evening," he says, eyeing the whip in Abu Khamani's right hand.

A second man, a stone-faced guard, stands behind Abu Khamani, holding an automatic rifle. The muzzle is trained on the floor, but it would take him only a heartbeat to raise his weapon and gun down everyone in the cell. Abu Khamani pays no attention to him, gesturing instead to the boy beside him who is carrying an allotment of MREs. The boy—he is maybe eight years old and Miles suspects he's one of Hussam's many children—drops the packaged meals on the floor. There are only three.

The four prisoners trade uneasy looks. Abu Khamani laughs. "You! Poulin!" He points at the missionary. "You lucky this night. You get to go home."

Noël shrinks deeper into his corner.

"Home," Abu Khamani repeats as if Noël is an idiot. "Your ransom is paid." He grabs Noël's arm, hauls him to his feet. Terror is inscribed on Noël's pale face. Miles understands that fear; he shares it. Once before, Abu Khamani promised a hostage that he could go home, but that man was executed, sent home to God.

Noël weeps as Abu Khamani drags him from the room. The door closes. Darkness returns.

There is a rustling noise as Ryan gropes for the MREs. He tosses one to Dano, one to Miles.

"Don't eat yet," he advises them. "You don't want to risk puking it all up when the screaming starts."

ASSEMBLE IN THIRTY

"ROACH IS ONLY stage one of Tamara's devious plan," Rohan is saying when True returns to the conference room just before the next scheduled meeting, due to start at 1300. "It's the beginning of the end for us, because she's going to automate us out of a job."

He's sprawled in a chair, his long legs stretched out under the table and a steaming mug of coffee in one hand, expounding his theory for the amusement of Felice, who sits two chairs away, arms crossed, eyeing him with a cynical smirk. Tamara herself is sedately arranging her cardigan on the back of a chair.

Rohan gives True a wink as he continues: "You heard it from me first. In a few more years, Tamara's going to field a bulletproof bot that can bound over walls, do backflips through firefights, sniff out IEDs, see the terrain in an expanded spectrum." He puts the mug down so he can gesture with both hands. "It'll have two legs that never get tired. Six arms—four of them configured as guns—and instead of blood and guts under the skin, it'll be loaded with ammo—enough to melt its fucking carapace if it ever goes postal."

"Don't worry, dawg," Felice tells him. "You gonna be retired by then."

True pours coffee, side-eyeing Tamara as she settles into a chair. True can feel the coming counterpunch like a static charge on the air.

"Rohan, dear," Tamara says, sounding like a disappointed preschool teacher—a tone that causes Felice to snicker again. "You've got it wrong. I'm not planning to replace you with a humanoid robot. Why bother? An aggressive, diverse swarm is more dangerous than any traditional soldier and easy to print up."

"Give it up, Rohan," True advises. "Tamara's going to retire all of us."

Any argument he might have made is precluded by the arrival of Lincoln and Chris, the rest of the QRF coming in behind them.

Chris is the field commander. He goes over the mission plan, including a review of vehicles and surveillance devices they'll be leasing from a partner company. "Like everything else," he says, "this is time-critical. I've got a twelve-hour hold on the equipment, but we'll need to make a fat payment to reserve it beyond that." He turns to True. "We really need to hear from State on whether or not we're looking at a closed area."

"I'm on it. I've been promised a call back by end of day."

By 1400, True is back in her office—and she's getting worried. On the east coast, the end of the workday is imminent and she still hasn't heard back from her contact at the State Department. Brooke Kanegawa is a good friend and reliable. That she hasn't called yet tells True that there *is* a conflicting mission, and it's taking Brooke time to get the specifics and the authorization to speak.

True scowls at a framed map of the world hanging on her office wall—and decides to check in. If nothing else, she can find out how late Brooke intends to be in the office. "Heads up, Ripley," she says, addressing her digital assistant, "call Brooke."

Ripley responds through her TINSL: "Calling Brooke Kanegawa. Please stand by." Thirty seconds pass. Then: "I'm sorry. There is no answer."

True starts to get up but sits down again when the soft chime that announces an incoming call sounds in her ear. "Answer it," she says, not waiting for Ripley to announce the caller's name. Then: "Brooke?"

Instead, she hears a low, old-man's voice edged with criticism: "You need to ID your calls before you pick up, True. Thought you knew that."

Colonel Colt Brighton, retired. True's mouth quirks in a bitter smile. The old man still has a knack for getting under her skin. "Hey, Dad," she says in what she hopes is a neutral voice.

"Waiting on an important call?" he asks.

"Need to know," she tells him.

"Huh. Not everyone's so circumspect. Word's out that Defense just awarded a billion-dollar contract to one of your competitors. You tell Lincoln he needs to show face in DC if he wants in on that kind of pork."

"We're a small company, Dad."

"Get a contract like that and you won't have to be."

"I'll tell him you said so." The call chime sounds again. Ripley whispers in the background, "Caller is Brooke Kanegawa."

"Got to go, Dad," True says. "Talk to you soon."

"Stay out of trouble," he warns her.

"You too, old man." She shifts to the new call. "Hey."

Brooke's voice sounds clipped, tense as she says, "I finally got your answer. Short version: stay the hell away from Mosul."

True is surprised. Mosul is nowhere near their intended target. She strives to keep the excitement out of her voice as she asks, "What's the long version?"

"You know I can't provide details, but I am to communicate to you in no uncertain terms that you will not operate in Mosul or surrounding areas. I'll email you the coordinates of the closed zone."

"I'd appreciate it."

Brooke continues in a formal voice. "Within that designated area you will undertake no offensive action. Not until a general clearance is issued. Should Requisite Operations defy this mandate, you will lose your license." Brooke draws a quick breath. "Hey, True," she says apologetically. "You know it's nothing personal."

"No worries. I appreciate it." Brooke is a good friend, but they are both constrained in what they can share. True has told her only that ReqOps is planning an offensive operation in the TEZ, providing no details on their objective. Lincoln has the option to file a notification, but he probably won't do it, because the risk of data leakage is too great.

"Any estimate on how long Mosul will be closed?" True asks, hoping to get a feel for when the State Department's operation might launch. If they're after Hussam, they're looking in the wrong place—but she can't tell Brooke that.

"No estimate at this time," Brooke says.

Maybe State is still prospecting. Maybe they won't go at all.

"Thanks, Brooke."

"You be careful."

"You know it."

True messages Chris, and a few minutes later they meet in Lincoln's office. In hurried words, she relates what she's learned, concluding by saying, "The field is clear. The risk at this point is that Hussam could decide to move on tomorrow and be gone before we get there."

"We'll have eyes on him," Chris says. "Once we're in the region, we can amend the plan. Hit him on the road if we have to, or follow him to his new hole."

Chris makes it sound easy, but True knows that a change of venue will present new dangers and that any delay will drive up costs—but Lincoln knows this too and it's his decision. So she resists the urge to play devil's advocate. She wants the mission to go. Her heart hammers in anticipation.

Lincoln doesn't leave them in suspense. "Let's do it," he says. "And the sooner we're on site, the more options we'll have. So alert the team. I'll notify the flight crew. We assemble in thirty at the loading docks for transportation to the airfield. Clear?"

"Roger that," True responds.

Chris answers, "You got it, boss." He turns his head, looking away as he speaks to his digital assistant. "Hey Charlie, set up a group text, QRF." True can't hear the acknowledgment, but almost immediately, Chris is repeating Lincoln's order. "We are a go. Assemble with gear, 1435, loading docks." Three seconds pass— the time it takes the assistant to read back the message—then Chris says, "Send it."

The text goes to everyone in the QRF. True hears a chime as her copy arrives. The adrenaline is pumping. She bumps fists with Chris. "See you in thirty."

True's identity is tracked by the house AI, Friday. That, matched with a swipe of her finger, releases the biometric lock on her office door. Her gear is ready and waiting inside.

She's got a slim, body-hugging pack stuffed with a selection of mini-robotics, spare button batteries, spare TINSLs, recharging units, RF-shielded collection bags, medical supplies, food, water, and ammo.

In a larger duffel she has more food and water, an armored vest, and an assortment of clothes—regionally appropriate civilian attire to wear in-country, the unmarked uniform she'll use on the mission, and an extra set of civvies, western-style, to wear on the way home.

A case holds her MARC visor—MARC being a compression of "Mission Arcana"—an augmented reality and audio communications headset. It's a lightweight half-visor worn like oversized eyeglasses, with a top bar housing most of the electronics and a magnetic dock for her ear TINSL.

True picks it up, slips it on. It boots automatically in a couple of seconds, projecting a default date/time display and brightening the shadows under the desk. The MARC is too big, awkward, intrusive, and costly to be popular with the consumer market, but it's a hell of an enhancement on missions. She slips on a black data glove that lets her select menu options with minimal hand movements. Voice input works too, but that can be problematic in a combat zone where commands may need to be issued in perfect silence or during the clamor of a firefight.

She twitches her index finger, running through a brief calibration sequence. Then she undertakes a short checklist, making sure the mission plan and supporting documents are up to date, and that the personnel list is complete. Right now everyone shows as offline, but that's expected.

She powers down, packs the MARC back into its case, and shoves it into the duffel. Minimal gear with minimal weight for what is intended to be a short, fast-moving mission.

Next she opens a closet and pulls out a light jacket with ReqOps' logo on the breast: a tan rectangle bordered in black, containing the company's chiseled initials, ROI, the full name written out beneath.

She takes a second to check her reflection in a mirror on the inside of the door, smoothing a few stray silver strands of hair. Her fair skin shows the evidence of years, but she can still run five miles in under forty-five minutes, so fuck it.

She shrugs the jacket on, then turns to the gun safe, swiping its biometric lock. Yesterday afternoon she spent an hour on the indoor range with her Kieffer-Obermark assault rifle. Her KO is modified with an underslung shotgun. That makes it heavy, but she wants the option of clearing drone swarms at close range, so she'll suffer the extra weight. She pulls out the hard plastic case that holds the weapon, sets it on her desk, and opens it, just to reassure herself that all is ready. She takes a 9 mm pistol too, wrapped up in a chest holster.

Only one more step and she can go.

She slips her tablet out of her thigh pocket, flips the cover open, and slips on her reading glasses. "Heads up, Ripley," she says. "Video call to Alex."

When the call comes through, Alex Delgado is heading out the door, due to start his shift as a county paramedic. He is fifty-one years old, two years older than True, though they share the same birthday—a coincidence that brought them together on the night they met, thirty-two years ago.

Back then, Alex was a newly minted army medic who'd enlisted for the GI Bill. He left the service four years later when his contract was up, using the education benefits he'd earned—generous in those days—to complete his paramedic's certification. Since then, he's worked in nine different US municipalities and even once in England, as True's army career took the family to new postings across the country and around the world.

In Japan he was a stay-at-home dad, looking after the kids—Diego, Treasure, and Connor. In the US, his mother lived with them off and on, helping with childcare. It was a chaotic life, and there were days soaked through with debilitating fear when True was deployed and didn't call home and he didn't know why.

She was a woman, and in those early years she wasn't supposed to be frontline combat—but she'd been frontline anyway. More often, he suspected, than she ever admitted to him. When the services technically opened all positions to women, she just kept doing what she'd been doing. It didn't make a difference to her. He would complain: *How do you think it feels to sit here and wonder if I'm ever going to see you again?* And they'd talk it out. But in the end it came down to the same thing every time: *Alex, this is what I was born to do.*

Maybe that was true.

When she retired at forty-five, he let himself believe that part of her life was over. When she went to work for Lincoln she said she was going to be a trainer, that's all. But within a year she was deploying again, overseas, on security operations, and this past year she'd participated in combat missions.

He taps his phone to accept the call. Video. She's wearing her reading glasses. Her head is canted as she gazes down at the tablet she's holding, a posture that enhances the lines in her cheeks—something he's sure she doesn't realize, or she'd hold the tablet higher. It's a portrait view, but he doesn't need help visualizing her figure. She's taller than most women, and determinedly lean, her well-defined muscles honed by hours in the gym, refurbished after every pregnancy. She is forty-nine years old, the mother of three adult children, and she is still the only one he wants.

"Alex," she says.

"You're on, aren't you?" Ghosts of old arguments lurk in his tone, making it sharper than he intended.

"It shouldn't be more than a few days."

She'd warned him a mission was possible. Another hostage rescue, this time on the other side of the world.

Now it's real. He knows the risks, the grim possibilities. He would keep her at home if he could but that's not an option she'll allow.

He says, "I need you back, True."

"I'll be back," she promises. "Don't worry. I got to go."

She isn't one to prolong goodbyes. She ends the call, leaving him with that last admonition echoing in his mind: *Don't worry.*

Their oldest son, Diego, said the same thing. *I'll be back, Dad. Don't worry.* That was eight years ago. Sergeant Diego Delgado, twenty-four years old. He was shot up in a firefight in Burma, and then captured, and executed—slowly—the ordeal recorded on video and released to the world.

But Alex is not to worry.

Not to wish ill on anyone, but as he opens the kitchen door and steps out into the garage, he hopes things aren't too quiet tonight. Better to keep busy and not think too hard about where True might be and what she might be going through.

True climbs into the backseat of a passenger van, still feeling the weight of Alex's disapproval. He objected to her frontline service when she was in the army, and he doesn't like her participation in the QRF now. The pressure has been worse in the years since Diego's death. She understands where it's coming from. But this is what she does. It's who she is.

For now.

She's still strong, still agile, but no denying reality. Sooner rather than later, age will put an end to her deployments. She won't be able to pass the physical qualifications and she'll have to stand down.

Until then, she doesn't plan to stop.

She slides across the bench seat to the window.

Experience has taught her that the best way to handle goodbyes is to keep them short, then put the guilt and the doubt away so that she can focus on the mission and what is required of her and of her teammates to meet their goals and come home safe.

Chris and Rohan slide into the seat in front of her. Chris hasn't trimmed his beard since the interview with Yusri Atwan, and he's looking scruffy. Rohan always wears a full beard, and he always looks scruffy. They both turn around to trade fist bumps with True.

"Right action," Chris says quietly.

"Right action," she echoes.

Rohan treats them to a wolfish grin. "Gotta love Lincoln. We are going to lose so much money on this operation."

"Truth," Chris mutters, shaking his head at the profligacy of it all, as if to shore up his reputation for fiscal prudence.

Hypocrite, True thinks wryly. He is just as eager to undertake this venture as any of them.

As Chris turns to face forward, Juliet Holliday climbs into the van. She takes the seat beside True and they trade the traditional fist bump—"Right action."

Juliet is only thirty-five, married just two years to a game developer whose only experience with the military is through first-person shooters. She leans in close, whispers in True's ear, "I lied to him. I told him this is a training mission."

True rolls her eyes. From the seat in front, Rohan says, "A fucking live-fire training mission."

Rohan lost most of his natural hearing during an extended firefight in Ukraine. Now he uses cybernetic enhancements wired into his auditory nerve, giving him a range of hearing far greater than the human norm, and with components that can be easily swapped out if his ears ever get blown again. Juliet punches him lightly in the shoulder. "Stop eavesdropping," she warns while Lincoln opens the driver's door and slides behind the wheel. Jameson takes shotgun.

The other four members of the QRF—Felice Farr, Nasir Peters, Ted Vargas, and Nate Gilbert—are in a second van.

It's a twenty-minute drive from the ReqOps campus to a private airfield. When they get there, no one barks orders. All are experienced; they know what they're doing and they don't need instruction. Moving quickly, quietly, they board a chartered business jet that will fly them in stages to Cyprus.

Lincoln boards last. He will not be going with them but wants this chance for a few final words. There will, of course, be continuous communication throughout the mission, but it's his belief, his experience, that it is easier to forge a deeper connection, a more unified purpose, when words are spoken in real time, face to face.

The team works quickly to stow their gear in cargo closets and in overhead bins while Lincoln waits at the head of the aisle.

The idea of organizing a quick reaction force was born out of a spirited discussion in a bar at a conference in DC. Lincoln can't remember who first proposed it. It might have been Chris or True. Hell, it could have been him. He'd had a few drinks. He remembers sketching out an organizational structure on the screen of his tablet, outlining the necessary equipment, the number of personnel, the potential market, and then following that with a rough and dirty budget calculation to show it could never be profitable.

But all three of them grew up in a tradition of service—they wanted to do it—so they went ahead anyway and the team has done good work. They've saved lives. That matters.

The bitter ambivalence Lincoln feels is because he has to stay behind. His burn injuries and his hand make him a weaker man than he used to be, and his bionic eye does not come close to replicating his natural vision. It lets him see only in gray scale, a monochrome world on his left that blends into a color spectrum where his good eye takes over. And it's a low-resolution interface—enough to distinguish objects on his left but not to see them clearly. Despite his experience, he would be a liability on this mission.

So instead of going himself, he is sending his soldiers. Enabling them, encouraging them to take on a potentially deadly task without any authority behind them, just their own will to do it.

More than any of the rest, Lincoln is aware that Requisite Operations is challenging a century-old tradition of national authority in which it is the duty of the state to protect its citizens. That tradition is collapsing in a world of failed states and ungoverned territories. When legitimate governments cannot or dare not intervene to protect the welfare of their citizens, or when no legitimate government exists, then hiring a private military company—a company of mercenaries—becomes the only realistic option for corporations, NGOs, or individuals who find themselves in trouble.

Someone's got to do the dirty work.

Lincoln waits for the team to settle, his prosthetic fingers tapping restlessly, thumb to index, middle, ring, and pinkie. It's a nervous habit. No predicting the direction events will take. But Chris is an excellent commander and Lincoln will follow virtually, offering any assistance he can.

Seat belts click. The rustling subsides. Nine faces look up at him, alert, expectant. They know what's at stake, but Lincoln wants to hammer it home. In his raspy voice he impresses upon them: "The first goal of this mission is to extract Fatima Atwan and return her to her home and family. But the lives of four other hostages also depend on your actions. I want every one of them extracted."

This earns him a low chorus of *yes, sirs*, serious faces all around.

He nods to acknowledge this and continues. "The mission plan you've been given is preliminary. Be assured we will continue to surveil the site and gather the intel needed to carry this off. As you are aware, the situation is live and evolving. Don't expect a final go/no-go determination until you are present in the region." He senses the copilot behind him, and the passing seconds. They cannot risk any delay. "Good luck," he tells them. "Make us proud."

Then he turns and descends the stairs.

IN THE REMAINS OF THE CALIPHATE

THE WESTERN TEZ is guarded, though not by a central authority. It's the local militias that hold power. The borders between their domains are fluid as they skirmish over the right to collect taxes and tolls. But it's not all treasonous deals and bloody death. The checkpoint guards, especially, are an open-minded crew, more inclined to grant passage than to ask questions, so long as the requested fee is paid.

In their defense, it's hard to tell an enemy from a friend.

A friend today might be an enemy tomorrow.

Besides, it's no easy thing to ask questions amid the Babel of languages in the TEZ. Foreigners are everywhere, wandering the shattered remains of the Caliphate, still looking for God or looking for trouble or just looking for a way out. The reasons they are here don't matter to ReqOps' mission, but their presence makes it easier for the teams to blend in.

True is part of Gold Team. They've been assigned to enter the TEZ from the west, all of them packed into a battered taxi with underpowered air conditioning. They bump and rattle through an overnight journey across the poisoned remains of Syria, on a road that should have been straight but instead snakes around bomb craters. On the road's shoulders is the detritus of years of conflict:

burned and twisted remnants of vehicles, many of them technicals—pickup trucks converted to carry machine guns or missile
launchers. Civilian cars, too, that might have belonged to families
fleeing the horrors of war, but who can say? Some of the wrecks
are partly buried in sand and grit. Others look like they burned
last night. That's an illusion, True knows. A deceptive effect of the
taxi's headlights. There hasn't been military action on this road for
at least three weeks.

The only signs of life are occasional headlights blasting up the
highway out of the east.

As they near the last junction before Tadmur, they come upon
a ruined tank, and after that another, and another. Fourteen in
all, many blown apart, all blackened by fire—the sordid remnants
of a hired army that tried to enter the conflict two years before,
only to be taken apart by aerial bombardment. The sight is not a
surprise. True has seen the pictures. But in the night, glimpsed on
the periphery of the headlights, those dead tanks bring home the
hubris of the PMC that fielded them. It's never been made clear
who hired the mercenary army or why. Afterward the company
evaporated, the executives became fugitives, and the surviving staff
scattered to the four winds.

Requisite Operations is a mercenary company too, though it's
not part of their business plan to mount a brazen invasion on the
back of a billion dollars of surplus military equipment. But if they
were going to do it, True would make damn sure they had a competent air force in play.

A few more kilometers, and a faint, rosy glow paints the eastern
horizon, visible past the swaying heads and shoulders of the men
in the front bench seat. True is in the back of the taxi, braced
between Felice and Juliet. It's hot, close, and cramped, and the seat
is doing her ass no favors. She's looking forward to making her
escape. So it's a relief to finally glimpse the lights of their destination shining against the brightening dawn: the war-scarred town
of Tadmur.

Their regional contractor, Khalid Naim, is driving the taxi. He's
a lean, lightly built young man, dressed in a neat button-down

shirt and brown slacks, adept at playing the role of a world-weary intellectual. Early on, he had remarked with a shrug, "Being a taxi driver here is like having a front seat to observe humanity's long fall."

But his is a kind of techno-aggressive weariness. Once they reached the highway, he pulled a battered AR visor from under the dash—not a high-end MARC, just an inexpensive AltWrld model, a piece of equipment even a taxi driver could plausibly afford. He donned the ugly eyeglasses with a grin. All AR visors, with their screen offset four centimeters from the user's eyes, are notorious for their geek mad-scientist vibe. "It'll never get me a girlfriend," Khalid explained. "But all the truck drivers in the TEZ use AR. They made an app that highlights the wrecks, the bomb craters, the potholes. It's a community project."

Rohan Valeski sits next to Khalid, squeezed into the middle of the front seat. He too wears civilian attire, though his appearance is not as neat. His collar is dusty and sweat-stained, and his thick ginger beard is untrimmed. He wears a MARC visor—it's black-market gear here and a status symbol. In contrast, his weapon is a Fortuna 762 assault rifle, which he holds in the crook of his arm, muzzle pointed at the roof. A Fortuna is a cheap firearm, common in the region, nothing that will draw notice.

Jameson Adams carries a Fortuna too. He sits beside the window. Every time the taxi sways, the Fortuna's muzzle taps against the window glass. Jameson is tall, broad, and intimidating. He's chosen to dress like a local tough, utility vest over a loose tunic and brown combat trousers that are Russian in origin. His beard is trimmed into a neat goatee, black against his black skin. He too wears a MARC. From her seat in the back, True can glimpse the flickers of his light-amplified view of the road. For men, both the technology and the weapons are standard.

The women, confined to the back seat, play a different role. All three are wrapped up in abayas, the traditional black robes worn outside the home by many Muslim women in this part of the world, with hijabs to cover their heads. In the ultra-conservative TEZ this is expected and will get no questions. None of them wear MARCs or TINSLs, nor do they carry any visible weapons, because women should be protected from such things.

But—as women do—they've stowed a few essentials out of sight. True has her subcompact 9 mm in a shoulder holster, a thin blade under her sleeve, and in her pocket, a Taser.

Red Team is driving in from the south. They are all men: Chris, Nasir, Ted, and Nate. Wandering troublemakers. Nothing unusual. Not here.

The taxi reaches Tadmur just as dawn's light infiltrates the town. Khalid sheds his AltWrld visor, stashing it under the dash. "It's not polite to wear a visor in town," he explains. "It's tough-guy gear. Marks you as a soldier—for hire, or already in someone's private army."

They see only a few people about, walking, or riding bikes. Khalid drives slowly anyway, past walls that shelter family compounds, then two- and three-story apartment buildings, closely spaced, with black windows and undecorated faces. They pass a block of ruined buildings: one bombed-out shell still standing, the rest collapsed into rubble. Then they roll into a livelier neighborhood of recently rebuilt houses, two and three stories high, most surrounded by concrete walls enclosing protected yards, the dark-green fronds of date palms just visible over the tops.

Here the streets are busy. Small pickup trucks and taxis scoot past, dodging one another and the donkey carts, the goats, the people. Skeletal dogs with crooked backs skulk in the sparse shadows, keeping away from the men who stand about in small groups, three and four together, the smoke from their cigarettes reflecting the soft dawn light. Most are dressed in loose-fitting sand-colored garments. Some wear belted robes. All carry weapons. They don't seem to have any pressing business.

True doesn't see nearly so many women. The ones in the streets move purposefully, at a fast pace, eyes down. They all wear the hijab and like the men, they keep to groups. Safety in numbers.

True keeps her eyes down too, shifting her gaze surreptitiously to take in the sights and get a feel for the town. Even this early, the air blowing through the taxi's vents smells of diesel exhaust, dust, and decaying things.

"Look to the left," Khalid says. "See the house at the end? With the photovoltaic roof? That's our target."

True turns to look down a street that runs for a block before ending at a cross street. Situated on that cross street is a walled compound with a rust-colored, paneled steel gate flanked by young date palms only seven or eight feet high. Beyond the wall, a glassy roof of flat photovoltaic tiles glistens in the early light.

"Can't wait," Felice growls between gritted teeth.

On the flight over they had learned time ran out for one of the hostages. A beetle, secreted beneath the anti-surveillance canopy that covers the courtyard, emerged with video of Noël Poulin's brutal ritual execution.

True thought the execution meant Hussam was ready to move on to a new safe house; she expected him to be gone even before they landed in Cyprus. She was sure the mission would be delayed and eventually scrubbed.

But Hussam has *not* left the house in Tadmur. Not yet.

Now that they are here, they need him to stay just one more night.

She lowers her gaze, crosses her fingers. "I hope Hussam's comfortable in that house," she says. "Reluctant to leave. Feeling a little lazy, maybe."

"Don't worry, Mama," Rohan says in a rough undertone without turning around. "We've got him."

"Truth," Juliet affirms. "Hussam's had his fun. Tonight we have ours."

Jameson's laugh is soft, but deep and reverberant. "Roger that shit."

"Amen," Felice adds.

True raises her gaze again, in time to see the rearview mirror capture Khalid's slight, approving smile. His reflected gaze meets hers. "It's getting real," he says, before looking back to the dusty street. "I can't fucking wait to ship that bastard out of here."

Khalid did six years of US Army service, first in the infantry and then in intelligence where his sharp mind and fluency in Arabic earned him steady promotion. Those skills have let him continue to thrive in the two years since, working on his own.

He steers the cab onto a side street. "The house where Hussam is staying belongs to a war tourist from eastern Europe. Real prick. But I didn't figure out that Hussam had rolled in until the call came from ReqOps and I went looking."

The cab pulls alongside a three-story apartment building. "Home, sweet home," Khalid says. The building is only a few years old, but bullets have already chewed up its concrete walls. Khalid parks in an alley, just outside a ground-floor apartment's weathered door. "Everyone around here wanted to believe I sold drugs, maybe weapons. So I left the door unlocked a few times. Now I'm just Khalid the taxi driver."

It's a relief to escape the cramped cab. This late in the year the air is pleasantly cool, and True takes a few seconds to stretch and enjoy it while Rohan and Felice fetch two large, mismatched suitcases from the trunk.

They follow Khalid inside to find a single room with smooth concrete walls. There is a counter with a sink, a small microwave oven, a double-burner propane stove. Beneath the counter is a case of bottled water. A toilet cubicle is in the back corner. A low, electrical buzz emanates from a ceiling fan as it turns at an easy clip above furnishings limited to a worn rug and a mattress on the floor. The only windows are narrow clerestories at the top of the outer wall; they give no view of the alley and admit only a little light, but they do make it difficult for anyone in the alley to see inside.

"We clear in here?" Juliet asks in a quiet voice barely audible above the buzzing white noise of the ceiling fan.

"Just your own equipment," Khalid assures her.

True eyes the upper walls and ceiling, looking for a surveillance beetle. It takes her practiced eye only a few seconds to spot it flattened against the concrete in an upper corner of the window. The little device is positioned so that its camera eye can swivel to watch the room or the alley outside.

"Everything is ready on my end," Khalid says quietly, tension in his voice. "If you don't want to wait, if you want to do this in daylight, we can."

"Less possibility of civilian casualties if we go late," True points out as she turns to check the room's inner corners for other micro-devices. "We got any reason to hurry? Any sign of the target bugging out?"

Jameson looks at her, eyes barely visible past the screen of his visor. "Boss says steady so far." He grins. "He also says to tell you, don't worry. The place is clean and he's watching over you."

That's the QRF's standard operating procedure. Lincoln watches over everything. He tracks their positions, monitors the video feeds gathered by their visors, surveils their surroundings, and keeps an eye on relevant regional politics.

Still, True can't resist trading a sly look with Juliet, who nods knowingly and says, "I bet every man in this neighborhood whispers the same sweet promises. 'I'll watch over you, baby. You don't need your freedom or your MARC.'"

"They're all full of shit," True says.

"All of them," Felice agrees.

"Ladies, *ladies*," Rohan says. "Let me come to your rescue."

He drops to his knees beside the suitcases, pops them open. Inside are camouflage uniforms, body armor, disassembled assault rifles, a collection of grenades, tiny surveillance robots, and fist-sized kamikaze robots—both scuttling crabs and hovering cop-ters—armed with small explosive payloads. But it's the visors Rohan retrieves, three of them, stored in their hard cases. "Plug in quick," he says, tossing True hers, and distributing the others to Felice and Juliet. "Hurry up, now. I do not want to see you get the shakes."

"You're such an asshole, Valeski," Felice says, snapping the case open and sliding her MARC over her eyes. "Never change."

True puts hers aside long enough to peel off her restricting abaya. Beneath it she wears a second full-coverage layer: a long-sleeved pullover, ankle-length athletic tights, and army boots. She is still hot from the car, so she unhooks her shoulder holster and unstraps the arm sheath holding her knife. With those out of the way, she peels off the pullover, releasing a flush of heat. Her skin is shiny with sweat, sports bra soaked with dark patches.

"Sexy mama," Jameson says, sitting with easy grace cross-legged on the mattress. "You look ready to kick ass tonight."

The contrast of the cool morning air sends a shiver running through her. "I'm a cartoon superhero in a brass bra," she agrees, strapping the shoulder holster on again. "Now move over." She pulls on her data glove and slides on her visor. "My ass needs a cushion while I confer with the boss."

Their communications are set up to bypass the local cell network, relaying instead through a solar-powered surveillance drone operating at high altitude, beyond the range of casual weaponry. The drone, like much of the equipment they'll be using on this mission, is leased from a regional company called Eden Transit that specializes in support services for PMCs.

Lincoln confirms that everything is on track. He posts a satellite map to her display, with Red Team's location marked—they're in a hostel a few blocks away. Lincoln says, "The surveillance drone is set to red alert if it detects more than foot traffic at the target house. If it looks like Hussam has decided to bug out, we'll know it—and we can launch with seven minutes' notice, but it won't be a clean hit."

"Yeah," True says. "We'd guarantee civilian casualties."

"Roger that. So we're working out the details of an alternate plan. If it comes to it, it's better to hit them outside of town."

"Agreed."

Afterward True returns the MARC to its case, but she continues to wear her TINSL so she can receive alerts and maintain voice communication.

She gets up again, to help Khalid, who's preparing breakfast. A skillet of reconstituted eggs, with bread and chopped dates to round out the meal. Whether the mission goes off or not, his career as a taxi driver is over. He'll be returning with them to the United States.

"Are you ready to go home?" she'd asked him, when they'd been on the road only a few minutes and were getting to know one another.

He flashed a shy smile, just visible in the dash lights. "Hell, yes. I've been ready for months, but I wanted to burn the last of my currency on something worthwhile." He nodded. "As soon as I confirmed with Chris who you were after, I knew this was it."

KEEPING WATCH

THERE ARE ADVANTAGES to being nearly fifty. One of them is a face that shows some mileage. Not that this is *always* an advantage, but once True puts on a hijab, without the prosthetic of makeup, those features she has earned through time—the slender white scar on her right cheek, the dark brown age spot on her left jaw, her mother's jowls that gravity insists on pulling into wrinkled relief—ensure that no man on the street looks at her twice. Not even those two youths slouching beside the gate of the house where Hussam is staying, automatic rifles in hand.

The two young Al-Furat guards exchange terse greetings with the townsmen who walk by, but both look right past True. Really, they should know better. Older women can be dangerous too. In the TEZ they have smuggled weapons, carried information, served as spies and as suicide bombers. Perhaps these two don't know that. Or maybe they've heard of such things but they don't believe it or don't believe it's important. True suspects they are simply selectively blind to a woman, any woman, over a certain age who is not a close relative.

On another day in another place, that might irritate her. Today she is cheered that not a single man takes notice as she hobbles past in her black abaya, walking with short steps as if suffering arthritic knees. If they see her at all, she wants them to see her as a harmless grandmother with a shapeless waistline—courtesy of the body armor she wears—and stooped shoulders that disguise her height.

The two guards are watching the street through Sasszem lenses—a Hungarian version of augmented reality glasses specialized for security officers. 'Zems offer only a few options, but they're far cheaper than MARCs, they're not constrained by stringent export restrictions, and they're good at what they do—which is to visually monitor a shifting milieu for weapons and for aberrant behavior. In addition, a facial recognition service is available by subscription.

It's likely these guards are subscribed—so there is one more possible reason they overlook True, a more excusable reason: Their software will have failed to tag her with a name, because Lincoln purchased identity restrictions from Global Asset Tracking.

GAT is a profiling company that specializes in matching names and faces around the world. Most of the hundreds of apps designed to identify strangers work from GAT's database and those that don't aren't worth a damn outside of limited regions. The faces GAT fails to recognize are nearly all of two kinds: those with the money to buy anonymity, and those at the opposite end of the social spectrum, with no choices, no money, and no future. An old woman with arthritic knees, for example, hobbling on some errand through the dusty streets of Tadmur.

True milks the role, moving slowly, biding her time, waiting for elements to shift. When a white sedan approaches the compound's gate, she hobbles a little faster. The sedan is new, four doors, black-tinted windows, a hood ornament. Dust hazes its reflective shine. As it noses up to the gate, the driver's window slides down. One of the guards steps up to confer while True ambles past the back bumper, one hand in a pocket of her abaya.

The sun's reflection flares in the chrome, blinding her. She squints, ducks her head, stumbles—and shoves two kamikaze crabs through a slit in the bottom of her pocket. Hidden by her abaya, they strike the road's dusty surface with a light clatter.

They are sand-colored robots, made of two hard plastic ovals with a layer of C4 sandwiched between. Remotely operated, they have just enough processing power to move quickly on their four jointed legs. Guided by Lincoln, or someone on staff at ReqOps' command post, they scuttle from beneath the abaya's hem into the shadow of the car.

As the car rolls through the gate, the kamikaze crabs go with it, using the vehicle for cover. Their targets are the two trucks parked inside. They will attach to the engine blocks and then, if Hussam decides to leave Tadmur today, it will be an easy matter to detonate the crabs and disable the vehicles in the open desert. If not, the engines will be blown up tonight after the hostages are recovered, eliminating the trucks as a means of pursuit.

True hobbles away from the target house without looking back, an old woman, unnoticed by anyone.

Eventually she makes her way back to Khalid's apartment where Rohan greets her with a wolfish smile.

"It worked, Mama," he tells her. "The kamikazes are in position."

By afternoon, the buzzing ceiling fan in Khalid's little apartment is stirring unseasonably warm ninety-degree air. True lies on her back, distracted by the ceaseless movement of the fan's spinning blades just visible past the edge of a three-dimensional schematic projected by her visor, and by the weird warmth of the generated breeze, like breath against her skin.

She occupies exactly half the mattress, refusing to let Jameson squeeze her out of her turf. He's asleep—she's sure he's asleep because he's been snoring softly for a good ten minutes, but every time he shifts position his massive shoulder presses a little harder against her. His T-shirt is damp with sweat, its scent sweet, thick. Vaguely arousing.

Rohan has taken his shirt off. Somewhere on the other side of the mountain that is Jameson, he sleeps on the floor, head pillowed against a neatly folded jacket. Felice and Juliet share the worn carpet's thin padding. Felice has stripped down to shorts and sports bra. Sweat gleams on her bare brown skin. She's awake, lying on her back like True, eyes blinking occasionally behind the screen of her visor. Her hands are at her sides, her fingers curling and twitching within data gloves as she studies some scenario. Juliet, wearing T-shirt and shorts, is curled beside her. Her MARC is in its case; her eyes are closed in sleep.

Khalid is out, rustling up fares. Nothing unusual here.

No one is on watch. They don't need to be, because ReqOps' staff, half a world away, has the entire town under surveillance.

Specific surveillance continues to be directed at the target property. The schematic True is studying is a three-dimensional projection of the house showing the outlines of rooms, the layout of furnishings, and the ghostly figures of people. It was developed from a radar sweep conducted by an Eden Transit UAV. No way to know for sure which of the six figures on the ground floor is Fatima. But the three individuals on the second floor, confined in a storeroom, are certainly the surviving male hostages.

A mosquito drone collected shadowy, low-res images of their faces. The three men are thin, haggard. But are they injured? Are they ambulatory? She hopes like hell they can get themselves down the stairs.

"Wireless communications layer," she says softly.

All active devices in the target house are pinpointed. Three mobile devices downstairs are certainly phones. An additional node of activity is a first-floor room, likely an office. The video of Noël's execution was probably sent out for professional editing from that room.

She drops the communications layer, extends her overview to the outside of the house. Multiple images captured by wandering beetles combine to create a three-dimensional projection of the compound sheltered beneath the anti-surveillance canopy. A small fountain sits at the center of the tiled court. Around the periphery, little potted cypresses look to be thriving despite the canopy's filtered light. The two large trucks are parked at the front of the house, to the left of the door. Two sedans are parked on the right, but those are visitors. They should be gone by the time the mission launches.

Placed among the cypresses are eight identical boxes. They are rectangular, around ten inches long, seven inches high, and seven wide. They have a recessed handle in the top to make them easy to carry. All around the handle, tiling the top of each box, are photovoltaic cells. Tiny camera lenses glint in each visible side.

The boxes are surely more than motion sensors. True suspects some kind of defensive system. She hasn't seen anything quite like them before, and despite the projection's excellent resolution, she can't see any manufacturer's mark.

Highlighting one of the boxes, she whispers a note, annotating the projection: **Add task: Eliminate PV boxes before we go over the wall.**

Khalid has had the house under surveillance for three nights. On each of those nights, two armed sentries stood watch within the compound on opposite sides of the house. In addition to the men, a tethered UAV circles three hundred meters above the compound. Its tether anchors it against wind gusting off the desert, ensuring it's always in position to use its excellent optics to watch the streets around the compound. It would certainly observe their approach and sound an alarm the moment they start over the wall . . . if it remains operational. The mission plan calls for it to suffer a sudden, catastrophic failure just as the QRF arrives on scene. The PV boxes need to share a similar fate.

A new annotation pops up on the projection, color-coded to Lincoln: **PV boxes are on target list.**

"Hey," True whispers to him. "It's 0400 where you are. You should be asleep."

His hoarse voice mutters in her ear: "I'll sleep when all of you are safe and on the way home."

Beetles still cling to the inner walls of the compound, hiding in plain sight thanks to their flat profiles and camouflage coloration. They upload images in intermittent, energy-conserving bursts. Lincoln studies each one, alert for changes.

By 1500 he has observed six different men taking turns standing watch at the gate. There is also a boy, maybe eight years old, who has come twice out of the house, looking bored.

At 1600 a local sheikh emerges from the house accompanied by four other men. They get into the two parked sedans, the gate opens, and they drive off. Only the two trucks remain.

He has seen nothing to indicate the household is preparing to move to a different location.

At 1620 he messages Chris and True: **Conditions nominal. Final authorization is pending, but best guess is, we're a go.**

Khalid returns after sunset prayer. The apartment is cooling off rapidly, while outside the wind picks up, whistling through the alley. "Are we on?" Khalid asks.

"It's looking good," True concedes.

As night sets in, they grow restless. Rohan obsesses over his Fortuna, using a soft cloth to wipe every square millimeter of its surface over and over again. Juliet is alert for footsteps, voices, or an engine in the alley outside and whenever she hears anything she moves to stand by the door, listening, even though the beetle keeps a constant watch. Felice packs and repacks her gear. Jameson taps keys on a virtual keyboard, taking notes for a novel he swears he's going to write one day. True covers her nervousness by handing out protein bars, double-checking everyone's equipment, insisting that Khalid lie down to rest, and generally making herself annoying.

Three hours after nightfall, Lincoln speaks to both teams, his voice arriving over their TINSLs. "Authorization granted. Chris, initiate the operation."

OVER THE WALL

RED TEAM SETS out first: Chris, Nasir, Ted, and Nate, strolling together in the dark wind-scoured streets, cigarettes lit, wearing the belted, sand-colored robes that have become the affectation of so many former holy warriors, mercenaries now, available for hire, odd jobs, no questions asked. The robes ripple and snap in the frantic wind. Each man carries a weapon, either a Fortuna or Triple-Y assault rifle, balanced casually over a shoulder or resting in the crook of an arm, and they speak together softly in foreign-inflected Arabic.

Sitting cross-legged on the mattress within Khalid's apartment, True watches a projection of the streets, tracking Red Team's progress. She is on edge, as she is before any mission. Her heart thuds in heavy, slow beats. A knot tightens her belly.

She listens to Red Team talk—about women and the terrible taste of the cigarettes they are smoking and the impossibility of ever returning home. It's a convincing portrayal of the exiles they are pretending to be, common soldiers left behind when the cause that drew them to the TEZ spun apart and the promises made to them were forgotten.

They play the role too well, True thinks, disturbed by the nihilism behind their words. What future can there be for men like these?

Lincoln puts an end to her melancholy spiral when he announces over comms: "Your turn, Gold Team."

True's heart rate spikes. She leaves on her data glove and her TINSL, but she slides off her visor, *carefully*, so as not to displace her hijab. She slips the visor into an expandable pocket on the front of a lightly armored utility vest that she wears over a high-necked commando shirt. Stuffed into loops on the vest are two thumb-sized capsules containing miniature members of the origami army: mayflies in one, a spare beetle in the other.

The vest, the shirt, and her matching trousers all have an outer layer of flame-resistant adaptive fabric woven for nocturnal camouflage. The black abaya covers it all. Rising to her feet, she fastens the last of the abaya's snaps. Then she fetches her weapon, checks the load.

"Right action," Jameson whispers, holding up a fist.

True raises a hand and their gloved knuckles kiss. Jameson has switched from the Fortuna assault rifle he carried on the way in, to a Kieffer-Obermark like True's, with an underslung shotgun. Rohan still has his Fortuna. Felice and Juliet both have KOs but without the shotgun, making them lighter. Like True, they wear abayas over their combat gear. The men wear loose gauze tunics and trousers as an outer layer. For now, the MARCs are stashed in hidden bags and pockets.

More fist bumps are traded, everyone murmuring, "Right action."

They pick up their packs. True has stashed a couple of kamikazes in hers. Khalid grabs the suitcases, now mostly empty. He exits first. The cab is parked just steps away. True holds her KO close to her body, letting her robe's wind-blown billows hide it. She gets into the cab's backseat. Felice comes in behind her. Juliet gets in from the other side.

The doors close. The trunk slams shut. Khalid takes a few seconds to lock the apartment door, then he slips into the driver's seat. Rohan and Jameson crowd in beside him, making no effort to hide their weapons.

True watches Khalid in the rearview mirror as he starts the engine. He looks tense, excited, eager. Khalid's reputation is solid, but he's the rookie on this operation. He's done intelligence work for ReqOps, but none of them have worked directly with him before. She catches his eye in the mirror. "We're not in any hurry," she reminds him.

He answers with a short-burst smile. "Not yet."

She nods tacit agreement, saying nothing else, reassured by the knowledge that Lincoln is in the loop, ready to talk him through any complications.

Khalid triggers the cab's silent electric engine and they pull out.

True watches the street ahead, wishing she could observe it with the light-enhancing function of her visor. She relies on the headlights instead and the electric lights escaping the houses. Skidding trash and little whirlwinds of dust. The day's foot traffic is gone, but knots of men still stand about despite the wind, three and four together, leaning on parked cars or in open doorways, the screens of their phones and tablets lighting up tired, bearded faces. Some look up, eyeing the cab as it rolls past. Jameson makes sure the silhouette of his KO is visible to discourage banditry and adventurism.

True keeps her head bowed, careful never to make eye contact. It's a posture that allows her to eye the dusty screen on the taxi's dash. Khalid has hacked the rearview camera so it's always on. He keeps the screen's brightness minimized, but the shadowy illumination is still enough to show a vehicle following them.

"Let's change our route," True says, her tension reflected in her voice. "Take a different street."

"I think it's no one," Khalid responds, his voice low. "But we can turn here, then go right at the next corner. It's almost the same."

They turn. The car behind them—a battered old sedan—drives on.

They turn twice more, roll past yet another group of men, and then stop, still a few meters from the target house. Khalid performs the role of taxi driver, holding out a biometric tablet to Rohan to collect payment. Rohan enters a code, presses his index finger to the scanner.

"I'll be back in six minutes," Khalid says softly. "Good luck."

"Watch your back," True warns him.

Rohan adds, "And don't be late."

Khalid flashes a smile. "Wouldn't miss it."

The men exit the cab. Jameson turns and opens the back door. True follows Juliet out into the driving wind, hauling her pack in one hand and holding her weapon close with the other. Felice comes behind. The wind carries the smell of smoke and of roasted meats and spices, but the taste it leaves in True's mouth is dust, and the sound of it is a white noise that muddles a background track of howling dogs and distant engines.

Then on the edge of hearing: a faint thrum of helicopter blades.

Right on time, True thinks. It's Blackbird, ReqOps' little 900-s stealth autonomous helicopter, newly purchased from Eden Transit in a deal that will let it be sold back if it's returned undamaged.

Blackbird comes armed with a sniper rifle, a light machine gun, and a set of behavioral algorithms developed by Tamara. The ship is the mission's designated sharpshooter, and once the QRF has Hussam in custody, it's up to Blackbird to haul the prisoner away. Success depends on Blackbird.

Rohan moves swiftly, quietly into the dark mouth of an alley. True swings her pack onto one shoulder as she follows in his wake. Juliet and Felice are on her heels. No doubt they've incurred the attention of the loitering men. Their goal is to be over the wall before those men agree on what is happening and make up their minds on how they will react.

Gravel pops under tires as Khalid drives away. True doesn't look back. It's Jameson's assignment to linger in the shadows at the alley's mouth, discouraging anyone who might be tempted to follow them.

On the other side of the world, Lincoln stands in ReqOps' command post. He wears an audio headset and holds a tablet in his prosthetic hand that lets him control multiple channels of communication.

Renata Ballard is with him in the command post, strapped into a padded recliner with VR goggles over her eyes and black-lace data gloves on both hands. She's ready for a long night in the chair, dressed in informal trousers and a baggy tunic, her blonde hair loose.

Engineering director Tamara Thomas is at a desk on the opposite side of the room along with her assistants, Naomi and Michelle. Each has her own workstation. They are ready to research and reprogram at need.

At the front of the room is Hayden Rees, a sharp kid, just a year out of high school, assigned to organize the video feeds displayed on a wall-mounted monitor. He sits at a narrow desk, using a tablet to rearrange them as priorities shift. Feeds from the QRF's visors have been pushed into a ring of small tiles around the monitor's periphery. Three larger tiles fill the center. One displays a three-dimensional map of the house, the result of the most recent radar scan. It shows six ghostly figures downstairs in two different back rooms, and upstairs, the three prisoners in their cell and four more individuals believed to be Hussam's soldiers.

The other two tiles display infrared feeds from the leased surveillance drone circling at high altitude. One feed shows an overview of Tadmur. The other is zoomed in on the target compound so that Lincoln's people are visible outside the wall.

Gold Team is in the alley. Red Team is in the narrow street behind the house. Both are presently hidden from the enemy's tethered surveillance drone, which is struggling to complete its circuit against the wind.

The wind isn't a problem for Blackbird's powerful engine. ReqOps' autonomous helicopter moves in swiftly, flying against the wind to minimize its sound profile. The plan calls for Blackbird to take the first shots, clearing the field for the QRF to advance.

It's time.

Lincoln looks down at the tablet he's holding. On its screen is a stack of colored bars. He taps the one labeled *Blackbird* and speaks to the AI pilot, giving final clearance: "Blackbird, engage Phase Green Nickel One."

A synthesized female voice responds, "Roger that."

Lincoln watches the wall monitor, counting silently. When he reaches five, a faint flash erupts downwind of the compound. "Aerial target one down," Hayden reports in an excited voice.

The enemy drone is gone.

The alley is so narrow and cluttered it forces Gold Team to go single file. The wind races past, whooshing and sighing against the concrete walls, sweeping cigarette butts into ugly little drifts that pile against discarded junk: TVs and automotive parts and broken plastic crates that True has to step over or make her way around.

Without slowing down, she strips off her hijab. Beneath it she wears a close-fitting skullcap that she unrolls into a camouflaged mask. The hijab she lets fall, and for a few steps it follows her, fluttering at her feet until it catches on an old car battery.

Next, she unsnaps the top of her abaya, retrieving her MARC and slipping it on. For a second she's blind. Then the visor boots. The screen comes to life, automatically enhancing the available light so that the alley brightens and the brand names printed on the scattered junk pop into clarity. A tag confirms her TINSL is linked.

Lincoln speaks over comms: "Aerial Target One confirmed down."

True resists the urge to look up. She didn't hear Blackbird take the shot; she didn't hear the impact. Both sounds were suppressed by the white noise of the wind—but Hussam's surveillance drone is gone. She receives the news with grim satisfaction, imagining a technician inside the house frowning over a suddenly absent video feed.

Rohan holds up a hand to signal a stop. True repeats the gesture for Felice.

Time for their final mission prep.

She presses the sticky backing of her mask against her cheeks to ensure it can't shift and obscure her vision. Dropping into a crouch, she lets her pack thump gently against the ground. Without ever losing contact with her KO, she peels off the abaya and lets the wind take it. Then she shrugs the pack on again and stands.

They are all dressed alike now in the microscopically textured fabric of their adaptive camouflage. Even seen through their light-gathering visors, they are ghosts, outlines blurred and blended into their shadowy surroundings.

The transformation has taken forty-five seconds.

In the control room, Lincoln says, "Hayden, let's get Blackbird's front camera on screen."

"Yes, sir."

The overview of Tadmur winks out, replaced by a gray-scale video showing a rapid, low-elevation approach to the town. Taking down the enemy's surveillance drone was only the initial step of Phase Green Nickel One. Blackbird is operating on its own to optimize step two: eliminating the suspect PV boxes in the courtyard. The camera can't see past the anti-surveillance canopy, but Blackbird doesn't need a visual target. The beetles have precisely mapped the location of each box.

Blackbird maneuvers into position and starts shooting.

True slings her KO. Her heart is racing but her mind is calm as she turns to Rohan, ready to execute the next step in the mission plan. From his field bag he takes a climbing hook sized for the wall. Attached to it is a short rope festooned with looped handholds. He unfolds the hook, locks it open, and hands it to her along with a Kevlar mat.

He stoops, lacing his gloved fingers together. She places one boot in the proffered step. Juliet and Felice move in to help her balance as Rohan boosts her up.

In a smooth, practiced sequence, True stretches up, sets the hook over the top of the wall and drapes the mat beside it, covering the broken glass set there to discourage thieves. Still rising on the momentum of three pairs of hands, she hauls out, belly down on the mat, the crunch of glass underneath.

As expected, her view across the courtyard is blocked by the fluttering, multilayered ribbons of the anti-surveillance canopy, shimmering inches below her face like the dark surface of a wind-

rippled pond. But the canopy is attached to the wall only at intervals, held in place by steel loops set three meters apart. Between
those points, the edge is loose, and as the canopy billows, a gap
opens allowing True to look straight down at a slice of the tiled
courtyard, with a potted cypress off to the side and one of the PV
boxes directly below.

She flinches at the hair-raising buzz of bullets zipping close
at supersonic speeds. She almost kicks off the wall but steadies
herself: The fusillade is expected. Four quick shots and then a fifth.
The bullets tear through the canopy, hitting unseen targets with
sharp *paks!* easily audible even over the wind. A sixth shot, and
the PV box below her shatters, fragments spinning halfway up the
wall. Mech parts: gears and wings and featureless chips of what
she suspects are plastic explosives.

Goddamn. Her mouth shapes the word though she doesn't say
it aloud. *Goddamn.* No sound of gunshots follows; these were
sniper rounds, fired by Blackbird at such a distance that the wind
has swept the noise away. Barely audible: the buzz of Blackbird's
blades as it swings around to target the compound from a different
angle.

Beside her, the grappling hook shifts; its rope pulls tight as
Rohan starts to climb.

True hurries to retrieve one of the capsules from her vest even
as Lincoln says, "Prep the swarm." She shoves the capsule down
under the canopy.

"Release it," Lincoln orders over comms.

She pops the capsule open. She can't see the swarm but she
can hear the buzz as four mechanical mayflies take flight. They
are fast and aggressive. They have to be, because they are short-
lived. Operating autonomously, they are programmed to seek out
anything human.

She pockets the capsule. Pulling the knife from the sheath on
her forearm, she uses it to slice an opening in the canopy even as
she scrambles to get a knee on the Kevlar mat.

Rohan pops up beside her. He grips her arm, steadying her as
she swivels to drop over the other side. The toe of her boot knocks

fragments of broken glass into the courtyard, but it doesn't matter. Anyone down there will already know the compound is under attack. She kicks off the wall, landing with a jarring impact in the debris field of the PV box.

Lincoln watches the four mayflies disperse. Or rather, he watches the videos collected by their cameras. Each camera sends a distorted, super-wide-angle view. Hayden has arranged all four feeds side by side on the wall monitor.

The mayflies have been tested extensively, but this is the first time they've been used in the field. They're tiny devices, small enough to balance on a quarter. Their brown oval wings are a crisp film made of woven spider silk and powered by an electric motor. An articulated tail trails two wires: one an antenna, the other a barb loaded with neurotoxin.

Tamara rises from her desk, comes to stand beside him.

Comes to interpret, Lincoln hopes, because he is having a hard time understanding what he's seeing. Everything onscreen looks miles away. Tamara points to a feed. "The third mayfly isn't going to find a target. The others are in line."

Lincoln makes out a tiny human figure at the distant center of one of the videos and then, with shocking speed, the view zooms in, strikes something solid.

"Got 'em," Tamara says in satisfaction.

Lincoln scans the video array. All four feeds are frozen. Three show a solid surface that he presumes to be the skin of the targeted sentries. The other, a distant wall. He says, "Hayden, I need a fresh overview of the courtyard."

Tamara pats him on the shoulder. "Don't worry, Lincoln," she says. "There were two sentries and both of them are down."

"*Status?*" True whispers.

No cry of alarm has greeted her arrival. She crouches in the two-meter-wide space between the wall and a parked truck. A glance up shows her the cut canopy flapping and Rohan's looming silhouette, the muzzle of his Fortuna a spike against the night sky's dusty blur.

"Sentries are down," Lincoln says. He doesn't sound sure, though. "Tamara says they are," he amends. "I'm waiting on confirmation."

Blackbird rumbles in the distance and two more shots sizzle through the air, hitting targets somewhere in the back of the courtyard.

True moves out, staying low, using the truck for shelter as she approaches the house, her KO ready. Rohan drops from the wall, lands behind her with a soft thump. She reaches the truck's bumper, pauses there to peer at the house.

The windows on this side are two vertical slits. Faint white light seeps through them. Tall potted shrubs flank the front door. Between them, a sprawled body.

The mayfly would have gone for the face, delivering its cargo of neurotoxin with machine speed, its whip tail curling, jabbing a barb through clothing if necessary and into flesh, dropping its target in seconds.

"*Door guard confirmed down,*" she whispers.

Rohan has moved in the opposite direction. "*Confirming—*"

A harsh buzz interrupts him. True's visor highlights a streak of motion, racing through the air alongside the wall, coming straight toward her. No time to think, but she thinks anyway. She thinks, *I don't want to make noise.* Then her brain registers a bleating alarm from within the house, a signal that they are done with stealth. Violence of action is all they have left.

She targets the object racing toward her, hand sliding forward on the stock of her rifle. She finds the shotgun trigger—

Whatever it is, the thing in the air, it blows apart with a now-familiar *pak!*

Blackbird took out the threat before she could pull the trigger. "*God damn it,*" she swears, whispering despite the alarm. She would have had that one. She could have taken it out herself. The noise wouldn't have mattered, because the damn alarm is still ringing.

She glances back to check on her team. Felice and Juliet are over the wall and moving up behind her. Even with her visor, True sees them only as suggestions of shadowy motion, but she can tell them apart because they're tagged with names projected in faint red. Jameson drops next into the courtyard.

True says, "Felice, you ready?"

"On your word, ma'am."

"Right behind you," Rohan says.

A warning comes in from Lincoln: "Guard your fire as you advance. Only friendlies in the courtyard."

"Juliet, you set?" True asks.

"Yes, ma'am."

Juliet will stay back to provide cover, control the courtyard, and prepare for their exit.

True's heart thunders as she growls at Felice, "*Let's go.*"

With her weapon held ready to fire, it's a two-second sprint to the door. During that span the alarm cuts out and True hears a shout from inside the house. Over comms she hears glass shattering and Chris yelling: "*Go, go, go!*"

Chris is at the opposite corner of the house, detailed to breach a window into the downstairs room where Fatima is believed to be, and likely Hussam with her.

True reaches the fallen sentry, glances down. He's on his back, legs bent, eyes staring in fixed, unblinking horror. Two mayflies are pinned to his cheeks by the barbs at the end of their whip tails. The toxin they deliver is nonlethal, fast-acting, and good to keep a man down for thirty minutes—though she isn't sure how a double dose will play out. Papers she's read indicate residual neurological effects, but that's better than a bullet to the brain.

Lincoln says, "Blackbird reports all targets accounted for."

"Roger that." She stoops to close the sentry's eyes with a gloved hand. Then she moves up to the door, with Felice right behind her, a hand on her shoulder.

"Breach it, Mama," Felice whispers. "You got the big gun."

True half-smiles. "Gonna try it first." Surveillance showed sentries moving freely into and out of the house. She's got a hunch the door is not secure.

She reaches out, works the latch. The door opens. She kicks it wide, steps in, swings right, hunting for opposition. Her visor eas-

ily gathers enough light to show her a large room beautifully furnished in sofas, upholstered chairs, and tables of fine, dark wood.
The MARC's threat assessment function finds nothing to highlight. No one in sight. No shots fired. She's conscious of Felice
covering the room's left side.

Jameson and Rohan dart in, pivoting right and left.

"Clear!" True yells.

In the back of the room, a stairway climbs to the next floor.
To the left, a wide passage leads to the rear of the house. Gunfire there. Following their assigned roles, Felice and Rohan move
toward the sound.

On the right, a closed door hides what they believe to be an
office. True advances on it, gets ready to enter. Jameson kicks the
door open. True pivots inside, Jameson right behind her.

No one's there. Just electronics filling the room with the glow
of ready lights.

"Clear," she says.

Jameson is standing in the opposite corner. She meets his gaze.
They hear shouting from the back of the house. Footsteps running
on the floor above. "Let's go." Jameson says. She nods and follows.

Gold Team has been assigned to enter the empty quarter of the
house, but Red Team is entering hot, so Lincoln centers the video
feed from Chris's MARC on the big monitor and follows him
virtually as he explodes into a downstairs bedroom.

Inside, beneath the window, is a low bed, occupied by a couple,
both of them scrambling to be elsewhere as Chris comes in on top
of them. The bedroom door is closed. A man—naked, bearded,
loose heavy black hair to his shoulders—spills out of the bed,
rolling, coming up on one knee with his finger on the trigger of
an assault rifle. Friday identifies him with a name tag: *Hussam
El-Hashem*. The woman is screaming, protesting in Arabic, "La'a!
La'a, seeboo fi haloo." *No, no. Leave him alone.* Hussam gets off
two shots into the mattress before Chris plants a boot in his face,
knocking him to the floor.

But Chris doesn't go after him. He loses his balance, staggers on the bed. Looks down. The woman is there at his side, hanging on him, one hand on his arm, one on his weapon. She's dressed in a thin white shift. Her long black hair is loose, her dark eyes wide with terror.

"We will all die!" she screams in English. "All of us!"

Chris's gloved hand comes away from his weapon, closes into a fist. He's about to hit her. Lincoln can feel it. He wants to shout at Chris to back off. Friday tags the woman with a name: *Fatima Atwan.*

Gloved hands grab Fatima from behind, haul her off of Chris and out of the way. She keeps screaming, begging, as if the apocalypse will be ignited if any further disrespect is shown to Hussam El-Hashem—who is up again, hunched over his assault rifle, blood running from his nose and lips as he raises the muzzle of the weapon.

Lincoln hears a three-round burst as Chris jumps off the bed. He can't tell where the bullets hit. "*Fucker,*" Chris swears as he kicks Hussam in the gut, kicks his weapon away. Spares a glance for the door.

Nate gets there just as the door opens. A rifle muzzle pokes in. Nate grabs it, shoves it down as shots are fired. Holes explode in the floor. But he doesn't shoot back. Lincoln's gaze shifts to the feed from Nate's visor as he yanks a boy, no more than eight years old, into the bedroom. He separates the boy from the assault rifle and heaves the rifle out the window.

From the end of the hall, Rohan is shouting in Arabic, *Drop the gun! Drop the gun!*

Then shooting erupts.

True and Jameson move up the stairs to the first landing. Whispering voices from above give them a moment's warning. "Back against the wall!" True shouts. There's a flurry of shots, bullets buzzing down the stairs, shattering the tiles on the floor below. Jameson pulls a flash-bang. True leans out, squeezes off six quick shots to suppress enemy fire, ducks back. Jameson heaves the grenade. It goes off in a shattering of light and noise. They hurl themselves upstairs.

True's visor highlights four figures in the hallway. One lies prone, his weapon dropped. Two hunker against a wall, still clinging to their assault rifles. And the other staggers away, blinded and confused by the explosion.

Jameson and True go after them while they're still disoriented. Jameson takes the lead. He skips the first one, the one who's already down, using swift kicks to unseat the next two, wresting away their weapons.

True squeezes past him, pursuing the one still on his feet. The air stinks and she's breathing hard, as much from adrenaline as from exertion. She catches up to the man, swings her KO, and hammers him in the shoulder. He drops with a pained yelp, and she follows him down, groping in a pocket for zip ties. They spill out beside her. She puts a knee in his back. He tries to get up. She punches him in the ear, growling, "Not a good idea."

"How you doing, Mama?" Jameson asks.

"Having a fucking heart attack."

"That soldier give you any problems, put a bullet in his head."

"No need for that," she says in a low, hostile voice as she works to zip-tie his hands together. "He's just confused."

They secure all four men, hand and foot. Then they clear the rest of the rooms on the way to the closed steel door at the end of the hall.

Behind that door is a storeroom that must have been intended as a vault for gold or weapons or something of value. But not people. Standing outside of it, True smells the stink of the sump bucket. She tries the latch for the hell of it. Of course it's locked.

Lincoln looks at the 3-D map of the house. Only one room left to secure, three defenders inside. Rohan and Felice are hunkered down at the end of the hall, taking fire but not returning it. If they return fire, they run the risk of stray bullets and shrapnel penetrating the room where Chris's team is located.

He tells Chris, "Stay where you are. Shelter the prisoners."

He shifts to Rohan's video feed. All he sees is the large front room. Somewhere out of sight, a flash-bang goes off. Rohan pivots.

He charges into the hall. Reaches a door. It's ajar. He punches it open, pitches another flash-bang inside, drops back, drops flat to the ground.

Somewhere—in the room?—an assault rifle hammers out a string of bullets. The grenade goes off. The gun goes silent. Felice moves up, passing Rohan as he scrambles back to his feet. She is first into the room, pivoting with her weapon. She yells, "Face down on the floor!" and fires a single shot.

Rohan moves in behind her. The three men are down. It takes only a minute for the pair to secure their prisoners, binding wrists and ankles with zip ties. When it's done, Rohan flips each man over so he's facing up. "Hey," he says, crouching over the last one. "We know this guy."

On the video, a young man glares in defiance. His face is sharp-featured, shadowed by a sparse beard and neat, black brows. His right ear is slagged scar tissue, a scar that continues down his neck to his shoulder, disappearing under a white nightshirt. Gleaming in his deep-set dark eyes is a promise of murder. The system identifies him as Hussam's nineteen-year-old brother, Rihab. A young filmmaker, according to rumor, who specializes in execution videos.

"Should we take him with us?" Rohan wants to know.

"Another time," Lincoln says. "We've got no authority to take him now."

Rihab's glare becomes a grimace of frustrated rage as Rohan leans closer. "First one's free, pal," Rohan warns him from behind the anonymity of his mask and visor. "I've got a feeling we're going to meet again."

ONE CHANCE

MILES ISN'T SURPRISED when gunfire erupts downstairs. He's been expecting some kind of operation ever since he saw the mosquito drone, but, "*Shit*," he whispers to himself. "Why did they wait until Noël was dead?"

Then he's up, military training taking over. There isn't enough light in the stinking little room to see, but he's memorized the place, the positions of his companions. "Ryan, you up?"

"Right next to you."

Miles feels a hand on his shoulder. Ryan is alert and ready to act; he saw the mosquito drone too.

"Get in the corner," Miles says, giving him a gentle shove. "Face the wall. Cover your head."

"What the hell is going on?" Dano demands in his thick Brazilian accent.

"We're hoping it's a rescue."

"What rescue? What do you mean? How do you know it's a rescue?"

Miles hears doors open. Shouts, footsteps. Decides against debate. Groping in the dark, he finds Dano, grabs the front of his shirt—"Get over here"—hauls him into the corner. "Get down. Cover your head. Protect your eyes."

He huddles with Ryan and Dano. Flinches as a flurry of shots erupts. A loud bang. Running footsteps. New voices. American voices.

Dano tries to get up. Miles won't let him.

"Stay back from the door!" someone shouts. A woman's practiced command voice. "We're getting you out of here but we have to blow the lock. In five!"

"We're ready!" Miles shouts.

"Might want to cover your ears," the woman suggests.

The gunfire downstairs has ceased. Distant shouts and a car alarm's faraway bleat mingle with the heartbeat thump of her retreating footsteps.

Boom!

Miles winces, feeling like he's been punched in both ears. Then he's up again, hauling Dano with him, knowing Ryan will follow. He still can't see a damn thing. He gropes for the door anyway, finds it ajar, pulls it wider. A tiny red light flicks on in the hall outside. It casts shape into the world, defines the hallway, but it does no more than suggest the presence of a camouflaged figure behind the light. She is a conception, a sketch of a soldier drawn to confuse the eye. Definition exists only in her gloved hands, the screen of her MARC visor, and in the solid mass of the Kieffer-Obermark resting in the crook of her arm.

True, looking back at him, finds herself caught in a moment of weird dissociation. Her visor shows her a light-amplified view of this stranger, Miles Dushane. He's dressed in a shapeless tunic and stained trousers, face gaunt, beard tangled, his hair dirty and disheveled. She does not know him, has never met him before. And yet between one heartbeat and the next it feels to her as if both time and space are folding around him, bringing forward a more familiar presence.

Haven't I dreamed this? she asks herself. *Of opening this locked door?*

Yes. And though it is Miles Dushane who looks back at her from beyond the doorway, she sees through him into a parallel past, to another prisoner, a young man not so different from him, also slated for brutal execution.

Her heart beats again. Time restarts. The past falls away. It is forever beyond reach, and still, a connection remains. It leaves a pressure behind her eyes, a tightness in her chest as she resolves that what happened before will not happen again. *Not this time.* Miles is not her son, but he is someone's child, a good man from all that she's heard, and it consoles her to be here tonight, to ensure that he, at least, survives.

She speaks in a voice purposely brusque, businesslike, no reflection at all of that space between heartbeats. "What's your condition?" she asks. "Any significant injuries? Broken bones? Anything that will prevent you from getting down the stairs?"

Miles too uses brusque words, but his voice is husky with emotion. "No," he tells her. "We're all ambulatory." He watches the red light move closer. It takes him a few seconds to realize she is holding it out to him. He accepts it by instinct.

"Step out here," she instructs him. "You first. The others to follow one at a time. I need to pat you down."

"Yes, ma'am." He does as she says, stepping into the hall. Only then does he notice a second soldier, a big man waiting halfway down the hall, keeping close watch on the proceedings, ready to bring his weapon into play. Beyond him, four men are on the floor, bound and therefore presumably alive. Miles holds his arms out. The woman runs her hands over him, quickly, professionally, stooping to check his legs and crotch.

Behind him, in the stinking cell, Dano protests. "I don't understand. Who is this woman? How do we know we can trust her?"

Miles answers with an impatience verging on anger. "I know she's not fucking Hussam and that's good enough for me."

"You're clear," the soldier tells him. "Who's next? Let's move."

"Go on, Dano," Ryan growls from the dark. "Or get the fuck out of my way."

Dano stumbles into sight, off balance like he's been pushed. Miles catches his arm, pulls him into the hallway, and tells him, "Stand still."

He stands frozen, staring at the men on the floor while the soldier pats him down. She finds nothing, turns to Ryan, and repeats the procedure.

"All right," she says when she's done. "My name is True Brighton. I'm here with an American PMC called Requisite Operations. If you cooperate and move fast, we will get you out of here. But it's all or nothing. There won't be a second chance. If you want to live, follow Jameson." She gestures at the second soldier. "*Move out.*"

She doesn't seek their agreement. She doesn't need it. This is their one chance at freedom. Ryan understands that. When Jameson starts down the hall, Ryan totters after him, unsteady for lack of exercise but determined. Miles keeps his grip on Dano's arm and follows.

But Dano still isn't sure. Shock and confusion piled on top of months of stress have left him adrift, focused on the wrong things, on things he can't control. After two steps he plants his feet and demands, "What about Fatima? Fatima Atwan? Dr. Atwan is my colleague. She is a prisoner too. We can't leave her behind."

Miles doesn't have an answer. This isn't his operation. For all he knows, Fatima is dead. "Right now, Dano, you need to shut up and do as you're told. I swear if you slow me down I will leave you behind."

"I just—"

"Dr. Atwan is downstairs," True says, crowding behind them. "She's coming with us. Now move."

Dano gives in. He allows Miles to steer him. The little red light picks out the men on the floor, picks out the face of Abu Khamani glaring at them as they stumble past. *Aloha, asshole,* Miles thinks, but he's too disciplined to say it aloud—or maybe he's too superstitious. They're not home yet.

His light finds the top of the stairs. He directs the beam down. The dim red glow wraps around an indistinct figure. "Ryan, is that you?"

Ryan confirms it. "Right here, pal."

Miles follows with Dano, the red light revealing one step, then the next. He can't see Jameson. Wrapped in darkness and camouflage, the soldier has become invisible.

But though Miles can't see much, he hears things. Male voices. A hard percussion of footsteps. The throaty rush of wind.

He reaches a landing. From somewhere below comes a woman's wailing wordless cry, one that shifts suddenly to a screaming protest in American-accented English. *"No, no, you don't understand. It won't help. It's too late."*

Dano is energized by that voice. "Fatima!" he yells in response. He picks up his pace, rushing Miles to the bottom of the stairs. "Fatima, where are you?"

Miles tightens his grip. "Leave it to the professionals," he warns.

True peels off at the bottom of the stairs, leaving the three hostages to make their own way to the door.

"Lincoln."

"Here."

"Going to pick up a few souvenirs."

"Do it. But be at the door in ninety seconds."

"Roger that."

She returns to the office that she and Jameson cleared on the way in. The door hangs open, its latch broken from when Jameson kicked it. She slips off her pack, digs out two radio-frequency shielded collection bags, and loads them with the obvious storage media: a laptop, a tablet, drives, sticks. That's all she can take. She seals the bags.

"Lincoln."

"Here."

"I'm going to leave a kamikaze crab."

He's silent for almost five seconds. Then he says, "All right. Do it. The structure of the house should support it."

She shrugs the pack back on, slings her KO over her shoulder, and with the two bags in hand, heads for the door. It's been a few minutes since she checked in with Juliet, who was posted to the courtyard. Time to catch up.

"Juliet," she says over comms. "What's your status?"

"Prepped and ready. I've got the canopy sliced open and our bots collected."

"You got all the mayflies?"

"Roger that. Recovered all four."

Good. True is concerned about the legality of the mayflies. The neurotoxin they deliver might be considered chemical warfare. Best not to leave evidence behind.

Miles follows the beam of his red light around furnishings set up like obstacles in a large room. Ahead is an open doorway with a thin slice of dusty night sky visible beyond. Jameson waits there. Ryan heads for the door but the soldier says, "Hold up. Stand on the side. Keep the door clear. We exit last."

Miles moves up, stands behind Jameson. From outside he hears the muted roar of powerful engines. A distant jet? And another aircraft, closer.

Boom!

He drops into a crouch, pulling Dano down with him as searing light flickers in the slice of night sky. A courtyard and two parked trucks are briefly revealed, along with a canopy, sliced open, loose edges rippling in the wind.

"That was us," Jameson says. "Just clearing the skies of cameras."

Miles stands up again, shaking. Ryan is right beside him, breathing in labored gasps. "Hey," Miles says. "You okay?"

"Ask me in ten."

"Right."

A clatter of motion draws his attention back to the house's interior. A shadowy tide of soldiers, more sensed than seen, flows from a hallway to the left of the stairs. As they reach the door, glints from their visors and red sparks reflected from his little light give them vague definition. Miles counts four of them and realizes they are carrying a body. He gets only a glimpse before they're out the door, but that's enough for a mental snapshot. The body is confined in a canvas bag zipped up to the chin; a black hood covers its head. The sight makes the hair on the back of his neck stand on end. He is sure the body is Hussam's.

All or nothing, he thinks. Either they get out of here in the next few minutes or every one of them is dead. He grits his teeth and waits for the signal to move out.

Aircraft noise gets louder, deafening, as a helicopter comes in. No navigation lights. No spotlight. It hovers over the courtyard, rotor wash blasting dust in through the open doorway.

Miles leans over to get a better look at the operation, but it's too dark to see what's going on. All he can make out are shadows and glints. Then an oblong object rises into the slice of open sky, its shape silhouetted against charcoal clouds. Hussam's corpse. It's lifted over the wall as the unseen helicopter roars away.

With the engine noise in retreat, Miles hears something else, something closer: a woman breathing in tiny, high-pitched gasps. She sounds as if she's just inches away. Cautiously, he raises his light.

Dano turns to look too. "*Fatima,*" he whispers.

She is dressed in a thin white shift. A broad Velcro restraining strap secures her arms against her body. A soldier stands behind her, gloved hands on her shoulders. Fatima wears no veil, no hijab. Her black hair hangs loose and wild, and in the red light her eyes have the appearance of unnatural black pits, haunted, in a face that is waxy and drawn.

"Dushane, are you ready?" True Brighton asks him.

He startles at the question, having lost track of her. He turns, finds her beside him, and answers, "Yes, ma'am. Are we getting the fuck out of here now, ma'am?"

"Roger that. We are crossing the courtyard and exiting through the gate, into the street. You will get your people into the back of the waiting truck. Understood?"

"Absolutely, ma'am."

"Switch off your light."

"Yes, ma'am."

"Let's go."

Miles can't see a damn thing as they move out across the courtyard. All he can do is follow the sound of the soldiers ahead of him while keeping a hand on Ryan's shoulder and a grip on Dano's arm.

Grit under his bare feet and the occasional thorn make him wince, but he doesn't slow down. Ahead he hears shouts and the ripping thunder of over-accelerating gasoline engines racing toward their position. It sounds like this escape attempt is going to run straight into the enemy's arms. But there's no going back.

The shooting starts as they reach the gate. He sees distant muzzle flashes like sideways candles. Hears bullets buzzing down the street, tumbling against the walls. Answering fire erupts, deafening in its proximity. The attackers fall back.

There is no moon, and there are no houselights to be seen anywhere along the street. Blowing dust shrouds all but the brightest stars. He can see a waiting truck only by the dim red light that spills from its open doors. It's a double-cab pickup with a high clearance and a rigid canopy enclosing the cargo bed. One of the soldiers opens the tailgate doors. "Get inside! Strap into a harness if you can. If not, fucking hold on."

Ryan doesn't hesitate; he scrambles right in. Miles pushes Dano after him and then crawls in behind.

It's a good-sized space. There are side windows in the canopy and a skylight four and a half feet above the cargo bed. A thick mat covers the bed and the walls.

Ryan raps his knuckles against the canopy. "Solid," he announces. "Fucker's armored."

Canvas seats and harnesses are anchored to the sidewalls. Nets stretched across the ceiling hold gear. Miles can see these details because red light from the cab wells through an intervening window, providing a baseline illumination. There's not enough light for him to be sure, but it looks like one net holds spare magazines and another has packs of what could be C-4. One thing he is certain about is a collection of helmets. He pops that net and pulls them out.

Ryan has moved all the way in, taking a seat closest to the cab. He pulls on a harness. Dano straps in next to him.

"Put these on," Miles says, handing them helmets. Then he straps in too, facing them, shoulder against the cab window.

Six soldiers climb in after them, vague shapes crowding in the near dark. The cargo bed fills with the heat of bodies and the smell of fresh sweat. The tailgate doors slam shut, muting the sound of gunfire. Facemasks come off, helmets go on.

In the cab, more soldiers. Miles watches them through the window. He recognizes Jameson riding shotgun. A leaner guy already strapped in behind the wheel. Two more in the backseat, wrestling with Fatima. She is struggling in her restraints, resisting their efforts to get her strapped safely in. Does she even understand this is a rescue? Or in her mind is she being kidnapped again?

Harnesses are secured. Doors close. The engine revs and the truck surges forward. Somewhere behind them, a muffled explosion. Outside, the shooting starts up again.

A side window close to Miles is shoved open. He ducks, not wanting to catch a stray bullet. Faint red highlights let him identify a KO in the hands of the soldier beside him. The weapon is aimed out the window, but the soldier isn't shooting. No one in the truck is shooting. The gunfire outside fades into intermittent firecracker pops, barely audible over the rush of air past the open window.

The window gets slammed shut.

A hearty masculine voice rises above the road noise. "Listen up, friends. My name is Rohan and this is a Requisite Operations mission. Things are going to get ugly in the next few minutes, but don't worry. The air force is looking out for us, and we *will* get you home. So hold on and don't get in the way."

LEAVING TOWN

KHALID IS BEHIND the wheel of the DF-21, a rugged, lightly armored truck that the QRF is relying on to get them out of Tadmur. True is squeezed into the backseat. She's behind Jameson, who's up front riding shotgun because he's too damn big to sit anywhere else. Fatima is next to her, with Chris on the far side.

True is braced against the DF-21's acceleration, holding her KO in a one-handed grip, her other hand poised above the switch that will lower the window if she needs to shoot. She has used her weapon only once over the course of the mission. She hopes she won't have to use it again. A street battle would guarantee civilian casualties. Not something they want.

They'll engage only if they are trapped and have no choice.

She leans forward to look at the dash display, where there's a feed from a rearview camera. She can see muzzle flash and she gets a glimpse of what might be a pursuing truck before Khalid wrenches the DF-21 around a corner.

Damn.

True had hoped to stave off pursuit. When they pulled out, she triggered the kamikazes. The devices, designed to deliver small controlled explosions, would have taken out the electronics in the downstairs office and disabled both trucks in the compound without damaging any neighboring homes.

But Hussam was the head of the Al-Furat Coalition. He had allies and soldiers in the surrounding neighborhood. No way to sabotage all their vehicles.

Fatima too is watching the rearview display, her expression fixed except for her lips which move as she speaks too softly to be heard over the road noise. A prayer, maybe.

Chris had summarized her condition over comms as he worked with True to get her strapped into a safety harness.

"No gross physical injuries," he said, speaking just loud enough for the mic to pick up his voice, but not so loud that Fatima could hear. "But he's fucked with her head. When we came in, she tried to protect him. I don't think she understands why we're here."

"She's in shock," True said.

"Yeah. And unpredictable. That's why she's in restraints. You need to talk her down."

It isn't a good time for talking. True grabs a handhold, bracing herself as Khalid whips the DF-21 hard around a traffic circle. He's riding an adrenaline high, racing to get them out into open desert. "We got fucking Hussam!" he shouts, his voice amplified over comms. "I can't believe it. We got the self-righteous bastard. And we got him *alive*."

Rohan answers over comms, annoyingly matter-of-fact, given the circumstances: "Bounty pays either way."

True turns to look in the back. The light-amplifying property of her visor reveals the tense faces of the three rescued hostages, and beyond them Juliet, Nate, Nasir, Felice, and Rohan, all strapped into canvas seats and swaying in unison as Khalid uses speed to smooth the bumps in the road. Rohan notices her gaze and flashes a thumbs-up. Shadows hide his smile but she knows it's there.

Gunfire rips overhead. Her first instinct is to duck. Her second is to trigger the window to open so she can return fire. The thick glass drops out of sight, the roaring of jet engines pours in on the dusty air. Lincoln yells over comms: "No threat! Reseal the truck. That was just RQ-3 discouraging a rooftop shooter."

"*Fuck*," True whispers, all too aware of her booming heart. She triggers the window to close again. Jameson and Chris close their windows too.

RQ-3 is one of a trio of Hai-Lin UF-29s—unmanned fighters—that make up ReqOps' air force. Lincoln has assigned all three to this mission to provide an escort for the DF-21 and for Blackbird as it carries Hussam away.

True calls up Blackbird's status on her display. The Kobrin 900-s reports itself at twelve hundred feet and still climbing. Hussam is suspended beneath the little autonomous helicopter, in a Kevlar cargo pouch at the end of a tether. If Blackbird is shot down, Hussam will go down with it. Under no circumstances will he be released alive back into the wild.

RQ-3 continues to shadow the DF-21. True hears its engine even past the armored sanctity of the cab and the blast of its air conditioning. She watches the buildings flash past, but there is no more gunfire. No resistance.

Abruptly they are past the last compound and into open desert. The DF-21's headlights are off. Khalid is no longer wearing his AltWrld visor. He's got a MARC instead, to help him see in the dark. True doesn't envy his task. She can hardly see the road past the streamers of sand that skitter across it—but it's easy to see where the road is going, because its path is marked in the distance by the fierce silhouettes of the burned-out tanks they passed on the way in.

This desert: ravaged by war and not much left to fight over. There's petroleum in the ground still, though it's not worth what it used to be. It's not worth the hell this region has become. Here, now, the fighting is an end in itself, a way of life, and that cold fact is one reason why PMCs like ReqOps exist.

"Couple of technicals behind us," Rohan says over comms.

True leans forward to look again at the dash display. The feed from the rearview camera is a kind of night vision, but shifted to display in dull red. It shows two small pickup trucks pursuing them out of Tadmur. Both are running with lights off. Machine guns are mounted in their cargo beds.

Lincoln assures the team, "We're on it."

The command post's wall monitor displays a continuously updated three-dimensional map of the desert outside Tadmur. It lets Lincoln track the shifting positions of ReqOps' equipment: the squadron of three Hai-Lin fighters, Blackbird, and the DF-21 racing up the highway. Also, a civilian convoy moving south. And of course the enemy, currently represented by two technicals speeding past Tadmur's outlying neighborhood.

"Targets acquired," Renata announces in a stern voice, operating from behind VR goggles. "Authorization?"

"Stand by," Lincoln tells her. "Let's give them a few more seconds to clear the town."

Hayden, at his desk in front of the monitor, drags RQ-3's feed from the screen's periphery, depositing it beside the map. It shows only desert and mountains as the UAV circles, getting in position for a strike. Onboard AIs pilot the Hai-Lins, but it's Renata who commands the squadron through the twitching, tapping motion of her fingers inside their black-lace gloves. She provides instruction, oversight, and authorization for the use of weapons.

"Okay," Lincoln tells her. "You're authorized. Take the shot at your discretion."

"Acknowledging authorization."

Hayden looks back, wide-eyed in excitement. He's never seen the Hai-Lins used in combat before. None of them have. This is the first time the UAVs will fire weapons in a live operation.

Lincoln feels a touch against his arm and glances down to find Tamara beside him, come to watch.

RQ-3 completes its turn. The technicals are dead ahead.

Renata says, "Missiles away."

Even as she speaks, their leased surveillance drone, cruising high above the action, issues a red alert.

On the dash screen, True glimpses a missile streaking in from the southern sky, almost too fast to see, and then sequential explosions erupt: billowing fireballs that swallow the two technicals, spitting out hard pieces, gun turrets and engine blocks that tumble into the night. She feels the concussion in her ears, in her bones.

The DF-21 jumps as Khalid leans harder on the accelerator.

"Take it easy," Chris snaps. "We're clear. No one left back there."

Lincoln says, "Premature assessment, Chris. We are *not* clear. Three bogies inbound from the southeast. Silhouetting as Arkinson XOs. No transponders."

"*Fuck*," Chris whispers in high-definition audio.

True's grip tightens on the armrest, tightens around the stock of her KO as she pushes back against lurching fear. None of their pre-mission intelligence indicated Al-Furat possessed Arkinsons—cheap and disposable jet-powered UAVs with a per-unit cost of just over five million American. They're designed to carry a payload of four slim Tau Hammer missiles—self-guided hunters that can obliterate a lightly armed ground vehicle like the DF-21 as easily as RQ-3 took out the technicals and the soldiers who rode in them. The absence of transponders means there's no telling who the Arkinsons belong to, though it's a damn good indication they're not friendlies.

The worst part: there's nothing anyone in the DF-21 can do to defend themselves. No need to look farther than the scattered debris of the technicals behind them or the looming silhouettes of the burned-out tanks ahead for evidence of that. It's on Renata to serve as their champion, wielding her squadron of Hai-Lins. True is grateful the Hai-Lins are out there, but it's a hard truth that her life and the lives of everyone in the DF-21 rely on the battle skills of machines, of competing AIs, to determine if they ever get home.

Lincoln's first move is to simplify the battle space.

He opens a voice link to the Kobrin 900-s carrying Hussam. "Blackbird," he orders, "move out. West along the highway, maximum speed while maintaining current elevation."

"You want an escort with that?" Renata asks from behind her VR goggles.

"Negative." Blackbird is slow compared to the oncoming Arkinsons and it's only lightly armed, making it as vulnerable as the DF-21, but it's not carrying ReqOps personnel, so it's not a priority. Hussam El-Hashem is its only cargo, and while Lincoln would like to deliver him alive, it isn't necessary. The bounty will still pay and it'll cover the loss of the helicopter. He tells Renata, "Focus defensive operations on our people. Set up for autonomous defense, standard protocol, and hold."

"Roger that, boss," she responds. "Three on three."

Lincoln's gaze fixes on the three-dimensional map. "Tamara, check known armaments for the Iraqi government."

"Already on it, Lincoln," she answers. "And . . . negative. Arkinsons are not part of the Iraqi arsenal. Probably a private registration. Checking area PMCs."

Lincoln's jaw sets. He got into the business of soldiering when he was eighteen, in part because it was what he knew, what he'd grown up with. But he also wanted to serve. Serve his country, serve the greater good, using the skills he was blessed with to do it. The QRF is a new phase in that tradition of service. His people are out there at the risk of their lives. It is his duty to support them to the extent of his abilities and the limit of his credit line. If it comes to a dogfight, ReqOps could lose a Hai-Lin, maybe more than one, escalating the cost of the operation. But if so, he'll make it up in other business. He'll take the chance, because he is all in.

That's the promise he makes to his people. No halfway measures.

Without waiting for Tamara's search results, he issues his next order. "Renata, initiate defensive response."

The rules of private combat are mostly unwritten but well understood among companies that regularly operate in the TEZ. A neutral PMC would not send equipment into the field to interfere with a third-party action. So the Arkinsons' presence in their area of operation marks them as enemy combatants, freeing Lincoln to take defensive actions, confident that he will not incur sanctions from the US government or ReqOps' allied contractors.

In all circumstances, right action demands that the welfare of civilian bystanders be taken into account, and as a practical matter, any PMC concerned with maintaining a viable reputation, one that allows it to operate openly, would strive to avoid collateral damage and loss of life. But in the real world, war is a messy business— which is why there is a thriving regional company specializing in the negotiation of financial compensation for incidental deaths, injuries, and the destruction of property.

But on the desert highway there are no innocent civilians to be caught in the line of fire and the only property involved is the already war-torn road.

"I don't care who the Arkinsons belong to," Lincoln says. "Neutralize them. Do not let them get off a shot."

"Roger that. Initiating autonomous defense, standard protocol, targeting Bogie-1, Bogie-2, Bogie-3. Weapons are active."

With the standard protocol in effect, the squadron AIs will operate on an instruction set written to minimize collateral property damage and avoid all civilian casualties. Excessive safeguards, tonight. "Correction," Lincoln intones. "Friend or foe."

"Confirming friend-or-foe protocol," Renata echoes in a crisp, emotionless voice. The squadron AIs will no longer have to calculate the probability of collateral damage, a change that will speed up their response time. As Renata cedes control, her hands go still.

The map shows the trio of Hai-Lins peeling apart. Lincoln doesn't know what their next move will be. Neither does Renata. Unless the Arkinsons withdraw, they are about to witness a dogfight between AIs. The Hai-Lins are technically superior, but they're not fully loaded. RQ-3 has already spent missiles against the technicals. And the AIs that fly the squadron have never before engaged in actual aerial combat. Up until now, all their battle experience has been in simulations. Their training will meet reality tonight.

True doesn't see the unmanned jets engaging over the desert, but she hears them despite the DF-21's insulation, despite its armor, the rumble of its engine, the rattling of its frame as Khalid leans on the accelerator, racing west to escape the battle. But there's no way he can outrun combat aircraft. The drone fighters scream in the night, nearer, farther. Loud enough to shake the stars.

She braces with one hand on the back of Jameson's seat, thinking of Alex and how angry he'll be if it ends here for her, if she doesn't make it home.

The DF-21 shoots over a slight rise. It goes briefly airborne, then comes down hard, skidding across a patch of sand. True feels the jolt in her spine as she's held down by the bruising grip of her harness. Beside her, Fatima gasps. Angry yells erupt in back.

It takes True a second to get her harness to loosen up enough that she can move again. When she does, she turns to check Fatima, who sits hunched in her restraints, loose hair hiding her face. True looks next into the cargo bed. If anyone back there got bounced around, it could mean a broken neck, a broken back. But everyone is strapped in, strapped down. Saved by their restraints but furious all the same.

True looks to the front again and shouts over the road noise. "Khalid, you in a hurry?"

"We're okay, Mama," he yells back. He doesn't slow down. "I just want to make sure we get home!" Fear lurks beneath the bravado in his voice.

"I want to get home too," Jameson warns him from an arm's reach away in the shotgun seat. "If you roll us, kid, I swear I'm gonna break your neck."

Fatima raises her head. She cannot raise her hands—her restraints prevent it—so she shakes her head to get the lank hair off her face. Her oily cheeks reflect the console's red gleam. Red glints give an unholy aura to her eyes.

"He *will* come," she warns in a despairing voice. "You cannot win. He will burn us all. He will."

"Fatima," True says, not quite touching her. When Fatima turns, True tries to meet that hopeless gaze, despite the jerky jumpy motion of the racing truck. She tries to plant hope, saying, "He wants you to believe that, but *I* think we can win. And this much

I know for sure: Hussam will be a prisoner of US forces by dawn, or he will be dead. For him there is no escape."

Fatima opens her mouth as if to argue, but whatever words she intends are crushed by the thunder of a jet passing directly above them. Animal instinct kicks in and everyone ducks. Even Khalid, behind the wheel.

But no autocannon fires. No missile hits them. True grasps the reason first: "Must have been one of ours. If an Arkinson passed that close, we'd be dead."

"*Fuck!*" Khalid swears as he straightens in his seat. His fingers hold the wheel in a bony grip while on his cheeks, rivulets of sweat trap the red light.

Rohan's laugh belts out over comms. Pumped up, riding an adrenaline high he says, "Take it easy, Khalid! There's no way we can outrun this fight. We live or die by the grace of our squadron AIs."

"*Truth,*" True whispers.

Ahead of them, electric-white light bursts across the desert. Briefly, it illuminates nearly a mile of empty road. Inside the truck the chatter dies. They listen: to road noise, to the throaty bellow of the engine, the dopplered roar of jets. Waiting to learn who won.

The concussive rumble of an explosion rolls in, background soundtrack to Lincoln's stern voice. "One enemy aircraft down. The other two are in retreat. The sky is ours."

Cheers ring out in both cab and cargo bed, but True does not take part. "What's Blackbird's status?" she asks, voice cutting through the celebration.

Lincoln says: "Blackbird has overrun the rendezvous. Heading back now. Otherwise nominal."

True's fingers twitch as she calls up their position on her display. It's twelve K to the rendezvous and the next phase of this mission.

"All the pieces in place?" Chris wants to know.

"On the way," Lincoln assures him. "We delayed the transport helicopter pending the outcome of the air war, but it's inbound now. We'll be back on schedule soon."

"And the merchandise?" Chris asks.

"Blackbird's camera shows it still kicking."

Wrapped in the backseat's shadows, True allows herself a small private smile. Machines dominate the battlefield, but it took human soldiers to snatch a bad guy from his bedroom and recover four captives from their prison.

It's a moment of contentment that doesn't last.

"Shit," Khalid says. "I see lights. Ahead of us. Goddamn army's worth."

PRO BONO

WHAT NOW?

True leans forward to get a look at the lights and swears softly to herself. Khalid was not exaggerating. A long line of traffic is coming toward them, headlights yellowed by the dust.

"Take it easy, everyone," Lincoln says in his gravelly, one-note voice. "That is not an army. It's a merchant convoy, still a few klicks out."

"Lincoln is watching over us," Chris reminds Khalid. "We've got high-altitude surveillance, and the Hai-Lins patrolling the road."

"Okay," Khalid says. "Good. But convoys out here run armed. There are guards on those trucks, and a lot more of them than us."

Chris says, "Just because they have weapons doesn't mean they're looking for trouble."

Lincoln speaks again: "Khalid, I want you to turn your headlights on. Let the convoy see you. Let them know you're not a threat."

Khalid doesn't rush to embrace this idea. "How about if we just wait off-road?"

Chris is first to reject the suggestion. "No. They'll assume we're waiting to pick off the last truck in the line. We don't want to look like bandits."

"Agreed," Lincoln says. "These are not Hussam's soldiers. They're merchants, and they know an op just went down. Guaranteed someone in Tadmur called them. And they've heard the jets. They are not going to risk their cargo or give us any reason to hit them. And if they do? The Hai-Lins are watching. We'll nail them before they get a window open. So turn on your headlights and make nice."

Khalid turns the headlights on.

"What else is out there?" Chris asks. "Are we going to have quiet time to make the transfer?"

"Time enough," Lincoln tells him. "Once the convoy is past, we're looking at a twenty-two-minute window with no traffic. That's your timeframe to rendezvous, transfer, and get clear."

"We'll get it done," Chris assures him.

True eyes the convoy. If a firefight *does* break out, she's in a bad position, on the wrong side of the DF-21 to return fire. No reason to think it will come to shooting, though.

As the convoy approaches, her visor filters the brightness of the headlights. The lead truck takes longer to arrive than she expects. "They slowing down, Lincoln?" she asks.

"Roger that," he says. "Looks like they're being cautious."

"They're as nervous as we are," Chris adds.

True thinks about it, imagining how they must look to the lead driver: this lone armored vehicle, racing away from a night raid in Tadmur.

The first of the headlights pierces the cab. Fatima turns her head away, hunching her shoulders and hiding her face against True's shoulder. The lead truck roars past, accelerating as it goes, rocking the DF-21 with its pressure wave. Khalid keeps their own speed steady, their course straight, as six more trucks sweep past.

Then the road ahead is empty.

"*Holy shit*," Khalid swears, switching the headlights off again.

Lincoln says, "It's good to remember not everyone in the world is out to kill us."

True knows he's right, but the tricky part comes in recognizing the enemy in time to thwart an attack—and that requires constant vigilance and a hair-trigger willingness to react in the face of partial evidence and half-imagined clues.

After another minute, Lincoln announces, "The H215 has reached the rendezvous."

Khalid acknowledges this: "I see it."

True leans forward to look. Her visor reveals a dust storm kicked up around the bulk of a large transport helicopter settling onto the highway maybe fifteen hundred meters out. It's an H215, another piece of equipment provided by their regional ally, Eden Transit, but this time with a flight crew.

She looks past the dust for Blackbird but doesn't see the little helicopter.

"You know your roles," Lincoln tells them. "Team Red receives the merchandise. Team Gold escorts the civilians."

"Blackbird in the vicinity?" Chris wants to know.

"Couple minutes out."

Fatima turns wide, fearful eyes to True. "What's going on? Is he here?"

"He's our prisoner, Fatima. He can't hurt you anymore. And we're going to get you home. That helicopter is going to get us out of here."

Khalid brakes hard, bringing the DF-21 to a skidding stop just outside the reach of the transport helicopter's rapidly spinning rotor. "Switching to self-driving mode," he announces.

True shoves her door open onto a night rumbling with the bass, bone-shaking sonics of multiple engines: the DF-21, the transport helicopter, the circling Hai-Lins. She exits the cab along with Chris and Jameson. Chris disappears into the night. Jameson slams the front door shut with help from the wind. Dust hazes the cold air, limiting True's night vision.

She shoulders her KO and speaks over comms. "Rohan, keep the civilians back there until I have a chance to talk to them."

"Yes, ma'am."

"Felice, I need you up here."

"On my way."

True returns her attention to Fatima, still in the cab's backseat.

Bound in her restraints, she looks dazed and lost. A prisoner still. True would like to remove the restraints, allow her some measure of control over her body, her fate. But if she balks or tries again to fight against her own rescue, she could endanger everyone.

"Fatima," True says, striving for a nurturing tone, although that's a challenge given that she has to shout over the engine noise. "We need to move you again, but no one is going to hurt you."

Fatima watches her with frightened eyes but says nothing. True can't tell if her words have gotten through. Nothing to do about it now.

She retrieves her pack from the floor, and then steps back, keeping one hand on the door to hold it open against the wind. Jameson is waiting. "Ready?" he asks.

True nods.

He leans in. Fatima rears back, trying to wriggle out of reach, her mouth open in a silent scream. He backs off, speaking to her in a low, confident, reassuring tone.

True crooks her fingers, signaling Felice to step in close so they can talk without comms. "You're taking care of Fatima," she instructs. "Jameson will get her aboard the flight, but I want you to stay with her. Make sure she's up front, and rig a shelter for her if you can. I do not want her to see the merchandise. And I don't want the rapist seeing her either."

"You got it, ma'am."

Jameson backs out of the cab, holding Fatima cradled in his arms. She isn't struggling anymore but whether that's because she's decided to trust him or because she's in shock, True can't say. He turns and carries her to the transport helicopter, Felice following a step behind.

True moves on to the next task. Opening her pack, she slips out her tablet and calls up a formal document. Then the roar of yet another engine draws her attention, and she looks up. Night vision shows her Blackbird coming in from the north, gliding slowly above the road, around forty meters away. It still carries its cargo suspended at the end of a long tether, dangling just above the pavement. *Right action*, she thinks with a grim smile.

But Chris and Red Team have the task of handling Hussam. Her job is to shepherd the civilians.

With her tablet in hand, True walks to the back of the DF-21 where Rohan is standing watch, facing the open tailgate doors. He looks menacing behind his MARC's half-visor, with his Fortuna held across his body. She gives him a skeptical look, one eyebrow raised. *I told you to keep them in place, not scare them to death.*

A smile quirks the corner of his mouth as he steps back, lowering the weapon.

All three civilians wait, crouched just inside the door, still wearing their borrowed helmets. They watch her with anxious expressions: Miles Dushane, former Ranger and more recently an independent journalist; Ryan Rogers, a petroleum engineer; and Dano Rodrigues, a Brazilian doctor kidnapped at the same time as Fatima.

Dushane grips the LED flashlight she gave him, holding it so the red beam points down at a haze of blowing sand. He starts to speak, but Blackbird roars overhead and for several seconds words become impossible. True turns to follow the little helicopter's flight, startled because there is a figure at the end of the tether and it's not Hussam. The Kevlar cargo pouch that carried him has been removed, and the troop carrier deployed. One of their soldiers rides standing up on the small platform, leaning against a short safety line.

This wasn't in the mission plan.

Her finger twitches as she links into comms. "Who's with Blackbird?"

It takes Lincoln a few seconds to answer. "I'm sending Juliet to look over the debris from the Arkinson. Status on the civilians?"

"Getting signatures now," she snaps, not pleased at being left out of the loop, but it's a gripe she'll save for the debriefing.

She drops out of comms. Though Blackbird is gone, the ambient noise is still overwhelming, and she has to shout just to be heard. "Don't talk," she warns the civilians. "Just listen." She turns the tablet so they can read the document on display. "This is your ticket out of here. It's a nondisclosure agreement. It says that you agree not to identify us or to describe the actions we undertook on this mission without prior written approval from our company's chief executive. There is of course an exception allowing you to speak to American officials with top-level security clearances in a confidential setting. Sign it if you want a seat on that helicopter."

No hesitation from Rogers. "Hey, not a problem. I'm in." He takes the tablet and scrawls a signature with his index finger, adding his fingerprint in the adjoining box. "Done," he says. "And what the fuck. I'm not going to write a book."

But Dushane looks suspicious while Rodrigues sputters in outrage. "This is coercion. You can't—"

True cuts him off. "We don't have time to argue," she shouts over the general cacophony. "Take it or leave it. We're here for Dr. Atwan, not for you. Your rescue is bonus points as far as we're concerned. But we're willing to handle it on a *pro bono* basis. We will not be sending you a bill." She takes the tablet back from Rogers, pulls up a fresh copy of the document, and hands it to Rodrigues. "All we're asking is your signatures on these documents. And you *can* write a book. You're free to tell the story of your captivity. That belongs to you. It's the details of your rescue that you won't be able to disclose. Small price to pay for your lives."

"Come on, Dano," Rogers urges. "Do it. So we can go."

Rodrigues glowers but he signs. Dushane goes next. When he hands the tablet back, he asks, "What about Dr. Atwan? You going to make her sign one of these?"

"She already has," True tells him. "Through a power of attorney. She just doesn't know it yet." She steps aside, clearing the way for them to exit the DF-21. "Rohan, escort them to the ship."

CONNECTIONS

MILES DOESN'T LIKE the idea of military companies. Private armies operating without legitimate authority are dangerous. Destabilizing. National armies have political and economic motivations to pursue peace, but private armies rely on a system of eternal war—and their rapid adoption of robotic weaponry only makes them more dangerous, more likely to engage.

Even so, even knowing that someone is paying Requisite Operations for the actions they've taken tonight, Miles is goddamn grateful to be out of that cell. Dano was right to say the maneuver with the NDA was coercion, but True was right too. It's a damn small price to pay.

He jumps down to the sand, dragging Dano with him, just in case the Brazilian is thinking of lodging another protest. But Dano stays quiet. Persuaded? Not likely. Probably in sensory shock from the ongoing engine noise, the stinging sand, the reek of dust and exhaust fumes jammed into their desiccated nasal passages by the wind.

Rohan waves at them to get moving. "This way to Liberty Air, gentlemen! Best service in the region, but we operate on a tight schedule, so double-time it!" In his night camo, he is a soft-focus shadow warrior.

Miles shifts into a jog, following Rohan around the still-idling DF-21. The pavement is cold and harsh against his bare feet, the whipping sand no kinder. His skull vibrates from the roar of the H215's engine as the transport helicopter's main rotor turns menacingly overhead and he's eager to get inside. It's just a few steps to the dull red light spilling from the open door.

But Rohan holds up a hand for them to stop.

The other soldiers jammed with them in the back of the DF-21 exited as soon as the truck jerked to a hard stop, disappearing into darkness, but now Miles sees them again, shadowy uniforms limned in red light as they move in unison to board the helicopter. They carry Hussam's body, still hooded and secured in a brown canvas bag. Rohan waits until they're aboard, then gestures for his charges to follow.

The cabin is cold and only faintly illuminated by the red lights. Every surface, the air itself, vibrates with the rumbling engine. Dust shimmers and dances on the seats, on the floor, in the air, a soft-focus filter that blurs every boundary.

The cabin is configured with rows of canvas seats. There's a pair of seats to the right of a narrow aisle and, in most of the rows, a single seat to the left. Near the door the single seats are missing, leaving an open area with cargo tie-downs. Hussam's body has been laid out partly in that space, his legs blocking access to the rear aisle. Miles is stunned to see a soldier crouched over him, unzipping the body bag.

The hood hides the body's face but the torso is revealed. It's unclothed. There is thick black hair on the chest and arms; the red light gives the skin the color of old bronze.

Miles's shock ramps up when he sees the body move. His heart jumps. He was sure Hussam was dead, but no. There's no mistake. Hussam's sinewy arms strain against the zip ties holding his wrists together and the Velcro restraints pinning his limbs to his body.

Rohan gestures Miles forward. A glance in that direction reveals a makeshift partition of casualty blankets that conceals the first pair of seats from the rest of the cabin. Dano and Ryan are settling into the seats behind it.

Miles feigns cooperation, moving a couple of steps, but he wants to know what's going on with Hussam. So he lingers, watching as the black hood is yanked off. Nothing gentle about the way Hussam is being handled. His neck arches, his mouth opens wide as his bloody, bearded face gasps for air. A black elastic band covers his eyes. His nose is swollen. He flops onto his side, coughing and retching.

Miles stiffens as a hand squeezes his arm. "Get your flight helmet on, Dushane," Rohan shouts over the engine noise. "And get strapped in."

Roger that, he mouths. But he delays still, watching as Hussam's naked body is hauled up and out of the bag. The man is limp, his head lolling. He's manhandled into a seat at the back of the cabin. A blanket is draped over him, the seat harness clipped over it. He sags, blindfolded head drooping. A man edging in and out of consciousness.

Miles decides he'd better sit before Rohan gets annoyed. He takes the seat behind Dano, swapping the combat helmet he's been wearing for a flight helmet. When he plugs it in, he finds himself party to a conversation.

A male voice, stern: "Road traffic approaching from the south at high speed, estimated four minutes out. Civilian traffic from the north, twelve minutes away."

Miles hesitates. He knows that voice. It's older now, raspy and scarred, and still, he remembers. He trained under that voice in Ranger School. *Lincoln Han.* So much has happened tonight that his mind has lost its capacity for surprise. He is a machine, taking in information. No room for anything else. Not yet.

He listens as another man speaks, impatient: "Let's go, True. Get that gear aboard."

"Working on it."

True Brighton. Miles ponders her full name. It's started to seem familiar, like Lincoln's voice. Something he's heard in the past. He's sure she's former army, though he can't remember why he knows that. He aches for a tablet that will let him question the Cloud.

Movement outside the door. A young man, an Arab. Dressed as a civilian, though the MARC visor he's wearing leaves Miles unconvinced. He comes in carrying a cargo net of supplies. Looks like gear stripped from the truck. True and the big soldier, Jameson, come in behind with more gear, which gets strapped to the cargo tie-downs.

Lincoln Han speaks again. "Go to work on the merchandise, Chris. I want him in shape to answer a few questions while he's still in our possession."

"I'm on it, Lincoln," Chris snaps. Miles recognizes the impatient voice, the one who was pushing True to hurry. Now Chris's tone communicates irritation—at the close oversight of command?

Been there, brother, Miles thinks.

The engine noise ramps up. A third male voice on the intercom, pilot or crew chief maybe: "Doors closing. Everyone take a seat."

Miles looks up, to see True eyeing the empty seat beside him. She's got a rangy build, bulked up by her armored vest, although in the dim light her uniform's adaptive camouflage works to blur her boundaries. Even the skullcap that confines her thick hair is night camo, leaving only her face to focus on. She takes off her MARC visor.

The red light, he decides, does her no favors, deepening the shadows around her mouth. He is curious to know how old she is, though he's not dumb enough to ask.

She drops her pack on the floor, unbuckles the flight helmet strapped to the empty seat, and flashes him a thumbs-up and a slight smile as she straps in beside him.

The helicopter lifts, swaying under the pressure of the buffeting wind. Out the window he glimpses the DF-21, headlights muted by dust, heading north again, no one at the wheel.

Once the transport is airborne, Tamara Thomas leans back in her chair in the ReqOps command post and allows herself a tired sigh. She's worn out from the stress of shadowing the mission. But it's almost done. Their preparation paid off. The equipment worked fine, and they got away with no casualties.

She waves off her two young assistants, telling them, "Take a break. Friday will let you know if we get busy again."

"You should go too," Lincoln says, not taking his eyes off the wall monitor.

"Not while Blackbird's in the air."

Tamara doesn't anticipate problems with the autonomous helicopter but she wants to observe its behavior and correct any perturbations that might show up. She also wants to review an event that took place in the courtyard.

The photovoltaic boxes were an unknown going in. Tamara guessed they housed the components of a defensive swarm. True had come to the same conclusion, so Blackbird was instructed to take them out before the QRF went over the wall. Only a single component survived long enough to launch. True saw it. It targeted her—and that gave her MARC a chance to capture it on video—a streak of motion moving too fast for details to be perceived.

Tamara hunts down that scrap of video, replays it on a desk monitor, slowing it down, studying each frame.

None of the frames are clear, but she makes out a flattened diamond-shaped fuselage, and tilt rotors on long swept-back wings.

The design stirs a sense of recognition. She runs an image search, trying to identify the model, but finds no matches. She tries a relational search, looking for UAVs that share a design heritage. That produces several results, all based on an early kamikaze developed more than five years ago by the Chinese defense contractor Kai Yun Strategic Technologies. Back when Tamara's colleague, Li Guiying, still worked for Kai Yun. It was possible, even likely, that Guiying had contributed to the design.

Tamara hisses softly, troubled at the way ideas travel and how they evolve. The Kai Yun device had a larger fuselage, and shorter wings set on ball joints. Its reported top speed didn't come close to the device in the video—but it's been five years.

Tamara considers sending the video segment to Guiying. She might be curious to see how the design has advanced. Tamara hesitates only because Guiying is sure to ask about the origin of the recording: where and when it was captured, under what circumstances, how the device performed, and if it was successful . . .

It came close to being successful.

Tamara shivers, frightened by what might have been. In an alternate timeline, where the PV boxes were hidden, the swarm might have survived to launch an attack. Under that scenario, the QRF could not have reacted fast enough to successfully defend themselves. They would have been overwhelmed.

She holds off on sending the video to Li Guiying.

Better to wait until after news of the raid goes public.

ROGUE LIGHTNING

LINCOLN WATCHES BLACKBIRD'S position shift north across the three-dimensional map, drawing closer to the wreckage of the downed Arkinson. With the wind behind it, the little Kobrin 900-s moves swiftly despite the drag caused by Juliet riding on the tether.

Displayed alongside the map is a feed from the helicopter's infrared nose camera. It shows a desolate plain cluttered with grit and stone, a line of barren hills ahead, and at the foot of those hills, the white-hot signature of burning fuel.

The appearance of the three Arkinsons is a puzzle that needs to be solved. None of ReqOps' pre-mission intelligence suggested Hussam controlled a sophisticated robotic air force. The absence argues for the existence of a third party, a hired gun with the resources and discipline to mount a serious response at a few minutes' notice.

Know your enemy.

Lincoln hopes to find clues in the wreckage that will tell him who that hired gun is.

It's a risk, of course. This side trip is going to chew into Blackbird's fuel, and if the two surviving Arkinsons return, Juliet will make an easy target. But Lincoln still has high-altitude eyes on the region. That will buy some warning time—enough for the Hai-Lins to circle back and engage.

Juliet speaks over comms. "Coming up on the debris field."

"Roger that."

A Hai-Lin overflew the crash site earlier, mapping debris strewn over two hundred meters. Lincoln mutes his mic. "You watching, Hayden?" he asks his young data wrangler.

Hayden flashes him a thumbs-up without turning around, repeating Lincoln's earlier instructions: "We're looking for identifying numbers, stickers, stuff like that."

"Exactly. But if you see anything you think is worth mentioning, mention it."

"Yes, sir."

"I'm watching too," Tamara says from her desk.

He glances at Renata. She's still strapped into the recliner, using the mediums of her VR goggles and black-lace gloves to guide the Hai-Lins as they escort the contracted transport helicopter.

Juliet speaks again: "Looks like the tail section."

Lincoln taps his mic back on, returns his attention to the monitor. Blackbird moves slowly, a hundred fifty feet above the desert. Its camera swivels, zooming in on a charred tail section embedded in a shallow trench plowed into the hardpan.

"Blackbird," Juliet says, "circle it."

Blackbird obeys, flying slowly around the object, recording it from all sides.

"Burned clean," Tamara says. "I don't see any identifiers."

There's no time to pull the wreck apart, look for serial numbers, so Lincoln says, "Juliet, move on. Let's take a look at the rest of it."

"Blackbird," she says, "survey next target."

Blackbird advances to circle a broken fuselage, crushed wings, and fire-blackened engines with low flames still flickering where fuel has soaked into the ground.

Hayden says, "I've got nothing, Lincoln. No numbers, no marks. If anything was there, it must have burned off. Wait—"

Lincoln sees it too: the edge of what might be a circular emblem. It's on a torn section of fuselage facing away from the fire. "Juliet, have Blackbird circle that section again, try to get in closer. We're looking at an emblem on the fuselage."

She repeats the instructions for Blackbird. The helicopter descends. As it does, Juliet disappears in a cloud of dust stirred up by the rotor wash. "Pull up!" Lincoln snaps. "We cannot risk engine failure."

Blackbird rises again as the wind carries the dust away.

"Blackbird," Juliet says, "switch on your searchlight. Let's see if that shows us anything."

Lincoln almost aborts the command—operating under lights always feels wrong to him, going against years of training—but he catches himself. Juliet is alone out there. High-altitude surveillance shows no other activity.

The bright beam of Blackbird's searchlight flashes on. It strikes the wreckage, finds the emblem. The curve of the fuselage hides most of it. Lincoln can see only the top of the design—twin lightning bolts intersecting a dark border—but that's enough to make him feel like he's just stepped off the map into unknown territory haunted by ghosts.

"I need to know what that is," he says in a clipped voice.

"Roger that, boss," Juliet answers. "I'm going to descend."

Lincoln checks the fuel. "You've got a three-minute margin before you need to head north," he warns her.

"Not a problem. Blackbird, put me on the ground."

The helicopter maintains its elevation but unspools the tether, lowering Juliet until she can step off the troop carrier. Hayden adds a feed from her helmet cam to the command post display.

Juliet is careful not to block the searchlight's beam as she crouches to look at the emblem. The wash of white light reveals all of its familiar details: a half-circle split into three sections by angled lightning bolts, spangled stars in the dark-blue outer fields, a bright orange sun in the center, and across the base, a name and a motto: *Rogue Lightning – Anywhere, Anytime.*

At the sight of it Lincoln shudders. Preternatural dread. His skin puckers, pulling unevenly at his scars, the pressure defining their shape, their presence, reminding him of things he's tried to forget.

Juliet doesn't share his turmoil. She just sounds puzzled. "That's your emblem, boss. What's it doing here? One of your guys on the other side now?"

His answer is terse and unhesitating. "No."

For three years Lincoln commanded Rogue Lightning, an elite Special Forces unit. "Rangers Squared" as their original commander, Shaw Walker, described it. The unit was dissolved after Lincoln's career-ending injuries, but he keeps track of the surviving veterans. Jameson and Chris work for him. All the others moved on to new postings or civilian life. "Someone copied it," he assures Juliet.

But the Rogue Lightning emblem, stolen and displayed out of place, has shaken him. He wants to know who's behind it. He wants to put a name on his enemy.

"How's the heat from the fire?" he asks.

"Not a problem. It's a cold wind."

"Okay. I'm giving you ninety seconds. I want you to take a look inside the fuselage. You see any electronics?"

Juliet climbs the wreck, looks inside. "Oh hell yeah. Mother lode. I'll grab the drives."

"Fans and filters too."

"Serious?"

"They'll contain microbiota. Could tell us where it's been, where it came from."

"Got it."

"Make it quick."

"Smash and grab. No problem." With ruthless efficiency, Juliet snaps drives out of their mounts, rips out filters, shoves it all into shielded collection bags. She clips the bags to her backpack.

"Nice job," Lincoln tells her.

"Did I make my time?"

He checks the clock. "You're only twelve seconds over."

"*Shit.*" She steps onto the troop carrier's little platform and hooks into a safety line. Automatic straps close over her boots.

"Get the hell out of there," he tells her.

"Blackbird, you heard the boss. Move out, best speed. Rest stop one."

Lincoln checks the map, confirming that Blackbird has plotted the correct route. Juliet will be checking too, using her heads-up display.

The 900-s responds, ascending straight up as it shortens the tether to cruising length. Then the craft turns north and lays on the speed. Juliet soars beneath it at the end of the curving tether, drawn almost prone by the wind.

"I'm taking a break," Lincoln announces in an angry growl. He heads for the command post door.

Tamara turns around, startled by his tone as much as by his sudden departure. The door closes behind him. When the latch clicks shut, Hayden says, "It was the emblem."

Tamara turns to him. He's a slightly built nineteen-year-old, fair-skinned and dark-haired, into video games and military history. Someone—maybe True?—said that he wanted to enlist in the army, but a severe allergy kept him out. ReqOps was almost as good. "You think?" she asks him. "He didn't seem bothered by it."

Hayden looks at her as if she's clueless. When it comes to reading people's moods, sometimes she is. "It was Rogue Lightning," he says. "That means everything to him."

Does it?

Tamara considers this as her gaze drifts up to the display. They've still got a high-altitude camera on the highway outside Tadmur. It shows a sedan and a small pickup truck stopped near the wreckage of the two technicals, with five individuals on foot exploring the debris field. A motorcycle from out of Tadmur approaches the vehicles, stopping fifty meters away. Tamara watches curiously, wondering if these people are friends or scavengers.

The motorcycle rider might not be either. He doesn't join the searchers. After thirty seconds or so, he rides on—*fast*—away from Tadmur. He pours on the speed like he's trying to catch up with the DF-21. That won't happen, but Tamara gives her assistant, Naomi, the task of tracking him anyway. "Let me know what he does."

Lincoln paces the hallway outside the command post. He still wears his headset, still listens to the chatter of ongoing communications, but he's granted himself a minute alone to settle his anger. His boots strike the floor in strict cadence. It's a display of discipline and control contradicted by the tremor that infects his hands—both the real one and the prosthetic.

In his mind the Rogue Lightning emblem is sacred, paid for in blood by men who risked their lives and who sometimes died doing work that was dark, remote, ruthless, and essential. Lincoln inherited command of the unit when Shaw Walker was killed with Diego Delgado and four other men. Lincoln rebuilt Rogue Lightning. He recruited new men, including Chris and Jameson, and for three more years they did what needed doing.

Then their gunship went down and Lincoln's injuries were severe enough to end his army career.

He thought a new commander would be named, new men recruited, that Rogue Lightning would go on. But instead the unit was dissolved and their emblem retired.

So what the hell is it doing decorating an otherwise anonymous Arkinson? One flying in defense of a murderous outlaw like Hussam?

He tells himself it doesn't mean anything. Someone stumbled across it, liked the look, and copied it, that's all—and it's not important to the outcome of the current mission.

He stops pacing. There is work to do. Phone calls to make. A procedure needs to be in place for transferring Hussam to American authorities.

He returns to the command post. There will be time for more questions when the mission is done.

VERBAL SPARRING

TRUE CLOSES HER eyes as the H215 levels off. She lets herself rest, just for a few minutes. She tries to relax. But snippets of memory pop up in her consciousness: the dark glittering surface of the anti-surveillance canopy; the crunch of glass and mechanical fragments under her boots; the hair-raising buzz of the defensive mech that targeted her; the *pak!* of Blackbird's precision kill shot . . . and her sense of a consolatory success as Miles—then Ryan and Dano Rodrigues—emerged from their stinking cell.

Ah, Diego.

Just that. A short, silent internal sigh. No more than that. She's learned to go lightly past those memories. Circle around, back to the here and now.

We take the victories we are given.

Her eyes blink, her chin lifts. She stretches her shoulders, acknowledging to herself that the mission *was* a victory. It went well. It went as planned . . . almost. The Arkinsons were a surprise, but the team was prepared for surprises. Preparation translated to survival—and success.

She loosens her harness and leans forward to check on the men in front of her. The Brazilian doctor is nodding off. Beside him, the engineer, Ryan Rogers, sits in perfect stillness, staring at nothing, like a man worried that the least wrong move could shatter the illusion that contains him.

She turns next to Miles, sitting beside her. His posture is tense. He's got one hand tight on the buckle of his harness like he's about to release it and spring out of his seat. He notices her gaze, returns it. His olive-drab flight helmet frames his bearded, dust-encrusted face. Behind the mic, his cracked lips move, asking, "Where to now?"

His question goes out over the intercom, as does her answer. She tells him, "It's under negotiation, but we'll probably take you as far as Cyprus."

He nods. "Sounds good. We can get home from there."

Rogers comes in over the intercom, voice hoarse, not quite steady. "Hey. I just want to say thank you. Thank you to everyone involved in this. Thank you for getting us the fuck out of that sub-basement of Hell. Seriously, man. I'd owe all of you my firstborn, if I had one."

Miles leans back in his seat, half-closes his eyes, and murmurs into the mic, "What Ryan said. You didn't have to pick us up. Thank you for doing it anyway."

Rohan cuts in with his usual, mocking humor. "Write us up pretty when you do the article."

"Love to," Miles tells him in a gruff voice, "as soon as True lifts that NDA."

She answers with a smile: "Sorry. That's above my pay grade."

She leans forward just far enough to grab her backpack from the floor. As she pulls the pack into her lap, a deep, throbbing ache in her knuckles catches her by surprise. *What now?* she thinks, disgusted at her own fragility. She flexes her gloved hand, testing the depth of the injury, and remembers punching a recalcitrant soldier while she and Jameson were securing the second floor. *No more fistfights for you, Brighton.*

Moving gingerly, she gets out her tablet. Noticing Miles's wary stare, she gives him a sideways look and a teasing smile. "No more signatures required. Promise."

The tablet uses its camera to scan her face. Identity confirmed, it allows her in. She fishes her reading glasses from a pocket and starts checking on the mission's digital back trail. No statement yet from Al-Furat, but three eyewitness reports have already been posted on a regional news aggregator. She starts to skim the English translations, then realizes Miles is looking, trying to read the tablet too.

A former Ranger, now an independent journalist—even in normal times he'd be afflicted with a deep, enduring hunger for information. After two months cut off from the world, he's got to be starving for it. She shifts the screen to give him a better view.

The initial reports are understandably short on details. They describe only the explosions in the compound, the hurried exodus from Tadmur, and the destruction of the two technicals. No mention of civilian casualties—hopefully there are none—or the soldiers left bound inside the house. None of the reports identify Requisite Operations by name, which suits True just fine.

She would prefer it if the company could work anonymously. That would make security easier and make them less of a target for both retribution and for the legal reformers at home. But it isn't possible. Requisite Operations' name will come out, and there will be a period of intense scrutiny. Their strategy will be to direct media interest toward the rescued hostages and the good that's been achieved. Given the speed of the global news cycle, interest should quickly fade—and everyone at ReqOps will be safer when that happens.

The intercom wakes up. It's Lincoln, speaking to them for the first time since the helicopter lifted off. "I've got a status update for you all. We are on schedule. Biometric data has gone to the State Department. They will need to confirm identity of the merchandise before they'll take him into custody, but that's a formality. Prisoner transfer *will* occur. USS *Keira Tegan* will be waiting for you. You'll offload the merchandise and depart for Cyprus, where the civilians will be admitted into the custody of their respective consulates."

"Including the target?" Chris asks.

"Roger that."

True cuts in, imagining the anxiety of the Atwans: "You notify the parents yet?"

"When you're out of harm's way," Lincoln says, "I'll make the call. For now we proceed with the interview. I want to know where those Arkinsons came from. Chris, get the merchandise plugged in."

But True sees a problem with this. "Let's assess our communications first. Right now we've got flight crew and passengers hooked in on this network."

"Roger that," Lincoln says. "We are sharing intelligence with Eden Transit. But good call on the civilians. Unplug 'em."

True slips off her reading glasses as she turns to Miles. He meets her look with a raised hand, palm out—a gesture that says *wait*.

"Lincoln," he says over the intercom. "It's been a long time. Seven years since I was in Ranger School. You remember me?"

In the ReqOps command post, Lincoln receives this question with a grudging smile. "I remember everyone, Dushane. Welcome back to the world."

"Thank you, sir. I'd like to listen in. Constrained by the NDA, if you want it that way, but I've been locked up in that bastard's care for two months. It's gotten personal."

Lincoln understands the sentiment. And Dushane is a Ranger, one of their own, after all. "Listen, not talk," he says sternly.

"Yes, sir."

"Let him stay in, True," Lincoln orders. "But get his friends unplugged."

"Roger that."

Rogers doesn't object. Rodrigues can't. The stress has gotten to him and he's passed out.

True speaks: "Felice, confirm the target is unplugged."

"Confirmed."

Lincoln shifts to the video feed from Chris's MARC. "Plug him in, Chris."

"Roger that." A moment later: "You hearing this, El-Hashem?"

Chris stands over Hussam, who is seated in the back of the helicopter with a blanket tucked around him, an olive-drab flight helmet on his head, and a black elastic band over his eyes. The boot sole Chris planted in his face has left him with a swollen nose, bruised cheeks, cracked lips, and dried blood in his neatly trimmed beard. Despite the rough handling, he answers Chris without hesitation, in Arabic. His voice is hoarse, strained: that of a man with a raw, bruised throat. But his words are clear: "*I hear a dead man talking to me.*"

Lincoln has enough proficiency in the language to understand the threat. "Not far from the truth," he acknowledges gruffly. "Let's talk."

Hussam doesn't need persuading. He looks up as if he can see past the black elastic blindfold to meet Lincoln's gaze. He has no way of knowing Lincoln is half a world away. Shifting to English, he says, "Yes, I will talk. Because I want you to know there is a price for what you've done and it's more, so much more, than the silver you're being paid for my head."

Lincoln notices Hayden eyeing him, reads the concern in the kid's expression, his unspoken question: *What can Hussam do?* Lincoln slides his hand through the air, palm down in a dismissive gesture. *Don't worry.*

Hayden nods and, forcing a smile, turns back to his display.

Men like Hussam cast spells with their words. They string words together and use those strings to bind others and make them dance to their will. Bold talk and ruthless violence. An age-old formula for those grasping at power. Right now words are all Hussam has left, so he's eager to spend them. But Lincoln has his own agenda for this conversation. "You know you're not going home," he says. "Not ever."

Hussam turns this statement around with a skill Lincoln can't help but admire. "When did I have a home?" he asks. "*Never. My father's home was made a blackened ruin. That's what the American occupation did for my family, my people. Nine of my father's sons are dead now.*" No fear in him. "Soon it will be ten."

"It would be, if it were up to me," Lincoln agrees congenially. "But we're turning you over to American authorities. If you're lucky they'll put you on trial. But I'm betting they've got a cage ready for you at some black-site prison and you'll never see the light of day again."

"As God wills." With the black elastic over his eyes, he looks like a blind prophet, pronouncing doom. "Either way I will outlive you. You know who Jon Helm is? No? You'll know soon enough."

Lincoln switches off his mic and turns to Tamara. She's transfixed by her screen, her fingers ghosting over a virtual keyboard. Her two assistants are similarly engaged. "Tamara, you got anything?" he asks her.

She checks with the assistants. Michelle shakes her head. Naomi says, "The name's too common. Must be a thousand Jon Helms out there."

Tamara tells them, "Assume it's a nom de guerre. Cross search on a security company or PMC." A few seconds later she pushes back from her desk. "Got it. Jon Helm, associated with a PMC, name of Variant Forces. Black hat. Not much data out in the light."

"Go dark."

"We're on it."

He turns his mic back on. "Was Jon Helm managing your security, El-Hashem? Did you pay Variant Forces to look out for you? I don't think you got your money's worth."

"You think it's over?" Hussam asks. He shows no fear: not in his voice and not in his manner. "No. You are marked. He will come after you. All of you."

"Are you worth that much to him?" Lincoln asks. "He's already lost an Arkinson. Are you more valuable than that?"

"*Yes.*" His lips draw back, exposing ivory teeth. "I am worth more to him than the money you will get for my head. And his reputation is worth more than that. He is . . . *relentless.* That is the word. He is one of your own. American. Special Forces. That's what you were, right? Both of you, mercenaries now. Jon Helm is his war name. I wonder if you know him by his true name?"

Lincoln doesn't like this thought, not at all, but he concedes to himself that it's possible. Plenty of former operators work in military and security companies. Still, it doesn't add up, because the Rogue Lightning emblem is stolen. He's certain of that. And if the emblem is stolen, maybe the backstory is stolen too, and "Jon Helm" is just some steroid-soaked wannabe badass who's concocted an ex–Special Forces origin story to boost his bottom line.

That's what he'd like to believe, but he can't get the theory to parse.

Long ago, he learned to trust an inner sense that perceives patterns, connections, and looming threats long before his conscious mind can map them—and that sense is telling him he's reading it wrong.

It's worth remembering that Variant Forces, the company behind this "Jon Helm," has a cash flow real enough to maintain a regional fleet of Arkinsons.

Hussam shifts restlessly, seeming puzzled, and then annoyed at the lack of an answer. When he speaks again, it's in the petulant tone of a man not accustomed to losing command of a conversation. "I think you *do* know him."

"Maybe. Why don't you tell me more about him?"

"I will tell you the kind of man he is. When I met him I saw that his left hand was crippled and scarred. I asked if he'd been shot through his hand. He said no. He said in Burma, his enemies tried to crucify him. They hammered in a spike through his left hand. Then he killed them. All of them."

Lincoln goes cold. The Burmese mission was the worst tragedy ever endured by Rogue Lightning. Diego Delgado was just one of six men lost, but his horrific death is the one everyone remembers. Eight years out, it lives on in the popular imagination through a video that persists in the Cloud despite all efforts to eradicate it. Hussam's story is a fictionalized retelling of what happened to Diego—same setup, better outcome—in other words, a lie. Lincoln understands now the reason for the Rogue Lightning emblem: some would-be tough guy co-opted and subverted the unit's history in a play to enhance his own reputation. Twisted fuck.

"Nice story," he says, determined to give nothing away, trusting his team to follow that lead. "And worthless without a name to back it up."

"Names change when war remakes us. But he will kill you."

It doesn't take an effort to sound unimpressed. "He missed his first shot."

Hussam shrugs. "You will never see the second shot coming."

Nice story.

True gives silent approval to Lincoln's acerbic assessment. Even now, eight years on, it's a gut punch every time she hears another callous reference to Diego's death. The consolation this time is that Hussam is out of the game. And this friend of his, this anonymous soldier of fortune, Jon Helm—she resolves she will not allow the idea of him to get under her skin.

Miles taps the back of her wrist—a gesture to draw her attention. He wants her to hand him the tablet. She turns it over, watching curiously as he opens a note-taking app. His fingers conjure a spell of words across the virtual keyboard. The screen is tipped at an angle that makes it hard for her to read, so when he's done, he hands it back.

Her eyes scan the message: **The American with the crippled hand is real. He led the raid when I was taken.**

Her eyebrows rise above the rim of her reading glasses. She is intrigued, sensing the possibility of valuable insight into Hussam's operation. She lowers the volume on the intercom, then with one hand types a single word: **Describe?**

She hands the tablet back to Miles. This time she leans over to watch the words appear: **Caucasian. Late 30s. Light eyes. Lean face. Lean build. Six-two? Weathered look. Tells: crooked upper lip, scarred. And a tattoo, left forearm. Inscription**

He sits back abruptly without finishing the sentence, lips parted, staring at nothing in a stunned expression that puts True on edge.

The verbal sparring between Lincoln and Hussam continues at low volume. True knows that Lincoln is trying to draw out hints and details on the status of other hostages in the region—but she isn't really listening anymore. Miles has come to some unexpected and—going by his expression—unwelcome realization, and she wants to know what it is.

Reaching out, she gestures at the tablet, fixing him with a demanding eye, saying without words, *Go on!*

He looks at her with a measuring gaze. There is something of caution, of wariness in his eyes that ignites in her a nascent anxiety. He returns his attention to the tablet. Types. This time, a question: **You said your name was True Brighton, right?**

It's a question so out of context it startles her. Her anxiety ramps up. That caution, still in his gaze. What the hell? And where is this going?

Fastest way to find out is to tell him what he wants to know. She nods.

He looks down. Types a brief phrase.

She reads it—**I'm sorry**—and her chest tightens.

He keeps typing. She watches the note take shape: **Inscription on his tattoo. "Diego Delgado. The Last Good Man."**

Prickling sweat flushes from her pores. An insurgency of emotion—anger, grief, regret—wells up, warring for the territory of her mind. She slides her glasses off, leans back, closes her eyes. She's had years of practice countering similar assaults. It takes seconds of concentration, a few deep breaths, but she steadies herself. When she opens her eyes again, she's back in operational mode and determined to learn more.

Taking the tablet from Miles, she types, **Would you recognize him, if you saw him again?**

Miles nods. No hesitation.

It's the answer she expected. The memory of his kidnapping is surely burned into his mind. That's the way of traumatic events. Eight years on, she still easily remembers the residential twilight, the clothes she was wearing, her breath white on the evening air as she jogged the last half-block home, and the first, vague tendril of dread when she realized it was Lincoln waiting with Alex on the porch, the two of them standing unnaturally still beneath an amber light, a few intrepid moths fluttering in the warm glow.

She shivers. She learned of the circumstances that led to Diego's capture only because Lincoln violated regulations and told her—

those words graven in her memory too—his voice gentle but matter of fact:

They were hunting Saomong CCA—the terrorists who'd brought down Flight 137. But they found far more enemy on the ground than we'd anticipated. Communication was compromised, and mechanical problems with the helicopter slowed the rescue effort. We believe four members of the team were killed in a running battle. Diego was wounded. Badly wounded, we think. He was captured along with Shaw Walker.

The Saomong Cooperative Cybernetic Army: True wasn't even sure what their political goal had been, or if they'd even had one, beyond fucking things up. The "cybernetic" part of their name was no joke. They were brilliant but brutal, into electronic sabotage and remote-control terrorism, sowing chaos all through Southeast Asia. And they really were an army, small but effective, financed by the drug trade and supplied by outlaw regimes.

Lincoln believed that because Diego was wounded and likely to die anyway, he was picked by his captors to die first. Crucified and burned on high-definition video. Lincoln warned her not to watch it. She watched it anyway. She wanted those scars.

Shaw Walker died several days later, incinerated when a Chinese cruise missile struck the village of Nungsan where he was being held.

What does it mean that an American mercenary with a crippled hand, who claims to have been in Burma, has her eldest son's name tattooed on his arm? Is Diego a fetish now? A secular saint in some twisted martial religion?

The Last Good Man.

Her anger turns in a slowly expanding gyre.

Just minutes ago she had resolved to keep an emotional distance from the idea of this ambiguous persona labeled "Jon Helm"—but that is impossible now.

She flinches at another touch against her wrist. Miles is watching her with a worried gaze, as if he suspects this is all too much for her. Her eyes narrow. She has seen that expression too many times in her career, but she is not so fragile—and she wants him to know it. So she turns to the tablet and types: **Thank you for telling me. We need to figure out who this Jon Helm is. Maybe there's a bounty on him.**

His lip curls. He takes the tablet and types: **Let me know. I'd love to hunt that fucker down.**

She gives him a sideways smile, unsure if that's bravado or if he really means it, but she approves of the sentiment all the same. She types, **We'll be on the ground in a few minutes—scheduled refueling stop. Let's pick up this conversation then.**

He nods and leans back, closing red-rimmed eyes.

True watches him. Of course he's exhausted. He's been through hell, although he's weathered it well—so far. Eventually his experiences will circle back on him. No way out of it. He's facing rough times ahead.

She cocks her head, listening, but the intercom is quiet. Lincoln's brief interrogation is done, at least for now. She's grateful for it, grateful for the silence as she considers her next best move.

REFUELING OPERATION

THEY SET DOWN at a small airfield on the edge of the desert. The pilot shuts down the engines—but that doesn't mean it's quiet. There is the low, rushing murmur of wind, the rumble of the fuel truck, the clatter of mechanics, the rustle of movement and the shuffle of boots on the floor, with Chris barking orders as he sets up a security perimeter. None of it wakes Miles, who has nodded off in the few minutes since his typed conversation with True.

She lets him sleep. There is no hurry now, not if circumstances work out as she intends. Besides, the mission is ongoing and, like Chris, she has duties.

She moves forward to check on Ryan Rogers and Dano Rodrigues. The Brazilian is asleep but the engineer is awake, alert. She gets him a bottle of water and trades a few words, letting him know they'll be on their way again in a few minutes.

Felice emerges from the next row where she's been sitting with Fatima, concealed behind the curtain of casualty blankets.

"How's she doing?" True asks, peering past the barrier.

Fatima is curled against the bulkhead. A blanket tucked around her hides both her safety harness and her restraints. Her eyes are open, blinking, but she doesn't look up. She gives no sign that she's heard True's question.

"She's not talking," Felice says. "But she's calm. I'd like to take the restraints off."

"I'd like that too." She squeezes past Felice and drops into the vacant seat.

"Dr. Atwan?" she asks, just loud enough to be heard over the ambient noise. "How are you doing?" Fatima doesn't respond, not by gesture or eye contact or words. "Talk to me, Dr. Atwan. I need to know that you understand. You're safe now, and you're on your way home."

This time, True's words have an effect. Maybe it's the mention of home, but Fatima shivers—a tremor that runs through her whole body—and without turning her head she asks in a plaintive voice, "Are my parents dead?"

"*No,*" True answers emphatically as a flush of outrage heats her cheeks. "If he told you that, he was lying. Your parents are fine. They are the reason we are here. They asked us to come find you, to bring you home. They miss you so much. They love you."

Fatima's lips tremble. She seems on the verge of tears but she still will not look at True.

"We'd like to take off your restraints," True tells her. "Okay?"

She doesn't answer right away. Instead she straightens, stretching as if testing her bonds. Then she says softly, "Thank you. I won't make trouble."

By the time True steps back out from behind the curtain, Miles is up and out of his seat, standing with Ryan Rogers at the open door, both of them watching the activity outside.

Hussam is still strapped into a seat at the back of the cabin, eyes hidden by the blindfold and mufflers over his ears to ensure he doesn't benefit from an overheard comment. Rohan is babysitting, sprawled casually in the next seat. He's still wearing his visor, his Fortuna held in a loose grip, the muzzle pointed at the floor. He notes True's gaze and flashes her a thumbs-up. She smiles.

The rest of the seats are empty. Everyone else is outside.

Miles gives Rogers a nudge. The engineer turns, takes note of True. "Hey," he says. "I think I'm going to sit down before I fall down." He shuffles back to his seat, water bottle in hand, swaying in exhaustion.

True joins Miles at the open door. "What'd you tell him?" she asks in amusement, indicating Rogers with a subtle tilt of her head.

Outside, the wind sweeps veils of dust through a pool of illumination cast onto the tarmac by a large rack of portable lights. The two-man Eden Transit ground crew works with keffiyehs wrapped around their faces. They've hooked up the fuel line; the pump is running with its grating noise. The pilot is with them, observing the operation. The copilot is up front, keeping an eye on the gauges. The entire refueling operation is watched over by two Eden Transit surveillance drones, backed up by Jameson, Nate, and Ted, patrolling beyond the reach of the lights.

Before they landed, True looked over a satellite map that placed the airfield in a dry, denuded plain, just a few scattered residences beyond the razor wire and chain-link fence. Abandoned residences, maybe. She can't see any lights.

Miles answers her question, saying, "I told him you wanted to do separate interviews." His lips barely move as he speaks. His voice is just loud enough for her to hear. She frowns. Did she give him the impression she was pursuing a private agenda? *Maybe.* She eyes Chris and Nasir talking together outside the pool of light. She considers Rohan in the cabin behind her, with his enhanced hearing. She pushes on anyway. There is nothing private about her next request.

"I'd like you to fly back to the States with us, if you're willing—though I guarantee the State Department won't like it. They'll want you in their custody. They'll want to interview you—but I want to interview you too, work with you during the flight home, see if we can figure out who Jon Helm really is. Interested?"

His voice returns to normal volume. "Sure. If you can make it happen. I owe you a lot more than that."

The lights of another aircraft appear in the night. It's flying low and slow as it approaches the field. Miles draws back, watching it with a tense gaze.

True recognizes Blackbird. "No worries," she tells Miles. "That one's ours. A Kobrin Remote Lift 900 stealth. Leased for the mission from Eden Transit and flown by one of our AIs."

The little ship buzzes in. As it draws closer, True makes out Juliet's figure suspended beneath it. She's laden with extra baggage beyond the standard backpack and weapon. Out beyond the fuel truck, Blackbird lowers her to the tarmac. Chris and Nasir set off to meet her while the 900-s moves away toward a line of three hangars.

"Juliet used to pilot machines like that," True muses. "So did I. Now the AIs get to do the flying and we've been demoted to cargo. Pretty soon this business of war won't involve humans at all—you know, except as targets."

Miles gives her a cool look. "And the PMC that fields the best robots wins the day?"

"You got that right," she says, crossing her arms. "It's the only reason you're here."

"Yeah, sorry. From what I've seen, your outfit is damn good at what you do."

She nods, too aware of the contradictions. "We're a private military, but we still serve our country. And we're in business only because there's a need for our services."

Some would make a counterargument that PMCs exist because they've created a need for their services: When one side buys protection, it encourages their rivals to seek armed protection too, and there's no financial incentive for military companies to seek peace.

Miles scratches at his dirty beard. "I got to ask you something."

Her lips quirk in cynical amusement. She can guess what's coming. It's what everyone asks eventually. *Why the hell are you working as a hired soldier? Especially after what happened to Diego?*

But he surprises her, asking something quite different, "How the hell are you old enough to be Diego Delgado's mother?"

His question stirs a faint, bitter echo of old battles—her father's harsh criticism, her own stubborn defiance. *I would do it all again,* she thinks as a melancholy smile tweaks the corner of her mouth.

She says, "I had him when I was still seventeen. Fell in love with a nineteen-year-old soldier. Dumbest thing a girl can do, you know? Thirty-one years later we're still married. Three kids. Like they say, through thick and thin." She whisks her hand through the air, a gesture that encompasses the helicopter, her fellow soldiers, the airfield, the entirety of the mission, maybe too, the historical weight of her marriage. "Alex hates all this. He's a paramedic now. Got out of the army after his first term."

Miles cocks his head, eyeing her uneasily. "At Ranger School, one of the instructors talked about Diego's execution."

"Yeah, I've heard that." She crosses her arms. It's not her favorite subject, but it's not one she hides from.

The pump has stopped. She watches the ground crew working together to reel the fuel hose back onto its spool at the side of the truck. "They *should* talk about it," she says. "Young soldiers need to understand that what they're taking on is not a game. Things get fucked up." She turns back to him. Hard shadows cast on his face by the blue-tinged lights make him seem older than his years. "*You* know how fucked up things get."

"I know."

The pilot signs off for the fuel. The ground crew wishes him well. They climb into the fuel truck's cab. The engine starts up with a rumble and the truck pulls away. In the distance, the little Kobrin is being pushed into a hangar lit with amber lights. Three figures walk together toward the H215—Chris, Nasir, and Juliet.

Miles glances over his shoulder to where Rogers is sitting, a row away, then tilts his head, indicating the tarmac. True nods. They jump down together and walk a few steps away. In an undertone, Miles tells her, "Every day in that cell we wondered if it was our last day. Maybe because I'd seen that tattoo, I kept thinking about Diego and that video and how people reacted to it. All the war talk that followed it. God forgive me, but I was angry about it— because Hussam was one sadistic bastard and I knew something like that could happen to me. And if it did? The world wouldn't notice. People are so jaded, that kind of stuff doesn't even make the news anymore."

True doesn't agree. "I don't think people are jaded," she says, surprising herself with the admission. "I think it's self-defense.

There are so many tragedies, who can process them all? You can't grieve for everyone."

"That tattoo though, what it said . . . 'The Last Good Man.' Doesn't that sound personal to you? It's like he knew Diego, admired him, grieved for him . . . you think?"

Her mind doesn't want to go there. "No, I don't believe that." Her voice has become as soft as his. "I'm not saying they never met. You meet a lot of people in the service. But I think it's a fetish. Fame and horror and martyrdom—they pull people in. Diego kept his friends close. I knew who they were, and I can account for every one."

He glances around at Chris and the others as they approach. "Maybe another prisoner at Nungsan?" he suggests. "Someone you never heard of?"

"*No.* No one got away. Shaw Walker was the only other prisoner and he died there. Everyone at Nungsan, everyone who saw Diego, who touched him, hurt him, all of them—they're dead. I made sure of it."

As she says it, she realizes how it must sound, so she adds a clarification. "Not dead by my hand," she says, moving back to the H215's open door. "I just looked into it, because yeah, for a while, I wanted revenge. But you've gotta let that stuff go."

"It must be hard not to hate."

A slight, bitter smile as she lingers on the tarmac beside the cabin door. "Who said I don't hate? The truth is I'm pretty indiscriminate about it. There are millions of people I could hate. Everyone who wants to give themselves rights they deny to others, who wants to fuck with self-determination, individual freedom—and a woman's freedom matters too. It's like this, Miles. We want to be friendly with people, but what I just said, that kind of philosophy? It's deadly to most traditional belief systems. Most of them, maybe all, require violent enforcement or, at the least, emotional blackmail, or they fall apart. Tolerance cannot coexist within intolerant systems. Not back home and not here. One of them has to die." She moves out of the way as Chris approaches, carrying two shielded collection bags.

"Personally, I'm voting we push the intolerant assholes out the airlock."

"You proselytizing again, True?" Chris asks.

"Always on," she assures him. She trades a fist bump with Juliet. "Did you find us some treasure?"

Juliet's expression has an electric intensity as she leans in close and grabs True's elbow. "Lincoln didn't tell you about the emblem, did he?"

The way she says it sends a shiver up True's spine. "What emblem?"

"Rogue Lightning. *Their* emblem. We found it on the crashed Arkinson."

"Remember that motorcycle you asked me to watch?" Naomi asks when Tamara returns to the command post after a short break.

Lincoln turns around, head cocked curiously.

"Sure," Tamara says. "What have you got?"

"He's freelance intelligence. Got to be. Look." Naomi gets up, walks over to Hayden's desk, and shifts a tile to the center of the screen. "See him? He's here, just off the highway." She shifts the view. "And way out here . . . is the wreckage of the Arkinson. He's sent a starburst copter out to look at it."

"I see it," Hayden says. "To the right of the main wreck."

"That's it," Naomi agrees. "He's circled every fragment twice. Got to be taking pictures to sell."

Lincoln shrugs. "Entrepreneurs are everywhere."

But something about the situation makes Tamara uneasy. "Hmm," she says. Just that. But it's enough to make Naomi whirl around, eyes wide.

"You think it's something else?"

"No," Tamara says thoughtfully. "I think your assessment is correct."

"Then what?"

Tamara isn't really sure. "*Damn*," she says softly. "I wish we'd destroyed that emblem."

"The Rogue Lightning emblem?" Naomi asks, side-eyeing Lincoln.

Lincoln is glaring at the screen. "You're right. We should have. There wasn't time, but we should have."

Hayden sounds puzzled when he asks, "You think it could come back to bite us? That wasn't even our ship."

"It's a coincidence," Lincoln explains. "That's all. But coincidences get misread all the time. Tamara's right. It's a loose end. We should have cleaned it up."

In the air again, heading north:

True broods over the question of Jon Helm—anonymous mercenary riding the reputation of Rogue Lightning, paying false homage to Diego's death.

She messages Lincoln: **You need to try Hussam again. He's got to know more about Jon Helm.**

Lincoln responds, **Fuck him. Hussam is done talking. We'll find out what we need to know on our own.**

True knows he's got queries out to his contacts and that he's assigned Tamara's team to do research, but so far it's like the man is invisible. Nothing more than a name. There isn't much on Variant Forces either and what there is, it's all from dark sites. Chatter leaves the impression that Variant Forces is a sophisticated operation, a PMC that's involved in finance as well as security, backing enterprises that deal in currency, drugs, petroleum, weapons, hostages.

They reach the coast, head out across the Mediterranean.

A message comes in from Tamara, addressed to both True and Chris: **Al-Furat finally issued a statement. They're claiming Hussam is dead. We gunned him down in cold blood.**

Chris responds: **Damn, I missed that part.**

True asks: **They worked out a successor yet?**

Tamara: **Looks like it's going to be Rihab. It says he swears revenge.**

True: **Hussam's little brother, right?**

Chris: **No worries. We'll get him next time.**

True sighs and leans back, closing her eyes. Twenty minutes later, they set down again, this time on the helicopter deck of a US Navy destroyer. Chris and Jameson escort the prisoner to the door, where Navy personnel take custody. They cover Hussam with an IR-opaque blanket and lead him away beneath the spinning rotors.

Seconds later, the H215 is in the air again and en route to Cyprus.

Lincoln messages the team's families, letting them know the mission is done and that everyone is safe and on the way home.

GHOST

THEY ARRIVE IN the middle of the night at a British Sovereign Base Area on Cyprus, setting down on an isolated concrete apron. No media waiting. No fanfare. Just a cluster of British officers and American officials, along with three gray vans.

In the deal worked out by Lincoln, the British have agreed to mediate the repatriation of the civilians but they want to stay outside of an anticipated legal squabble over the activities of mercenaries. So Requisite Operations is to depart immediately—a scenario that suits True just fine. Even better, Lincoln has worked a magic spell, persuading US officials to let Miles Dushane leave with them.

"Chris," True says over the intercom as the H215's engines wind down.

"Here."

"Hold the officials at the door. I want a couple of minutes to talk to Fatima."

"You got it."

The curtain of casualty blankets still hangs between the seats. True looks around it to find Felice helping Fatima out of her safety harness. Felice looks up. "Ready?" she asks.

"Just about."

Fatima appears tired but calm. Her face has been washed and her hair neatly tucked away beneath a thin orange cloth that she's using as a hijab. She meets True's questioning gaze and with a hoarse edge to her voice she says, "You want to know if I will throw another mad fit?"

True sits down beside her. "You seem past that."

"For now," Fatima agrees.

True says, "Felice has told you that there are US State Department personnel here, waiting to receive you."

"Yes."

"They'll see that you get medical treatment and that you get home. Your parents will be here tomorrow."

"I understand. Thank you." Her gaze cuts away. Her hand closes into a tight fist against her thigh. "I'm pregnant."

This is not a surprise. True tells her, "I'm sorry. I'm sorry he's laid that claim on you."

Fatima looks at her again. Her gaze is steady, focused. Angry. "You understand, then. If I bear this child, I will be a slave, *his* slave, for all my life. My body used by him, to his own ends. I *hate* it. I hate his voice in my head, so superior, lecturing me how it is all God's will. I hate this fear he has put into my heart. I hate *him*. I hate him."

"He deserves your hate," True says. "Never forget what he did to you. Never forgive it. Never forgive those who inflict such horror on others." Her focus slips. She hears again the soundtrack of Diego's agony—and her own hate bleeds as raw as ever.

She draws in a sharp breath, forces herself back to the surface. "Hate him," she advises Fatima. "But don't let him live inside your head. Don't let him make any decisions for you. It's on you to decide who you are and why you're here in the world."

The ghost of a bitter smile surfaces on Fatima's face. "Thank you for finding me," she says. "I am ready to go."

Chris gets the door open. There's an awkward moment as they say goodbye to Fatima, to Ryan Rogers, and to Dano Rodrigues. When they are gone, a pair of American intelligence officers comes aboard. Everyone signs an electronic document agreeing to submit to an interview within forty-eight hours of their return to the United States, and after that they transfer to a chartered jet. A cheer goes up as it lifts off. There are fist bumps and yells of "Right action!" Chris even gives a little speech: "We did what we came to do and we did it well. Be proud. This will be one to remember." He sniffs at the cabin air, shakes his head. "And damn, we stink. As soon as we reach cruising altitude, I want everyone to get cleaned up."

They use the kitchenette and the tiny restroom to wipe down. The clothes worn on the mission, smelling of sweat and smoke and gunfire, are packed away in plastic bags. They change into civilian clothes. An extra athletic shirt and trousers are found for Miles. He still doesn't have shoes but he's not going to complain.

"Who's got a razor?" he shouts down the aisle. He remembers the coarse length of his beard. "Maybe scissors too."

Rohan grins. "I've got just the thing." He reaches deep into his pack—and produces a straight-edge razor, of all things. Turning the blade so the cabin light flashes against it, he says, "Of course you might slash your own throat if we hit turbulence."

Miles shrugs and accepts the weapon. "I always wanted an ironic death."

He manages not to kill himself. Afterward, his face clean, he studies himself in the mirror, startled at how much he's aged. His face is thin, bony, reminding him of the way his father looked after a bout of pneumonia almost killed him. Miles was lean before this ordeal, but looking at his ribs, his hollow belly, he guesses he's lost thirty pounds. He pulls his borrowed shirt back on, returns to the cabin, returns the razor to Rohan. Khalid hands him a steaming microwaved meal.

Miles wants to ask about the mission, how ReqOps located Hussam, how they got inside the building, how they pulled it all off without taking casualties. He wants to ask who hired them, and what their relationship is to the US government, and what legal basis they had to do what they did. But the smell of hot food reminds him that he's thirty pounds underweight and starving. So he eats. Afterward he leans back in his seat, closing his eyes for just a minute—and doesn't wake up again until the plane touches down in Dublin. A brief refueling stop. Only the pilot is allowed to disembark. Miles goes back to sleep.

True gives in to post-mission fatigue, sleeping most of the way to Dublin. She's more alert as they set out across the Atlantic. It's 0400 on the west coast. Lincoln has gone home to sleep, but she knows someone will be staffing the command post, so she calls in. Michelle, one of Tamara's assistants, answers.

"Hey," True says. "We got anything new on Jon Helm?"

Michelle answers with a low, dejected sigh. "Not really. Any outfit with the resources to field those Arkinsons should have a bigger footprint, but there's a weird silence around his operation. We haven't even been able to track down the provenance of the Arkinsons."

It's disquieting news. "Do you have any idea why that might be?"

"He employs the right people. That's my guess. Wildcat cybertechs who make sure his name stays out of the Cloud."

"Jon Helm," she murmurs. "Still no idea what his real name is?"

"Not a clue."

"All right. Keep me posted."

On the east coast, it's just past 0700. The day's getting started. In a couple of hours, Lincoln will be on the phone. He has a long list of contacts—trusted friends and former associates—any one of whom might have insight on Jon Helm's identity. But True has Brooke Kanegawa—and Brooke has straight-line access to intelligence resources in the US Department of State.

It's a girl thing. True met Brooke when they were both pregnant—True with her third, Brooke with her first. True had been only twenty-seven—*Twenty-seven? My God, was that even possible?*—on temporary assignment in Washington DC, drafted onto a committee charged with producing a report on the sequence of blunders leading to the Mischief Reef incident. Brooke, a State Department employee with a master's degree in international relations, was assigned to the same committee. They've stayed close ever since.

True uses her tablet to compose a brief email:

> **Mission accomplished. But I'm trying to chase down an identity on a nom de guerre, "Jon Helm." Associated with a black-hat PMC, Variant Forces, based somewhere in Africa. Got anything you can share?**

She doesn't expect an immediate answer. It's too early. She waits five minutes. Nothing comes, so she gets up to get something to eat. She finds Chris awake. They talk, and then she returns to her seat. Just before 0900 EDT, a reply from Brooke drops into her tablet:

> **Holy F!!!! When you guys at ReqOps go head-hunting, you don't fool around! This place is buzzing. Some not happy, to be honest. You know how it is. Toes have gotten stepped on, so watch yourselves.**
>
> **Re: Jon Helm. You believe in ghosts, sister? People here do. And that's all I can say about that.**

True stares at the note. Reads the second paragraph a few more times. A shiver walks her spine. That second paragraph says a lot: Jon Helm is known to State, he's supposed to be dead, and he's someone True knows or at least knows of . . . If he was a stranger, Brooke would not have made it personal: *You believe in ghosts?*

So who is it?

True thinks back over twenty-seven years of service. She's met a lot of soldiers in that time. Some are dead, some still serve. Most have returned to civilian life. She keeps in touch with only a few.

Another email arrives from Brooke. As True's gaze alights on the subject line, she feels a feverish flush: *Diego.*

True didn't mention to Brooke anything about Jon Helm's tattoo. So why is Brooke thinking of Diego?

She opens the email to find a photo of Diego. Lincoln is on one side of him, face unscarred, Shaw Walker is on the other. All three of them drunk and Diego with a brilliant, carefree smile. He looked so much like his father: a lean face, chiseled Spanish features, dark eyes, dark eyebrows, and skin that turned a rich brown with just a hint of sunlight.

True remembers the day that picture was taken. She remembers taking it. A Fourth of July barbecue she and Alex put on a few weeks before Diego's first deployment with Rogue Lightning. They were bound for Kunar Province in Afghanistan. Gone three months. Near the end, Lincoln was seriously wounded. That was the first time he was seriously wounded, by gunfire. Diego took no visible wound but after he returned, he never smiled like that again.

Five months later, he was dead.

True blinks against welling pressure in her eyes. Scrolls past the photo to where Brooke has included a single line of text:

You have to wonder, if he'd lived, who would he be now?

True's heart skips as she scrolls back up to look at the photo again. Who would he be now? She enlarges the image. *If* he had lived . . .

She lets Lincoln drop off the screen. Then Diego, because there is no "if" about his death. True read the autopsy report. She examined the x-rays. She looked on his blackened and shrunken body.

Only Shaw Walker's image remains on the screen. He's laughing with Diego, but his eyes are narrow, his mouth quirked. His is a cynical humor. He's a good-looking man, with a high forehead and strong, balanced features. His eyes are light-colored. Easy to think the camera failed to capture their blue hue, but True knows it rendered them accurately: pale gray. His buzz-cut hair is dark blond. In the photograph, he's clean-shaven.

True studies his face, the set of his eyes, the details of his expression. She strives to see through to his soul. If Shaw had lived, who would he be now?

Brooke has an answer to that: He'd be Jon Helm.

JON HELM

TRUE NEEDS TO be sure. She spends twenty minutes in the Cloud, going through her albums and pulling out photos of soldiers who fit the description of Jon Helm that Miles provided—Caucasian, light eyes, lean face, lean build. She dumps them into a slideshow, putting Shaw Walker's photo sixth. The picture is eight years old. Shaw would have been in his early thirties.

They are halfway across the Atlantic when she wakes Miles. He sits up, bleary and apologetic. He looks years younger without his beard.

"We were supposed to talk about Jon Helm," he remembers.

She says, "I want you to look at some pictures."

"Sure. Happy to."

"Go wash your face. Drink some water. I need to know you're awake."

She waits in the aisle until he comes back with a cup of coffee. He returns to his window seat; she sits beside him.

"I've collected some pictures," she says. "Think of it as a photo lineup, okay? I'd like you to look at them. Let me know if anyone looks familiar." She wakes the tablet, hands it to him.

He puts his coffee in a cup holder, then studies the first photo. "Don't know him," he says.

"Swipe to see the next one."

He does, examines it carefully, shakes his head. The third portrait catches his attention. "I think I met this guy once in a bar." And the fourth photo: "That's Rick Hidalgo—he was an instructor at Ranger School."

"You're right," True says. "That's who that is." She strives to keep her voice flat, to show none of the anxiety she's feeling. She doesn't want to influence him, even on a subconscious level.

He looks at the fifth photo but makes no comment. He swipes to the sixth, Shaw's photo. "*Fuck*," he whispers.

True's stomach knots, but she says nothing, makes no move. She focuses on her breathing, keeping it soft and even.

In a husky voice, Miles says, "This is an old photo. The guy's older now. He has a scar on his lip. But it's him. The merc with the crippled hand. Jon Helm." He turns to her. "You know him? Who is it?"

"He's supposed to be dead," she says in a voice barely audible over the white noise of the engines. She takes back the tablet, taps out of the slideshow, and turns off the screen before reciting the facts like a whispering automaton. "Shaw Walker. Captured along with Diego. Held with him at Nungsan. Shaw was there when they murdered Diego. They made him watch the execution. You can't see him on the video but you can hear him screaming, pleading with them to stop, to stop . . ."

She's rambling. A sharp breath, a few seconds to steady herself. She doesn't look at Miles when she says, "Thank you for helping. That's what I needed to know."

She starts to get up but he catches her arm. Veins stand out on the back of his large hand as he holds her in a firm grip. "That bastard couldn't have been Shaw Walker," he says in a harsh whisper that escapes between clenched teeth. "Shaw Walker is a decorated combat veteran. Shaw Walker is fucking *dead*!"

"Let go of me," True says.

Miles looks confused. He releases his grip. His voice is soft, husky with anger as he says, "Hey, I'm sorry. But how the fuck could it be him?"

It occurs to True that the only thing she knows about the circumstances of Miles's kidnapping is that the raid was led by the merc with the crippled hand.

By Shaw Walker.

"I don't know how," she says, a tremor in her voice betraying her. She sits down beside him again. Not looking at him. *Breathe.* She gathers herself and when she speaks again, her voice is steady, calm, controlled. "The army identified remains found at Nungsan as those of Shaw Walker. That's what I was told."

She glances across the aisle to where Jameson is sleeping. This knowledge, it's as if she's stumbled onto the rusted shell of an unexploded bomb. Speak too loud and she might set it off. She leans close to Miles and whispers. "This is going to cause a lot of fallout among our veterans. A lot of bad feelings." Sweat glistens on his cheeks; his jaw is so taut it looks like he's holding back a scream. "I need to ask you one more favor."

"Don't ask me to keep this a secret, True."

"Just until we're home." She knows that Chris is in the back of the plane with Khalid. Everyone else is in their seats. Asleep, maybe. She hopes they're asleep. "I just think it's best to wait until we're on the ground."

He stares at her suspiciously, like it's a trap. "I'm going to be researching this," he warns her. "Writing about it."

She's surprised by the fierceness of her own response. "Think about that, Miles. This is a man who does not want the world to know he exists. You want him coming after you?"

"What the hell? What are you saying? You're going to let this go?"

"*Fuck* no. I'm saying you need to be careful. I understand you're a journalist now, not a Ranger. I understand your priorities are different. But take time to assess the situation."

"And you?" he asks suspiciously. "What are you going to do?"

She thinks about it. After a few seconds she says, "I buried what was left of my son eight years ago. I went to five more funerals—for Shaw, and for the other soldiers who did not survive that mission. I thought it was over—as if you can ever get over something like that. But if Walker is alive, I want to know why. I want to know how. I want to know what the hell he's doing preying on innocent people like you. And I want to know what *really* happened at Nungsan."

"Then we've got the same goals," Miles says. "Except I've got one more. I want to see him brought in. I want to see him stand trial. And when he's locked away in a super-max, I'm going to write a fucking book."

DANGEROUS GROUND

By the time they land at JFK, the news about the mission is out. Emails have started to arrive. Most are congratulatory but True knows that's only because her digital assistant, Ripley, files away the toxic missives—the insults, ill wishes, and death threats from digital terrorists, half of them generated by passionless trolls working under the direction of propaganda bureaus, the rest the irrational rants of awkward kids, or of narcissistic farts who imagine they can command the world from behind black curtains. Ripley forwards redacted copies of the toxic stuff to a nonprofit troll-hunting service with an AI that tries to engage the senders, while analyzing patterns and clues in their emails that get cross-matched to billions of forum posts until anonymity melts away. True scans the weekly reports, but otherwise she doesn't waste time on it.

As their plane taxis from the runway, she types a quick, smartass answer to a gruff note from her old man:

> Yes, I know what "retired" means. It means I get to choose my own missions. I'll let Lincoln know your opinion of his "loose cannon maneuvers."
> Love,
> True

A new email comes in. True grimaces when she sees it's from Tamara's too-friendly colleague, the roboticist Li Guiying. She endures a flush of embarrassment when she reads the subject line:

You are a hero among women!

For fuck's sake.

Eyes narrowed in irritation, she skims the congratulatory note, confirming that it contains the sort of flattery she's come to expect. In an uncharitable turn, she wonders if Guiying has trained a simple AI to write her correspondence, teaching it basic rules of echoing and praise. An easy project for someone with her skills, and it would let her maintain pseudo-friendships with thousands of potential colleagues.

True decides she likes the idea. It's a neat explanation for what she's always regarded as the inexplicable amount of attention Guiying has paid to her ever since they met at a London seminar . . . five or six or seven years ago? True's presentation at that seminar had been a brief, informal talk on the potential lethal impact of autonomous combat systems. She'd argued for the moral necessity of a human decision-maker in the kill chain.

Li Guiying—a stranger at the time—approached True afterward, a rosy blush coloring her face as she awkwardly introduced herself as a robotics engineer formerly employed by the Chinese firm, Kai Yun Strategic Technologies, but working now for a French corporation.

Guiying was in her late twenties then, a petite, finely dressed woman who seemed ill at ease despite her sterling credentials. "I very much agree with this fear you have expressed," she told True in crisp, Chinese-accented English. "I believe you are correct that some tragedy of machine error could occur. I have nightmares of such a thing."

Then she went on to counter everything True had said:

"You are an experienced soldier, a brave patriot. You are wise, and know a combat situation could demand a least-worst option. There must be contingency in the decision-making process for times when communications are disrupted. Then, the choice is to withdraw robotic weaponry and concede the battle, or to proceed, knowing there is risk, and the algorithms could be in error. But all war is risk. It is my experience that those who have the power to make such choices will choose to proceed."

This sounded to True like a well-rehearsed argument. She acknowledged its merit but added, "Command might back such technology, right up until the first time something goes terribly wrong and our frontline troops, along with those of our allies, have to pay the price."

At this, Guiying's flush deepened, her gaze drifted. Watching her, True felt as if the conversation had changed in some critical way, so that it was no longer theoretical but had somehow become personal. She was left puzzled and deeply uncomfortable, a feeling reinforced when Guiying said in a quiet, almost guilty tone, "Most often, advancing technology demands to be used. I think Command would say to fix it . . . but maybe it is different in America?"

Not so different, True thinks, taking off her reading glasses and rubbing her eyes. The plane has come to a stop, so she turns off the tablet's screen without bothering to reply to Li Guiying's email.

Looking back, it's clear to True that the roboticist regarded the rise of autonomous systems in the military as a given. She probably knew it would be only a few more years until True was out of a job but had been too polite to say so. Hell, maybe what True sensed in that long-ago conversation was the inevitable end of her own military career—but whatever the cause, she has never forgotten the odd, awkward feeling of that encounter. Ever since, she's looked on Guiying with a wary eye.

She puts the tablet away. Chris is already standing in the aisle. "Gather everything," he reminds them. "And make sure all the storage bins are open to inspection."

Every muscle in True's body has gone stiff. She's not the only one. There's a general groan as the team stands up to collect their gear. They exit the plane with their hand-carries and present themselves to US Customs. Passports are logged. Biometrics are crosschecked with database records. They queue up for the scanners: one to inspect for contraband and another seeking signs of infectious disease. Automated interviews follow, conducted individually in soundproof booths. True sits, facing a video screen, maintaining eye contact with a generated female persona in a customs officer's uniform. The persona projects an aura of stern suspicion as it asks in its synthesized voice, "What was the purpose of your travel, ma'am?"

"Business," True answers, aware that the AI behind the screening procedure is analyzing her voice and facial expression.

The persona follows the standard question tree: "What is the nature of your business?"

"Paramilitary activity."

"Do you have a license to conduct paramilitary activity?"

"Yes, I do."

A brief pause while the AI cross-checks government records. Then: "How long were you away?"

"Two days."

Another pause. This time the persona turns its head to look off-screen. True has seen this behavior before. She suspects the AI is awaiting results from the swarm of fast-moving, fist-sized robotic crawlers used to inspect all incoming aircraft, and from the baggage scanners, which will be logging the presence of their weapons.

After a few seconds the persona returns its gaze to True. "Confirming all necessary permits and licensing. Welcome home, Ms. Brighton."

The team gathers outside of Customs. Miles is the last to be cleared. He's looking shaky as he explains, "They weren't expecting me, so they had my profile flagged. It took a call to the State Department to confirm I'm legitimately me."

They return to the plane. Chris and True work with the flight crew to inventory the contents of the cargo hold, confirming all their gear has been returned to them. Then they take their seats.

Six more hours in the air and they'll be home.

True doesn't sleep on this last leg of the homeward journey. In the intervals between banal conversation and phone calls with Treasure and Connor, she stews over what she's learned. She turns it over and over in her mind—the implications, the possibilities.

This is dangerous ground, and not just for the reason she cautioned Miles. Shaw Walker might be a threat, yes, but that's a remote fear, something for the future.

Many times since Diego's death she has fallen into a pattern of obsessive thoughts, reliving over and over what was done to him, what he was made to go through. She appears quiet as she sits gazing out the window of the plane at the patterns of farmland far below. But as her mind walks that path again, there's panic at the cellular level. It's a frantic metabolic reaction, very real. It kicks up her core temperature and sends heat flushing through her as she considers his terror, the agony he must have known, all the while haunted by her own helplessness to intercede.

She shoves her sleeves up, presses a chilled bottle of water against her cheeks.

Don't go back there, she thinks.

"Hey, True," Juliet says, popping up to look at her from over the back of the next seat. "What's the best time you ever ran the mile?"

"It's your three-mile time that matters," True says, striving to keep her voice steady.

Juliet grins and drops back down into her seat to continue some inconsequential argument with Rohan.

Did Lincoln lie to me? True wonders.

She wants to hear his side, his explanation, but she doesn't call him. No chance of a private conversation on the plane. She schools herself to patience. She wants his raw reaction to this news of Shaw Walker; she wants to give him only a little time to prepare. So she waits until they're twenty minutes out from Paulson Field. Then she emails him the photo Brooke sent, with Shaw's face circled. Her accompanying note is terse:

> **Identified by Miles as Jon Helm. Brooke confirms. Have not shared with team yet. We need to talk.**

His answer comes in less than a minute:

> **This is bullshit. Shaw is dead. And Dushane is mistaken. I've got over fifty family members here, half of them kids, waiting for your plane to arrive. Do not throw a flash-bang into the middle of this reunion, True.**

Her reply goes out just as quickly:

I'm not planning to make an announcement. But when I step off this plane, you and me are going to talk.

He doesn't answer.

She doesn't follow up.

REUNION

THEIR CHARTERED JET touches down in early evening. They deplane down a stairway and cross the tarmac to a ground-floor terminal where their families and coworkers wait behind a glass wall, waving enthusiastically. No media are present. No journalists. This is a private airfield and a private reunion, though of course there are plenty of cameras.

Juliet reaches the door first. A cheer goes up when she pulls it open. Cries of greeting, hoo-yahs. The rest of the team crowds in. All but True. She lingers, watching through the glass, waiting for everyone else to get inside, giving Lincoln a chance to greet them.

Juliet throws herself into her husband's arms. Miles is met by his weeping parents and his grinning sister. Cameras flash amid a swirl of kisses and hugs and handshakes and small children lifted joyously over the crowd, and teenagers on the periphery, hanging back with embarrassed half-grins. True slips in behind it all.

Alex is there, just inside the door. She warned him something was up, no details. He looks wary as they share a ritual kiss.

Lincoln is with him, wearing his typical uniform: tan ReqOps polo shirt, brown slacks, and a casual jacket. "I don't want to talk here," he says, his artificial eye contributing to his intimidating glare. "It's not secure."

"You want to go to headquarters?" she challenges him. "That's fine with me. But I don't want the team hearing about this from Miles."

"About what?" Alex asks. "What does this have to do with me anyway?"

True turns a cold eye on Lincoln. He makes a good guess at what she's thinking. "I did not lie to you, True." He says it in an undertone, barely audible over the chatter around them. "I told you the truth. Shaw Walker was declared dead. That was the official conclusion."

True turns to Alex. "You remember Shaw?"

"Of course," he answers, cautious as a man circling an IED.

"He's alive. Brooke confirmed it. Which means someone in the State Department already knew. Maybe it's been known for years."

"I don't believe it," Lincoln insists. "It's a case of mistaken identity. I went to Nungsan. I went in with the forensics team, helped locate the bodies. I saw what was left of the structure where Shaw was held. It was incinerated. A smoking hole in the ground with the trace remains of at least three people. He did not survive."

True shakes her head. No way will she accept that conclusion, not anymore, not when she has two sources telling her that Shaw is alive. "Were those trace remains enough for a DNA identification? If not, you can't prove he was there, Lincoln."

"Come on! You know he was there. You heard him on the video."

"That was days before the village was targeted! That doesn't tell us where he was when the missile hit."

"True—"

"Hold on!" Alex interrupts. "God damn it, what are you saying?"

She turns to him, puts her hand on his arm. "There's a black-hat mercenary working in the TEZ who goes by the name of Jon Helm. It's a pseudonym, a nom de guerre. Miles picked him out of a photo lineup. It's Shaw."

Alex gives Lincoln a puzzled look. Then he returns his attention to True. "So what if it is Shaw?" he asks her.

She understands. He doesn't want to deal with it. Just like her, he's afraid of reliving the grief, the horror of that place and time when Diego's death was raw and new. His reluctance is plain to see—but she needs him on her side. She tells him, "If it is Shaw, he is the last living man who saw our son alive and I want to talk to him, ask him why *he's* alive, and what happened in that forest. What went wrong and what part he had in it and why he didn't come home."

Quickly, breathlessly, she sketches for Alex the story Hussam told of Jon Helm in Burma—how he killed his assailants when they tried to crucify him. "If the story is true, Shaw fought his way out of there. He could have come home. He *should* have, but he didn't. Why?"

"Because the story's not true," Lincoln says.

That's what he wants to believe. She tries to get him to reconsider. "When you were there, did you find the steel pipes of the cross they used?"

He presses his lips together. His living eye narrows. "Yeah," he admits in a wary voice. "I saw that. It was knocked over by the blast that took out the building where Shaw was being held."

"Did you find bodies near that cross?"

He glances around. Everyone else is clustered in front of the bar or alongside the buffet table, absorbed in their own conversations. His measuring gaze pauses on Alex before returning to True. "Two burned corpses. We don't know who they were."

"Saomong?" Alex asks.

"Yes."

True says, "That supports the story. What did you determine as cause of death?"

He scowls. "Nungsan was hit by a cruise missile, True. When it took out the target building, debris was flung in every direction."

She considers this for a few seconds. Leans in. "Sure. I know. Anyone in front of that building would have been pummeled by the debris. *But were they dead before that happened?*"

Seconds slide past as they glare at one another. Alex shifts restlessly, wondering, maybe, if he should intervene.

Lincoln breaks first. He tries to back out of the discussion, growling, "All of this is classified."

"No," True says. "No, you don't get to go there."

Lincoln has never been an expressive man. The burn scars and the artificial eye make him an even harder read, but True sees contrition on his face as he says, "Look, we can't know what happened. There were different factions among the Saomong. They were probably at each others' throats."

"Maybe," she allows. "Tell me what you saw. Tell *us*. I just want the truth."

He eyes her for several seconds. She holds her breath.

He raises his hand, taps the side of his head with two fingers. "One had his skull caved in here." He touches his forehead. "The other one, here. Like they'd been hit with a small sledgehammer."

She turns away, struggling to hold on to a semblance of calm. Beyond the glass, a ground crew services the plane. She feels the weight and warmth of Alex's hand on her shoulder.

Lincoln says in his habitual monotone, "We concluded that they'd been executed."

She rounds on him. Alex's hand falls away. "You want me to believe they were formally executed—with a hammer?"

"*Yes.*" He's willing her to believe what he chose to believe eight years ago.

That is not a game she can play. "Let's say Hussam's story is true."

"Okay! Fine. Let's do it that way. Shaw killed those two, disappeared into the forest, and died there—because if he'd lived, he would have checked in. He would have let us know."

"Let's say *all* of Hussam's story is true. Shaw lived, but he didn't check in. He took off on his own." She goes on to tell them about the tattoo Miles saw on Jon Helm's arm. She touches her own forearm. Her throat feels thick. Her voice is low. "The epitaph read, *Diego Delgado, The Last Good Man.*"

Alex steps back, shaken. Lincoln reacts in contempt. "That motherfucker—if it *is* him—even back then, True, he was not the hero you imagine."

This response is not what True expects. She didn't know Shaw well, but she's never before heard Lincoln say a word against him.

"No man is perfect," she says, surprised at her own desire to look back on Shaw in a clean light.

She's stunned when Alex tells her, "Shaw wasn't even close." Certainty lies behind his words, an implication that he knows more than he should, that he's kept things from her. She looks at him in shock, wanting the truth of it, but he doesn't see her. She's been sidelined. He trades a gaze with Lincoln as if they're conspirators in some crime and says, "If the story is true, he's sold his soul."

Lincoln acknowledges this with a slow nod.

True looks from one to the other, unsure what's going on, and that makes her angry. "I missed something," she says. "But I'm putting you both on notice. I intend to find him. I *need* to find him. He was there with Diego at the end."

SOME WORDS ARE LIKE BULLETS

TWENTY MINUTES LATER, True walks with Alex to the car. Neither speaks. He carries her pack and her duffel. She carries her weapons, stowed in cases. The parking lot is dark, the dull amber lights from the single-story terminal building insufficient to chase back the shadows. Past the parking lot, the black expanse of an empty field stands as a buffer between them and the bright headlights of a busy highway.

Out of habit, True scans the parking lot, on guard against anything that feels out of place. Alex makes his own survey. He's been out of the army twenty-five years, but situational awareness is a survival skill for paramedics as well as for soldiers.

The night is calm, peaceful. There's just a susurration of wind, and the traffic's muted growl.

Alex pops the trunk and drops her pack inside. She offloads her guns.

"Did you fire them?" he asks.

"A few rounds from the KO to discourage the bad guys while Jameson hit 'em with a flash-bang. Blackbird—the AI flying our Kobrin—did most of the shooting. Knocked out their automated defenses."

He grunts and closes the trunk. Then he follows her to the passenger door and, moving in practiced ritual, he opens it for her, shutting it after she slides in. Though she does not live a traditional life, old courtesies live on between them, reassuring gestures that ease their sometimes-stormy relationship.

True is all too aware of heavy weather incoming. They both know it. Back inside, the reception is still going on, but it took just a look from Alex and a word not even spoken aloud—*Ready?*—to forge an agreement to leave early.

That was right after Lincoln spoke to the gathering. He congratulated the QRF and read aloud a note of gratitude from Fatima's parents. He also warned everyone to be on their guard in the wake of the mission: "The guiding sentiment behind Requisite Operations is 'right action.' The work we do is honorable and within the bounds of the law. Even so, our existence is controversial. It brings out the crazies and the paranoid. That's why I prefer we operate under the radar when we can. Minimizing publicity lets us protect the privacy of our clients while enhancing our own safety. Public attention is a dangerous thing—and unfortunately, we're going to get a lot of it going forward."

True braced herself, afraid Lincoln would make an announcement about Shaw Walker—but that wasn't what he had in mind. His stern gaze picked out Miles among the listening crowd. "We made the mistake of rescuing a journalist."

This won a burst of laughter, and Rohan calling out, "Ah, he's just a Ranger gone wrong."

Lincoln acknowledged this with the ghost of a smile. "A press release has already gone out. There's no reason to say more, so if you receive a request for an interview, ignore it. And all of you, families included, be aware of your surroundings, exercise caution wherever you are, keep your fairy godmothers on duty at all times, and let me know if you even suspect trouble.

"And before I let you return to the buffet, one last bit of bad news. All QRF personnel will report to the office at 0800 for debriefing and interviews with federal officials." A groan ran through the gathering but Lincoln ignored it, pointing into the crowd. "That includes you, Khalid. Welcome to the Requisite Operations family."

True understands that being part of the Requisite Operations family is no easy task. She glances at Alex as they drive away from the airfield. His gaze is fixed on the strip of road that lies ahead. He's not ready to talk yet. True is content to wait him out, knowing it won't be long—and she's right.

He waits until they're on the highway, locked in the flow of evening traffic, before he says, "You need to let it go, True. Even if Shaw Walker really is out there playing mercenary badass, he's got nothing for you. Nothing he can tell you about Diego will make it hurt less."

"You've got it wrong," she tells him. "I'm not looking for comfort."

A soft, cynical hiss. "Yeah, I know. I just wish you were." He stares ahead at red taillights. "You know and I know . . . we can't ever escape it. What happened to him . . . it's got a gravity of its own. Like a black hole in our lives that we'll always be circling around."

It's a metaphor she hasn't heard before and she's startled at how well it resonates. "I never thought about it that way," she says. "But you're right. That's exactly how it feels."

"Don't let it pull you in," he warns.

She scowls at the implied assumption that she is fragile, vulnerable, prone to emotional decisions. "Look, I don't know what you think I'm going to do—"

He cuts her off. "You've already told me what you're going to do! You're planning to hunt down Shaw Walker. And I'm telling you, *no*. Don't do it." She doesn't interrupt; she lets him finish. But she's bristling, like she does every time she feels the leash tighten.

He says, "I remember Shaw. He was an arrogant son of a bitch who took things personally, even when it should have been just another part of the job—and he wasn't above revenge."

Her response is low and heated. "You think you know something about him, Alex? I didn't think you knew Shaw all that well."

They've reached their intersection. A turn lane takes them to the rural road leading to their home. A low, crowded forest looms on both sides of the road, mostly spindly maples, leaves half-gone this late in the season, with more falling, tumbling through the headlight beams.

Alex says, "Diego never talked to you about his first deployment with Rogue Lightning."

Some words are like bullets. True's heart lurches. She hears the low pounding of her pulse even over the road noise—and she doesn't know why. "Rogue Lightning missions were all classified," she says quietly, allowing no hint of distress into her voice. "He wasn't supposed to talk about it."

Alex pushes the accelerator, driving swiftly but carefully. They've lived here four years now, the longest they've lived anywhere in their long marriage. Time enough for him to memorize every curve, but he remains alert, eyeing each approaching car as a potential enemy. He's seen too many accidents to take the skills of other drivers for granted.

"He wasn't supposed to talk about it," Alex agrees. "But after he got back, he came to me. Said he needed to talk. Made me swear never to tell you. He didn't want you to think less of him."

Her pulse drums harder as fear overtakes her. Fear for Diego.

"*Oh God,*" she whispers, staring ahead into the night. Never mind that her son is far beyond all risk and all pain.

Memories roll in, all out of place for this conversation. She was deployed for so much of his childhood. His grandmother, Alex's mom, lived with them then, helping to raise him. A good kid. Smart and strong and generous, a team player. Endowed with joy . . .

But he came home from his first deployment with Rogue Lightning a different man. A more reserved man, quiet and cautious. No one returns from combat unchanged. Knowing that, she said nothing, but she wept secretly, mourning the child he'd been, even as she took pride in the man he became. And she reminded herself of one of Lincoln's favorite adages: *Someone's got to do the dirty work.* Better that a good man take on the task than a sadistic monster.

Alex senses her distress. He gives her time, driving half a mile before he speaks again. "I've kept that oath for eight years and I would have kept it to the grave, but I know you. You get an idea in your head that something needs to be done, and you can't let it go."

Maybe it's his criticism or maybe it's the way he has of drawing things out, but her temper triggers. "God damn it! If you've got something to say, say it."

He steps hard on the brake. "*Deer*," he announces. "On the right."

She looks up to see a dim shape stepping out from the shadow of the trees. Long spindly legs with too many joints, a lithe, segmented body in a matte-brown camouflage coloration, and a telescoping neck that retracts as she watches, drawing the head, with its stereoscopic eyes, downward until it fits in a niche at the front of the chest.

Alex is right that its shape suggests a deer, but it's much smaller, no more than two feet high. It reverses direction, stepping swiftly backward, locomotion so unnatural the hair on the back of her neck stands on end. "Stop the car," she says as it disappears into the dense shadows between the trees.

"Not a deer," Alex growls, steering onto the road's unpaved shoulder. "A mech. And not one of ours."

FALLOUT FROM THE MISSION

LINCOLN NOTES WHEN True and Alex leave the reception. He'd like to leave too, but leadership demands his presence. It's his duty to show confidence in his people and in his company. So he circulates. He talks to Khalid. "You're not officially employed yet. We've got paperwork to do. But I want you to come in tomorrow with everyone else and get your interview done."

"Yes, sir. That's what Chris said. I'll be there."

Miles is waiting to talk to him, his parents and sisters smiling behind him. "Lincoln, I'm heading out, but I want to thank you—"

Lincoln holds up his hand. "I just wish we'd come in sooner." He leans in and adds in a hoarse undertone, "I know True asked you to sit on this . . ." He hesitates, considering how to phrase it. ". . . this Jon Helm rumor. I'm asking you to keep it quiet for a little longer. You're going to get slammed with a thousand requests for interviews, but if you could keep this under wraps for another day, I'd appreciate it. I don't want to hit my team with the news tonight, but I want them to hear it from me."

Miles nods. "I can do that. Anyway, the name is going to stay 'Jon Helm' until I can confirm . . . well, the other."

"Okay. You take care."

As Lincoln turns away, Tamara intercepts him, reminding him

about the recovered electronics. "Who's got custody?" she asks. "We need to make sure those bags are not opened or there's no point doing a pollen and fungus analysis."

"I'll talk to Chris about it," he promises. "And I'll take the bags into headquarters tonight. Leave them in your lab for safekeeping."

He realizes this is a good excuse for making an early exit. With that in mind, he checks in on his two daughters—eight and ten years old—who are playing big sisters to Jameson's three-year-old twins. "We're going to leave soon," he warns them.

"*No*," Anna, the older, protests. "Everyone just got here."

"We're having fun," Camilla chimes in.

"Five minutes," he growls. "I don't want any argument."

God, he adores them. But he gets impatient anyway, too aware that they live in a different reality, blithely ignorant of the terrors of the world. That's a good thing. That's as it should be, but it's hard to make the shift between their world and his.

He continues around the room, shaking hands, thanking his people and their spouses. When Chris sees him coming, he whispers something to his wife, who melts away.

Lincoln doesn't like the idea that Chris has an agenda, not tonight. Tonight he just wants to get clear. "Let's save the analysis for tomorrow," he says. "I'm heading out. Hayden's got the key card. He's in charge of making sure everything gets cleaned up. I just need to round up the girls and get the recovered electronics from you."

"Sure," Chris says. "I've got the bags. They're with the rest of my gear. But I need to ask you: what the hell was going on with True, right after we got in? That did not look like a friendly conversation."

The fingers on Lincoln's prosthetic hand tap in quick rhythm: thumb to index, middle, ring, and little finger. "Fallout from the mission," he says gruffly, using truth as an evasion. He isn't ready to talk about Shaw. Hell, he isn't ready to believe it—and he's still burned by the way True ambushed him with her allegations. She did it that way on purpose, not saying anything until just before her plane touched down, a ploy aimed at shaking him up, shaking the truth out of him—but he's always told her the truth. And the truth is, he believed Shaw was dead.

This idea that he's not, that Shaw is alive—there's no joy in it. Not for him. Eight years ago, yes. Yes, he would have been happy to find Shaw, but now . . .

Far better that Shaw Walker died in the line of duty than that he walked out on that duty, walked out on the memory of the men of Rogue Lightning who followed him into that Burmese forest to die there—five of them, with Diego on the cross.

For all the differences Lincoln had with Shaw, and despite the falling-out after their last mission together, he meant every word of praise he spoke when he delivered the eulogy at Shaw's funeral. Shaw was a skilled warrior, daring, decisive, a fast thinker who could recast any mission the moment circumstances changed, and he was blessed with more than the usual share of luck. He was a hard man too—and that was appropriate. No sympathy for those who talked tough but couldn't measure up. His men admired that, and they loved him. They trusted him not to waste their lives.

But like any man, he had his flaws. He could be self-righteous, humility was never a strong point, and he resented being held back or overridden by commanders who did not have his experience in the field. Sometimes he refused to be held back. But Shaw's flaws were flaws of ego. Lincoln cannot believe he is the same man as the hostage-trading mercenary Miles described.

"Fallout from the mission?" Chris echoes. His gaze is intent, suspicious. "What fallout? If True had a problem with the mission, she should have come to me."

"She didn't have a problem with the mission."

Chris needs to hear this rumor about Shaw Walker. He's part of Rogue Lightning and so is Jameson. But they're not the original team. Both were brought in after Nungsan, and neither knew Shaw except by reputation.

"We'll go over everything tomorrow," he promises. Then he collects the electronics and his protesting daughters and makes his escape.

FAIRY GODMOTHERS

TRUE GRABS A flashlight from the car's center console and gets out, directing the bright beam into the forest.

Alex has the trunk open. "See anything?" he asks over the sound of a magazine being jammed into a pistol.

"No. But it's out there, watching us."

He steps up beside her, a 9 mm in hand. "Someone's fairy godmother?"

"Maybe. Definitely a biomimetic, but I've never seen one like it before."

"Didn't notice weapons on it."

"Nothing overt," she agrees.

He says, "Dash cam should have an image."

"Right. I'll send it in. Tamara should be able to track it down, check for registrations."

His gaze sweeps the woods. "It's giving me the creeps standing out here. Let's get back in the car and go."

"Okay."

Alex closes the trunk, but when he gets in, he still has the pistol. He passes it to her without a word, puts the car in gear, and accelerates onto the road.

"Probably just a fairy godmother," she says.

He grunts.

"Nice design." She's trying to sound casual. "Maybe we should get one like it."

"Damned sophisticated," he allows. "Not cheap."

"Not out of reach, either."

Biomimetic robots—mechanical animals—were more and more common, and why not? Millions of years of trial-and-error testing lay behind their shapes and the efficient physics of their motion. The mech they saw suggested a small deer—a nice option in rural areas, one that True had not considered before. A ground-based design like that would be less vulnerable to strong winds than a flying drone, and a well-made model could be both swift and stealthy in the woods, capable of standing still within the shadows and observing for hours while consuming very little energy. Something like it would be a nice addition to ReqOps' origami army.

Thinking out loud, she says, "It must have just been released. It shouldn't have allowed itself to be seen from the road. That suggests it hasn't had time to learn the terrain."

"Or it's lost."

If so, it won't last long. Personal drones aren't supposed to wander through or fly over private property. In rural areas, those that do tend to disappear. Over the past year, True shot down three that flew too close to the house. No way to know if they belonged to hobbyists, mediots, or an enemy. Hostile intent is assumed.

She and Alex keep their own menagerie, of course. Gargoyles—low-slung like crabs, with a carapace designed to shed the force of the wind—inhabit the roof, watching over the house and the surrounding sky. They have enough locomotive ability to keep themselves above any snow accumulation and to keep intruders in sight. The rest of the five-acre parcel is patrolled by two sets of fairy godmothers. The first are squirrel mimetics that can stealth-glide or -crawl in the forest canopy, and the second are turtles—ground-based devices that move faster than their name implies. As a rule, only three devices of each type are active, while a fourth recharges at the house. All are linked to a security AI.

True designed the system, selecting high-end components. Now she feels a sting knowing that none of her devices is as sophisticated as the deer mimetic.

Alex turns the car onto the long driveway. The gate is already open for them as the house senses their proximity and prepares for their arrival. Gravel crunches under the tires. Most of their land is forested in a tangle of regrowth that's come up in the thirty years since the area was last logged. Dark evergreens mix with alders and maples that are mostly bare this late in the year. The house is a neat two-story skirted by a wide lawn with trees beyond to screen them from their neighbors. True means to plant azaleas and rhododendrons at the forest's edge, but it hasn't happened yet.

Amber lights are already on in the house as they drive up. The garage door is open. Alex pulls in, parking next to True's SUV. They bought the place when she retired from the army, and both hope they never have to move again.

True retrieves her gear while Alex unloads his pistol and returns it to the trunk. She drops her pack in the mudroom, sits down to take off her boots, and then carries her gun cases into the kitchen, leaving them on the table.

She takes a moment to listen, but the house is quiet. Too quiet. It's like no one lives there.

"We should get a dog," she says as Alex follows her in.

"When you're ready to retire, we will."

She turns, leaning back against the counter, arms crossed, eyeing him, taking in his dark eyes, his high forehead, his lean weathered features. A handsome man, still. She fell so hard that night they met. After she knew she was pregnant, she told her parents, "It was meant to be. We share the same birthday." God, what a ridiculous tangle of passions she'd been, so defiant, so in love. She let the pregnancy happen, maybe in part to show Colt that her life was her own.

Not the smartest move she ever made, but not one she regrets.

"So tell me all of it," she says gruffly, brought low by the heartache of fractured trust.

His gaze is stern. "You heard what Lincoln said. Shaw wasn't the hero you imagine."

"So what happened? What did he get Diego to do?"

"He got him to cover up a war crime."

"Ah, *fuck*." True turns away. Diego's time in Kunar Province had cast a shadow over him, but she attributed it to combat's horrific reality. It doesn't take a war crime to affect a man that way.

"Wait," she says, puzzled by a new thought. "Lincoln was there. He must have known."

Alex meets her troubled gaze. "Yes."

A PRESENTIMENT OF DANGER

LINCOLN IS ALERT, scanning both ground and sky as he crosses the dark parking lot with his daughters—but it's Anna who spots the threat. She's chattering with her sister, a step ahead of him, when she stops, hand up, hissing at Camilla for quiet.

Lincoln is hit with a presentiment of danger.

He's coached his girls to be alert, encouraged them to always be aware of their surroundings. He's trained them how to recognize potential threats and how to react. It's a game for them. Not for him. He shifts both collection bags to his prosthetic hand. His skin prickles, puckering around his scars as he tries to figure out what's wrong.

Anna is partly on his blindside, cast half in amber by the building lights, half in black and white. She turns to look at him. He's confused to see her smiling—proud, excited—not scared at all. When she's sure she has his attention, she points—using just her finger, not extending her arm, exactly the way he's taught her. She indicates the unlighted access road that leads to the highway. Then she flattens her hand, wobbling her palm. It's their sign for a drone.

He sees it then, painted in light from the highway. It's gliding on meter-wide membranous wings, engines off as it drops in a long, slow arc toward the parking lot. He recognizes the model—a

Coriolis PR30. It's not much more than a toy, incapable of carrying a payload beyond the tiny camera that comes standard, but it's quiet and capable of stealth surveillance.

It's probably recording the thunderous pounding of his heart.

"Mediot?" Anna whispers.

All of them jump, and Camilla screeches, as a squadron of three defensive starburst copters shoots from hutches on the roof of the single-story terminal building. It's illegal to fly private drones this close to an airfield and the perimeter on this field is strictly enforced. It's one reason Lincoln uses it.

"Don't worry," he tells Camilla. "Those are just going to chase the mediot away."

He's wrong. The squadron's lead copter streaks toward the PR30. The winged drone tries to turn but it's slow. There's no way it can outrun the copter. There's a pop. The PR30 drops, disappearing into an open field. The starburst copters circle the site, moving with manic speed, then shoot back to the terminal building.

"Holy hemlock!" Anna exclaims, and Camilla immediately echoes her.

Holy hemlock? Lincoln wonders, but he knows better than to ask.

He scans the parking lot, the nearby fields. He's on edge, wondering what else might be out there. The airfield's defensive copters offer protection from aerial intruders, but would they detect a ground-crawling mech? An ambitious mediot might try both approaches in an effort to get first pictures of the team. An Al-Furat hired gun might choose a ground crawler too.

Anna fails to hold her position. Without waiting for permission, she starts for the truck, waving her hands to make sure the sensor sees her. Lincoln almost panics. He jumps after her, grabs her shoulder with his free hand.

"Stay put," he warns.

His grip is too tight. It makes her squirm. "*Dad!*"

He ignores her, heart racing as he eyes the truck suspiciously. He's picturing the kamikaze crabs True used in Tadmur. It's easy for a crawler to carry a payload, to get up into an undercarriage, and from there into the engine block . . . or the gas tank.

No. He rejects the idea with a sharp shake of his head. This is not Tadmur. It's not the TEZ. *Don't get paranoid.* The worst threat his girls face is mediot harassment.

"*Dad,*" Anna protests, "you're hurting my shoulder!"

He lets her go. Both girls stare at him, eyes wary, uncertain. "What's the matter, Dad?" Anna asks.

"Nothing," he says gruffly. "There's nothing to worry about."

It's the truth, and still, he's beset with anxiety. A sense of vulnerability. It's the way he used to feel in the weeks and months after a mission. It's this talk of Shaw Walker, he decides. It's the reality of Variant Forces. An outfit capable of fielding three Arkinsons on a few minutes' notice might have a long reach.

He parked his truck between two other vehicles. They're both still there, and nothing has approached since. If anything had—human, animal, mech—he would know about it. One of the tiny cameras mounted around the truck's frame and across its undercarriage would have captured the motion and sent him an alert.

He pulls out his phone and reviews his list of alerts, just to make sure he didn't miss anything. "We're okay for now," he concedes. "I want you two to move fast. In through the driver's door. Let's go."

They scamper for the truck, Lincoln right behind them. The truck unlocks for them and the girls climb in. He stashes the bags behind the seat. "Make sure you fasten your seat belts."

"We *know,* Dad," Anna says irritably. "We're not babies. Why are you acting so weird?"

"Always vigilant," he reminds her.

She rolls her eyes and, remembering that she's angry with him, flounces back in the seat, crosses her arms, and glares at the dash. "I wish we didn't have to leave early. We were having fun."

"Sorry," he says as they pull out.

Camilla gets her cell phone from the dash compartment and retreats into some comforting game world—Lincoln has no idea what game it is. Anna watches her for a few seconds, then gets her phone out too. "Let's link," she tells her sister. They tap their phones together.

Lincoln drives, thinking about Shaw Walker, remembering him

as a man who believes in revenge. *Relentless*, according to Hussam. His grip tightens on the steering wheel.

Hussam's brother, Rihab, swore to seek revenge, but Lincoln is skeptical, suspecting Rihab will first have to fight to secure his brother's operation. He's far more concerned about Shaw . . . if it is Shaw. Requisite Operations' name is already out in the media.

Are we at war? Lincoln wonders. And if they are, where is the war zone?

A memory. A mission in the Hindu Kush. Lincoln has called in targeting coordinates. A Reaper responds. It flies below them, entering the valley through a low pass. Shaw, speaking in an undertone scarcely audible over the wind: "If I was the enemy, I'd be gunning for that pilot."

Lincoln snorted at the absurdity. "Those pilots are seven thousand miles away."

"Yeah. I'd hit 'em where they live."

Lincoln thinks about this now, watching the red taillights ahead of him. Renata flew the Hai-Lins from out of ReqOps headquarters. Does that make her a target? Is the ReqOps campus a potential war zone?

He glances at the girls. They're preoccupied, plugged into their game. When he left the airfield, he planned to stop at the office, drop off the electronics, and then take the kids to their mom's house. Now he reconsiders, deciding it's better to take the kids straight home.

He's not worried. Not really. But he drives past the ReqOps exit anyway.

Farther on, traffic gets heavy. Slows to a crawl. Lincoln is frustrated, but the girls don't notice. They're happy in their electronic world. That's how kids are. Lincoln was the same. He regrets it now, thinking of his own dad. He wishes he'd known him better.

His parents were both army: his mom a rangy blonde, the descendant of Southern slaveholders, and his dad, not quite as tall but an outstanding athlete, the youngest son of Korean immigrants. Lincoln remembers him as quiet, determined. Remembers too the longing for his return when he was deployed, gone for months at a time—and then gone forever. A stupid accident during a training exercise, when the helicopter carrying his squad clipped a rotor and went down, leaving a trail of burning wreckage. It's a parallel Lincoln tries not to dwell on.

His mom left the service after that, but two years later she married back into the army—one of his dad's friends, a talkative good ol' boy, full of philosophy. The transition was rough, but Lincoln came around. In retrospect, he should have learned more from his stepdad about what it takes to stay married.

After he pulls into Claire's driveway, he walks the kids to the door. She's surprised to see them back so early.

"Something wrong?" she asks as they slip past her, disappearing into the house.

She's tall, full-figured, only a little heavy. Beautiful dark eyes. Teaches advanced math at a small prep school.

He speaks softly, his scarred voice a low burr. "We might be getting fallout from this latest mission."

"Come inside," she urges. "Tell me about it."

He's tempted. After six years apart, they've lately embarked on a slow and cautious rapprochement. But he's got the recovered electronics in the truck and he needs to get them safely locked up. "I can't. I've got to run by the office."

"Are you going to make it to the soccer game this weekend?"

"I don't know."

She presses her lips together and nods.

"I want to," he tells her.

"I know."

Lincoln would like to make it work with Claire and he intends to try. But in the long term? He doesn't give it much chance of succeeding.

WAR CRIME

A WAR CRIME—AND Lincoln knew.

True ponders this unsettling revelation while Alex splashes Irish whiskey over ice.

Alex tried for years to steer Diego away from military service, but Diego refused to be persuaded. He grew up wanting to be a warrior, a boots-on-the-ground protector, a defender of the tribe—and he wasn't willing to wait. "Give college a try," Alex urged him. "You can always enlist next year."

He wouldn't consider it. "Dad, if I don't go now, I might not get a chance. The army's cutting back. Robotics are going to take over combat jobs and pretty soon frontline soldiers will be obsolete."

He'd been wrong about the timeline but not about the process.

Alex hands her a glass. She takes a cautious sip, focusing on the sweet burn and her own culpability. Where would they be now if she'd made different choices? If she'd left the army early, put the military behind them. Kept Diego home those summers he'd spent with her old man?

Pointless questions.

She chose the life she wanted and Diego did the same. He worked hard and he took his chances—and she was proud of him. She's still proud of him. She will always be proud of him.

Alex is proud of him too. He looks across the great room at the cabinet with the eternally lighted shelf holding Diego's formal army portrait. A triangular flag case, set at an angle beside it, holds the neatly folded American flag that draped his coffin. On the other side of his portrait, a black-framed case displays his medals along with an embroidered patch. The patch bears the Rogue Lightning emblem. It's too far away to see the details, but True sees them in her mind's eye: a half-circle, with two star-filled fields flanking a bright orange sun, lightning bolts dividing them, the unit's name and the motto underneath.

Anywhere, Anytime.

Alex says, "I think he'd be okay with this if he was here now."

It's hard for True to speak against the pressure in her chest. She breathes in the vapors of the alcohol, letting it distract her. Alex is making this hard for her. He's doing it on purpose.

"Just tell me," she whispers.

Alex furrows his brow and complies. "They were in Kunar Province. The assignment was to kill or capture a Saudi radical rumored to be in the area. They were working with a contingent of highly trained Afghan National Army soldiers, supposed to be the best of the best. Except one of them tried to lead the team into an ambush. It didn't work. The team detected the presence of enemy soldiers in time to stage a counterattack. But the ANA soldier turned his weapon on our men. Lincoln was hit bad. Two of the Afghanis were killed. This, from a man they believed to be a friend.

"The enemy retreated but they had their wounded too, so they didn't go far. They took refuge in a house. It wasn't clear if the family was present as hostages or if they were collaborating. The surviving ANA soldiers insisted they were relatives of the traitor. But everyone knew there were children in the home."

Alex shrugs. "They were under a lot of pressure. Two dead, enemy soldiers in the area, evacuation delayed, and Lincoln bleeding out, slow but sure. Shaw let his temper off leash, turned into an avenging angel. On the terrain map, he marked the house as a known enemy position, no civilians present. Seconds later a drone strike took it out."

He scowls at his glass, takes a long sip, waits for the burn to pass. "Diego didn't understand at first what had happened, but Lincoln did. Despite his wounds, his wooziness, he was furious. Swore he'd report what Shaw had done. But he never did. None of them did. Tribal loyalty won out. Five months later, Shaw and Diego were in Burma."

Lincoln didn't go on the Burma mission; he was still recovering from his wounds.

Alex fixes her with a measuring gaze. "I'm certain Shaw did his damnedest to save Diego's life. But don't kid yourself. He was dangerous and unpredictable even then. If he really is this Jon Helm, he's not someone you want to get close to."

"Maybe not." She doesn't like the resentment that edges her voice. It's real though. She doesn't try to hide it. "But here we are, years later. Shaw's name comes up, and suddenly I'm finding out critical things I never knew about my son."

"Hey," he says. "I didn't like sitting on this. I would have told you before, but I promised him."

Her hand tightens around the cold glass. "What else don't I know? Shaw had that tattoo. 'The Last Good Man.' What was that about? Don't you want to find out?"

"*No.* No, I don't. And you need to let it go. We have two living children. Just because they aren't kids anymore, that doesn't mean they don't need you. Someday they're going to have children of their own. You need to be around for that. You owe us."

She sips the whiskey, holds it in her mouth as she focuses on keeping her temper in check. She hates it when Alex plays the guilt card. He knows she hates it. He does it anyway because sometimes it works.

Not this time. "I'm going to be blunt, love. There's a creed. No man left behind. In a day, maybe a week—it won't be long—Lincoln will remember that. And then we're going after Shaw. He was Rogue Lightning. Still is. He's still flying the colors. It's just a matter of time."

Alex scowls, but his tone is surprisingly conciliatory as he says,

"Lincoln might have things to make up for, but that doesn't mean you need to be part of it."

"I'm already part of it," she warns him. "So are you. We've been part of it since the day Diego died. Like you said, what happened is a black hole, and we can't ever escape it."

COLD MORNING

TRUE AND ALEX wake to an intrusion alarm. It's 0432. Both grab tablets from their respective sides of the bed. True holds hers at a distance so the image on the screen is sharp. The screen shows a video feed with the source labeled *Brighton-Delgado-3*. One of the squirrel mimetics. The device is moving in the forest canopy, skittering through low branches, gliding when it needs to, as it works to keep up with an intruder on the ground whose slender shape is intermittently visible past evergreen deadwood and half-gone autumn leaves.

True recognizes it. So does Alex. "It's the mech from last night," he says, anger edging his voice. "Heading straight for the house. Fucking mediots. What, they don't think we have defenses?"

True watches the feed, on edge, her heart racing after being startled awake. She is struck by the speed and grace of the device as it dashes through the rough terrain. It disappears into darkness. "Damn, it's fast," she says, with growing trepidation. "BD3 can't keep up."

"Did we just lose track of it?" Alex growls.

"'Fraid so, love." She tries to be reassuring. "The gargoyles will pick it up when it gets close to the house—but I don't like this." She shoves the blankets off. Stiff muscles protest the movement.

Chill air shocks her bare skin. She reaches for a thermal shirt and jeans. "That thing is no mediot's toy. It's too sophisticated."

He's up too, pulling on trousers he left draped over a chair, tablet abandoned on the nightstand. "Who, then?" he asks. "Are you thinking El-Hashem's people—"

"No," she says firmly, dressing as quickly as she can. "There is no way they could have tracked us down already, gotten a weapon in the field."

"A weapon?"

She pulls her shirt down over her belly and considers. "I don't *think* it's a weapon. I'm sure it's just a spy device. Fairly sure—but I don't want it close to the house."

"Neither do I," he growls. He doesn't bother putting on a shirt, disappearing out the bedroom door.

She grabs her tablet and follows him downstairs, leaning hard on the banister and hobbling to ease her painfully tight calves. He ducks into the office, where they keep the gun safe. A series of sharp beeps as he punches the combination on the electronic lock.

She heads for the mudroom. Just as she reaches it, the tablet trills a second alarm. A glance confirms that the gargoyles have detected the intruder.

Her heart rate ramps up. *It's not a weapon*, she thinks, reminding herself there was no visible gun, no room to hide one.

If it is a weapon, it's a kamikaze. *Fuck*. Not a reassuring thought.

The tablet's screen shifts to display a video feed streamed from a gargoyle on the roof. She watches it as she steps into a pair of rubber boots. The mech is thin, lithe, and nicely camouflaged, so even with adaptive night vision, it's hard to see as it moves slowly to the edge of the undergrowth separating the forest from their wide front lawn.

She's relieved to see it stop there. Its stick-thin legs bend as it sinks to the ground. Its torso can't be more than eighteen inches long, shaped like a flattened loaf. Processors don't take up much space, so most of that volume probably contains battery and sensors—or maybe explosives?

The neck retracts, leaving the stereoscopic camera only an inch and a half above the grass. It's like the mech is settling in, taking up an observation post from which it can keep the house under surveillance. Given its matte-brown camouflage, it would be damn hard to see, even at noon on a sunny day.

The mudroom is cold. It has a musty smell. One of its doors opens into the garage, the other onto a concrete pad outside the house. The mech will be able to see that door open.

Alex joins her. He still hasn't got a shirt on, but he's got a shotgun in hand.

True shows him the tablet. "It's at the edge of the lawn."

"Got it." Not bothering with boots or a jacket, he shoves the door open, brings the shotgun to his shoulder, and fires. True watches onscreen as a spray of leaves and dirt erupts from the spot where the mech was just a moment before.

"No good," True says, shivering in the frosty current of air flowing in through the open door. "It must have been trained to react to the sight of a weapon. It was gone as soon as it saw you."

"It'll be back," he says grimly, coming inside and slamming the door behind him. "Probably before we get the coffee brewed."

"The gargoyles will let us know."

But the gargoyles remain quiet. If the deer mech is out there, it's smart enough to stay beyond the range of their sensors.

The sky is beginning to lighten as Tamara speeds along the rural road to ReqOps, passing small farms and stands of young forest. She's heading into work early, but she's not the first to arrive. Four compact cars are there ahead of her, parked on the road's shoulder just outside the security gate. They've been there long enough to collect a sprinkling of yellow maple leaves. Worried that something is wrong, she approaches slowly.

Five people, wearing jackets against the cold, block the driveway. They turn to look at her. It's a geeky gathering. Two wear AR visors. The other three are recording video of her with their phones. Independent journalists, she decides.

She edges her car into the driveway. They move back, but one man taps on her window glass, shouts his request for a short interview. Tamara rolls forward far enough to trigger the gate's automatic inspection routine. Then she lowers the window, gives her best smile, and says, "I'm not authorized to speak for the company."

The journalist tries to press his case but the gate opens. Tamara makes her escape.

She gets her second surprise of the day when she sees Lincoln's truck already in the parking lot. As soon as she steps inside, she asks, "Friday, where's the boss?"

The upbeat, androgynous voice answers, "Lincoln is sleeping in his office."

"Has he been there all night?" she asks as she crosses the uninhabited lobby.

"He's been there since twenty-two hundred."

The security door behind the reception desk opens for her. "When he wakes up, tell him to take a shower before he comes to drink my coffee."

"I will do that, Tamara."

In the long south wing to the left of the lobby are classrooms, a bunkroom, and general storage. Tamara turns right, passes the large conference room, and approaches a second security door that also opens for her. She passes through it into a checkpoint. Her shoulder bag goes through an x-ray scanner. She walks through a body scanner. Results appear on wall screens but she doesn't bother to look. "Find anything suspicious, Friday?"

"No, Tamara. You are clean."

The system isn't calibrated to look for weapons, which pass in and out of the secure wing all the time. It's looking for surveillance devices. Tamara picks up her shoulder bag and heads down the hall, past the break room and suites of offices, doors closed and locked. Next is the tactical operations center for the ReqOps campus and across the hall from it, the mission command post. At the end of the north wing are utility rooms and the onsite network operations center, but Tamara exits the building through a side door before she reaches them, emerging into a section of the grounds kept secure by high fences and intense surveillance.

The cold morning air is moist and sharp with the scent of evergreens. Her breath steams as she follows a winding, wet concrete path down to the Robotics Center. On the way she messages Chris, asking him to assign someone to the front gate, to make sure the driveway stays clear.

Urgent tasks await her attention. Lincoln sent an email last night to let her know he'd locked up the recovered electronics in one of the robotics vaults and he wants an analysis ASAP. And True emailed an hour ago to report a very unusual and interesting mechanical intruder that needs to be identified.

But first things first: Tamara gets the coffee started.

While the coffee brews, she goes to collect the bags. She's laying them out on a lab table, the coffee just finishing, when Lincoln comes in, freshly shaved, wearing a clean shirt. She nods in approval. "Good morning, boss!"

He ignores this and says, "I want you to look at the shit we pulled out of the Arkinson before you do anything else."

Her eyebrows rise. Lincoln can be hard to read, but she has definitely seen him in better moods.

"Go over the drives," he continues. "See if you can extract anything interesting—"

She stops him there. "Anything interesting," she warns, "is going to be encrypted."

"Do what you can. Have you got a lab in mind for the microbiota analysis?"

"No, I don't. I have to research it. I've never done this before. Keep in mind though, that geographical analysis of microbiota is a highly specialized field. We could find ourselves caught in a backlog. We might have to wait days, even weeks for results."

A sideways shake of his head. "No. We don't have days or weeks. Find an outfit that will get it done. I don't care if you have to send it to China. I need to know where that Arkinson has been and where it was serviced. I need a lead on Jon Helm."

She puts one hand on her hip and cocks her head, troubled by his intensity. "Something else going on?" she asks him.

His answer is terse: "Yeah." He doesn't elaborate.

Tamara sighs, pours two cups of coffee, hands him one. "You got a budget for me?"

He gives her a figure.

"I can work with that," she says.

"Okay. Thank you." He turns to go, coffee in hand.

"Lincoln," she says in surprise.

He looks back. "Is there something else?"

"Yes, there's something else. True didn't call you?"

He looks puzzled, then worried. "What happened?" he asks. "Is she okay?"

"She's fine. She sent me a video. If you haven't seen it yet? You need to."

Lincoln walks back up to headquarters, breath steaming on the cold air, his color-gradient gaze scanning the shadows beneath the trees, the lowering gray sky.

The biomimetic deer is bad news, but more troubling to him is True's failure to notify him of it. A flagrant intrusion like that should have been reported. That she didn't do so—that she didn't even copy him on her email to Tamara—strikes him as a criticism, an indication of broken trust. Does she still believe he lied to her about Nungsan?

He wanted to devise another explanation for her failure to report the incident. Maybe she convinced herself the device belonged to a mediot or an independent journalist—someone relatively harmless—but Tamara put an end to that hope as they watched the video.

"I've never seen anything like it," she commented as the deer retreated on lithe stick legs, speeding backward into the forest. "Impressive agility, good speed, lightweight, and a versatile form. Just *gorgeous*."

Lincoln would never tell this to any of his other people, but he's seen the signs, read the writing on the wall, and he's aware that his initial business model—to provide conflict-area intelligence and security, as well as specialized security training—might not survive its first decade, not when he's in competition with gigantic corporations. So he has steadily boosted the financing behind the robotics department, seeing Tamara's work as the best hope for the future of the company. Her devices are already generating income. One good patent and they'll all enjoy an extravagant retirement.

In the meantime, he respects her opinion on all subjects and defers to it in the matter of robotics. If the deer was an off-the-shelf product, she would have recognized it—but she didn't. "You're saying the deer is a custom build."

"I want to research it, but that's my initial evaluation."

This is concerning. Mediots and journalists don't have the skill or the finances to bother with custom mechs. A custom build implies either a serious hobbyist or an operator with meaningful financial resources. A criminal organization, for example. Or another PMC.

Variant Forces?

If Variant Forces fielded that deer, it suggests they have resources or a network already in place in the Seattle area, and that they are way ahead of ReqOps in the intelligence game.

Lincoln wonders again: *Are we at war?*

Friday unlocks the door to the headquarters building as he approaches. After the chill of the outside air, the heat inside is oppressive. He strips off his jacket. Checks the time: 0728.

"Hello Friday," he says. "Anyone in yet?"

The AI replies through his TINSL. "Hayden is in the break room. Chris has just arrived in the parking lot."

A lesser AI would have mentioned Tamara too, but Friday's algorithms are clever enough to deduce that Lincoln already knows of her presence. More significant to Lincoln: True isn't in yet.

"Call True," he tells the AI.

She picks up on the first ring. "Hey."

"What's your ETA?" he asks.

"Seven fifty at the latest."

"I want to see you in my office."

"I'm on my way."

PRECISION STRIKE

TRUE IS SITTING behind the wheel of her SUV, stopped at a red light during the brief exchange with Lincoln. The abbreviated conversation reflects the tension, the mistrust that has surfaced between them. She doesn't like what she's learned about him in the past twelve hours. He withheld facts from her about Nungsan. He failed to report a war crime.

She wants to believe he had good reasons.

She feels cut off, isolated by the secrets of others. Alex swears he's withheld nothing more from her but the wound remains, while Lincoln might still have more secrets to confess.

Then there is Shaw Walker.

Did the deer mimetic belong to Shaw? Or to his outfit?

Variant Forces.

The light turns green and she's rolling again. Traffic is heavy, but over half the cars are autonomous, helping to smooth the flow. AIs are better drivers—more efficient, patient, and conservative than humans. True sometimes uses autonomous mode, but this morning she's driving. She needs the sense of control.

As she nears ReqOps she finds herself following Renata Ballard's sleek red two-seater electric. Renata's brake lights come on as she rounds the last curve. True slows in turn, surprised by the sight of several cars parked on the road's shoulder. A ReqOps maintenance worker stands watch at the end of the driveway. He waves at Renata to come in. True follows. Strangers are gathered at the entrance taking pictures, but no one tries to block the way.

Renata stops at the gate. An automated inspection clears her car and admits her. True goes next. The tall gate and a masonry wall screen the parking lot from view of the road. True pulls into her usual stall, then meets Renata. They trade fist bumps, knuckles stiff in the early morning cold.

"Missed you last night," True says.

A smile brightens Renata's graceful, fair-skinned face. Her perfectly groomed eyebrows rise in teasing challenge. "Hey, so I was a little late. You were already gone."

"Yeah," True concedes as they walk together across the damp pavement. "Had some things to deal with."

In an ideal world, a woman would be judged purely by her skill set, but both True and Renata live in the real world and they accept that looking good—in a way that is powerful and feminine, with no affectation of weakness or vulnerability—is an effective asset. True's ideal is a polished but relaxed look, mature and coolly competent. Faux military is a favorite and she's wearing that today: slim ankle boots, form-fitting slacks, silky shirt under a cardigan jacket, all in understated colors. Minimal makeup.

Renata is more flamboyant. Like True, she's taller than most women but where True is slim, Renata has curves, and dresses to enhance them. Today she's wearing gray slacks, a dusky-rose sweater, and heels of a height that True would never go near. Her honey-blond hair is pinned and braided in complex patterns.

True says, "That was one intense exit from Tadmur. I knew the technicals wouldn't be a problem for you, but when those Arkinsons showed up . . . we all sweated that one. Nice job holding them off. Spectacular fireworks when you took that one down."

Renata wrinkles her nose, shakes her head in disgust. "That wasn't me on the stick. I turned it all over to the AI when the Arkinsons showed up. Fully autonomous mode."

True stops at the edge of the terrace, disturbed, and a little angry too. "I didn't know that. I'm sorry to hear it." She shakes her head. "We really have ceded the battle space to programmers and engineers."

Renata answers this with a wry smile and a dismissive wave. "Inevitable. It's what we've been training the AI for and thank God it performed, or you wouldn't be here, sister. You and me, we were lucky we got into it when we did. Lucky we had a chance to fly. And now?" She shrugs. "I still get to be air force chief and you get to play commando, so what the fuck."

"What the fuck," True echoes agreeably. "And regardless, you're a great air force chief."

"Thanks, sweetie."

The door opens ahead of them. Hayden is at the reception desk. His cheery good morning is immediately countered by a gruff audio message from Lincoln, piped in through her TINSL: *Conference room. Now.*

Her gut clenches. Something has changed in the twenty minutes since his terse phone call. "Got to go," she tells Renata. "Lincoln's in a mood."

Renata lifts an eyebrow and taps her own TINSL. "I got the same message. Come on. I'll walk with you to the conference room."

Chris is there ahead of them, sprawled in a chair, a cup of coffee steaming on the table in front of him, his cheeks flushed like he's just finished a run. They crosscheck and confirm: None of them knows the topic of the meeting.

Swift, clattering footsteps in the hallway. Tamara enters, looking harried and impatient. She plops into the seat at the head of the table, rocks back, and says, "Someone want to tell me why we're here?"

Lincoln must have just stepped out of his office, because Tamara's question is still hanging in the air when his chiseled figure looms in the doorway. "I'll tell you," he says in clipped syllables. He slams the door behind him with a concussion that makes True jump. His artificial eye overlooks her. Overlooks Chris and Tamara, too. Fixes on Renata. "I just got off the phone with Eden

Transit. They've been hit. A pair of Arkinsons carried out a precision strike against the hangar where our Hai-Lins were housed—"

"*Fuck!*" Renata says. Her fist bangs the table, causing True to flinch again. She meets Chris's stunned gaze across the table's expanse as Renata rises to her feet. "What the hell kind of security—"

Lincoln holds up his right hand, his living hand, palm out. Renata breaks off, but her pretty face has darkened with ominous anger.

Chris speaks into the silence. "We got anything left?"

"Not a damn thing." Lincoln passes behind True's chair. As he does, she feels the prickling current of his anger on the back of her neck. He says, "The Hai-Lins are a total loss. They were being serviced, prepped for a move to Tel Aviv when an anonymous warning was called in, ninety seconds ahead of the strike." He reaches the end of the table, turns his scarred face to take in his senior staff. "The hangar is still on fire, but all Eden Transit personnel got out and are accounted for."

"*Sweet Jesus,*" Tamara says with conviction. "It was Variant Forces, wasn't it? It had to be. Thank God they had the professional courtesy to call in a warning—"

"Professional courtesy?" Renata echoes, contempt in her voice. "We took out one of theirs, so they take out three of ours? That's not courtesy. It's a declaration of war."

True is thinking the same thing. She remembers what Alex said, that Shaw Walker is not above revenge. "We didn't just take down one of his Arkinsons," she says. "We hit his reputation."

Chris asks Lincoln, "Do we know it's Jon Helm? Has there been a claim of responsibility?"

"Not so far."

Chris says, "We need to be absolutely sure before we react."

"I'm not sure we can afford to react," True says. She's feeling sick as she runs a mental tally of their losses. "We had the Hai-Lins insured for accidents but not for acts of war, so there is no way we are going to be able to recover their value. We've also lost the income they earned flying as armed escorts."

"This is a major, major loss," Lincoln agrees. "We are not going to be able to replace the Hai-Lins. Not right away." He looks at Renata.

She returns his gaze, hands on her hips. "Are you firing me?"

"No. We might have to subcontract you out, though. We've proved our AI can fight. Maybe we can run the software on some-one else's machines." He pulls out a chair and sits down. "Cash flow is an issue but the security of our people is a bigger concern." He rests his arms on the table, the riotous colors of his sleeve tat-toos enhanced by their contrast to the polished wood. True's gaze shifts from those illustrations of dragons and koi and snarling lions to find Lincoln studying her. "True, why the hell didn't you let me know the moment you detected an intrusion at your place?"

Chris leans forward. "You had trouble?"

"No trouble. Not really. It was just a surveillance device. Sophis-ticated. Not something I'd seen before so I sent video to Tamara." She turns to Tamara with a questioning gaze. "Did you find any-thing on it?"

"It's a custom job," Lincoln says coldly.

Tamara nods. "You should have copied the boss on it, True."

Lincoln takes it a step farther: "You should have called it in."

True doesn't like being put on the spot. She squares her shoul-ders, crosses her arms. "It was 0400. The thing had no weapons; it presented no threat. There was no reason to call it in."

"You think you're safe here?" Lincoln asks her. "What if that device was sent to confirm your presence in the house before a strike was called in?"

"This is not the TEZ," she snaps.

"What if similar devices were snooping around the homes of everyone else who just got back from the TEZ? Don't you think they might have liked a warning?"

True weighs this. It *was* just a surveillance device. Beyond that, the incident had felt personal—*just me and Alex bonding over a common enemy*—but she sees, in retrospect, that it was a mistake not to report the incident. "Okay, you're right," she says. "I've had surveillance drones fly over before but this was different. I should have called it in."

"I'd like to see the video," Chris says.

"I'll forward it."

Lincoln stands up. "It's 0800 and we've got a company meeting. Staff is already assembled in the auditorium. True, I want you to kick things off with an update on the status of the Hai-Lins. Chris, you'll follow with a review of at-home security protocols. I'll go over what not to say when we have our interviews with the feds. They're due at 0830. We push them through as quickly as we can, and once they're out of here we'll meet again and consider our options. Let's go."

INTERROGATIONS

ARE WE AT war?

Lincoln asked himself that question only last night. The destruction of the Hai-Lins has answered it affirmatively, emphatically.

He wondered as well where the warzone might be. Traditionally, wars have been fought along geographical fronts, but geography may not be a limiting factor in this conflict. *Hit 'em where they live*, Shaw Walker had said—even if they live seven thousand miles away.

He is returning to his office from the auditorium when he gets an alert that a black SUV with government plates is waiting at the automated security gate. The driver holds up a badge for the camera to see. Two other agents are in the vehicle.

"Let them in," Lincoln tells Friday.

By the time the trio walks in the door, he's waiting in the lobby. Handshakes are traded, introductions made. Lincoln scans their badges, confirming their identities, but he's disappointed. All three are young men, recent college graduates.

Lincoln asks what they know about Hussam's operation, about the security he had in place, and about regional military companies who might have done business with him—but they shake their heads. Their spokesman says, "We work out of the Seattle office, sir. Our focus is the Pacific. We're here today as puppets for the department's Middle East experts." He slides a tablet out of his coat pocket and holds it up. "They'll be looking in, overseeing the interviews."

"I'd like to talk to them," Lincoln says.

"You will be, when you're talking to us."

"I like to see who I'm talking to. Why don't we set it up?"

"We can't, sir. Security."

Lincoln considers this, staring down the young men, who appear increasingly uneasy under his half-mechanical gaze. He has his own questions to ask, but not of these kids. He considers refusing the interviews until he's allowed to talk to someone more senior. But his business requires a cooperative relationship with the State Department.

"How long do you expect these interviews to last?" he asks.

Their spokesman looks relieved at the concession. "Fifteen or twenty minutes per person, sir. That's assuming you're willing to turn over video of the operation."

"I'll need a confidentiality agreement and limited liability."

The youth hesitates, gaze unfocused as he listens to instructions from someone in authority. He nods. "Yes, sir, Mr. Han. I can have signatures by the time we're done here."

The legal documents are sent to the DC office, Lincoln assigns rooms for the agents to use, and the interviews commence. When his turn comes, he asks a question for every question he's asked—and some get answered.

"How did you locate Hussam El-Hashem?" his interviewer wants to know.

Lincoln addresses his answer to the tablet, set up on the table between them, knowing that a senior official is present behind its little camera lens. "I employed local contractors to track him down. What can you people tell me about an outfit known as Variant Forces?"

The kid listens to instructions Lincoln can't hear, then says, "We believe it's a syndicate of unlicensed military contractors operating in north and central Africa. Sir, how many local contractors did you employ in your operation?"

"Every reliable one I could find."

"Could you provide us with a specific number, sir?"

"Under twenty," Lincoln allows. He doesn't want to say three because that will lead to too many questions about the surveillance equipment he used—equipment the State Department is not allowed to use, not if they are operating legally. He moves immediately to his own question. "What information have you got on a mercenary with a crippled hand associated with Variant Forces, name of Jon Helm?"

The kid cocks his head, taking several seconds. Then he tells Lincoln, "They say no such man. Seven or eight warlords like to claim the identity. They use it to hide crimes or enhance their reputations. That's all."

"That's all?" Lincoln asks suspiciously.

"Yes, sir."

"What about a mercenary with a crippled hand, Caucasian, by any name?"

"There are a lot of mercenaries in the region, sir. Could you tell us how many fatalities occurred during your mission?"

Lincoln: "Not precisely, no. We're guessing at least four on the road. Those were defensive kills, undertaken to protect my people."

"This would be the personnel in the technicals that were hit by your squadron of Hai-Lins?"

"Yes."

"Were those UAVs operating under a customized artificial intelligence?"

"Absolutely. That AI is proprietary. I'm sure you're aware we had trouble from a squadron of Arkinsons."

"Yes, sir."

"Who was flying the Arkinsons?" Lincoln asks.

The young man hesitates. "I'm sorry, sir. That's classified."

This is not an answer Lincoln expected. "Are you telling me those Arkinsons were allied assets?"

The kid looks worried. He gives a slight shake of his head. "There are ongoing operations in the area, sir. The answer is classified."

Lincoln nods, hiding his frustration behind a neutral expression. What this agent is relaying to him . . . it doesn't make sense, not in the context of what Miles reported, of what True was told. But even disinformation can be useful. Jon Helm is not a fictional person. He's sure of that much.

He's sure too that the State Department would not lie about it unless the identity of Jon Helm mattered.

Later, the agents ask to take possession of the intelligence material recovered during the mission. This Lincoln denies. "We need time to look it over."

Given the backlog of evidence awaiting analysis in federal labs, he knows that if he turns over the recovered electronics now, it will be weeks, maybe months, before anyone bothers to look at it.

No, he'll let Tamara examine it first. In ten days or so, he'll hand it over to the feds as a goodwill gesture that might earn him favors down the road.

SENIOR STAFF

"WE CAN'T AFFORD a war," Chris is saying. "We need to contact Variant Forces. Work this out."

Lincoln has re-gathered his senior staff in the conference room: Chris, Tamara, True, and Renata. Tempers are short. Renata presented the results of her research on the replacement cost of the Hai-Lins: an impossible forty million for all three. ReqOps still owes several million on the loan used to purchase the now-destroyed equipment.

"Big profits only happen on the back of big risks," Lincoln reminded them. But no one anticipated a hole this deep.

Chris continues: "We've got major training contracts to fulfill. The next class gets here in three days. We need to be one hundred percent on our security before then, and if that means signing a peace treaty, I say we do it. We cannot run the risk of a vindictive hit harming our clients, and we cannot afford to lose this training contract."

Lincoln does not agree with this assessment. He hasn't announced it yet but he intends to postpone the training session. ReqOps can come back from the financial hit, but if they allow harm to come to their clients? The company will be finished, and deservedly so.

True says, "You've put this off long enough, Lincoln. You need to let our people know who we're dealing with."

He meets her gaze, nods. Chris realizes he's been kept on the outside of something, and the knowledge does not go over well. "What the fuck, Lincoln?"

Lincoln leans back, crossing his arms. Might as well do this right. His gaze drifts up to a tiny camera glistening in the corner of the room. "Hello, Friday," he says. "Call Jameson in here."

Chris eyes him warily but asks no more questions, willing to wait. Renata too says nothing, though her tension is revealed in the quiet tapping of her polished fingernails against the table top. Other than that, it's silent until Jameson walks in. He looks around the table, assesses the cool emotional climate, and scowls in suspicion.

"Take a seat," Lincoln tells him.

Jameson pulls out the chair next to True. They trade a glance. The chair creaks as he sits down.

Lincoln says, "You're here because you and Chris were part of Rogue Lightning."

"This have to do with our emblem?" Jameson asks in his deep voice. "Juliet told me about that."

"It's more than the emblem. It's about Shaw Walker, our original commander, before either of you were part of the team."

"We know who Shaw Walker is," Chris says. "We know how he died." He's careful not to look at True.

Lincoln says, "There's evidence that he's not dead, that he's Jon Helm, and that elements within the State Department are aware of his identity."

Neither believes it. After True provides details, neither *wants* to believe it.

"We were supposed to be the good guys," Jameson says. "How could Walker be tangled up in all the shit Hussam's been putting down? You knew him, Lincoln. You really think Walker is the same man as this asshole, Jon Helm?"

Lincoln chooses his words carefully. "Shaw Walker had his faults. We all do. If it *is* him, the time he spent in Nungsan must have fucked him up good." He turns to Chris. "We can't do a deal with Variant Forces. They're an unknown. We have no idea if they would honor an agreement."

"They called in a warning before they hit our air force," Chris reminds him. "That shows restraint. They were concerned with avoiding casualties. That tells me they can be reasoned with."

"They gave Eden Transit ninety seconds to clear out," Lincoln says in contempt. "That's not concern. That's one step north of *fuck you*."

"Come on. If he's known to the State Department—maybe on their payroll?—he's not going to—"

"We don't know what his relationship to the State Department is, but I'm betting 'deniable' describes it. We are going to postpone the upcoming training session—"

Chris's fist hits the table. "We *cannot* afford to do that! We will be liable for—"

Lincoln cuts him off. "Yes, we will be liable for costs! But we cannot take the risk that our clients will be targeted the same way the Hai-Lins were targeted, if Variant Forces decides to take it up a notch."

Tamara leans in, lends her support. "Lincoln's right. I don't know if Shaw Walker or Variant Forces was behind the intrusion at True's place. My gut instinct is that was a step up from the operation we encountered in the TEZ. Even so, if Variant Forces decides they want to scope us out, take a run at us, my guess is they have the personnel to pull it off."

"So you think Variant Forces is more than Shaw Walker?" Chris asks. "You think he's got his own development team?"

"Absolutely. We beat them in that dogfight but if we had to do it over again—"

"If we *could* do it over again," Renata interrupts in a bitter tone.

"Where's a renegade company like that going to find quality talent?" Jameson wants to know.

"Anywhere," Tamara tells him. "Everywhere. We're used to the university system. We expect the best programmers to come out of the best schools—but it's not always that way. To be really good at this stuff, you've got to have a mind wired for it, and you've got to be confident in your abilities and, sometimes, willing to take chances. Those traits can show up anywhere, including the ungoverned territories."

"I'm going to guess 'right action' is not their company motto," Chris says acidly.

Tamara shrugs. "I've seen people in this country explain away what looks to me like inexcusable behavior. But morality aside, Walker is running a successful operation that almost certainly relies on wildcat talent with no accountability. I imagine his people are not overly concerned about mistakes. So a few bystanders get killed; so what? They just update the system and move on to the next job. An attitude like that will produce breakthroughs at a faster pace than a highly educated team working under the general liability of a big defense contractor. That's why, in my opinion, wildcat systems are game changers."

"More reason," Lincoln says, "that we need to handle this straight up and handle it now. First we assess, confirm the identity of our enemy, and evaluate his resources. Then we go after him."

"You're going to hunt down Shaw Walker?" Chris asks in a harshly skeptical tone. "That's where you want to focus our resources? And if you find him, what? You planning to bring him home?"

"Yes," Lincoln affirms. "One way or another. We don't leave anyone behind."

CROSS PURPOSES

ONE WAY OR *another*.

An innocuous statement, but True doesn't miss his meaning. She studies him from across the table, wondering: *Are we at cross purposes?*

He notices the intensity of her gaze. "Speak," he tells her.

"I don't want him dead."

Lincoln crosses his arms, considers this for several seconds, then says, "I don't either. That's not my objective."

"But it *is* an option?"

"Not an option," he insists. "But a possible outcome? Sure. You know how it works. We'll draw up the best plan we can, but once we're in the field anything can happen."

She nods. "That's what I'm afraid of. You're focused on removing the threat of Shaw Walker. I want that too, but more than that I need to hear from him his story of what happened in Burma."

She feels everyone's eyes on her, no one daring to talk until Lincoln says, "I get that. I know it's important to you. But it's too early to have this debate. Right now we have no idea where he is or what his circumstances are."

"I'm going to back True on this one," Tamara says. "That kind of closure matters."

True hears this with gratitude. Tamara is their lone civilian voice and Lincoln respects her, seeks out her opinion.

Tamara continues. "I also need to insist that this company have a legal basis for whatever we decide to do. We cannot engage in a vigilante operation."

"We won't need to," Renata says. She cocks her head, crosses her arms. She's still spoiling for a fight. "We start by looking for an existing bounty on Jon Helm—"

Tamara shuts this down. "No bounty turned up in my early research."

Renata shrugs. "So we be proactive. Get some puppet government to sponsor one and give us the cover we need."

"No," Chris says. "I am not going to play that game. If we do this, we do it right."

Lincoln looks impatient with the debate. "We'll work out the legal structure," he says dismissively. "But we can't do anything—we can't know what's possible to do—until we find him and understand how he's situated. That's our initial task and we need to do it quietly. Carefully. If we want to control the situation, he can't know we're coming."

True is left uneasy, unhappy, as the meeting breaks up. Nothing is decided, not officially, but she's worried that her concerns will be dismissed, and that this chance, *her* chance, to understand what happened at Nungsan will be taken away from her—if she allows it to be taken away.

It's unsettling to feel so at odds with the people she trusts.

She'd like to retreat to her office. Instead she tells Lincoln, "I'm going to talk to our people."

"Do it."

She takes Jameson with her. They gather the team in the break room and True goes over it all again, laying down what's happened and what's known of Shaw Walker, and warning them to be careful. She listens to their disgruntled talk.

Felice lets her sarcasm spill over: "So we know the guy who burned our air force? Shit, with friends like that . . ."

Khalid looks to the future: "We going after him?"

Jameson eyes True. He didn't say much in the conference room, but that look, it's an apology. *Sorry I gotta do this, Mama.* He turns to the others and says, "It needs to be done."

"One way or another," True says coldly.

Rohan's usual good humor has evaporated. His ginger eyebrows meet in a cynical glare. "Revenge sucks as a motive, Mama. Tell me we've got a major bounty in play?"

"No bounty," True answers. "Not that we know of."

"So it's a question of honor?" Felice wants to know, her tone making it clear what she thinks of honor as a motivation.

"Ah, Jesus," Rohan says with a roll of his eyes. "Fucking save me."

"This stays within these walls," True warns them. "It stays within the QRF. You got any concerns, come see me."

After that she does retreat to her office, though she leaves the door ajar as an invitation to anyone with questions.

It's not yet noon, but she's tired: physically spent from the mission and emotionally worn by the fallout. She's edgy, too. Now that she knows he's out there, *Shaw Walker,* she can't imagine relaxing until she finds him, gets her answers.

That's all right. She's got too much to do to relax anyway.

She starts by calling Miles. She wants to check in with him, see how he's doing, and to thank him for keeping silent about Shaw. "Heads up, Ripley," she says to alert her personal agent. "Call Miles Dushane."

His phone rings several times, then goes to voice mail. She leaves a basic message: "Miles, it's True Brighton. Call me when you get a chance."

A footstep outside her office door alerts her. She looks up as Jameson comes in. At the moment her feelings toward him are less than friendly—and apparently it shows.

"Don't give me that look," he says in his low voice, closing the door firmly behind him.

"I thought maybe you'd get it," she tells him.

He sits down in the guest chair. Leans forward. "I *do* get it. I got kids of my own. I know where you're coming from. In your place I'd feel the same way."

"*It needs to be done,*" she quotes him. "One way or another."

He considers this, rocking in the chair while she watches him. When he speaks again, it's in precise, carefully chosen words. "When a brother wanders off the path, it's right action to go after him, bring him home, bring him to justice if that's needed. But I don't know this bastard. He's not my brother. He wiped out our Hai-Lins and that makes him the enemy. I've gotta believe he's hunting us, Mama. That fucked-up mechanical deer you saw— who you think that belongs to? He's mapping out your life. He's probably mapping out all our lives so he can hit us. I don't care 'bout bringing the brother home. I want to bring the battle to him. Hit him before he hits us here at our home. I've got to think of my kids, True. They're only three years old. I've got to think of my wife."

True sighs and leans back, lacing her fingers together, pondering what little they know. Shaw led the raid to kidnap Miles; he had a contract to protect Hussam. Logical to assume the two were partners on a kidnapping-and-ransom gig. A criminal business, to be sure, but a business all the same. And the hit against the Hai-Lins, wasn't that just business too?

"It might already be over," she says. "The Hai-Lins might have balanced the scales."

"Not a chance I want to take."

"This is Shaw Walker," she reminds him. "If we swing and we miss, *guaranteed* he's coming after us."

"I got that, Mama. And that's why I think we need to do it off the books. Do it mean. Ensure the threat is neutralized."

She shakes her head. "You heard Tamara. This can't be a vigilante action. He has ties to the State Department. You don't think they'd notice?"

"They might thank us."

This is about his kids. She makes herself remember that and adopts a conciliatory tone. "Let's see how it plays out. Nothing we can do anyway until we know where he is."

"Yeah. Until then, we are targets in his scope."

———

Khalid spent two years in the TEZ, listening to gossip and chasing rumors. Jon Helm was one of those rumors. It was generally agreed he was an American mercenary and you did not want to be in a conflict if he was hired by the other side. But Khalid had never gotten anyone to admit that they'd met Jon Helm. Rumor insisted he was an American but nothing else was certain. He was a black guy or a white guy. He was a drunk, he was disciplined. He lived in Sudan, Algeria, Chad, maybe Mali. Somewhere far away, but he could turn up without warning and make warlords disappear.

Khalid had assumed Jon Helm was a story, the kind used to scare your rivals. Only when he heard Hussam El-Hashem's description of Jon Helm did he begin to think the man might be real. So he listened attentively when True explained what was known of Jon Helm, and he chided himself for not following up on the rumors he'd heard.

It doesn't have to be too late.

He takes a few minutes to consider and compose a plan. Then he goes to see True in her office—but Jameson is there ahead of him. When the door closes, he moves on to knock on Lincoln's door.

He half-expects to be ignored. After all, he's the new guy, bottom of the hierarchy, and Lincoln is busy. But the door unlocks.

Lincoln is seated behind his desk, a laptop open in front of him. "What's up?" he asks gruffly. "Did Chris give you all the employment forms?"

"Yes, sir."

He met Lincoln last night at the reception. When Chris introduced him, he stood there like an idiot, frozen in surprise, taking in the fire-scarred face with its artificial eye, the weird, semitranslucent prosthetic hand with its fingers rippling in nervous motion, and the violent colors of the tattoos on his arms, so unnatural they suggested his arms might be artificial too.

Khalid was used to seeing scarred and disfigured men in the TEZ, but there, war was a way of life. He hadn't expected the scars to be so visible at home where war was distant—although here, too, it's a way of life for some.

The scars no longer command Khalid's attention, but he still hesitates before he speaks—a few seconds spent trying to read the mood behind that ravaged face. It's not easy. He's got a feeling Lincoln was hard to read even before his injuries.

Finally, Khalid says, "I wanted to talk to you about Jon Helm, sir. Or Shaw Walker, if that's what it is."

"Go ahead. You know anything about him?"

"Nothing solid. I heard rumors in the TEZ, though. I could make inquiries."

Lincoln nods thoughtfully. "You don't need to do this face to face?"

"No, sir. I know a couple of guys I trust pretty far. They trust me. I won't need to tell them why I'm looking or mention ReqOps at all."

"You'll need a budget," Lincoln says.

Khalid nods. "A couple grand?" he suggests. "It could be dangerous work for them."

"Set it up. I'll arrange for the money."

NO MORAL ARGUMENT

MILES SITS AT a desk in the guest room of his parents' house in Seattle, an old keyboard and tablet in front of him. He is typing swiftly, steadily. He's been typing for most of the twenty hours since he's been back, pouring out every memory of the past two months, first in broad strokes but then revisiting his narrative, over and over, filling in the finer details of his experiences: textures, scents, sounds; the words that were spoken—brutal, commanding, mocking, misleading—rendered as exactly as he can remember them; harsh gallows humor among the prisoners and desperate promises; the absurdities he witnessed, and the agonies; the lofty philosophies spawned out of hopelessness and terror.

Alongside the keyboard is a phone. It's been activated with the number he's used since he was a kid. When he turned the phone on, a call rang through. A harbinger of the myriad to come. So he turned the phone off again, letting his parents field the calls—calls from mediots, from news agencies, from publishers who never before showed an interest in his work. Calls from friends.

He answered none. He wasn't ready to talk. Not even to the State Department officials who visited the house.

"Tell them I'm asleep."

It wasn't the truth, but it wasn't entirely a lie either. He was hardly conscious of himself, of the room, the house, his worried parents. Instead, for most of that time, he existed within his memories—not as himself, but as a disembodied observer wandering through the hours of his captivity, reviewing it all with what felt like perfect recall.

But at last his mind is winding down, his fingers slowing, new words no longer appearing on the screen.

He is nodding in exhaustion, hardly able to hold himself up when a man's voice speaks from out of nowhere, low, rough, regretful. "You shouldn't have come here, Dushane."

The voice doesn't frighten him because he knows it's a dream. And because it is a dream, *his* dream, he gets to ask a question that he didn't know to ask when he first heard those words. "Why are *you* here?"

The mercenary—Jon Helm, Shaw Walker, whatever the fuck his name is—ignores the question, if he hears it at all. He moves off to supervise the execution of the Iraqi laborers who'd been heading home from the western desert and who'd given Miles a ride.

Worst mistake of their lives.

Last mistake.

No point in holding on to them. None will fetch a worthwhile ransom. No point even trying to collect. "Why the fuck don't you just let them go?" Miles screams, but this too is a revisionary memory. He only wishes he'd said that.

The reality of that day is that Miles said nothing.

Slide it back. Play it through again, more detail.

He is on his knees. The thick fabric of his trousers fails to stop the bite of small stones against his flesh. His feet are numb, his back aches, his eyes burn with dust and the glare of the sun against the gray desert grit. His mouth is dry, throat swollen, and not just from the fear that his blood and brains are about to be redistributed in a spray pattern, a transient marker of his presence written on sand, but also because the afternoon temperature has climbed to one hundred eighteen degrees Fahrenheit and he's been kneeling for some immeasurable period, and if it gets any hotter he fully expects the air to ignite and maybe that wouldn't be a bad thing. Maybe this fucking world deserves it.

By the time the mercenary stops to look at him, Miles has given up on moral argument. He recognizes that there is no moral argument that can save him when the men who were kneeling on either side of him are already dead. The best he can do is look up to meet death's gaze, a last act of defiance.

The mercenary is tall and lean. A long face, narrow nose, light-colored eyes just visible behind the tinted lenses of his sunglasses. His skin is burned dark by the sun but lightened again by dust caked in his sweat. His brown beard is frosted by dust. He wears combat fatigues, an armored vest, a helmet. The sleeves of his combat jacket are rolled up. He holds an assault rifle in his right hand. The fingers of his left hand are long and thin and contorted—half-curled—around a mass of scar tissue. There is a multicolored tattoo on his left forearm.

Miles means to look him in the eye, to look death in the eye, but the tattoo distracts him. It's a thin black cross, wreathed in fire and wrapped in a loose, floating banner. *Diego Delgado*, it reads. *The Last Good Man.*

It's an anomaly. So out of place it's weirdly annoying. It distracts Miles from the imminence of his own death so that for a moment all he can think is *What the fuck?*

He turns to the mercenary for an explanation and Shaw Walker speaks the only words that Miles heard from him that day: "You shouldn't have come here, Dushane." He gestures with his crippled hand and Miles braces, expecting a bullet in his skull. A gag goes into his mouth instead. A hood goes over his head. He is barely able to breathe as rough hands shove him into an enclosed space with two other men.

A cold voice, speaking Arabic, warns that if any of them makes a sound, all will be shot.

Miles finds himself thinking, *This is a fucking awful dream.* He forces his eyes open. He has somehow made it from the desk into bed, though the light is still on.

With a shaking hand he turns it off, plunging the room into darkness.

Darkness is a reprieve. As long as the cell door is closed, he's safe.

He imagines Shaw Walker, locked up at Nungsan.

What'd they do to you there? he wonders. He doesn't know the full story but he knows how it turned out. He envisions a shock wave, generated by a soul's cataclysmic collapse, exploding out of Nungsan in a karmic blast that is still igniting violent repercussions.

He hears Noël weeping, a distant, hopeless sound. Even farther off, gunshots in an unhurried rhythm, each one speaking the death of a man.

And it's not over, Miles thinks.

But if he can, he'd like to finish it.

TRANSITIONS

TRUE'S AFTERNOON IS consumed by reports and research and brief discussions. Lincoln calls to let her know that Fatima Atwan and Ryan Rogers are both back home in the United States.

"I talked to Rogers," he says. "The State Department grilled him on Hussam's operation but there wasn't much he could tell them. Fatima probably witnessed more. I'd like to interview her, but Yusri doesn't think she's ready to answer questions."

"Do you think it's okay if I call her?" True asks. "Just to check in?"

"Do it. Keep the lines of communication open."

Yusri answers her call. He expresses his gratitude, but he's hesitant to let her talk to Fatima. "She is distraught," he explains. A worried father.

"I understand, sir. I just want to let her know we're on her side, we're thinking of her."

"I'll ask her," Yusri agrees, and soon Fatima is on the phone.

She sounds distant and tired. "I cannot sleep," she admits. "Every time I do, I'm back there again."

"It'll get better," True assures her. "Give it time."

"My mother says the same thing. She insists I am stronger than this."

"You are. You're brave and brilliant, Dr. Atwan, and you have so much still to give to the world, so much life ahead of you."

Maybe this is the wrong thing to say because Fatima responds in a despondent whisper. "It is my obligation, I know. A debt I owe to all those women who will never be free. I am the lucky one."

Maybe there are no right words.

Fatima does not mention her pregnancy; True does not inquire, recognizing it as a private matter.

Afterward True loses herself for a time in banal tasks, so that it's close to 1700 when she tries Miles again. This time a message says his voicemail is full.

She leans back, thinking about him, about Fatima. Thirty-six hours ago both were captive; they'd seen other captives murdered.

For Miles, the prospect of his own gruesome death was never far away.

Now he's safe at home, but the sudden transition from captivity to conventional civilian life, with no chance to decompress, can't be easy.

Restless, she stands up, stretching stiff joints, sore muscles—minor aftereffects of the mission and easy to dismiss. It's the anxiety like a slow-drip amphetamine in her blood that's got her on edge. She's not sure Requisite Operations has the financial depth to survive the loss of the Hai-Lins. Worse, she's no longer sure of her own loyalty.

Fuck this day anyway.

"Hello, Friday," she says aloud. "Is Tamara still in?"

The office AI answers over her earpiece. "Yes, Tamara is in her office."

True grabs her shoulder bag off the desk and walks out. Lincoln, Jameson, Renata—they all want to go hunting. Tamara's was the lone voice of caution in the meeting today. Tamara is still an ally.

It's late in the day. The air is cold, the sky cloudy. Wind rustles in the evergreens as True walks down the concrete path to the Robotics Center. She finds Tamara in her office.

"Hey," True says, dropping into the guest chair. "Thanks for backing me up today."

"I didn't like the mood in that meeting," Tamara tells her. Her brow creases with concern. "How are you holding up?"

"I'm good."

"You don't look good," Tamara says. "You look exhausted."

"Heh. Thanks."

"Come on. We're past the age of vanity."

"Speak for yourself, ma'am."

Tamara smiles. A thin cover for her disquiet. "Any more alarms go off at your house today?"

"Not so far. Maybe it *was* a mediot and they pulled out rather than risk their fancy tech."

Tamara doesn't argue but neither does she agree. "I sent video of the mech deer to some colleagues. No one recognized it, but Li Guiying said she's worked on similar quadrupedal systems."

"Is she still private-sector?"

"Mostly university now. Splits her time between China and France."

True says, "I didn't tell you my new theory about her."

Tamara leans back, crossing her arms. "Why do I get the feeling I'm not going to like this?"

"I think she has an AI handling her correspondence. I got a note from her yesterday, *minutes* after news of the mission went public. 'You are a hero among women.' That sort of thing."

Tamara's eyes narrow. "You just told me you're not past the age of vanity. Surely you're not going to argue with that?"

True refuses to be drawn off point. "Who would write an email like that? She's got to be using an AI. It probably tracks a list of correspondents, generates hundreds of congratulatory emails a day."

Tamara rolls her eyes. "She *likes* you, True. I can't imagine why, but she does. She admires you. She mentions you all the time. She thinks of you as a friend."

True shakes her head. "Everything about her feels fake to me. Always has."

"You're really standoffish, you know that?"

True cocks her head in wry acknowledgment. "Safer that way."

———————

On the drive home, True finds herself pondering the obsolete nature of the laws of war. The QRF's actions in the TEZ could be considered an act of war—if ReqOps was a sovereign nation. "Which we're not," she says aloud. Neither is Variant Forces. Both are private military companies—but does that matter?

If this conflict is allowed to escalate, each company could designate the employees of the other as enemy combatants, making them legitimate targets—for an adaptive definition of "legitimate"—even here, within the sovereign borders of the United States of America.

If someone with Shaw Walker's experience and resources decides he is going to target and kill an individual, it *will* happen, and it won't require a human hand. A sniper drone, a bomb in an autonomous car, a crab mech carrying explosives, a mayfly with a toxic payload. Lots of ways to get the job done. That's the reality of their situation. It's why Jameson wants a preemptive strike and why Chris wants a peace treaty.

Requisite Operations is not a sovereign nation, but it's starting to act like one.

THE UNOFFICIAL STORY

ALEX IS ALREADY home when True arrives. The shotgun is out. "Just in case," he says, but he doesn't look worried. He pours her a glass of wine and they sit down to high-end Italian takeout that he picked up on the way home. For a few minutes life feels almost normal.

True is pouring more wine when the intrusion alarm goes off: a shiver-inducing bleat that emanates from Alex's phone on the dining table and from her tablet, left on the kitchen counter.

She gets up, furious. "Get me a location on it," she tells Alex as she scoops up the shotgun and heads for the mudroom.

"Hold on," he says, phone in hand as he rises from his chair. "It's not our robotic stalker. There's a car at the gate."

"A *car*?" she asks suspiciously, because no one ever stops by their house without calling first.

"Looks like Brooke Kanegawa."

Courier mode: that's what Brooke calls it. "When information is so sensitive it can't be conveyed electronically for fear it will be intercepted."

"So you came in person," True says wonderingly. She's also a little afraid.

"Let's go downstairs," Brooke says, "into the basement. Leave all your electronics here."

Lights come on automatically when Alex opens the door. The three of them tramp down the hardwood stairs. The basement is finished but unfurnished. A few forgotten boxes are stacked in a corner. There's not much else.

Brooke looks around. She's still not satisfied, so she heads for the furnace room. "In here," she says, opening the door. The furnace is running, providing white noise, though True doesn't think that will defeat any truly sophisticated listening device.

They squeeze in. Alex closes the door behind them.

Brooke is a couple of years older than True—a compact woman, only five-foot-two—still attractive, with a soft, round figure, frosty blond hair, and blue-gray eyes that project a no-nonsense attitude. Those eyes are bright as she looks up at True and says, "I don't have any proof of what I'm about to tell you, but it was told to me by someone I trust, someone in a position to know. And maybe it involves Diego. That's the reason I came."

True nods. Brooke knew Diego as a ten-year-old, that year in DC. "We understand," she says, grateful for Alex's presence beside her.

Brooke leans closer, eyeing both of them. "There's a suspicion our Chinese allies knew our men had been taken to Nungsan—but they failed to share that intelligence."

Below the surface, True feels the stir of an old, familiar panic, a metabolic rush, the demand that she do *something*. Stiff knuckles resist the tight squeeze of her fist.

Brooke continues, "Diego was held overnight before he was executed. There might have been time enough to go in after him, *if* we knew where he was. *If* the Chinese had shared that knowledge with us, but they did not. Worse, they diverted our forces away from Nungsan."

"But *why?*" True interrupts in a plaintive tone. "Why would they do that? The hunt for Saomong was a cooperative action. We weren't at odds. We were sharing intelligence. Both sides wanted them taken out."

Brooke raises her hand, requesting patience. "You know the official story. The story that was worked out afterward. Right? That no one knew an American prisoner was being held at Nungsan. So when Chinese forces received intel that a Saomong warlord on their hit list was in the village—and that the civilians had fled—they took unilateral action and eliminated Nungsan with a missile strike. In their position we might have done the same."

Alex says, "I thought this had to do with Diego. He was murdered days before that happened."

"The unofficial story is different," Brooke says. "It's now believed that the warlord, if he existed at all, was an excuse, a cover story for the real goal. The Chinese wanted that village erased along with everyone in it—militants *and* prisoners."

This is such a departure from True's understanding of the Burma operation that she struggles to make sense of it. "You're saying the Chinese wanted Shaw dead?"

"And Diego. And everyone else."

"*Why?*"

"No one knows."

Alex says, "Someone knows."

True thinks about it. She has a feeling Jon Helm could tell them why.

THE HUNT

MILES AWAKES TO gray daylight seeping through the bedroom curtain. He watches the shadow of a cheap quadcopter drift past and wonders if his parents' Internet connection has been hacked.

Probably.

He gets up, showers. His mom is in the kitchen, watching him with worried eyes. "I'm all right," he tells her, giving her a kiss on the cheek.

She's not convinced, but for now she's willing to pretend. She cooks breakfast for him, eggs and bacon and pancakes, while he sits at the kitchen table and listens to his dad and his sister describe the phone calls, the government agents, the surveillance drones, and the mediots parked out front.

"I don't want you to have to deal with this," he tells them. He explains his plan to find a short-term rental in a secure tower.

Of course they protest, until he tells them, "I'm going to need the quiet anyway. I'm writing a book."

This is what they expect to hear. It wins their cooperation. His sister offers to call a friend who deals in real estate; by noon he's put his electronic signature on a month-to-month lease for a fully furnished condo.

He's got a few boxes stored in the garage—mostly clothes. His dad's going to drive him over to the new place, so he loads the boxes into the trunk of his parents' car. Before he leaves, he pulls his sister aside. "As soon as I get a secure connection, I'm going to send you a copy of the manuscript so far. Don't open it, but stash it somewhere for safekeeping. I'll give you the name of a literary agent you can trust. If anything happens to me, forward the manuscript to him. He'll hire someone to finish it and he'll get you a good deal."

Her hazel eyes widen. "Miles, what do you mean, *if something happens to you*? You're home now. What's going to happen?"

He smiles, brushes it off. "Sorry. I'm still a little paranoid."

She wants to believe the story he's writing is over, but it's not. He intends to look into what happened at Nungsan and prove a connection between that event, his own brutal kidnapping, and a mercenary known as Jon Helm. If things work out, he'll end the book with Jon Helm being brought to justice.

He doesn't tell his sister that the real reason he wants his own place is so that she and their parents will be out of the line of fire if Jon Helm decides that the story should end in a different way.

Brooke made sure she had an official reason for her sudden visit. Since she's served as liaison between the State Department and Requisite Operations in the past, she's been assigned to conduct additional follow-up interviews and make recommendations to improve relations and communications in the future.

It's busy work but True is happy to comply. She takes Brooke on a tour of the Requisite Operations campus and introduces her to Lincoln and Chris and Tamara. No insider information is mentioned and Brooke departs at 1300, in time to make her flight back to DC.

True stands beside Lincoln outside the lobby door, waving as Brooke pulls out of the parking lot. "Did you get something from her?" Lincoln asks as the automated gate closes behind the rental car.

True nods.

They retreat to the security of his office, where she tells him the unofficial story—the speculation from deep inside the State Department that the Chinese took extreme measures to ensure no witnesses survived Nungsan.

Lincoln is deeply shaken. "If that's true, they betrayed our men. They betrayed the mission." He looks at True. "We don't know why?"

"We don't know," she confirms.

He gropes for an explanation. "Maybe they had an agent on the ground. A double agent. Someone who betrayed them and they didn't want that fact to get out."

True leans in to make her point. "There's one witness still alive who might be able to tell us."

Lincoln gives her a measuring look. "If Shaw wanted to talk, he would have come home eight years ago. He's wrapped up in this somehow, in a way you're not going to like."

"I want the truth," she says. "I know it won't be pretty."

She'd told Alex the same thing last night when he tried again to convince her to stay clear of any pursuit of Shaw. They'd been sitting around the fireplace with Brooke, who immediately picked up on their tension. She and True traded a look. Silent agreement passed between them. They would talk later, just the two of them.

True had waited until the morning. After Alex left for work, she asked Brooke, "Is Shaw a department asset?"

Brooke furrowed her brow, uncertain. "I don't think so. It's hard to know, though."

"Do you have access to any contact information for him?"

"No."

"You're aware he hit our fighter squadron."

"Yes, I heard that."

"Those were legal aircraft," True said. "Could we get State to offer a bounty on him against that action? Make it live-capture only, in respect for his past service?"

True thought this approach might prove ideal. Lincoln would have to respect a live-capture order. But Brooke voided the idea. "No. That is not going to happen."

"You're certain?" True pressed.

"Look at it this way. To acknowledge Shaw Walker's past service would require State to admit he's alive, and if he's alive, then the investigation into what happened at Nungsan has to be reopened. And if Shaw is brought in, he could testify in a manner that might play hell with our diplomatic relations with the Chinese. The same thing applies to Jon Helm. State won't issue a bounty on that name either, because they cannot take the chance that he'll come home alive, under any name."

An unpopular man, True thought. State didn't want him alive and the early sentiment at ReqOps echoed that. It left True feeling protective of him. And why shouldn't she? Hadn't he been the last man to defend Diego?

"I need him alive, Brooke," she insisted. "I need to find him alive. That's the only way I'll ever know what really happened."

But Brooke cautioned her too. "I know you don't want to hear this, but Alex is right to worry."

"I understand that," True answered. "I know Shaw Walker is a dangerous man."

He was a decorated war hero . . . but Nungsan broke him. Shaw could not be seen on the video of Diego's execution, but he'd been there. True had listened to his voice coming from off screen, heard him begging for mercy. Not for himself. Never for himself. *Let him live*, he'd screamed. *Take me instead.*

Tiny wrinkles in Brooke's brow reflected her concern. "Promise me you'll be careful."

"Eyes wide open," True assured her. "I can promise that."

Now, sitting in Lincoln's office, True recalls that conversation, distills it in her mind, and tells Lincoln only what he needs to know. "Don't expect any bounty on Jon Helm. Not from State, anyway."

"Noted. We're still early in the intelligence-gathering phase. Let's keep at it. Something will shake loose."

A robotic beetle is perched outside Miles's twenty-third floor apartment. It clings to the jutting rib of a slight overhang above the picture window. He noticed it the day after he moved in. Two days have passed since then and it's still there. He tried to reach it with a broom handle to knock it down. No go.

Farther out, in the gulf of air above the surrounding buildings, a raptor wheels in suspiciously tight and consistent figure eights. It's been there for hours, unperturbed by the steady traffic of passing delivery drones and easily outmaneuvering the occasional thug drone that tries to knock it from the sky. He watches it, feeling both anger and admiration. Biomimetic robots have gotten so damned sophisticated.

His phone rings. The call IDs to a woman he once did a story on, who works for an environmental NGO. He walks into the bedroom, where heavy blinds are drawn across the window, closing the door before he takes the call. "Hello, Elena?"

"Miles!" She sounds surprised that he answered the phone.

Wherever Elena is calling from, it's noisy with the sounds of an open market. People chattering, yelling back and forth, pop music blaring, and the crow of roosters. "I'm heading into the field," she says, "but I might have something for you."

Miles began his hunt for Jon Helm with basic reconnaissance: a search of public resources, publications, and private databases. He didn't find much—he didn't expect to—but it was a necessary step.

No doubt the team at Requisite Operations was already far ahead of him.

He thought they were likely to focus on North Africa and the Middle East—the region where Jon Helm was known to conduct his operations. ReqOps would have intelligence resources in place, people they could hire to pursue rumors—though it would be a dangerous assignment.

Jon Helm didn't want to be found. No doubt he discouraged people from looking.

Miles had decided to approach the problem from another direction: He would go back to Nungsan.

He knew the official story of what had happened there was wrong. Diego Delgado had died in that village but Shaw Walker had not. What else about the official story might be mistaken? What had been left out? He had only press accounts to go on—he didn't have access to the official report—but he could find no indication that interviews had been undertaken, not with people living in the area or with surviving soldiers of the Saomong Cooperative Cybernetic Army who might have insight on the details of what happened at Nungsan. It wasn't hard to imagine that in the eagerness to wrap up an investigation without incurring more casualties in the war-torn region, some critical fact had been overlooked.

So Miles turned to his contact list, picking out people with experience in the region. He sent them an email saying he was back, recovering, and writing a book as therapy. Given what he'd witnessed during his captivity, he wanted to document the history of execution videos and their exploitation of violence for political influence. Nungsan was part of that.

Elena shouts over the background market noise. "I had no idea what you were going through until I got your email. I'm so glad. *So glad* to know you're safe at home."

"Hey, me too. But you said you had something for me?"

"Maybe. It's not much."

"Tell me."

"I don't have a source. It's something I remembered after I got your email. Years ago—five years, six? Something like that. It was when I was working in the Philippines. I remember reading a profile about a priest, a Catholic missionary in Myanmar. He was kidnapped, held for some days, supposedly with an American prisoner. I can't remember the details. I don't know if it had anything to do with Nungsan, or if it was some other incident, but it would have been when Saomong was active."

"Do you remember where the article was published?" he asks.

"Not really. I think it was a little socialist revolutionary site. It probably doesn't even exist anymore. I'm sorry. I know that's not very helpful."

"No, it is," he says, not really believing his own words. "It's something to follow up on."

Miles scribbles a note. They talk for another minute, then say goodbye.

For two years, Khalid worked as a freelance operator in the business of acquiring and selling intelligence in the TEZ. He made friends in that time, and a lot of connections. In his mind, he developed a complex map of who his connections might be connected to.

After getting authorization from Lincoln, he establishes an open contract for significant information on the activity, associates, or whereabouts of Jon Helm, a principal of the PMC known as Variant Forces. He sends the offer out to his most trusted friends and associates.

Khalid knows how the gossip network operates in the TEZ. He imagines pointed questions whispered here and there, and fading text messages sent to trusted sources. The queries rippling from one individual to many . . . and maybe disappearing?

He hopes not. He hopes to get an answer back.

After several days, he does.

REVISED STRATEGY

NINE DAYS HAVE passed since Lincoln defined his strategy: *confirm the identity of our enemy, evaluate his resources, and if it's Shaw, bring him home.*

Despite staff hours devoted to the task, and thousands of dollars paid out for research and intelligence, after nine days, Shaw Walker, aka Jon Helm, remains a ghost, and Variant Forces a mirage flickering into a transient existence on the basis of rumor and guesswork, none of it confirmed.

Lincoln has been thinking of Variant Forces as a corporation like ReqOps. But the State Department suggested it was a syndicate and Lincoln thinks that is a good description.

The word "corporation" derives from the Latin, *corpus*, for body. But Lincoln considers it likely that Variant Forces has no corporate body in the sense he is accustomed to, that it has no central location. Its structure is more fluid.

The model he thinks of is a swarm: small independent units that can function on their own or come together as a coordinated whole when need demands it.

He flinches at the hard rap of knuckles on his office door. Friday announces, "Chris would like to enter."

"Let him in," he mutters irritably.

The lock clicks. Chris comes in, slamming the door closed behind him. His face is flushed. He exudes disapproval—but that's his duty.

"God damn it, Lincoln," he says, "we are hemorrhaging funds." He yanks the guest chair to the center of the desk and sits down. "Renata is busting her ass getting bids on our Hai-Lin AI, but that is not going to save us. We have to resume our training schedule. We cannot reschedule any more sessions. If we do, we are going to lose the company. It's that simple. If that's the direction you want to go, let me know, because I will start laying people off today."

Lincoln is well aware of the financial situation. He knows Chris is not exaggerating. He's aware of Renata's activities too. She went against company policy and consented to an interview in a defense publication. Her flamboyant personality shone through as she described the dogfight outside Tadmur, her own authority as squadron leader, and the autonomous action of the AI pilot. Her purpose was to generate interest and drive up bids for the AI's services. She succeeded, but the publicity came at a cost: Her name and face now represent the mission. It's the kind of exposure Lincoln wants his people to avoid—and he's determined it won't happen again.

"Reinitiate the training schedule," he tells Chris.

"*What?*"

"You heard me."

"Just like that?"

"Yes."

"Why?"

"You wanted a peace treaty?" Lincoln asks him. "Well, we've been handed one."

"What the hell?"

"Shaw is invisible. We are not."

It started with True and the mimetic deer. Since then, everyone who participated in the operation against Hussam reported similar incidents. The devices varied from insect mimetics, sighted on eaves and windowsills, to a raptor that Lincoln watched as it watched him, floating on an updraft past his seventh-floor balcony.

Everyone has been allowed to *see* the devices watching. It's a clear statement.

He says, "Variant Forces has us mapped. They could hit us—hit our personnel, hit our families—anytime they want to."

"But they won't do it unless we give them a reason. That's how you're reading this?"

"It's not a guess anymore. Khalid made contact. Not directly with Shaw. The message came through an intermediary."

"You *know* that? You've got confirmation?"

"Yes. On the Burma mission, Shaw's last mission, the identity confirmation code was 'perfect field.' That was appended to the message Khalid received. Who would know that? Who would bother to remember it except Shaw?"

"What was the message?"

Lincoln activates the tablet that's lying on his desk and reads aloud in a flat voice: "For old times' sake, I'm going to call it even and let this one go. You know I can get to you. Fuck with me again and the blade goes in."

Chris leans back, looks to the heavens. "Jesus."

"I'm stepping aside as executive officer at ReqOps," Lincoln says. "I'm appointing you interim CEO. I want you to get us back on schedule, get the cash flow going again."

"So you're not accepting this peace treaty? Do you really think dissociating yourself from ReqOps is going to make a difference?"

"No. And I'm not dissociating myself. But the day-to-day operation of this company is a full-time job and I can't give it my full-time attention right now. So it's on you, Chris, to keep us in business."

"While you go after Shaw?"

"While I attend to our long-term security. What this incident has made clear is that the world we thought we were living in doesn't exist anymore. We've always emphasized personal security among our people, but up until now we've operated on the naïve assumption that the threats we face at home are minor. We guard against intruders. We use security cameras and alarms. But we've got nothing in place to protect our homes and our families from a raid like the one we ran against Hussam."

"It's not a realistic worry," Chris objects. "We're behind an active shield of federal surveillance, antiterrorist investigations, government checkpoints. Some AI, somewhere, is going to trigger an alarm at any hint of an unlicensed private military operation on that scale."

"How confident are you of that? Really? Think about it. Think how you would do it."

He gives Chris time to consider this.

"It would be easy for you," Lincoln continues. "You're one man. A lone wolf. You're not after publicity. You don't want to promote a political or religious cause. You don't want to negotiate. All you want to do is hit a soft target. You don't need to be present to do it. An armed drone with a kamikaze function wouldn't even leave evidence."

"That's a path to paranoia," Chris says. "Yes, it's possible. But what you're saying—it means Shaw is not our only problem. We can make enemies with anything we do—a defensive security operation, even training someone else's jackboots. If we're that vulnerable to low-cost retribution, our business model is blown, because we will never have the budget or the legal protections of a state-sponsored military operation."

"Exactly," Lincoln says. "We are vulnerable to anyone, anywhere, anytime."

"Unless we go into hiding, adopt a bunker mentality. Is that what you're saying?"

"No. None of us wants to live that way. In the long run, we're going to have to live by our reputation. We offer no quarter. We respond to every threat. So bringing Shaw home is essential . . . in the long term. For now though, we play along. We respect the peace treaty. We get the company back on a stable financial footing."

"While you prepare for war."

"Eight years ago, in Kunar Province, I was present when Shaw knowingly called in a drone strike on a house full of noncombatants, women and children. I did not report the incident. I told myself it was for the good of the unit and I stood aside. That was a mistake. Not one I plan to repeat. Everything that's happened since, from Burma to the TEZ—"

Chris cuts him off. "You don't get to put that on your shoulders!"

Lincoln shakes his head. "Let's just say I don't like loose ends."

A LEAD

MILES DRIVES OUT to the ReqOps campus on a gloomy morning, with the windshield wipers of his rented car swiping at a light rain. He's feeling jumpy, like he's in the TEZ, going to meet an activist, knowing the local warlord might have a checkpoint set up just for him.

No warlord here, he reminds himself.

From the other shoulder: *Modern warlords don't need to co-locate to kick your ass.*

The surveillance is constant and oppressive. Some of it is mediots trying to get his story before it fades from the public consciousness. He can understand that; he can handle it. It's the raptor that bothers him, wheeling outside his window night and day, its battery recharged through sun-tracking photovoltaic feathers.

Most of the time, surveillance is surreptitious. But sometimes a watcher will want the subject to know they're being watched. It makes them cautious. It makes them think twice. It lets them know they're vulnerable. Whoever is flying the raptor wants Miles to know he's vulnerable.

He assumes it's Variant Forces, though he has no proof.

The question that haunts him: *Does Shaw already know I'm looking?*

He reaches the ReqOps campus. He reviewed the route before he came, so the automated gate that guards the entrance is no surprise. Lowering his window, he lets the guardian camera get a look at him. From beneath the car, the soft whirr of an electronic motor. Something moving down there. Probably a wheeled robot with a chemical sensor, sniffing the undercarriage for explosives. He starts to open the door to look, but the gate opens and he's allowed in.

The number of cars in the parking lot surprises him. Almost thirty. He has to hunt for an empty stall. He finds one in a far corner, rain-soaked shrubbery leaning into it. Branches scrape the passenger side as he backs in.

He gets out but lingers beside the car, studying the parking lot, looking for potential hazards. Roving biomimetics, for example.

Rain beads in fine droplets on his closely cropped hair, his face, the gray collar of his coat. He doesn't see any biomimetics.

He studies the building: two long wings curving away from a central lobby. Security cameras aren't obvious but he knows they're there. He feels safer under their gaze. ReqOps security is surely on alert for free-ranging autonomous devices . . . at least the ground-based variety.

He lifts his gaze to the gray sky. Tiny raindrops tingle against his face as he watches a raptor circle beneath the dark gray clouds.

Shit.

He tells himself, *It's not suspicious that I'm here.* It's natural to visit the people who saved his life. It's expected. It'd be suspicious if he *didn't* come.

He walks to the building. Two sets of glass doors slide open in quick succession, admitting him to a small lobby furnished with twin sofas, a low table, and several glass exhibit cases. The cases hold battlefield photos, outdated weapons, battered equipment, tattered flags. A young man—he can't be more than eighteen—with a button-down shirt and a military haircut stands behind a long reception desk, watching him with a friendly gaze. Miles realizes he's seen the kid before. At the reception at the airfield. Hayden. That was his name.

"Sergeant Dushane, welcome to Requisite Operations—"

"It's Mister Dushane, but you can call me Miles."

"Yes, sir."

"I don't have an appointment—"

"That's all right, sir. Ms. Brighton is on her way out to meet you."

Even as Hayden says it, electronic locks hum, a security door beside the desk opens, and True steps out with a smile. "Miles, good to see you."

He flashes back on the first time he saw her: a soldier obscured into uncertainty by her camouflage clothing so that her visor and her Kieffer-Obermark were the only solid things about her. Today she's cast in another role: civilian representative.

She is dressed to flatter her willowy figure, tight slacks, a clingy black T-shirt, and flowing jacket. Her silver-brown hair is confined in a thick French braid and her eyes are bright, enhanced by the subtle shadowing of makeup. An office warrior, he thinks. Let the badass boys lurk in the background. The image she presents is sharp, competent, mature—an ideal public face for a private military company.

He can't imagine Rohan or Jameson or Chris cleaning up so well. Maybe it's something only a woman would be asked to do.

She holds out her hand and he clasps it. There's real concern in her voice when she asks, "How are you doing?"

"Good enough. Sleeping a lot. Writing."

"You look like you've gained back some weight."

"A little. Can we talk?"

"Of course. Come inside."

He follows her through the security door. On the other side is a glass-walled conference room with an oval table and upholstered chairs. No one's in it. No one else is in sight, though he can hear a male voice—he thinks it's Chris—lecturing from somewhere down a hallway that curves away to the left.

"Training session today," True says in explanation. "That's why the parking lot's full."

"You don't work directly with students?"

"Not this round. Chris has most of the staff with him, leaving me the joy of office work."

Behind them, the door closes with a heavy thud. Soft buzz and click of electronic locks: a comforting sound, a promise that the watchers are locked outside.

True gestures to the right, where the hallway ends at a second security door. "I'm going to take you into the restricted area. That's where we have our offices. Lincoln's the only one in there right now. He's on a call but he wants to see you."

"Hold on, just a minute," Miles says. He takes off his overcoat and examines it, checking the lining, the pockets, the pocket flaps.

She watches him, an eyebrow raised. "Been feeling itchy lately?" she asks.

"You know how it is." When he feels a knot of hard plastic under the collar of the overcoat, the hair on his neck stands on end. He flips the collar up, exposing a teardrop-shaped device with four tiny articulated legs hooked into the fabric. He wrests it off, drops it on the floor, flattens it under his heel, then kneels to pick up the crushed shell. He holds it up for True to see. She wrinkles her nose in distaste.

"Could be mediots, trying to scoop your story," she suggests.

"That's what I keep telling myself but it's been ten days. I should be old news."

"Right. Well, come with me. We've got a scanner set up. We'll make sure you're clean."

He's startled to discover an automated security checkpoint beyond the next door. He follows True through a body scanner, while his coat rides a belt through an X-ray machine.

"Got anything, Friday?" True asks, addressing the walls.

"No, True. You and Mr. Dushane are clean."

A wall screen shows a slowly rotating three-dimensional image of Miles's body. Highlighted details include the zipper on his pullover shirt, the rivets in his boots, and the titanium plate that held his left wrist bone together after a bad break—but no more hidden electronic devices. Some of the tension goes out of his shoulders.

"Are you okay?" True asks, a worried note in her voice.

"Post-traumatic jitters."

"You getting any help with that? Counseling?"

He shrugs. "Been busy looking into things. That's what I want to talk to you about."

"Sure. We've got a shielded conference room. Come. I'll make you some coffee."

Lincoln comes into the conference room just as the coffee finishes brewing. He's wearing a tan ReqOps polo shirt and brown slacks—the same thing he wore the night of the reception. Miles suspects he has a closet full of the same shirts and slacks, and that he wears them as a uniform. Some guys like that strategy; it saves them the mental energy of picking out clothes every day.

Miles stands up and they shake hands across the table. Coffee is poured, pleasantries exchanged, then Miles gets to the point of his visit. He says, "I'm going to guess you've been hard on the trail of Jon Helm, or Shaw Walker—whichever you want to call him."

"That'd be a fair assessment," Lincoln agrees. "And the evidence we have from multiple sources supports the identity of Shaw Walker, so that's what we're going with."

"Can I ask, have you been able to contact him?"

He watches Lincoln trade a look with True, who sits at the end of the table cradling her coffee mug in two hands. Lincoln says, "We're not in direct contact and we haven't been able to pin down his location."

"He's a ghost," True adds.

Miles nods. "I did an initial search for him. Didn't come up with anything. So I decided to focus on Burma, research the incident and reach out to my contacts. See if I could shake loose any leads."

Lincoln draws back. True puts her mug on the table with a sharp crack. Miles's heart skips with trepidation. "What?" he asks. "You know something?"

Lincoln nods at True, agreeing to some unspoken question. She says, "Friendly warning: If Chinese intelligence picks up on inquiries like that, they might not react well."

"Chinese?" Miles is incredulous. "What the hell do the Chinese have to do with Shaw Walker?"

"We've heard a theory that Chinese intelligence knew Shaw was in Nungsan, and they hit the site anyway, because they wanted to make sure there were no survivors."

"You're kidding," he says blankly.

"Nope."

"*Shit.* Maybe that explains the surveillance."

"Most of our people are under surveillance too," True says. "Whoever it is, they're not trying to keep their interest a secret."

"It's a threat," Lincoln agrees. "I think it's Variant Forces, letting us know we're mapped, that we're targets."

Miles draws a deep breath, focusing on slowing his heartbeat. "Okay, well, Variant Forces isn't going to like this next bit. A friend gave me a lead. She remembered reading a story about a missionary priest held in Burma along with an American prisoner. I finally found the piece in a restricted archive." He turns an uncertain gaze on True. "It profiles a priest who gave up his Catholic faith after witnessing what happened to Diego Delgado."

True shrugs. Not the reaction Miles expected. "It's bullshit," she says. "I've heard that kind of thing before. People claim they've talked to an eyewitness, someone who was there—it makes them feel important. But push them on it and their facts don't hold up; they can't produce the witness."

Miles understands her skepticism. Diego Delgado's horrifying death—bound and bleeding and burned on a cross of steel pipe—set the Cloud boiling with useless analyses, pointless criticisms, rebukes, mockery, and of course with posts celebrating the defeat and death of an American soldier. Millions of words spent in reaction; no value in any of it. But what he's found is different.

He says, "I know it sounds farfetched. I dropped it to the bottom of my research list because I figured it would be a fabricated propaganda piece, if I could find it all. But when I was out of other leads, I went looking—and it was an interesting read. The village isn't named—I don't think the priest ever knew the name—but the details felt right. And the description of the American soldier brought in along with Diego—it struck me as a plausible description of Shaw Walker. He can't be seen on the video. His name was never released in association with that operation, so how could anyone know about him unless they were there?

"But I wanted corroboration before I went farther. So I contacted Rick—you know, Rick Hidalgo from Ranger School. He knew Walker. I read him the description. He said it was accurate, down to the 'infidel' tattoo on his chest and the Rogue Lightning tattoo on his upper arm."

True looks shell-shocked, just like she did after he'd first pointed to Shaw Walker's picture as the face of Jon Helm. In contrast, Lincoln's expression has gone icy. "You should have called me," he growls. "Not Rick."

"I wanted to make sure I really had something before I brought it to you."

Miles eyes True, worried how all of this will affect her, but Lincoln has already moved on. "When was the article originally published?" he asks.

"Six years ago."

"Does it name Shaw?"

"No. The priest—his name is Daniel Ocampo—he just calls him 'the American.'"

"How did Ocampo escape?" True wants to know. "Or was he ransomed?"

"He says he was left in a cage in the forest. Left there to die. But the American escaped somehow, found him, freed him from the cage. Daniel called it a miracle."

True looks doubtful. "I thought you said he lost his faith."

"He's not a priest anymore. I guess it was the kind of miracle that convinces a man to change his faith."

"Have you found Ocampo?" Lincoln asks.

"I found the writer, Reynaldo—Rey—Gabriel. I talked to him. He said Ocampo is back living in the Philippines. I asked him to put me in touch. He said no, that wasn't going to happen. Ocampo was in and out of trouble with the government for a few years after he got back. He was part of a leftist party, pushing for land reform, the rights of the poor, that sort of thing. He wound up in jail. He's out now, with a wife and kid. That's made him cautious. He's still involved in politics but behind the scenes. He doesn't do interviews and he doesn't like being reminded of Burma."

"So it's a dead end," Lincoln says.

"No. Rey Gabriel talked to him, told him that I was trying to learn more about the American soldier who was there with him . . . and that I was in touch with Diego Delgado's parents and they had questions too. That tipped the balance. He's agreed to talk. Rey says he wouldn't have done this for anyone else. Even so, he'll only talk if it's face to face, and not for publication."

True turns to Lincoln. "I need to go down there."

He gives her a slow nod. "Yes. If it all checks out. I want to talk to him too. You and me. And Alex?"

"He'll want to go," True agrees. "And Miles?" She cocks an eyebrow at him. "Are you going? Even if you can't write about it?"

"Yes." He started planning the trip even before Reynaldo Gabriel interceded on his behalf. He looked at flights and drafted a schedule, knowing that if he shows up in person he has a good chance of getting even an uncooperative subject to talk—and he desperately wants to talk to Ocampo. He wants to hear what the ex-priest can tell him about the American, because Miles needs to understand how a war hero like Shaw Walker came to order the murder of innocent, inconsequential men on that day in the TEZ, when Miles knelt in the grit and said nothing.

Miles will go on this trip alone if it comes to that. Working alone is nothing new for him; most of the reporting he's done post-army was on his own. But the ordeal in the TEZ left him scarred, on edge. Scared. He prefers reliable company if he can get it—and ReqOps will have connections, and more options for security than he'll have alone.

Still, he doesn't want to deceive True or encourage false expectations. "You need to understand," he tells her. "This is just a lead. Ocampo isn't going to be able to tell you where Walker is. It says in the article that he never saw the American again."

It's Lincoln who answers. "We'll find Walker on our own. That's a matter of time. What we need from Ocampo is the backstory. He'll know details of what happened at Nungsan. If he talked to Shaw, he might have learned what happened to turn our men into targets. The more we know about what Shaw went through, the better prepared we'll be when we find him."

UNKNOWN TERRITORY

FUCK WITH ME again and the blade goes in.

Lincoln keeps these words in mind as he steps outside the secure customs area at Ninoy Aquino International Airport, with Miles, True, and Alex a couple of steps behind him. He scans the brightly lit terminal left to right; black and white in his gradient vision, blending into color. Alert but not afraid.

It's early morning in Manila and the terminal is busy. Passengers from the Seattle flight, most with phones pressed to their ears, move toward the doors, eager to escape after the sixteen-hour flight. Progress is slow. They're forced to weave through a barrier of tour guides, hotel drivers, and eager families. People begin to notice Lincoln. There are murmurs. Startled eyes fix on his scars. Frank gazes don't turn away even when he meets them. He doesn't let the attention rattle him. He stays aloof, on task, surveying the crowd for potential threats.

He'd like to be wearing a MARC visor, running apps to analyze the identity and intent of the faces around him, but the devices are unpopular and unwelcome here. So he relies on his own judgment and experience. He considers the distribution of individuals, their focus, their baggage. He looks past them to consider the traffic outside. None of it registers in his mind as a threat. All appears normal, acceptable.

So far.

"There's Rey Gabriel," Miles says.

Lincoln follows his gaze and sees a face, grown familiar during two video calls, moving toward them through the throng. "Got him."

The leftist writer has spotted them as well. He raises a hand over his head, waving in greeting and calling out, "Welcome to Manila!" in a voice so unrestrained that people turn to look for the source of commotion.

Lincoln had hoped to keep a low profile, to *not* draw attention. Wishful thinking.

True's disapproval takes the form of quiet sarcasm. "Hel-*lo*, world. Here we are."

It's been just three days since Miles proposed this trip. Even so, events haven't moved fast enough to suit True. Lincoln is all too aware she's been on edge, affected by a paranoid strain of worry that says another day, another hour, could bring on something unforeseen, and she might never get to meet Daniel Ocampo. Alex's efforts to get her to de-escalate, to relax, just irritate her. It's unbelievable to Lincoln that, after thirty-plus years of marriage, Alex still hasn't figured out when to leave her the hell alone. *Never*, he reminds himself, *travel with a married couple*.

Miles takes the lead, extending his hand to Rey, who's agreed to act as their guide and go-between with Daniel Ocampo. "Good to meet you, and thanks again for setting this up."

Rey Gabriel is a slight, wiry man, wearing a dark-red button-front shirt, worn cargo pants, and battered sandals on his feet. His complexion is dark brown and he's clean-shaven, but his thick black hair, down over his ears, could use a trim. There's a cynical edge to his smile that warns Lincoln not to underestimate him.

"I spoke to our friend yesterday," Rey assures them in excellent English delivered at enthusiastic speed. "He is expecting us but he was surprised you got here so soon. I told him it was a challenge to get everything ready in time, but of course you were eager"—he pauses to take a breath, getting dual use out of the moment by nodding at True—"this is about your son."

"He was my oldest child," True tells Rey in a soft, somber voice. "He was subjected to a horrific death and his memory was exploited for political ends all around the globe. So you will understand why it's important to us to keep this visit discreet. No attention, no publicity. No photos. That was our agreement."

Lincoln doesn't miss the implicit threat in her voice. Rey hears it too. He responds with a quick and nervous smile, but his enthusiasm still bubbles through. "Yes, True. May I call you True? It's hard for me to resist thinking of this as a story, I admit. I'm an investigative journalist down to my soul! And this—it will be like opening a letter written years ago and only now delivered." He sighs wistfully. "But I promise discretion. No worries. I will abide by our agreement."

An agreement for which Rey is being well paid.

Having made her point, True smiles, putting Rey at ease. "Thank you so much for understanding."

It's already day's end at home—*the end of yesterday*, Lincoln reminds himself. He is stiff from the long flight and still feels a lingering lethargy, but with the help of drugs and soothing white noise he was able to front-load on sleep. They all were.

The plan is to make the long drive to Daniel Ocampo's home, arriving in the afternoon, and when the interview is done, return to the city, where they'll catch a few hours of sleep at a hotel before flying home in the morning.

As they follow Rey's lead to the parking structure, Lincoln monitors their surroundings. He notes security cameras and looks for phones and for video eyewear that might be turned in their direction, but sees nothing that makes him suspicious.

The parking structure is packed with mostly new cars, reflecting a growing business class. Rey brings them to a black midsize SUV so clean and shining it looks like it just left a dealer's lot.

"I borrowed it!" he exclaims, his voice echoing faintly against the concrete. "We will trade it for another when we are partway there. You are concerned about security. So is our friend. He's worked hard on behalf of the common man, and he's suffered for it. Now he is cautious. He does not want strangers coming uninvited, asking questions. So I am making it harder to follow us." With a cynical wink, he adds, "Maybe!"

"We'd like to monitor that," True says. She gets a hemispherical camera pod from her daypack. "It's a traffic cam," she tells Rey, and as he watches wide-eyed, she secures it with a suction mount to the roof above the lift gate.

"That's going to tell if someone is following us?" he asks.

"That's what it does," Lincoln assures him. He checks his tablet, confirming a connection. "An app assesses the video feed for suspicious vehicles."

"Does it watch the sky too?"

Lincoln shrugs. "Visible light only. The camera won't be able to see through clouds and it doesn't have the resolution to pick up high-altitude UAVs, even if the sky is clear. But if there are municipal UAVs monitoring traffic, it should find them." He takes the shotgun seat, and when Rey gets in behind the wheel, he asks, "Have you noticed any extra attention since we got in touch?"

"There is always someone," Rey says with such energy that Lincoln suspects him for an adrenaline junkie. He might be disappointed if this visit *doesn't* stir unwanted attention.

From the backseat, True asks, "Did you find a printing service we can use? We'd like to finalize our preparations before heading out to see Mr. Ocampo."

"I have!" Rey assures her as they get underway. "I have reserved three hours at the printer's. Is that enough?"

"It's enough," Lincoln agrees. But adds, as he gets his first look at traffic, "If we get there in time."

The roads are packed. It's crazy. All kinds of vehicles—high-end glittering sedans, mud-splattered trucks, jeepneys, scooters, motorcycles with sidecars or trailers, bicycles—all jockeying for position, with brave or foolhardy pedestrians wading into the chaos. Horns sound constantly, near and far, varying between quick warning taps and prolonged angry blasts. Rey is an aggressive participant, accelerating, braking, avoiding collisions by a whisper as a dash cam records their progress.

At least the road monitor stays quiet.

It takes them an hour to get to the printer's but that's all right, because Rey planned for an hour—but there's a delay. Customers ahead of them are running late. The machines are still in use. They wait fifty minutes in the lobby before they're issued a key card— and their schedule is blown. "Rey," Lincoln says, "I need you to call Mr. Ocampo, let him know we're going to be late."

Rey shakes his head, rocks his palm back and forth in the air. "Mr. Ocampo is . . . *nervous*. He did not want this meeting. You change a thing, he might say no way, call it off."

"We don't need the full complement," True says softly.

Lincoln considers this. He's not happy about it, but she's right. They can make do. "Come on," he tells her. "Let's go check out the equipment. Rey, I'll be right back."

"I'll be here."

The printers are in little cubicles with opaque glass doors. True swipes the lock on their assigned room. Lincoln follows her inside. He's relieved to see that the printer is the promised Mae-muki Quick-Task 3000, with multiple stages allowing parts to be printed simultaneously. "Looks good," he says.

"So far."

The facility advertises "fast, private, personal printing." Street speak to let customers know their activities will not be closely monitored. To verify this promise, they both get out their MARC visors, using the devices to survey the room's clean white walls, its smooth ceiling.

"I don't see any cameras," True says. "You?"

"No. Not detecting microphones either. Let's do it."

Lax oversight, combined with computer-aided design, 3-D printing, and amateur engineering guilds, has fed a continuous proliferation in the type and availability of armaments. What they are about to do has no doubt been done here many times before.

The visors go back in their cases. Then True slots an instruction card, one that Tamara prepared. *This is an anarchist hack,* Tamara told them. *It overrides the printer's logging function and sets a value of zero to the list of restricted manufactures. You'll be able to print your gun parts without leaving any record of it.*

Lincoln watches over her shoulder as she runs a short series of system checks that Tamara instructed her to undertake. "Looks good," she tells him as she pulls up the project list. They intended to print four handguns. "But we've got time to print just two."

"Do it. It's just an insurance policy."

Shaw Walker might or might not know they're here, might or might not give a damn—but on this mission, Shaw is only one in a trio of potential hazards. Equally concerning is the possibility of Chinese interest, stirred up by Miles in his research on Nungsan, or being caught in the crossfire of the radical politics supported by both Rey and Daniel. No way to know where any of it could lead.

True initiates the print run. The process is hidden behind shields as lasers melt and fuse metal alloy powders to slowly form the necessary parts.

"How do you feel about Rey?" she asks Lincoln.

"He's cocky. Confident. Not a bad thing."

"This is a game for him."

"I think that's his personality. We hired him to keep a secret and he likes being on the inside. Don't worry. We're going to pull this off."

"Sooner or later he's going to ask what we're printing."

"I'm sure he *knows* what we're printing. But it's best for him if we don't confirm or deny."

She nods. "You better go get the ammunition."

He sends Alex and Miles to keep her company while he goes with Rey to a courier's office to claim the package of ammunition he sent in-country. He goes in alone, wanting to limit their exposure on the slim chance that some law enforcement agency has flagged the shipment—but he takes delivery with no questions asked, and an hour later, he's back at the printer's.

He tells the others, "Take Rey and get something to eat."

True returns just as he finishes assembling the newly printed parts into two snub-nosed all-metal handguns. He gives her one. She checks the load, slips it into the deep pocket of a hip-length beige utility vest.

"Did you pull the card?" she asks.

Lincoln hands her the anarchist's hack. "Let's go."

True sits in the SUV's backseat. She's behind Lincoln, with Alex beside her and Miles next to him. Rey has decided he is their tour guide. She obediently turns to look whenever he points out sights or names the districts and neighborhoods through which they're passing. She pretends to be interested, pretends that she's calm. So much of her emotional life is pretending. Putting on a face, playing a role, because the personal cannot be allowed to interfere with the professional.

She long ago learned to live by the mantra of military life: *Focus on what needs to be done, and do it.*

Right now she needs to play along, but the truth is that nothing Rey says makes any difference to her. They are less than two hours away from meeting Daniel Ocampo. *That* is all that matters.

After it was decided that they'd go to the Philippines, she called Alex to share what they'd learned of Daniel.

Alex was skeptical. "An ex-priest? You think this is real?"

"I do. But he won't do a remote interview. We have to go down there and talk to him."

Alex was incredulous. "Come on. This has got to be a setup."

"No. I don't think so. The journalist checks out. He's credentialed. Alex, I told Lincoln you would want to go."

"Yeah. Of course. If you think this is real."

People at work owed him favors, so he was able to adjust his schedule, trading shifts to get the time off.

That night as they lay together in the dark, he asked her, "What are you hoping for?"

"Not a lot," she answered. "I just . . . I want to know how it was for Diego in those last hours. I want to know if Shaw was with him, if he took care of him. And how did Shaw get away? I want to know that too." She sighed at her own neediness. "*Fuck.* I want to know everything about that mission. I want to know what went wrong, and I want to know who's responsible."

They waited until they were at SeaTac to call the kids, letting them know they'd be out of the country for a few days.

"Another mission already?" Connor asked in the stern, disapproving tone only a twenty-one-year-old can muster.

"It's not a mission," True told him. "Dad doesn't go on missions. This is a fact-finding tour. No bad guys." *We hope*, she added silently. Aloud, she said, "Don't tell anyone, okay?"

"You mean don't tell Grandpa?" Connor asked.

"Smart kid."

They will be in the Philippines just overnight—twenty-eight hours between arrival and departure. So she brought only what would fit in her daypack: a change of clothes, a jacket for the plane, a utility vest for her gear, a few toiletries, a small first-aid kit, her MARC visor, and an assortment of small robotics from the origami army—to the amusement of the Filipino customs officer who inspected her bag. "Cool stuff! You sure this is not a boy's backpack?"

She put on a teasing smile as she explained to him, "Other women pack clothes. I pack toys."

All harmless of course, surveillance only. The customs officer admitted her to the country with a grin and no further questions.

They've been forty minutes on the road, crawling through traffic, when Rey startles her with an enthusiastic announcement. "Okay, this is it! Stage two. We trade cars in case someone is following us."

He turns off into a large gated parking lot roofed with banks of photovoltaic panels, parking the black SUV in an empty stall. They transfer their gear and the traffic cam, then drive off in another SUV—a much older, tan-colored model. It's less comfortable, less impressive, and far more practical, with a high clearance and an everyday look that won't draw unwanted attention.

They leave the city behind, and the chaotic traffic with it. So far as the camera can tell, no one is following as Rey drives on a neat concrete road, past small towns and rice fields, with mountains visible in the distance beyond drifting curtains of light rain.

As they put more kilometers behind them, Rey's tour-guide narrative gives out. He tries to engage Lincoln in a discussion of the business structure and ethics of private military companies, but he doesn't get far. Miles talks to him for a while about the travails of independent journalism. Eventually, though, silence takes over. True is grateful for it.

An hour slides past. They leave the highway to follow a narrow road flanked by towering tropical growth, little homes half-hidden in the vegetation.

She watches their progress, charted on a map displayed on her tablet. They are entering unknown territory. If this was a mission, she would have requisitioned a UAV to do advance surveillance. She would have real-time coverage of the route and the destination. She would have deployed beetle and mosquito drones to do reconnaissance: mapping potential hazards and identifying the people who live there.

But it's not a mission. It's just an interview.

Still, they will not be going in blind.

Right on schedule—a planned two kilometers from their destination—Lincoln speaks. "Let's stop for a few minutes," he tells Rey.

It's the first anyone has spoken in some time. Rey is startled. "Stop? But we're almost there."

"Just for a few minutes," Lincoln says reassuringly. "And stay away from any houses."

Rey pulls off the road alongside towering bushes—an unfamiliar species that True can't identify. A misty rain is falling, but she's not too worried about it. The clouds are breaking up, and she expects a return of blazing sunshine in another minute or two. In the meantime, she retrieves a small biomimetic bird from her daypack and unfolds its long, narrow wings.

Tamara calls the device a blue gull. Its dorsal surface is dark with a photovoltaic skin, but its belly is coated with a light-blue paint containing tiny reflective chips that simulate the complex range of subtle colors in a living bird. The wings are long, thin, and adjustable, but it doesn't fly by flapping. It uses quiet electric engines to drive tilt rotors. Blue gulls are an old design, not very agile, and only vaguely birdlike. But on a calm day like today, with sunshine to supplement its batteries, the device should be able to soar for up to two hours.

Without a word, she wades out into the searing humidity and launches the blue gull, sending it ahead through the steaming air to reconnoiter.

When she returns to the air-conditioned comfort of the SUV's cabin, Rey has turned around. He's watching her, looking confused and very curious—but she offers no explanation. They are minutes away from meeting Daniel and she is too tense to speak. So she just smiles an apologetic smile, slides on her reading glasses, and calls up the gull's video feed on her tablet.

Alex leans over to look, telling Rey, "It's just reconnaissance." When she makes no comment, he prods her: "Right, True?"

"Yes."

Hearing her voice, even a word, reassures him. Alex does not like it when she goes silent. It's been a point of conflict between them. "When you get too quiet," he's told her, "there's a reason for it—usually not a good one."

He's probably right.

Silence gripped her hard in the early days after Diego's death, when all words sounded trite and pointless. Alex didn't understand that. He interpreted her silence as guilt. "You can't blame yourself for what happened," he eventually lectured her. "You didn't make him go army. You didn't even encourage him to do it."

That was the day she realized how frightened he was—*for her*. He had no way of knowing what thoughts roiled behind the cold walls of her inward-facing grief. So she kissed him in gentle apology and gave the counterargument: "I didn't need to encourage him. I let my old man do it."

A harsh joke, but it won a snort of bitter laughter.

"I don't feel guilty, love," she promised him. "Brokenhearted, that's all."

Slowly, slowly, the pain faded. And still, eight years on, she sometimes awakens at three AM, her heart catching in panic, desperate to run to Diego, knowing he needs her but not knowing where he is or how to reach him. When that happens, she pulls on a shirt and wanders the house until the feeling subsides. If Alex wakes up, comes looking for her, she tells him it's just insomnia, never letting him know what's going on in her head.

It isn't guilt she carries from one day to the next. It's the frustrated, horrifying sense of knowing she can never comfort Diego, never reach him, never undo what was done.

And the bitter knowledge that she will feel this way for the rest of her life.

The blue gull soars sedately past houses and small farms, rain wet and glittering in the sun. True waits until Daniel Ocampo's little estate comes into sight, then slides her finger around the screen, cueing the gull to circle.

She half-expects to see camouflaged guerillas in the woods, or maybe uniformed police officers. But there is only the neat pink house, a gravel driveway, a covered parking area with a small sedan, and white goats in a fenced pasture out back.

Lincoln watches the feed on his own tablet. "We're good," he says after a couple of minutes. "He's got no one here. I don't think he knows we're here."

Rey looks at all of them with narrowed eyes. "It's not Mr. Ocampo you're worried about . . . is it?"

"Let's go," Lincoln says. "We don't want to be late."

DANIEL

REY PARKS JUST off the gravel driveway beneath the shade of a massive mango tree. As True gets out, black hens and two colorful roosters nervously retreat into the surrounding bushes.

The house is a modest wooden one-story, pastel pink with white trim and a gray corrugated roof with mounted photovoltaic panels. Red hibiscus bushes flank three wide steps leading up to a screened porch.

True is aware of the blue gull circling above them, but she doesn't look at it, not wanting to draw attention to its existence. Rey is not so reserved. He pulls his phone out and takes pictures of it—though he doesn't take pictures of them since that would be a violation of their agreement. True doesn't like it, but there's not much she can say without getting into an argument.

They gather in a loose group to walk toward the house, except for Rey, who stays behind. Miles turns back, asks curiously, "Aren't you coming?"

Rey flashes a grin. "Didn't I mention it? Mr. Ocampo has asked me not to attend. He doesn't trust me to *not* publish this interview."

True is sympathetic to Mr. Ocampo's caution. She too does not entirely trust Rey to keep quiet.

Alex takes her hand. "You okay?"

"I'm good."

Nervous as hell, but good.

They walk together through the oppressive afternoon heat, Lincoln and Miles following. They climb the steps to the screened porch, pull open the door. The porch is spotlessly clean, gleaming with fresh paint. A petite woman in a blue dress waits for them, her smile friendly as she holds open a screen door into the house. Neat black hair frames her smooth face.

"Please," she says in heavily accented English. "Come inside."

The floor is linoleum, the furniture wicker. Fans blow hot air around. Sheer white curtains sway in the breezes. Framed photographs are on the walls and an acrylic pitcher of juice garnished with citrus slices sits on a low coffee table, wearing a thin skin of condensation. Everything in the room is neat and clean—including the man seated on the wicker sofa.

He uses a cane to stand up from the faded green cushions. He's short and slight, dark-skinned, with a broad nose and a face pitted by acne. No gray yet in his black hair, which he wears parted on the side and neatly combed. He's dressed in brown slacks and a white shirt embroidered on the sleeves and around the neck with floral patterns. True is startled to notice that both his feet have been replaced with prosthetics, dark brown in color and designed to look like natural feet, but too perfect and too motionless to pull off the deception.

She forces her gaze back to his face as he looks them over, caution in his eyes.

"Welcome," he concludes after several seconds, leaving True with the impression that until this moment he had not quite decided if he would welcome them at all. "I am Daniel Ocampo." The woman in the blue dress moves to his side. Her smile is warm, but her eyes are wary. He says, "This is my wife, Carina." Daniel's voice is soft and a little hoarse. His words are pronounced with an accent that True finds challenging to understand. He acknowledges this, saying, "My English is not so good."

"No, it's fine," they all say. Apologies are made, because while between them they speak Arabic, Farsi, Spanish, and some Russian, English is the only language they have in common with Daniel.

Lincoln introduces everyone. Carina urges them to sit. True hesitates, her attention drawn by movement beyond one of the windows, but it's just Rey, wandering toward the goat pasture in back.

Miles and Lincoln sit in padded chairs. True sits on a small sofa alongside Alex, her pack at her feet and tablet in her lap. The tablet's screen is blank, but at a touch it will display the feed from the circling gull. Carina serves everyone a glass of juice, explaining that it is calamansi juice, a Filipino version of lemonade. She joins her husband on the larger sofa, their shoulders touching.

"Delgado and . . . Brighton?" Daniel asks, looking thoughtfully at Alex and True. "You are not married?"

Carina pats his hand, clearly embarrassed, while Alex answers. "We're married. True kept her own name."

"Is it all right if I record this conversation?" True asks. "It's just for myself, to keep the details clear."

Daniel inclines his head in reluctant approval, perhaps guessing that she is already recording. He looks somber as he says, "It's been many years since that terrible time but I offer my condolences. What was done to your son . . . it is beyond the understanding of good men."

True says, "We would like to learn more about your time there. Of course we've read Reynaldo Gabriel's interview—"

Daniel waves his hand dismissively. "Mr. Gabriel made me seem like a brave man in the story he wrote, like a hero. It isn't true."

True glances at the window. Rey is no longer in sight. She wakes the tablet to check the blue gull's video feed. She is able to see it well enough without her glasses, and quickly locates him out back, leaning on a fence post, watching the goats.

"He admires you," Miles says.

Daniel shrugs this off. "We both want to see reform."

True is determined not to let the conversation drift. "Anything you can tell us," she says, "about what you saw, or heard, or were told while you were being held at Nungsan—we want to hear it."

He resists this idea with a slow shake of his head. "I cannot speak of what was done to your son. It is beyond words."

"You don't need to speak of that," Alex says quickly.

Daniel regards him for many seconds. "You're thinking of that video," he decides. "So you know that part of the story. I never watched it. I pray I will never witness a thing like that again." He sips his juice, puts his glass on the table, takes Carina's hand. He says, "I don't like to talk about my time in that place. It's not a thing I want to remember, or be remembered for. I agreed to speak to you now only because your son was there—but I don't think what I have to say will bring you comfort."

Echoing Daniel's gesture, Alex reaches for True's hand. He squeezes it, letting her know he's aware of what she's thinking: *I am not here for comfort.*

If Daniel *could* offer her comfort, if there was something he could say that would ease the horror of what was done and smooth the scars that mark her life, True would refuse to hear it. For eight years she's rejected all such words. She does not need comfort. She needs her scars. But she keeps these thoughts to herself.

She says, "We know what they did to Diego. We want to know the rest."

Daniel looks deeply unhappy, but he says, "I will tell you what I can."

He speaks slowly at first, groping for words: "The Saomong prison . . . it was under the ground. Part of a concrete bunker. Filthy and wet. Black mold on the walls. It would flood. The floor was plastic shipping pallets sinking in mud. At first I was alone, and I was sick. I could not hold anything inside me. My bowels ran. I vomited. So of course it stank. It was hot. So hot. Just the memory makes me feel sick again."

Sweat has appeared on his forehead. He reaches for his glass. True watches his hand and notes a tremble that she's sure wasn't there before. He takes two long swallows of the calamansi juice, then continues, speaking faster now. "I think they tried to ransom me, but there was no money, and this made them angry. They began to beat me. Every day they order me outside and I am whipped or beaten with sticks. One day I refuse to leave my prison. They come down the stairs and drag me out and it is worse. They told me I must renounce God, but I refuse. I tell myself I am ready to die. I thought it was true.

"Eight or nine days like that. It does not sound like a long time, does it?" His face squeezes as if he's perplexed, struggling to make sense of the nonsensical. "I prayed for strength, for forgiveness, for pity. I was granted none of those things. Then they brought the two American soldiers in.

"The one was wounded. Shot three times." Daniel points to his own body as he says, "His side, his leg, his shoulder."

Alex's fingers tighten around True's hand. Their gazes meet in shared affirmation. Those were the wounds they saw on the video. It's what the autopsy reported.

Daniel continues, saying, "Later I learned his name was Diego, but his friend never called him that. He called him 'D,' just the letter.

"D was feverish and very weak. The other soldier tried to comfort him. 'D, D,' he whispered. 'I promise you, they know where we are and they are coming for us. You have to hold on, D. They will come.'

"Both of these soldiers, they wore only trousers. Their boots and their shirts had been taken away. Their wrists were tied. I could see all this because light came in through a steel grate that was like a trapdoor at the top of the stairs. I thought that D would die that night. I wanted to give him last rites, but the other American, he told me to fuck off. He told D, 'You are not going to die. They'll come tonight. You'll be okay.'

"That night after the lantern was put out, it was very dark, and after a time, very quiet. No rescue came. I thought D had passed, but that was wrong. He was still alive in the morning. He looked a little stronger. I thought maybe he will live after all."

True's thoughts flutter past half-noticed things: the restless motion of the white curtains, the slick film of sweat between Alex's hand and hers, the terrible pressure behind her eyes.

He might have lived. Even then, even that last morning, it was not too late.

"D was a strong man," Daniel says, his gaze fixed on the runnels of condensation drawing slow lines on the pitcher of juice. "That was his curse. Better for him if he had died that night with his friend at his side.

"The Saomong, they argued in the room above us. I could not understand what they said. But at noon, they came for him. The American tried to get in their way, to fight them, but they had a Taser. One of them brought a syringe. He gave D a shot. I don't know what it was, but it made him awake. Alert. It made him seem stronger than he was."

Daniel goes silent, brows shifting, gaze unfocused as if enduring some internal battle. After several seconds, a coarse sigh. He says, "They made us watch. After . . . after it was over the American was amok. I thought he might kill me. He needed to kill someone. I stayed in a corner. Finally the guerillas came in and beat him unconscious.

"I do not understand such evil as we were made to witness. I will not pretend to understand it."

Daniel falls silent. There is the sound of the fans, the tap of the blowing curtains. One of the men, Lincoln maybe, softly clears his throat. True feels adrift, only marginally present as she watches Carina stroke Daniel's hand. All wait. When Daniel speaks again, it's in a different voice, more detached, as if he's achieved a needed distance from the past.

"They did not feed us after that," he says. "For two days the only water we had was what dripped from the walls. When they finally lifted the grate again, they called to me to come out. I thought they would kill me the same way . . . But no. It was just a beating.

"When they returned me to the prison the American spoke to me for the first time since he'd told me to fuck off. He asked, 'What do they want from you?'

"I told him they wanted me to renounce God.

"He said I should do it. He said renouncing God is easy. We talked more about it. I never knew his name. He said we had no need of names. I came to trust him though. There was no one else.

"And finally I did it. I did what he said. I renounced God in front of their video camera. And they laughed at me. They told me, 'Good job. You are a smart man.' They took me out of the village, along a path in the forest. Not far. I thought they meant to shoot me, but even that was more mercy than they would give. Along the path was a bamboo cage, half-sunk in the mud. They forced me into it and left. I never saw them again after that.

"I was feverish. I don't know how long I was there. More than a day. I remember hearing them away in the village, practicing their soldier skills, but mostly it was quiet. Just the sounds of the forest, the birds, the rain.

"It was raining hard when the American came, but not hard enough yet to wash away all the blood splashed on his face, caught in his beard, running in streams on his chest.

"I think he was surprised to find me there because when he saw me, he stopped on the trail. We looked at each other, both of us dazed. Me from my fever. Him . . ." Daniel shakes his head. "I said nothing. I thought it must be a dream of mine that he was there. I was resigned to my death, wishing for it. So I did not ask him to help me. But he helped anyway. He did not have a gun, but he carried a hammer that he used to break the cage open.

"Then he left.

"I crawled away. I don't know where I went. I remember terrible dreams. I thought I was in hell, but I was just very sick. When I finally woke, I found I was in the care of Good Samaritans. They found me and took me in." He gestures at his prosthetics. "I lost my feet from gangrene. But by the grace of God, I made it home. I gave up the priesthood. That calling was over for me. But because the American stopped for me, I lived. And now I have Carina, and we have a daughter."

The room's heat has gotten inside True. Soothing, distancing. Her thoughts run like hot oil as she takes in every word, every tic in Daniel's expression. "Did he speak to you of other things than God?" she asks him in a husky voice.

"We spoke," Daniel concedes. "But not about D."

She sips cold calamansi juice to ease a throat swollen with emotion, then asks, "Did he talk about the mission? About what he'd been doing before he was captured?"

"He said some things," Daniel acknowledges. "But I was feverish. Maybe I don't remember it all. Or maybe I don't remember it right."

"Tell us what you remember," Lincoln urges.

Daniel looks . . . he looks *embarrassed*, True decides. She holds her breath, waiting to find out why.

"The American hated the guerillas," Daniel tells them. "He called them cowards. He said, 'We were beat, but not by them.'"

Lincoln is getting impatient. "By who, then?" he presses.

Daniel's cheeks puff out as he expels a breath. "By killer robots." His eyebrows knit as if reconsidering his choice of words. He looks like a man struggling to remember what was really said, what really happened eight years ago when he was feverish, dying . . . but he shrugs. This is the best he can come up with. "Killer robots," he says again. His body rocks with a contagious uneasiness that leaps to True. "The American said two of his men died within seconds of the robots' attack. They fought the attack, but the guerillas heard the gunfire. They came hunting him and his men. Sixty, hunting the four who still lived."

True allows herself to consider only this surface description, to think only about the tactics, to look on the scenario Daniel has described as if it were a chess game and not the fucked-up travesty that killed her son. She turns to Lincoln. Her voice is still husky when she says: "Did they have a combat robot on that mission?"

"Not eight years ago," he tells her. "They might have had surveillance, even an armed UAV. If so, it would have been called a UAV, not a killer robot. That tells me it was something he had never seen before."

Lincoln means "something Shaw had never seen before." But he doesn't say Shaw's name aloud. Daniel does not know who the American was. When this visit was planned, it was agreed no one would tell him. Shaw's identity is dangerous knowledge. No reason to burden Daniel with it.

Miles says, "The Saomong could have been running North Korean hardware. Something new. Unknown at the time."

Lincoln shakes his head. "I've seen a hundred intelligence reports from conflicts involving Saomong. None mentioned a robotic fighting system."

True thinks about the Chinese and the speculation that they interfered in the recovery of the prisoners because they wanted no witnesses . . . but no witnesses to what? Could the Chinese have been running an experimental combat system in the forest around Nungsan? A robotic system that went disastrously wrong—and wound up targeting allied troops?

Her heart hammers, flushing out the lethargy of her grief, allowing outrage to blossom. Was Rogue Lightning sacrificed to keep an embarrassing failure secret? Had someone, somewhere, made that decision?

Comfort, True decides, can have many definitions. Over the years she has taken some comfort in the simple fact that all those involved in Diego's death are themselves now dead and gone. But the existence of a killer robot means she's been wrong about that.

It's not something she can discuss here, now, in front of the Ocampos, but that's all right. She has only one more question. She leans in, gaze locked on Daniel. "Have you ever heard from the American, or heard of him, since that day he broke open the cage?"

"No. Never. I have never heard from him, never heard of him, never seen him again."

True stands up. She is ready to go. She *needs* to go before her anger becomes visible. "I want to thank you, Mr. Ocampo—"

"Just one more thing," Alex interjects. "Mr. Ocampo, do you remember what kind of a hammer the American was using when he broke the cage?"

Despite the heat, True shivers. She looks to Daniel to find his head cocked, expression puzzled. "Is it important?" he asks.

Alex says, "Maybe."

Daniel looks like he wants to ask why, but he doesn't. "I remember it clearly," he tells Alex. "Because I saw it before. It was the kind of hammer with a large, heavy head, like this." He touches the tips of his fingers together, enclosing a space with his hands. "The kind of hammer used to drive stakes into the ground. Or into a man."

True refuses to even consider that image. Instead she recalls Lincoln's description of the two bodies the forensics team found in the village, close to the pyre, both with crushing skull injuries. And she remembers Hussam's story of Jon Helm killing the men who tried to crucify him. She does not doubt the truth of it anymore.

Lincoln asks, "Where were you when the village was destroyed?"

Daniel shakes his head. "Those who cared for me told me that place was blown up. I don't remember it. It must have been after I crawled away from the cage. But I don't remember."

"Thank you, sir," Lincoln says. He leans forward in his chair, extending his hand across the low table. "We appreciate your willingness to discuss—"

From outside, there's a sound like glass breaking, followed by a startled cry from Rey, "*Ai!*"

Lagging by half a second, the sharp crack of a gunshot.

BIOMIMETICS

LINCOLN SWIVELS OUT of his chair. Keeping low, he scuttles to the window. True shoves her tablet into her pack, swapping it for her MARC visor as she moves to the door. She slips the visor on. It boots, syncing with the earpiece. She shrugs on her pack. Her hand slides into the front pocket of her utility vest where she's got her pistol, but she doesn't pull it out yet.

As she reaches the screened porch, Rey appears from around the corner of the house. He's in a panic. "Someone shot your drone," he blurts as he bounds up the porch steps. "It came down in pieces over the goat pen."

She scans the yard and the bushes around it, but sees no one. The MARC's threat assessment function doesn't highlight anything.

Lincoln comes out of the house. He passes her, passes Rey, strides down the steps. That's when a kid comes into sight from the direction of the driveway—a petite teenage girl dressed in jeans and a body-hugging green-camo T-shirt, a .22 rifle carried comfortably in her hands. The MARC scans her face, tags her as unknown. Tags the make and model of her weapon.

She backpedals when she sees Lincoln, looking like she's about to turn and run. But Daniel has come out to the porch too. He sees the girl and shouts to her. "Divina! What did you see? Has someone come?"

His presence emboldens her. Holding the weapon with the muzzle toward the ground, she approaches, pausing to stare wide-eyed at Lincoln's scarred face and artificial eye.

"You shot down our bird," Lincoln concludes in a tone half-annoyed, half-amused.

"Your bird?" Daniel asks. He is not at all amused.

"A surveillance drone," Lincoln says. He looks at True. "Take Rey. Have him show you where the pieces came down."

She moves down the steps, gesturing at Rey to follow, while Daniel speaks in an angry voice, "You had me under surveillance? For how long?"

True does not stay to hear Lincoln's answer. But as Rey follows her, he murmurs, "I didn't think of it to warn you, but he is angry because he's been harassed by political enemies, spied on, his home vandalized."

True is angry herself, emotionally worn, her mood brittle. "No one's been hurt," she snaps, seizing on cold practicality. "I'm sorry he's upset, but it was a matter of security."

She studies the bushes, and the trees beyond, allowing the MARC to survey for hazards, but detects none.

They reach the side of the house. Out of habit she scans the wall, the windows, the eaves. This time the MARC finds something to highlight. It's at the top of the white window frame. The object looks like a dark-gray leaf that's gotten hung up in a spider's web, but it's not a leaf. It's a mech designed to mimic one.

She averts her gaze, keeping the leaf mech in sight but not looking directly at it, not wanting to warn its operator—or its algorithms—that it's been noticed. Still moving slowly, breath gone shallow, body tense, she considers her strategy. There is a waist-high hibiscus hedge alongside the house. She will not be able to get past that before the leaf mech alerts—and she's certain it's capable of flight. She will have to intercept it in the air.

Despite the example of the teenage Divina, True rejects the idea of shooting down the little mech as too dangerous, and too likely to result in a miss. What she needs is a net, but she doesn't have one so she's going to have to improvise.

Quickly—still without looking directly at the mech—she unbuttons her utility vest and drops it on the grass. "Don't touch that," she warns Rey, not wanting him to pick it up and wonder at the pistol's weight.

Rey is behind her. He sounds confused when he says, "Your broken drone is in the goat pasture."

"I know where it is."

She peels off her shirt. Why not? It's the closest thing she has to a net and there's nothing shocking underneath. Just a beige bra precisely engineered to secure her small breasts while making her look good. She calculates her best line of attack. Then she bounds toward the window, shirt clutched in one hand, ready to swing.

She's almost at the hedge when the leaf mech reacts. It emits a sharp *pop!* True ducks at the noise—she can't help herself. "*Fuck!*" she swears, already guessing the sound is harmless, an effect meant to startle, like the furious burst of a pheasant's wings when it springs from dense grass. Works damn well.

Her momentary hesitation allows the leaf mech time to deploy a buzzing propeller that lofts it from the window frame. True leaps after it, swinging her shirt to try to bring it down, but it's already out of reach, streaking away toward the goat pasture. Her MARC tracks it, highlighting its shifting position.

She takes off after it. A device that small and fast won't have the battery life to fly far. If she can track its flight path, she'll have a real chance of catching up with it. She stoops to scoop up her vest, shrugs it back on while she runs, and stuffs her shirt into one of its large pockets.

The fence that surrounds the goat pasture is coming up. It's made of wooden posts with four-foot-high field wire strung between them. She gets one hand on a post, climbs the wire in two steps, and drops on the other side—just as a blue-gray biomimetic hawk shoots across the pasture propelled by silent bird wings.

The hawk is on a path aimed to intercept the tiny surveillance device. The two mechs collide—they seem to collide—then the hawk wheels and streaks off toward distant trees while the leaf mech is simply gone.

"*Shit*," True whispers, staring after the hawk. "What the *fuck*? That was fucking amazing."

The interaction was too fast for her to follow. She'll be able to analyze the video later, but she is sure the hawk collected the leaf mech out of the air and carried it away, extending its range, possibly by miles—which means the operator could be anywhere . . . even on the other side of the world?

No.

She rejects this thought as soon as it comes. She does not want to believe Shaw is behind the hawk or that his network is so sophisticated and widespread that he was able to detect their destination and deploy surveillance ahead of their arrival.

Rey has caught up with her. He is leaning over the fence, eyes wide as he searches the trees like he's hoping the hawk will reappear. "What *was* that?" he asks.

She arches an eyebrow. "Not yours, huh?"

"Are you *kidding?*" He turns to look at her, and even though her eyes are hard to see past her MARC's tinted half-visor, he can read her expression well enough that he looks chagrined. "Yeah, you are kidding," he concludes. "But hey, I didn't know bots could do that. That thing moved like a real bird."

True nods agreement, except she *has* seen similar raptors before—videos of them, anyway. Both Lincoln and Miles recorded biomimetic hawks turning in gyres outside their apartments—but those videos did not show the model's full capabilities. The quality of its engineering calls to mind the deer mimetic.

Rey says, "You can see why Mr. Ocampo is touchy. Always someone trying to know his business."

True would like to believe Rey is right, that the leaf mech was here as part of a regular surveillance operation targeting Daniel Ocampo—but she doesn't believe it.

She looks out across the pasture. She still needs to recover whatever is left of the blue gull. So she gets her shirt back on and with Rey helping, she starts to look—though she feels vulnerable out in the open among the white goats. The MARC detects no threats but she can't see far and she feels like a target. The animals are friendly and curious, nibbling at her clothes, but beyond the trees is an unknown enemy.

Brooke's words come back to her: *The Chinese wanted that village erased along with everyone in it.*

Why? Just because they wanted to keep the secret of a killer robot?

True can't believe it. Even given a desire to save face, it doesn't make sense. Friendly fire incidents happen. They're an unfortunate fact of war. An inquiry might have led to punishment for those individuals held responsible, but no one would have considered such an incident a breach of the alliance or an act of war. The reaction—providing misinformation on the location of the surviving soldiers, allowing Diego's death, and ultimately destroying Nungsan—it's all out of proportion to what happened . . . at least as Daniel recounted it.

There is more going on.

The presence of the biomimetic hawk suggests that someone besides herself is still very concerned about the incident at Nungsan. As she wanders the pasture, True feels the intensity of that concern like crosshairs on the back of her neck.

Rey startles her with a shout from the pasture's back corner. "Here it is! Some of the wrecked parts anyway. I think maybe the goats have taken the rest."

True goes to see what he has found.

RAMPING UP

QUICKLY, QUIETLY, IN a huddle beside the black SUV, Lincoln and Miles listen as True describes what she saw. "I don't think it's Shaw who fielded that hawk," she concludes as she packs her MARC away. "It's like we were told. The Chinese have a concern."

Her face is flushed, there's a sheen of sweat on her cheeks, and her eyes are bright—almost fever bright. Lincoln watches that intense gaze shift to Miles. "Some branch of their intelligence network is probably monitoring chatter on Nungsan."

Miles leans in, speaks sharp words at low volume. "I drew their attention. I get that. But I can't do my work anonymously—"

"It's not the time to debate it," Lincoln interrupts, eyeing the porch where Rey and Alex still talk quietly with Daniel.

Their host's burst of temper over the blue gull was mostly soothed when Lincoln explained his concern about outsiders following them here and eavesdropping. Daniel's answer was bitter: "You've heard of my troubles, then. The government is always watching me. They won't leave me alone."

It wasn't the government watching today. Lincoln is sure of that.

He crooks a mechanical finger at Alex. Now that True has reported on what she saw, it's time to go.

Alex acknowledges the signal with a nod. A few more words,

handshakes exchanged on the porch, and then Alex and Rey cross the lawn.

Lincoln murmurs, "No mention of a Chinese connection in front of Rey, understood?"

Miles nods. True whispers, "You got it." She adds, "I can't wait to get out of here."

Lincoln is in full agreement. "We need to move," he tells Rey, speaking louder now. "It's late. I want to get to the hotel so we can eat and get some sleep before tomorrow's flight."

It's late afternoon. The sun has broken out past rainclouds to shine on the towering, glistening green vegetation hemming in the narrow road. Occasionally visible beyond that living barricade are rice fields and coconut plantations. Miles stares out the window, watching the countryside roll past—but his thoughts are turned inward.

He is uneasy, uncertain, and unhappy. Coming here, he decides, was a mistake. They intruded on the peace and privacy of a man who has already suffered too much in life, and for what? They knew already that Shaw Walker is alive. All they've really learned is that Rogue Lightning may have fallen to "killer robots" and for that fragment of knowledge, they may have exposed Daniel Ocampo to an uncompromising enemy.

True put it delicately: *The Chinese have a concern.*

That scares the fuck out of Miles. The village of Nungsan was incinerated to eliminate witnesses and, eight years on, someone is still on guard, monitoring interest in the Nungsan incident.

Miles woke up a monster when he went digging for long-buried rumors—and he's deeply worried there could be blowback against Daniel, even though the man knows nothing dangerous, nothing that could compromise anyone. All he really remembers is a fever-hazed image of Shaw Walker, and maybe Walker never really said those words, *killer robots.* Daniel might have misheard or misremembered or dreamed it as he lay dying in the mud.

Daniel is no threat to anyone.

For fuck's sake, Miles prays, *let the enemy understand that.*

A new idea occurs to him. Maybe it's not Daniel they've endangered by coming here. Maybe what they've done is to shine a light on Shaw Walker. If so? If this enemy decides to finish what should have been finished eight years ago?

Fuck it. That bastard deserves whatever he gets.

Lincoln sits in the front seat, swaying as the SUV rolls past the bumps and swales of the rough country road. He thinks about True's report—the leaf mech perched on the window frame, the biomimetic hawk that intercepted it—and assumes that everything Daniel related to them is known.

But known by who? True's answer is a Chinese faction. A logical deduction, given the information relayed to them by Brooke. The question Lincoln faces now is whether the activity will be limited to surveillance, or if it will escalate to active interference. They encountered no trouble on the way out. They detected no vehicle following them, but a ground vehicle wouldn't be necessary to an enemy with sophisticated aerial surveillance.

He studies the narrow road ahead, uneasy. Traffic is light, but he can't see far. No way to know what's around the next bend, or a few more kilometers down the road. He asks himself, *What can be gained by attacking us?*

Nothing.

An assault would lead to an investigation, and eventually the reason they came here would be made public. No one involved in this tangled operation, whether known or unknown, wants that. And still his anxiety is ramping up. He's got a feeling trouble is coming—and that's a feeling he's learned to trust.

The SUV rocks as it plows through a rain-filled pothole. Lincoln is abruptly conscious of the pistol's weight in his pocket. They printed the guns as an insurance policy in case Shaw had a presence on the ground. But the situation is changed and Lincoln senses the weapons are now a liability.

He glances at Rey behind the wheel. The journalist, focused on driving, doesn't notice the attention.

Lincoln returns his gaze to the road. He slides his right hand, his organic hand, into his pocket. His fingers close on the pistol. He pulls it out and surreptitiously passes it back to True, who's sitting behind him. He feels her take the weapon.

Next, he pulls out his tablet, taps out a text, and sends it to her: **Break it down. We're done with them.**

He glances back to see her eyeing her tablet, an anxious flush heating her cheeks. She looks up, nods.

He consults his tablet again, reviewing a satellite map of the road ahead. Then he turns to Rey. "Let's stop."

Rey looks around in surprise. So does Miles. Rey says, "Sure, we can stop. There's a store just—"

Lincoln interrupts him. "The map shows a bridge five hundred meters ahead. I remember crossing it. Let's stop there. I need to conference with True."

He's barely gotten the words out when it starts to rain again, a heavier shower than before. "Crap," True says from the backseat.

Lincoln laughs at the sincerity in her comment. "Pass me my jacket," he tells her.

She takes off her seat belt and turns around. Their packs are in the back. She rummages among them. Alex turns to help out. Miles is alert, looking around, looking for danger.

They're almost at the bridge when True hands a raincoat to Lincoln. "I'm ready," she says.

The bridge is modern, wider than the road, low concrete sides topped with steel railings. Rey drives across it, then eases the SUV into a muddy pullout. Lincoln and True get out. She pulls up the hood of her rain jacket. Their boots stick in a fine, sucking mud as they walk back to the bridge. A sweet scent of flowers and spice defies the rain. For now, there is no other traffic.

Lincoln gestures her to go ahead. She pulls her hood off again. "Can't hear anything with that up," she mutters. The rain beads on her hair as they stand at the railing. Lincoln has positioned himself to hide her from Rey's sight if he's looking in the rearview mirror.

The stream below is running fast from the intermittent rain, water brown with suspended silt. True has disassembled both pistols, removing the magazines and separating the slides from the lower receivers. She leans down to rest her forearms on the railing and drops the pieces in. They vanish in the brown current. The extra ammo follows.

"What are you thinking?" she asks, just loud enough to be heard over the rushing water.

"I don't think a Chinese intelligence agency fielded that hawk."

She looks up in surprise. "No?"

"It doesn't feel right. This whole thing feels off."

She straightens up, pushing a few strands of wet hair off her forehead. "Targeting Nungsan was extreme."

"Agreed. So is running a surveillance program eight years out. That's why I'm starting to think it's personal. Someone with influence who would be affected if the truth got out. Someone with resources, used to outsourcing on-the-ground activity. The biomimetic hawk was the same here as back home."

She thinks about this, then says, "I'm not sure if that's better or worse. You have any idea who we're talking about?"

He follows her gaze to the muddy water. No sign of the gun parts. He hopes they're working their way downstream. "Not a clue."

She says, "They'll be hunting for Shaw just like we are, but we have the advantage. We know for sure he's alive. We know the name he's using. All they'll learn from our conversation with Daniel is that he escaped Nungsan."

The rain paints cool tracks down his face and the back of his neck. His shirt is getting wet. "They're determined," he reminds her. "They'll figure it out." He juts his chin, indicating the stream. "I'm thinking they'll try to slow us down in the meantime."

She looks up at him again. That fever-bright gaze. "You thought Rey must have guessed about the guns. You think he said something?"

"No. But Rey and Daniel have enemies. It wouldn't be hard to get the cops curious about why we're here, why we're talking to them. But we're clean now. It won't matter." He cocks his head toward the car. "Come on. Let's go."

She catches his sleeve. "Lincoln. Do you think Shaw knew he was marked for death?"

The question comes out of nowhere. He puzzles over it as the rain begins to abate. "How could he know?"

"He couldn't," she says. "But he knew something. I mean, he got away. He got out. But he didn't come home. There must have been a reason. What reason, Lincoln?"

She asks him that, but she's already guessed why—and he has too. "We can talk about it later. Let's go." He starts back toward the SUV.

"He was abandoned in that place," she says from behind him, still in that voice so soft he has to turn around to hear her clearly. "He was abandoned and he knew it. No rescue came. His brothers didn't come for him."

"*God damn it*. We looked for him. You know we did, but we were sent on a false trail."

"Yes," she says, letting him know that this is the point she wants to make. "All of us were betrayed. Shaw needs to know that."

Her eyes are wide and bright, *too* bright, with a warrior's focus—as if she's sizing him up the way she'd size up an enemy. She wants to find Shaw—so does he—but their reasons are not the same. "You're feeling protective of him, True."

"I am."

"You need to be careful of that. Whatever his reason for not coming home, it doesn't excuse what he's done since." He jerks his chin at the car. "Let's get the fuck out of here while we can."

Miles watches out the rear window of the SUV as Lincoln and True walk back from the bridge. He's not sure what's going on between them but it's a relief to know the guns are gone.

When they get back in, they bring with them the odors of mud and rain-wet clothing and a sense of tension as thick as the tropical humidity. Neither offers an explanation.

"Let's go," Lincoln says. Rey obeys.

Alex helps True squirm out of her raincoat. "We okay?" he asks her.

She raises her hand, fingers crossed, a serious look in her eyes.

Miles feels his jaw tighten; his heart rate kicks up.

Alex whispers, "*Shit.*"

Rey glances around, a hint of worry on his brow. "Something up?"

"Let's all relax," Lincoln tells them. "We'll be fine."

Will we? Miles wonders.

Clearly trouble is coming. That knowledge scares him. He wants to question Lincoln, but not in front of Rey. So he says nothing. He returns to staring out the window, stewing over what might be going on. It irritates the fuck out of him that Lincoln wants to pretend things are okay.

They've gone on for maybe twenty kilometers when two chimes ring. Miles flinches at the noise. True and Lincoln react too, both reaching for their tablets. As the chimes go silent, Miles asks, "What is it?"

Alex leans over, eyeing True's tablet. He asks her, "Is that the traffic cam?"

Miles twists around to look behind them, but if anyone is following, they're not in sight.

"Something overhead," True says. "A UAV. Identifies as national police."

"Following us?" Rey asks from upfront.

"It's a good bet."

They're rounding a long curve, almost back to the main highway, when Lincoln says in a preternaturally calm voice, "Rey, let's slow down."

Rey touches the brakes, shaving their speed. "Oh," he says as a roadblock comes into sight ahead of them. "Oh, *fuck.*"

A sentiment Miles shares.

Three police cars, lights flashing, are staggered diagonally across the road, right up to the vegetation on either side, blocking all possibility of getting past them. At least eight officers armed with long rifles crouch behind the cars. More police cars wait farther down the road.

The sight brings Miles to the edge of panic, a physical memory of the last time he was waylaid on a remote road. His heartbeat ramps up but there's nowhere to go.

Lincoln tries to reassure Rey. "Take it easy. We're going to be okay."

It's not looking that way to Miles. Rey isn't convinced either. He sounds distraught as he says, "But you're carrying—"

"No, it's okay," Lincoln insists. "Just do as they direct."

Rey stops well short of the barricade. He's ordered to get out of the vehicle first, hands on his head. Then he's told to walk to the police cars.

Alex turns to True and with undisguised suspicion he demands, "What the *fuck*?"

True responds with an exasperated eye roll, as if it's all obvious and she is not in the least surprised. "Lincoln predicted this."

"Predicted what?" Miles wants to know. "What is going on?"

"It's a setup," Lincoln explains. "Someone called in a tip, accused us of some high crime."

"Are we guilty?" Alex asks. Nothing in his tone suggests he's joking.

"Fuck, no," True answers. She looks annoyed, not frightened at all. "Right now, the opposition is just scrambling to figure out what they can about the 'American'"—her fingers move in air quotes—"and they want to take us out of the hunt while they do."

"Take us out for how long? I have to be on that plane tomorrow morning. I need to be back at work."

True responds to this with terse sarcasm. "I'm sure the police will take your work schedule into consideration."

Outside, Rey has reached the barricade. He's hustled out of sight. New orders are issued by megaphone: "*One at a time! Exit the car. Hands on head.*"

"Who's first?" Alex asks, like he just wants to get this over with. He can't go first because he's trapped in the middle of the seat.

"Me," Lincoln says, opening the door. "Remember, we're here for personal reasons. That's what we need to tell them, and it has the advantage of being the truth."

"*Step away from the vehicle! Face down on the ground.*"

"Fuck," Alex says in disgust. "If we get gunned down, the kids are going to be *pissed*."

True gives him a scathing look. "Get a grip," she says. "They don't have any reason to shoot us."

"They don't have any reason to *stop* us," he counters.

"I'll go next," Miles volunteers. Despite his effort to put up a stern front, he hears a tremor in his voice. *Fuck it all.* He starts to open his door.

"Miles," True says.

He turns to her.

"This is not like before," she tells him. "They'll ask you a few questions. That's all."

"Yeah, I know," he says softly. "I understand that."

But what happens if the police have figured out that Lincoln printed up those guns?

DETAINED

Two hours later they're back in Manila. Alex hasn't seen True since the roadblock, when they were escorted to separate police cars. "Where's my wife?" he's asked more than once. "Why are we being detained?"

No one consented to answer.

He sits now at a battered steel table in an austere interview room that stinks of disinfectants. Cameras in the ceiling corners are protected by hemispherical pods. Across the table from him is a uniformed police officer, a man in his thirties, bulked up like a weightlifter, with dark eyebrows knit in a puzzled but not unfriendly expression as he asks Alex, "You are a US Army veteran, Mr. Delgado?"

Alex frowns. Not a question he expected. What the fuck is going on?

"Yes, I'm an army veteran, but it's been a long time. I work now as a paramedic and I'm due back at work in about thirty-four hours. We're scheduled to fly out in the morning."

The officer cocks his head as if he's having a problem parsing this answer. "You don't work as a mercenary for this private militia, Requisite Operations?"

Alex narrows his eyes. "You've been misinformed, sir. Requisite

Operations is not a militia. It's a military contractor. And no, I don't work for them. I'm not a mercenary. I'm a paramedic."

"But you are married to True Brighton?"

"Yes, True is my wife."

"Your wife, she is part owner of Requisite Operations?"

Alex inclines his head. "She has an interest, yes. But we're here in your country for personal reasons. Nothing to do with the company."

The officer looks suddenly stern. "Is your wife a mercenary, Mr. Delgado?"

Lincoln is in a nearby room. He's been deprived of all electronics except for his left hand and his artificial eye, although the eye caused concern among the officers, who worried it might be capable of recording the interview. Lincoln assured them this was not the case, but they asked him to wear an eye patch anyway. He agreed to this.

He's already answered a few innocuous questions asked by a senior officer whose sun-worn face is flecked with dark moles. *Time to get serious,* he thinks as she leans forward, resting her ring-encrusted right hand on the table between them, her dark-eyed gaze fixed on him. "You control your own private militia. Is that correct, Mr. Han?"

"No, ma'am. I'm the owner and chief executive of Requisite Operations Incorporated, a private military and security company. We are not a private militia. We are a United States government contractor and a signatory of the internationally enforced Military Company Code of Conduct. I can confirm for you that True Brighton, whom your people also took into custody, is my Director of Operations. That said, we are here in the Philippines for personal reasons unrelated to company business. The other members of our party, Miles Dushane, Alex Delgado, and Reynaldo Gabriel, are *not* employees of Requisite Operations."

The officer nods solemnly throughout this explanation, letting him know he has her full attention. She speaks her next question slowly, as if she's carefully choosing her words. "You understand that it is concerning to us that a 'private military company' should come into this country for the single purpose of consorting with a known radical element?"

Lincoln echoes the officer's precise manner of speaking. "Ma'am, as I have explained, we are not here on company business. We've come to see a Filipino citizen by the name of Daniel Ocampo. Our purpose was to interview him about his time as a prisoner of the Saomong Cooperative Cybernetic Army—an experience that took place eight years ago, in a distant country."

Later that night, True sits with her arms crossed, facing the same officer, presenting a confident, self-contained front. The simmering anger underneath well disguised.

She has already answered questions about Requisite Operations, and about her knowledge of Daniel Ocampo and Reynaldo Gabriel. The questions she dreaded, about the time spent at the printer's, have not materialized. They may have gotten lucky. That operation was paid for with pre-purchased codes that are not immediately traceable, so it's possible the police don't know they were there.

True has finally gotten the senior officer to confirm why they were detained. She had already guessed the answer, but to hear it spoken . . .

Her voice remains soft but there is a fiery edge to her words. "Eight years ago, my son, a United States Army soldier, was captured and murdered by the terrorist organization known as the Saomong CCA. He died fighting terrorism, ma'am. And here, tonight, you tell me that I have been detained on suspicion of terrorism, simply for asking questions of Daniel Ocampo, another victim of the Saomong and a witness to my son's execution."

There is real sympathy in the officer's eyes as she says, "I understand your passion, Ms. Brighton. My own son was killed in action in Mindanao."

True inclines her head. "I'm sorry to hear it. You have my deepest sympathies." She lets her shoulders relax; she rests her hands on the table. "I don't mean to cause trouble for you, but you need to understand that the American media is going to have a field day with this story."

"Yes," Miles says in answer to a question from the slim, neatly uniformed young officer conducting his interview. "I am a freelance journalist. I discovered Daniel Ocampo's existence while working on another story. Rey Gabriel arranged the interview. He's acted as our guide."

His voice is calm. He is calm. Silently he repeats True's words, telling himself, *This is not like before.*

Miles has used those words over and over, a comforting mantra that allowed him to hide his panic when a cell door closed behind him. The national police have their own reputation, but they are not Al-Furat. He is not in the custody of Hussam El-Hashem. This is not like before.

The officer proves it by speaking in a polite, conversational tone. "Were you aware of Mr. Ocampo's radical associations?"

"Yes, in a general way."

"Are you aware that Mr. Ocampo is interested in hiring the services of Requisite Operations?"

Miles is stunned at the accusation—but he's pleased too, because their innocence will be easy to prove. "No," he says firmly. "That's not true. It's not remotely credible. What you need to do is contact the United States Department of State. I'm sure you'll find officials eager to vouch for the integrity of both Lincoln Han and Requisite Operations."

"Yes, Mr. Dushane," the young officer agrees. "That will be part of our investigation. Can you tell me, is it your intention to write about this interview that took place with Mr. Ocampo?"

Miles hesitates, pondering the motive behind this question. Have the police realized they've got nothing? No evidence? Just a looming propaganda nightmare . . .

If what they need now is a graceful way out of this situation, he'll do what he can to help. "No, I won't be writing about the interview," Miles says. "Mr. Ocampo stipulated that what he had to say was not for publication. He spoke to us only as a personal favor to True Brighton and Alex Delgado." He gives the officer a knowing look. "So far, I don't have a story to report on. Let's not change that, okay?"

INTO THIN AIR

THEY ARE HELD overnight. No hotel. No shower. No sleep. But at 0400, word comes that they will be released. The senior officer who spoke yesterday with True comes to see her, and personally escorts her to a police van waiting in a garage behind the station. On the way she explains the confusion: "We received faulty intelligence, facts confused, dates wrong, names inconsistent, but it came from a credible source so we had to treat it seriously. I'm sure you understand."

True plays the required role, speaking politely, communicating that they are both rational women who understand the complexities inherited from the War on Terror. "A perfect storm of inadvertent errors."

"Yes. But we have been in discussions with your Department of State and have assurance that you and your companions are respectable and do not threaten our security here."

True considers several responses but judges them all too acerbic, too sarcastic, too patronizing. In the end, she simply inclines her head as if in thanks. "May I get my things back?"

"All possessions are waiting for you in the van. Your friends too, your husband. We will drive you to the airport, where you will wait for your flight, and leave our country as you have already planned."

"Yes ma'am." *Can't fucking wait.*

Shaw is out there somewhere in the wide world. True hopes that by the time they get home, Tamara will have a lead on where to look for him.

As soon as she steps into the garage, she sees the little van—white, with no police lights, no markings—Alex waiting outside. "Oh, thank God," he says when he sees her. He meets her, they trade a quick hug, then he pulls back, studying her with an anxious gaze. "Are you okay?"

"Tired and dirty but otherwise fine. Let's go.' Lincoln and Miles are already seated in the van. "Where's my pack?" she asks them.

Miles hands it to her. She spot-checks the contents, confirming her combat lenses and tablet are still there. She switches the tablet on as Alex closes the van door.

A uniformed officer is behind the wheel, another rides shotgun. Both wear sidearms.

"Any word on Rey?" True asks as the van exits the garage.

"Yeah," Miles says. "I got a message. They kicked him loose last night. He said it was a fun party. Call him anytime."

The police officers stick with them until they're through security. After that they've got a five-hour wait until their flight departs. True checks in with Ripley, reviews her messages and emails. Lincoln calls home, checks in with Chris. They clean up as well as they can in the bathrooms, have breakfast, and sit down to wait. It's early enough that only a few people are waiting at the gate.

Alex and Miles nod off—soldier's instinct: sleep while you can. Lincoln is engrossed in his tablet. Lack of sleep has left True brittle, coffee has got her wired, uncertainty has sharpened the edge. She paces, watching Lincoln out of the corner of her eye as his living fingers tap and slide on his tablet.

Nothing they learned from Daniel has changed his mind or softened his resolve. He'll go after Shaw and bring him home—one way or another.

She recalls the accusation in his words when they stood together on the bridge: *You're feeling protective of him, True.*

And her blunt response: *I am.*

Lincoln is not the only one hunting Shaw. Someone with deep links within the global intelligence community is interested. Someone with the resources to engineer a police roadblock.

Their detention was brief, just overnight. Not even long enough to make them miss their plane. But if they didn't have the State Department to vouch for them? If they didn't have a backstory that let them threaten a public relations nightmare? They might have been held up for days.

Just the idea of the delay eats at her.

Shaw has been invisible for eight years, but now the existence of "the American" is revealed. A survivor of the Rogue Lightning mission. A witness to events that have been, until now, successfully concealed.

Finding Shaw has become time-critical.

True needs to reach him before the opposition does. She needs to know what he knows—what went wrong on that mission, why he and Diego were abandoned in Nungsan, why he never came home.

It chills her soul to think that whoever condemned Diego might still be in a position of power, able and willing to trade the lives of good, brave soldiers just to protect their own welfare. More than Shaw, that person needs to be brought into the light.

Phones and tablets chime: a bright chorus of simultaneous beeps. True stops pacing, checks her screen to find a message from the airline. Their flight is delayed due to the crew's late arrival last night. Departure has been pushed back six hours.

Lincoln gets up, grabs his pack. "There's an earlier flight to Los Angeles," he tells her. "I'm going to find a gate agent. See if we can get on that."

She nods, casting her gaze over Alex and Miles, still asleep.

A new thought stirs: *Why go back at all?*

They aren't going to find Shaw in Seattle or anywhere in North America.

Curious to know what options might be available, she connects to the airport's website, pulls up the departures schedule, and finds flights leaving for all over the world.

Alex wakes up. She tells him about the flight delay. "Lincoln's trying to get us on an earlier flight."

Half an hour later Lincoln returns, the slight lift at the corner of his mouth hinting at cautious optimism. "We're on a standby list for the Los Angeles flight, leaving in fifty minutes. The agent thinks we'll get seats, but we won't be together."

Alex turns a tired gaze on True.

She shrugs. "That's all right. We'll be sleeping anyway." She wakes up Miles and they walk to a new gate, this one packed with milling passengers. Kids scamper among the bags and backpacks and the buzz of a hundred conversations in Tagalog and English. The odors of coffee and damp carpet are thick in the air.

There are no empty seats, so they retreat, taking up a position at the edge of crowd, but still close enough to hear the gate agent's announcements.

Lincoln's tablet chimes with an incoming call. True turns an idle gaze on him, but her interest picks up when he says, "It's Tamara."

"Put her on speaker," True says.

He taps the screen. They cluster around. "We're all here listening," he tells Tamara. "Me, True, Alex, Miles."

Tamara has heard about their adventures from Chris. She's full of questions, almost breathless with worry and relief. It takes several minutes for her to get to the point, but finally she tells them, "I got the lab results back on those filters we recovered from the crashed Arkinson. The analysis looked at mineral dust as well as microbiota. No surprise, it indicates low-altitude flight in the TEZ. But pollen in the filters points much farther west. Best guess: that Arkinson was last serviced near the western reach of the Atlas Mountains."

True shuffles through her knowledge of geography. "So that would put it in—"

She meant to say *Morocco*, but she's interrupted by interference in the call—a muted background roar—then Tamara, her voice pitched high, "Jesus, what was that? It sounded like an explosion."

"What?" Lincoln asks. "Where?"

"I don't know! I'm in the Robotics Center. I think it was up at headquarters. Hold on. I'm checking security feeds." Her voice is shaking. Then it gets whispery. "*Oh God.* Lobby cameras are out. Front door cameras are out. Oh . . . I see it now. Lincoln, it's the front gate. The security gate. Two cars are burning. I've got to go up there. I've got to see if I can help."

"No!" Lincoln says, sharply enough that heads turn in their direction. He lowers his voice to a gruff whisper. "Stay where you are. There could be a second bomb. Wait for the police—"

"No, I'm going. Someone could be hurt." She's breathing hard. It sounds like she's running. "Lincoln, come home."

"I am. I'm coming."

"We need you," she insists as if he said nothing.

"I'm coming," he repeats.

The call ends.

Lincoln immediately puts another call through, this time to Chris. It's the middle of the afternoon at home. A weekday. Everyone should be in, at work somewhere on the ReqOps campus. There should be a class in session.

Chris doesn't answer. Neither does Jameson. He finally gets Hayden on the phone. The kid sounds shaky but coherent. "It was a car bomb at the front gate. We're on lockdown."

"Tamara's with you?"

"Yeah. Chris did a roll call. None of the clients are hurt."

"And our people?"

He hesitates. "Everybody was down at the range except me and . . . and Renata. She was in the city, talking to potential clients."

"You've been in touch with her?"

"No. She's not answering her phone."

Two cars, burning at the front gate.

True feels Alex's arm encircle her waist. His calm proximity is a shield, a brace against the crushing pressure of grim expectation.

"Find Chris," Lincoln says. "Tell him to call."

They hear nothing for an anxious ten minutes—then all their tablets chime. True is sure it's a group message from Chris—but she's wrong. It's their seat assignments for the Los Angeles flight.

They're in line to board when Chris finally calls. "Hold on a second," Lincoln growls into the tiny mic. He leaves the boarding line. True follows. So do Alex and Miles. They huddle in an empty corner while the other passengers continue to file onto the plane. Lincoln shifts the call from his TINSL to the tablet's speaker. He tells Chris, "Report."

Chris's voice is flat, hard. "They must have followed Renata's car back here. They used another vehicle to trap her at the security gate. She was their target, Lincoln. That's what their message said. A combat pilot. Fair game. It was that interview she did. It made her the public face of the mission."

"What is her *status*?" Lincoln demands in a hoarse whisper.

"She's dead."

True reaches for Alex, returning to the comfort of his embrace. Miles swears softly. Lincoln pushes on. "Any other casualties?" he asks Chris.

"No. The second car was empty. The gate's destroyed, of course, and at least twelve parked cars have been damaged, but there's no structural damage to the building. Police are outside. FBI are on the way. Lincoln, I've got to go."

But Lincoln has another question. "Who signed the message?"

"Al-Furat."

Hussam's organization, supposedly taken over by his brother, Rihab. For True, this is a glimmer of good news. She leans in, wanting to be sure. "Not Variant Forces?" she asks.

"You think there's a difference?" Lincoln snaps.

She turns to him, guarded, cautious in the face of his anger. She would like to believe that there is a difference, that this was not Shaw's doing—but she answers him honestly: "I don't know."

Chris speaks up again. "Lincoln, I've got to go. I've got to talk to the cops."

"Do it," Lincoln agrees. "We have to board our flight anyway—but message me with any updates."

Chris's voice is low, his tone dangerous when he says: "We need to deal with this. We need to hit back hard."

Lincoln assures him, "We will."

True feels the pressure of Alex's arm around her shoulders. He whispers, "Come on. We need to board."

But she resists, unwilling to retreat in the face of Lincoln's quiet anger because she knows what it portends. "You want to believe it's Shaw," she accuses.

He wants to get on that plane. He doesn't want airport security brought in. So he speaks softly, his words confined to their circle. Even so, True feels his fury straining at the leash when he says, "Renata is *dead*. A fucking car bomb."

True gulps air. Renata was a good person, a good friend, but she is not going to cry for her. Not here. Not now. "He didn't want a war," she insists. "He gave you a peace treaty. Out of respect for the past."

"Maybe he changed his mind," Alex says reasonably.

Miles jumps on this. "Yeah. If he worked out where we are and who we've talked to—he might not like it."

"Al-Furat took credit," True insists. "*Not* Shaw. Not Variant Forces."

Beneath Lincoln's scars, the muscles tighten, drawing seams across his face. His anger is contained, but when he speaks, acid edges each quiet word: "There is *no such thing* as Variant Forces. It's not a company. It's a syndicate. Independent operators. Maybe Shaw didn't order it but it doesn't matter. Al-Furat must have used his network, his connections. They don't have the reach to do something like this on their own."

True listens—and with each word she can feel Shaw's existence, never quite real anyway, dissolving into thin air and everything he knows going with him.

"You *want* him to be responsible for it," she says. "You want all the doubt scrubbed away. Make it easy for yourself when you finally corner him, when you finally have a chance to make up for your silence about what happened in Kunar. You don't want to bring him home."

"*Jesus,*" Alex whispers. "Come on. You're upset. We're all upset. Let's just go."

It's good advice. They need to go. The last of the passengers has disappeared into the jetway. But she is not going to retreat. She wants to hear Lincoln confirm or deny what she has said, but he does neither, only watches her with a predator's intensity. She feels it, the threat. It's a chemical in her bloodstream, sending her heart racing, pushing a sickly heat through her pores, but still she doesn't back off. She raises her chin instead, daring him, *Deny it.*

He says nothing.

Her lip curls as she guesses why. It's Alex. Lincoln is furious with her but he is not going to risk a confrontation with Alex minutes before their flight is due to leave.

Miles tries to tip the balance. "Does it matter?" he asks with startling bitterness. "Even if that bastard had nothing to do with this, he's done enough. He—"

The public address system interrupts: "*Last call. All passengers booked on flight 422 bound for Los Angeles should now be aboard.*"

Alex reacts first, a paramedic accustomed to de-escalating volatile situations. "That's it," he says. "You can fight this out when we get home, but right now we are getting on that plane. Let's go."

True cooperates this time as he steers her toward the gate. Lincoln and Miles fall in behind them. She gets out her tablet, calls up her electronic boarding pass on the screen, and lets the red laser light of the scanner read it. The rest of them brandish their phones. They walk quickly, boots thumping the jetway, until they catch up with a line of passengers still queued at the boarding door.

After that they shuffle forward, making slow progress as the aisle clears. True's seat is on the aisle, close to the front. She hugs Alex, kisses him goodbye, while Miles slips past.

"We'll get through this," Alex murmurs.

"I know. Don't worry."

He moves on toward the rear of the huge aircraft, leaving her to face Lincoln's cold gaze.

Lincoln says, "When we get back, we're going to talk." It's not a friendly invitation.

She nods and takes her seat. He moves on.

For a few seconds True just sits there, hugging her pack, with her tablet still in hand. She is flushed, nervous. Afraid. She glances at the young woman in the seat next to her who is stead-fastly ignoring her presence. Then she looks ahead, toward the boarding door. The aisle is clear. No one else has gotten on, but the door remains open. She leans into the aisle and looks toward the back. Several passengers are still on their feet, frantically sort-ing through their bags in the overhead compartments. Alex has already gone past them. She can't see him. She can't see Lincoln, or Miles.

A resolve comes over her. She doesn't examine it too closely. The circumstances call for action. Quick action. *Right action?* No time to judge.

She gets up, shoulders her pack, and moves swiftly, quietly, toward the boarding door. What matters now, what matters most, is that she finds Shaw first, before Lincoln can get to him.

Two rows ahead, a short, round, aged woman shoves herself up and into the aisle. She tries to lift a bag into the overhead compartment. "Let me," True says quietly. She lifts the bag, shoves it into place, then squeezes past the woman, ignoring her effusive thanks.

A flight attendant is the next obstacle in her path. "Miss, we need everyone—"

"The term is 'ma'am'," True says softly. "Not 'Miss.' I'm not a child. And I'm getting off the plane."

"Yes, uh . . . *ma'am*, there's no time. The boarding doors are about to close."

"I know." Her voice is still very soft. "That's why I need to get off *now*."

"Ma'am, you'll delay the flight."

"I don't have checked baggage."

She looks stunned. "But if you're getting off, we need to scan your boarding pass."

True holds up her tablet. "I'll scan it at the end of the ramp."

"Are you . . . flying alone?"

True doesn't answer. She turns sideways and forces her way past the flight attendant. Steps through the door, strides up the jetway. Thinks, *Jesus, Brighton, you are a fucking idiot.*

But she learned to read Lincoln years ago and she knows: The worst kind of war is a civil war, brother against brother, and that's what's coming. It's what she read in Lincoln's glare.

And Miles is no ally. *Does it matter?* he asked, not caring what crime Shaw hangs for, so long as he hangs.

But the truth does matter. It matters to her. She *needs* to know, not only what happened in Burma, but why, and who's responsible. Shaw Walker may be the only one left alive who can help her find out.

Behind her, the boarding door closes. Ahead, a security officer waits. She walks boldly up to him, shows him the tablet with her boarding pass displayed. "Emergency," she says. "I need to fly to Morocco instead."

The officer scans it as other officials converge. The tablet is handed back to her just as a text from Alex arrives: **I'm next to an infant! God help me. I'll come visit you when we're in the air.**

She thinks maybe she just threw her marriage away. She thinks maybe she's going to vomit. This was a stupid, stupid, stupid thing to do. But none of her inner turmoil can be seen in her face or heard in her voice. She speaks softly, her tone calm, words measured as she persuades the officials that she needs to book a flight to Morocco. After some discussion, they decide to help her. After all, her credit is good and the sooner she's gone from their jurisdiction, the better. The tide turns her way, and she gets a seat on a plane bound for Madrid, leaving in ninety minutes. Easier to get to Morocco from there.

She is standing at the concourse window, watching the runway, when the flight to Los Angeles takes off.

She watches it climb into the air, recede into the hazy distance. Another plane barrels after it down the runway. She thinks, *After this, I'm done.*

She tells Ripley to put those words into a text and she sends them to Alex: **After this, I'm done.**

Then she calls up the tablet's settings. Ruthlessly, she switches off phone and text functions, logs out of her ReqOps account, and sets her profile to anonymous to prevent any apps from reporting on her location, her availability, her activity. All automatic backups get switched off. She has a credit account in her own name that Alex won't be able to access.

She can still get email.

She's not looking forward to that.

I'm sorry for taking off like this, but you heard Lincoln. War is coming. And I need answers while it is still possible to get them. The best—the fastest—way to make that happen is to go on my own. That's how I see it. I am sorry I didn't say anything to you. The truth is, I didn't know I was going to do it until I stood up and walked off that plane.

I'm going to be out of touch for a while. Not long. A few days maybe. When it's done, I'll call you. I hope you'll be there. I hope you forgive me.

Love you,

True

NORTH AFRICA

PRIVATE MILITARY COMPANIES exist around the world. Some are small, some immense. Many provide only support and training services. Others include armed security. And some are mercenaries in the classic sense: soldiers for hire, willing to work in offensive military operations that might include frontline combat or the overthrow of vulnerable governments.

It's a secretive world. Even the white-hat companies are publicity-shy and cautious of new contacts.

True has worked four years in the industry. She's done a lot of networking, developed alliances, but only among white-hat companies that are signatories in good standing to the Military Company Code of Conduct. She is sure, though, that in the volatile regions of North Africa and the Middle East, even those local companies with sterling reputations will have connections reaching into the darker side of the industry. She needs to tap those connections. It's the only way she'll ever find Shaw Walker.

She targets a company she's worked with before, one based in Rabat, Morocco, and run by a middle-aged Egyptian expatriate known as Dove Barhoum. She sets up a clean email account for the purpose.

She doesn't want to mislead, so when she contacts Dove, she

is careful to say that she is not representing Requisite Operations Inc. and that she is not seeking services. To her surprise, the approach piques his interest. Sixty minutes after clearing customs in Rabat, she is sitting across a desk from him, in a windowless room within a large training complex on the city's edge.

He is a man of stern posture, with dark eyes, a neat beard, and a weathered, sun-blackened visage. His wavy hair is streaked with gray. "We have all heard of Requisite Operations' recent job in the TEZ," he says. "And of the troubles that followed—at Eden Transit, and at your company headquarters in America. There has been talk that a retaliatory strike is sure to follow. Yet you are here on your own?"

True's response is blunt, and honest. "I'm here ahead of the war," she says. "I can't tell you what form it's going to take or when it's going to happen—because I don't know. But I don't deny it's coming. Too many lines have been crossed. But I'm not here to reconnoiter, or to cultivate allies. Like I said in my email, I'm on personal business. All I'm looking for is an introduction."

"You understand that my company abides by the code of conduct?"

"Yes, of course. I would not imply otherwise. But while you and I operate by that code, we can't afford to ignore those who don't. I don't doubt that you sit at the nexus of an intelligence operation that is aware of every other PMC in this region, legitimate or not. How could you successfully serve your clients otherwise? I am not asking to access that operation. All I'm looking for is an introduction, or a referral. Someone able and willing to get a message to Jon Helm."

"Jon Helm," Dove repeats, slow and thoughtful.

"Do you know him?" True asks.

Dove shrugs. He tugs at his beard. He asks, "You are not seeking a negotiated peace?"

True's thoughts go to Renata. "It's gone too far for that."

"So you wish to speak with this Jon Helm."

"Yes. About something that happened a long time ago. He'll know what I mean."

He reverses her earlier question. "Do *you* know him?" he asks, doubt in his voice.

"Yes, Dove, I do. At least, I *knew* him—in another life. He'll know me."

This brings a scowl to Dove's weathered face. His mouth knots as if with a sudden, bad taste. "I prefer dealing with the young," he finally says. "Their lives are simple and their secrets are trivial."

"Can you help me?" she presses.

"I cannot. Not directly. But I know someone. He is an agent who knows all kinds of people. I will share your contact card. How long will you be here?"

"No longer than necessary."

She thinks of Lincoln, home by now and surely occupied in setting ReqOps' house in order. Right or wrong, he blames Shaw for Renata's death and eventually he will come. She needs to find Shaw before then. It's that simple.

She gives Dove the number of a burner phone she purchased at the local airport. She knows that he will call Lincoln, mention her visit, in case it matters. There's nothing she can do about that.

They both stand. "I appreciate this courtesy," she tells Dove. "I will not forget it."

Several seconds pass as he studies her. It's easy to see he would like to ask more questions, but he does not. "Be cautious," he advises as he walks her to the door.

He means well, but it's not advice she can follow. To do this, she'll have to do it on Shaw Walker's terms, if he's willing to offer terms at all. She's gambling, no question. Risking her life on a promise implied by the tattoo Miles saw. *The Last Good Man.*

She's convinced Shaw did his best for Diego; he would have died for Diego.

Take me instead.

It's Diego's memory that links them. She's gambling that will be enough to keep her alive.

It's late afternoon when True strolls into the hotel lobby, her gaze taking in the décor—sleek and modern—and the clientele, the same. It's a hotel intended for business travelers, not tourists. She evaluates the layout, picking out places a beetle could be concealed.

It's just habit. She already left one perched on a tiny ledge in the façade outside, positioned so that it can collect images of everyone entering the hotel or passing by the front doors. Her inventory of surveillance devices is limited. She won't risk a second beetle in the lobby—especially given a real possibility that hotel security runs regular checks for unauthorized electronics.

She checks in, and then buys a change of clothes from the hotel store so she'll have something to wear while she sends her other clothes to be cleaned. She settles on khaki slacks made for hiking and a gray athletic pullover.

The room is large and comfortable, furnished in the usual hotel style. Floor-to-ceiling windows look across low-rise shops and cafés to the glittering ocean.

She orders dinner in her room. A facial recognition program has sorted the images of hotel guests, staff, and visitors gathered by the beetle, appending names to many. True reviews them on her tablet but none seem meaningful. It's comforting to remember that her own identity is protected. ReqOps paid for the privilege of anonymity—something she appreciates now more than ever.

After a shower, she settles in to wait.

She startles awake at the sound of an alarm, sure that she's been asleep for hours. The curtains are still open. Light from a full moon and from the street below spills into the room, creating a shadowy twilight. She slides out of bed to crouch on the floor. A quick look around confirms she's alone. The trilling continues. It's not an alarm. It's the ring tone of her burner phone.

She gets to her feet. Picks it up from the nightstand. The time flashes: 2300. Unknown number. It's a new phone, of course. It doesn't know anyone else's number.

"Hello," she says, believing the caller to be Dove's mysterious agent. For a moment she wonders if this person will be a man or a woman. Then too many moments slip past, all of them silent.

Is no one there?

She has no evidence, but she *believes* someone is there, listening. Probably not the agent. Next best conclusion: Events have progressed faster than she anticipated. It's Shaw Walker, reconnoitering, making a cautious approach. She speaks with that possibility in mind, with the hope that he'll remember her voice. "This is True Brighton. We've met before. Diego Delgado is my son and I want to know what really happened."

Silence.

She checks the phone's display. The call has ended. Annoyed now, frustrated, she tosses it onto the bed and heads for the bathroom. But as soon as she comes out, she picks it up again. A text message has arrived from the same unknown number. GPS coordinates, along with a time, 2330. That's twenty-six minutes from now. She checks a map. The coordinates correspond to a street corner several blocks from the hotel.

A rush of emotions dumps a smothering weight on her heart. There is a flash of peevishness at being called out in such a peremptory fashion. There is fear too: Anyone could have sent that message, and even if it *is* him? There is still fear. Strongest, though, is a sense of triumph. This is why she came.

She runs wet fingers through her hair and re-braids it. Gets dressed in her newly purchased clothes, puts her tablet and her reading glasses in a thigh pocket, works her hand into a snug data glove, and pulls on her jacket. Her new phone and her MARC visor go into the jacket's front pockets; her daypack goes over her shoulder. The pack holds a first-aid kit and a remnant collection of robotics from the origami army—a sparrow, two beetles, two off-the-shelf tracking discs popularly known as "mother's helpers," and a small snake—all that's left.

She is unarmed.

Guilt works on her as she waits for the elevator. Doubt . . . not over what she's doing but doubt about her right to do it, to take this chance. She's risking more than her own life. Alex is in her head, reminding her: *We have two living children. Just because they aren't kids anymore, that doesn't mean they don't need you.*

But when the elevator doors open, she steps aboard. No one else there. She watches the numbers count down as she descends. She tries to imagine *not* going out tonight . . . and can't.

She's been drawn here by the gravity of Nungsan. No turning away now. No second chance. One way or another, she'll see this through.

It's cold outside, but she resists the urge to put her hands in her jacket pockets. *Be ready for anything.* Her pace is swift as she sets off up the block, senses alert. Listening, looking at everything around her. Feeling too visible in the bright moonlight.

At this hour traffic is light, and there aren't many people about. Dark-haired boys lean out the windows of a passing sedan, yelling shrill invitations. She turns her head to watch them, hoping they will notice her age, hoping their friends will notice and give them hell for it.

When they're gone, she takes out her MARC visor. It boots, linking to her anonymous profile. The optics kick in, brightening shadows and blunting the glare of headlights, making it easy to see details of the occasional passersby. A few European couples. They nod as they pass. A gray-haired businessman, identified by her visor as a city resident. He looks her over with a disapproving glower. Five dark-eyed young men, teenagers, joking with each other and smelling of cigarettes. They crowd around her, shoulders brushing, bumping. Playing at intimidation.

She murmurs in Arabic, "Tara aaraf ommak, enta we howa." *I know your mother, you and him.*

They respond with shrill, nervous laughter and go their way.

Another man, ahead of her, walks in the same direction, but he disappears into a club, swallowed up by a burst of electronic music. No one else is near.

She watches the sidewalks, the street, the buildings, the night sky. Every few steps she glances back to check for interesting things that might be following behind, but she sees only a few stray cats. Nothing suspicious, nothing threatening, until the traffic lulls. Then she hears a faint hum from overhead—like a wet electrical line or a stealthy surveillance drone.

A glance up confirms there are no electrical lines. This is a new neighborhood. Utilities are underground.

She activates one of the MARC's search programs, designed to inventory artificial objects in the sky—both those that self-identify with transponder signals, and those that don't. Stealth objects are found by analyzing video from the MARC's cams. She looks up, turning in a slow circle to scan the entire arc of sky visible between the eclipsing bulk of the buildings. The program can visually distinguish objects presenting at least thirty seconds of arc—but that's in clear air. There's a haze of dust over the city tonight. Still, the MARC picks out some low-flying drones, listing them in her visual field:

Transponder identification Aquila-East municipal monitor, serial #Z-3423AEVK

Transponder identification Kishori network booster, serial #C-67808EWJS

85% probability Sibolt RS, no transponder

87% probability Sibolt RS, no transponder

The two unidentified Sibolts concern her. They're quiet, off-the-shelf surveillance devices, half a meter in diameter, capable of autonomous navigation, and cheap enough that almost any urban sky survey will turn up at least one. Easy to use, too. Register a target and they'll follow it until their power reserves drain to the red line and they have to return to their charging station.

Just because there are two in the sky, it doesn't mean they're interested in her. But they might be.

She reaches the end of the block and turns onto the cross street. When there's a break in traffic she trots across to the opposite curb, turns the next corner, and scans the sky again. One Sibolt is still in sight. She cuts beneath a canopy sheltering the front of a closed bakery and listens. It's a quiet street. This time she's sure she can hear the whispery hum of stealth propellers.

Who? she wonders.

A Sibolt is such a basic tool she can't believe one was fielded by the same crew who flew the biomimetic hawk in the Philippines. She doubts it belongs to Shaw either. A man who can command Arkinsons would surely field more sophisticated surveillance. Another possibility occurs to her: Maybe Lincoln is behind it.

Maybe Dove contacted him, told him about her visit. Or maybe he just worked out where she'd gone and hired a local company to monitor her movements.

The thought angers her. Lincoln is a friend, one she respects, but in the matter of Shaw Walker their goals are not the same. That's why she's here by herself—and she is not going to tolerate interference.

Using her phone, she dictates a text: "I'm being watched. Aerial surveillance. A Sibolt. If it's not yours, be cautious."

She waits under the canopy for another minute but gets no answer. Her gaze shifts to the lower right, cueing the time display on her visor to brighten. 2328. She has two minutes to reach the rendezvous point.

She walks swiftly, and soon she can see the corner where she has been instructed to wait. The surrounding buildings are four and five story apartments, shops and a restaurant at street level. The restaurant is still open. Parked cars line the curbs. Traffic is sparse. She sees no other pedestrians, no one waiting at the corner. It's possible someone is waiting inside one of the parked cars. The idea disturbs her. It makes the hair on her neck stand up. She eyes each car as she passes, determined not to be taken by surprise. But no one's there.

She reaches the corner, looks up and down the cross street. Half a block away, two young men smoking outside a club. No one else in sight. No one gets out of the vehicles. There's a corner café—closed now—with large glass windows. She retreats into the shadow of its canopy, a position that lets her watch both streets.

A few cars pass, their headlight beams sliding over her. An expensive sedan slows almost to a stop as the driver takes a look. She lets her MARC record an image of his face and of his car, uploading it to a secure folder—a resource that will be emailed to both Alex and Lincoln should she disappear.

A fierce faint buzz from overhead seizes her attention. She looks up in time to see the golden burst of a small explosion no more than ten meters above the building diagonally across the intersection. The sound is like a firecracker. She drops into a crouch as the concussion echoes back and forth between the buildings. The luxury sedan accelerates hard and disappears. True remains down, unsure what happened until her visor inventories the sky again.

The Sibolt is gone.

"*Holy shit*," she whispers, venting tension. He took out the Sibolt. He must have had some kind of kamikaze up there and he took out the Sibolt.

The realization brings with it a crazy kind of relief, because he could have targeted her with the kamikaze if he wanted to. She knows now that's not his purpose.

She checks the time. The digital display brightens under her gaze. 2329 shifts to 2330.

Cautiously, she stands up. A van rolls past, followed by a scooter with a helmeted rider. An old beat-up SUV with tinted windows turns into sight a block away. It advances toward her at a moderate pace, stopping briefly on the other side of the intersection. Instinct tells her this is it. Sweat prickles under her arms. Her heart booms. When the SUV rolls forward again, she moves out into the street to meet it.

She approaches from the passenger side. As she does, the window slides down. She is ready to drop, or to turn and run, but she tries not to show it as she peers inside.

Dim light cast by a dash video screen illuminates the driver. He's dressed like a civilian, khaki trousers and a darker, long-sleeved pullover. His large hands are on the steering wheel but his left hand—the hand Miles described as crippled—holds the wheel in a distorted grip. It's his index and little finger that curl to meet his thumb. The two middle fingers don't help out, standing off instead, stiffly curved.

He wears a data glove on his right hand, and on his right wrist, a bracelet that looks like something a child would wear. It's made of clear, colorless, flat plastic links with embedded wiring. A tracking device? Maybe.

His face is weathered, his eyebrows thinner than she remembers, his hair darker but maybe that's just the light. His hair has been buzz-cut, but it could use another trim. So could his beard.

He's wearing an augmented reality visor—not a MARC, some other brand. He's not looking at her but she can see through the screen to his spooky, pale eyes. Their focus shifts, taking in the street, and maybe the rearview mirror, or the data streamed on his display. He's watchful, on guard. She notes the tension in the set of his mouth and wonders if he's expecting an assault.

But is it *him*? It's been so long, she's not sure. "You got this right?" she asks him, her voice soft but urgent.

A cold smile crooks his lips. He still doesn't look at her. "Get in, True, if you want this to happen."

Goddamn, she thinks. It's as if a ghost has spoken. Goosebumps rise on her arms, on her neck, at that rough, raspy voice. She remembers that voice more clearly than she remembers his face. She glances into the backseat. As best she can see, it's empty. She opens the door and gets in, settling her daypack into her lap.

He drives. The window closes and cool air from the vents blows against her flushed cheeks. The cabin smells of sweat, dust, and a faint lingering odor of cigarette smoke. She twists around to get a better look at the backseat. No one's there. No one's on the road behind them. Still, she doesn't believe he's alone.

Motion draws her gaze to his bracelet. It's stirring. It's no longer a closed circle. Instead it's crawling around his wrist like an agitated centipede. She can see mandibles. He ignores it and asks her, "You got a tracking signal?"

"Nothing running."

"You recording?"

"No. I had a sky survey going but that's done now."

The centipede settles down, transforming back into a bracelet. He says, "I'd feel better if you put the visor away."

"Not a problem." She shoves her pack to the floor beside her feet, where there's a rubber mat filthy with grit and pale dust. She takes off her MARC, making a show of powering it down, folding it, sliding it into her jacket pocket. "What the hell is that thing on your wrist?"

"Personal defense," he says as he turns onto a different street. "It's got biomarkers on you now, so you've got nothing to worry about."

"Good to know."

He drives sedately but without hesitation, familiar with where he is and where he's going. She notes the streets and passing buildings, trying to assemble a map of their route in her mind.

"Other devices?" he asks her.

"Sure."

"Power them down. It's not that I don't trust you, but you never know who's hacked in."

It's a reasonable precaution. She gets out her phone and her tablet, and shuts them off. The origami army is already dormant, so she leaves those devices untouched in her pack. "You worried about being identified?" she asks.

He drawls, "No, I've got no reason to worry. This is my town. One of 'em. I'm just a tourist who forgot to go home. An expatriate."

"Jon Helm is a tourist?"

"Yeah."

"I heard he's a notorious mercenary, head of a black-hat PMC."

His mouth quirks. The motion highlights a scar on his lip, visible even in the low light from the dash. Miles mentioned that scar. Shaw says, "It's a common name."

She considers this, wondering how many versions of Jon Helm he controls. Each one no doubt supplied with a flawless history, full documentation, biometric confirmation. She wonders if someone in the American intelligence community helped him set it all up, or if he bought versions of the name on the black market.

"I thought it would take longer to find you," she says. "Were you already here in Rabat?"

"No. I wasn't here."

She nods. Of course he wouldn't keep his operation here. He's probably based on the other side of the Atlas Mountains, in ungoverned territory. Did he come alone? Unlikely. Somewhere not far off there must be at least a few Variant Forces soldiers, assigned to guard his flanks. He implies as much when he tells her, "I've had assets out, looking for your crew." There is uncertainty in his voice. Maybe she's bait in a trap? He isn't sure yet.

She decides to play on his doubt. "You didn't find my people, did you?"

His right hand tightens on the wheel. "No."

"That's because I'm alone."

Again that tense quirk of his lips, scar flashing white. "That's hardcore, True."

"Spur-of-the-moment resolve," she admits, certain now that he has his own crew nearby, watching the approaches.

"You rogue, then?" he asks. "Not Lincoln's girl anymore?"

"For now."

"How does he feel about that?"

"I don't know. I ghosted."

A low whistle of surprise. "He won't like that."

She doesn't need Shaw to tell her that. The knot in her gut is doing the job nicely, thank you. "I did what I had to do."

"That's what it comes down to," he agrees. He asks, "You think it was Lincoln who commissioned that Sibolt to follow you?"

She's suspicious but doesn't want to admit it. "I don't know. Maybe it was Dove. Maybe he got curious."

"No. Dove's been warned to be discreet."

She touches the phone in her pocket. She assumed Dove would report her visit to Lincoln—but maybe that didn't happen and she really is on her own, with no chance of backup at all.

You chose it, she reminds herself.

But she's also reminded of Shaw's associates, and it comes to her that Hussam's little brother, Rihab, might want to know about a Requisite Operations soldier gone astray. Rihab was supposed to be the filmmaker behind Hussam's execution videos.

Shaw senses something. A change in her breathing maybe, or the sudden fixed focus of her gaze. Or her hand on the door latch. "Something I need to know about?" he asks.

"No." In her mind she reviews the moves she'd have to make to open the door, to roll out into the street, even as she turns her head to meet his gaze. "It's something *I* need to know. Is Rihab here somewhere, with you?"

"Late to be asking that question."

"I didn't get to ask a lot of questions."

"Yeah, you took a hell of a chance, that's for sure." He adds, "Rihab doesn't know about you, and I sure as fuck am not going to tell him. He knows better than to show up here."

"He's not your client?"

"No. He'd rather kill me than pay me money. Revenge for his beloved brother, even though the prick hates Hussam almost as much as I do."

"Hussam said you worked for him."

"I took his money. I take anyone's money." His voice grows harsh. "I help them make money. Because what fascinates me, True, are the levels of depravity people are willing to engage in to earn a few dollars. No sense of perspective. Full throttle, over the cliff."

Her cheeks heat up in the wake of this outburst. Her mouth is dry with tension.

He adds, "I saw your crew got busted in the PI."

She breathes deeply, striving for calm. He must have seen a news report. He must have a digital assistant searching for mentions of ReqOps, of Lincoln . . . and of her? "A misunderstanding," she tells him softly.

"You found an ex-priest tortured by Saomong."

"Yes." Her heart races. She fears for Daniel. "He's no harm to you."

"He told you what happened?"

"Some of it."

"Tough bastard," Shaw says with grudging admiration. "Thought sure he wouldn't live out that day."

Her voice is soft, soothing, almost submissive when she says, "You weren't all that surprised to get my message."

"No, I was. Not what I was expecting. But I'm not surprised someone's following you. You got any other guesses about the Sibolts?"

She considers mentioning the biomimetic hawk in the Philippines but rejects the idea, not wanting to feed his suspicions. "No. No other guesses."

A pause. She turns in her seat, looking back, but the street behind is dark.

"You expecting someone, True?"

She settles back in her seat. "I think we're both trying to understand the terrain, the potential threats."

"Yeah, that's always the trick."

"You're part of the terrain." Her voice is cautious, feeling her way. "You've got people out there covering you, guarding your flanks. Don't you? Variant Forces soldiers."

A grunt of amusement or annoyance. She can't tell. He hesitates as if weighing his words. Then tells her, "It's a modern company. Relies heavily on automation."

So maybe they are alone?

"The State Department described Variant Forces as a syndicate of independent operators." She looks at him sideways. "Financed and organized by you?"

"You want to know how to set up a pirate PMC, True? I'll tell you the secret. Don't trust anyone. And make sure you hold all the keys."

She thinks about this. Considers the little she knows of his operation. Then speculates: "The first key, that's cash. You control it and distribute it generously. That lets you sit at the center of an intelligence network, fed by contractors. That's how we do it, anyway. Human intelligence. Machine surveillance. Here, in your theater of operations, you know everybody who's in the business, either directly or through intermediaries. They know you. Or they know your reputation. You're reliable. Again, that's how we do it. But our IT is in-house. I'm going to guess yours is freelance. Your programmers are probably from all over the world. No personal interest, paid well. Even so, you run an AI to check their code, confirm its security. Ensure you've got password overrides or backdoors on all the software. That how it works?"

The knuckles on his right hand whiten as he holds the wheel. "You left out one thing."

"No qualms," she says quietly. "But you already told me that."

They enter a warehouse district. Lights are on in a few buildings, but most are dark. Shaw weaves through the streets. Ahead of them, a panel door at the front of a tall warehouse begins to open. Lights come on inside, spilling out to paint the street. Shaw drives in, parking on a concrete pad just large enough for two vans. It's a loading space, surrounded by modular walls that hide the bulk of the warehouse's interior. Only a small glass-walled office is visible.

"Anyone here?" True asks.

"Still scoping the terrain?"

"Yes."

"No one's here. The way I see it, this is between you and me. No one else. Right?"

"Yes."

The panel door rattles shut behind them. He opens his door, admitting a familiar noise: the soft, rhythmic, integrated hum of precision machinery driven by quiet electric motors. She opens her own door, sniffs at air that is cool and a little dusty. Not air conditioned and even so, there's no scent of industrial chemicals or exhaust. "Printer factory?" she asks.

"That's what most of these warehouses are."

She studies him across the hood of the SUV, under the day-light glow of ceiling lights. He's six-two, maybe six-three. Lean to the point of being underweight. His cheeks are gaunt, his dark blond hair shot through with gray and starting to thin. If he's carrying a weapon, she can't see it . . . except of course the centipede bracelet, its mandible presently hidden. "Is this place secure?" she asks him.

"Good enough."

"You aren't worried we'll be followed here?"

He studies her in turn through the gleaming transparent screen of his AR visor. A wary gaze, but coolly rational. "I'm expecting it. I like to know who my enemies are."

"Then you do have someone watching over us?"

"Not someone."

She recalls his description of Variant Forces as a modern com-pany relying on automation. "Autonomous surveillance, sure. But you've got someone in the control room?"

"Autonomous response, too. You sound worried, True."

Of course she's worried. She's remembering the Sibolt, and she thinks of Renata, too. "You're saying you trust your mechs with a lethal response?"

"No qualms," he reminds her.

Lincoln believes Shaw to be behind the car bomb at ReqOps headquarters. True would like to hear Shaw deny it—but does it matter?

Not tonight, she decides. She is the first to look away, reminding herself she's not here to judge his guilt or innocence. But he's good at reading people. She knows that when he asks, "Are you my enemy, True?"

She answers honestly, "Maybe later. Not tonight."

"Good. I need a drink. Come on."

A door opens as if in response to his gaze. The whispering of electronic machinery jumps in volume.

She follows him onto a factory floor that is only a little larger than a backyard swimming pool. Four midsize factory printers hum pleasantly, but she can't see what they're producing because their work stages are shielded—which means it's hot work, involving lasers. At the back of the factory floor, a stairway takes them to a loft that must have been intended as an office, but it's set up as a Spartan apartment with a cot, a couple of folding chairs, a small refrigerator, a few glasses, and a bottle of vodka, barely touched. "You're not here much," she says.

"No." He pours a shot. Gives her an inquiring look. "One for you?"

She shakes her head. Moves to the window to look out over the factory floor. A trolley is in the aisle. With precise movements of its robotic arms, it extracts a product from one of the printers: the narrow, matte-gray barrel of a rifle.

Where to start? Maybe he's wondering the same thing. He moves up beside her, making no noise so that she startles at his unexpected proximity. She smells the vodka, feels the heat of his skin, senses his gravity. Instinct warns her to retreat. But she ignores instinct's good advice.

Moving slowly, deliberately, hoping not to startle either him or the centipede bracelet into a defensive reaction, she turns and touches the back of his left hand, his scarred hand—not the hand with the centipede.

He doesn't like it. He pulls away but she grasps his wrist—her grip firm, insistent—while she watches his face, watches the corded muscles of his neck, ready to dodge a blow if it comes to that, although she's not sure she could move fast enough. His skin is warm, slightly damp beneath coarse hair.

She feels him give in, the tension in his arm easing just a little. She releases a breath she wasn't aware of holding and turns his arm over, pushes his sleeve up. He growls, "Who the fuck told you?"

There on his forearm is the tattoo exactly as Miles described it: the cross, the flames, the banner inscribed with her son's name and the epithet *The Last Good Man*. In a husky voice she says, "Tell me a story, Shaw Walker. The story of what really happened in that Burmese forest. All these years, I thought it was just a mission gone bad. But it was worse than that." She looks up again, her gaze meeting his through the screen of his AR visor. "Wasn't it?"

"*Shit*," he whispers. Gently, he reclaims his arm, moves away. She steps back too, leans against the glass, crosses her arms. Waiting.

He retreats into a corner at the opposite end of the window. "Short version," he says, pulling his sleeve back down. "We were caught by surprise and we got hammered. When we tried to retreat, we were outnumbered, outmaneuvered, and they killed us."

A perfect summary of what True has been told but she knows there's more. "The plot is in the details."

He looks out across the factory floor. "You ever go there?" he asks. "After?"

"No."

His chest rises and falls in a long sigh. "We were left there to die. That's the first truth you need to know."

"I've learned that much already."

He looks surprised at these words, almost grateful . . . as if he had not expected her to believe it.

"Tell me the rest," she urges. "Tell me what really happened. Tell me why Diego had to die."

IN THE FOREST

We were on a punitive mission.

The Saomong Cooperative Cybernetic Army had claimed responsibility for the shoot-down of Flight 137, and the president decided to believe them. No one wanted a trial. So Rogue Lightning was tasked with rendering justice. No prisoners. Just take out Saomong CCA's leadership quickly, quietly, with minimal collateral damage.

We went in on a dark night under heavy clouds. Lightning on the horizon and no lights at all visible on the ground. We came in low, across contested territory, on a stealthed bird—crewed in those days, not autonomous. I was sitting in the open door, ready to drop when we reached our insertion point, with my team set to follow. There were six of us. Diego was behind me, his hand a solid weight on my shoulder. After him were Francis Hue, Jesse Powers, Hector Chapin, and Mason Abanov.

We slowed, drifted, went into a hover. The crew chief trying to sell me on the idea that we'd reached the drop point. I couldn't see a damn thing. Not until I pulled down my night vision lenses, and that was worse.

We were twenty meters above a tangled regrowth forest—all bamboo and spindly trees—weedy shit that had popped up after the old forest was logged out. Under the rotor wash it looked like a seething, rain-blurred, bottomless chaos. The rain was coming down like nails. A gust hit us and rocked the ship. Diego's hand tightened on my shoulder. He wanted to make sure I didn't go over the edge before we had a rope.

The crew chief pitched the rope out and signaled me. Time to bail.

I must have weighed close to three hundred pounds with my armor, my pack, my weapon, but I was riding the adrenaline of the mission and I felt good. I grabbed onto the rope, hands and feet, and dropped into the night. Hard rain. Like static against my helmet. I was soaked before I was halfway to the ground but it didn't matter.

I wanted that mission. I'd told myself it was going to be like reliving history. We'd be on our own, going in under radio silence because we knew if we made noise, Saomong would detect it and come looking. We carried the comm equipment anyway, of course—even if we weren't talking, we were going to try to listen for updates from Command—but no calls home until we were done.

The CCA was vicious, no question, but they were smart bastards. Better at electronic warfare than us and this was their home territory. We knew they had aerial assets in place. Sophisticated UAV platforms, equipped for detection, jamming, spoofing. Quality toys that were probably going to prevent Command from easily talking to us.

We could have sent in fighters to take them out, but if we did that, Saomong would know we were coming. The brain trust we were after would disappear, and we'd be escalating a hidden war into something visible—so that wasn't going to happen.

It was up to us to infiltrate, catch their leadership in the open, and take care of things quietly. If we couldn't get an incoming signal, that meant we wouldn't have even a surveillance drone to watch the activity around us. I was okay with that. The mission was going to test our skills and I was looking forward to it.

A jerk in the rope just before I hit told me Diego was on his way down. The insertion site was a tiny patch of water-smoothed rock alongside a muddy, rushing stream, with the sapling forest leaning in around it. It was like landing a skydive. That fast. As soon as my boots touched ground I scrambled out of the way. Diego was right behind me. He cleared out quick, blazing a path into the trees, while I stood by to make sure everybody got down okay.

In just a few seconds, we were all on the ground. I gave the crew chief a thumbs-up and followed Mason into cover, listening to the engine noise as our ride pulled out. I couldn't hear it for long. Not with the wind. It gushed through the trees, sounding like a river flowing overhead, with the squeaks and groans of branches grinding against each other. Every breath I took smelled of rain and sweet rot. And it was cold—a chill on the air that surprised me.

The terrain wasn't what we'd expected either. Like I said, it was regrowth forest and it was tight. All young trees, just inches between them. We had to weave our way. Slow going. And the rain, blurring our lenses. We couldn't see three meters.

Diego was on point, steering by GPS, but after twenty minutes he pulled up and we conferenced, our helmets close together so we could keep our voices low.

"GPS isn't corresponding to terrain," he said. "Saomong's got it spoofed." He knew the electronics better than any of us, so I wasn't going to question him.

"You remember how to use a map?" I asked.

He cracked a smile. "That's how I know we're off course."

"You're our scout, then. Get us there."

It wasn't easy in the dark, in the rain, but it wasn't the navigation that really slowed us down. It was the forest. Why the fuck did no one tell us the trees would be like that? We scraped our packs, squeezing between them. And we kept getting hung up. We'd have to drop back and find another way. I started to worry we wouldn't make our destination in time.

Going in, we were following solid intelligence. That's what I thought. Detailed intelligence. It was a cooperative mission, American and Chinese.

Somehow the field operatives had learned that our target would be passing a known point on a road, just after dawn. We needed to get there in time to set up an ambush. That was going to be our chance to quietly cut off Saomong's head and we could not be late.

But nowhere in the pre-mission briefing did anyone think to mention the trees.

And we couldn't go in by road, we couldn't use any roads, because the roads were mined and electronically monitored. Anyone without proper credentials wasn't going to get far. The local civilians didn't even try anymore. If they wanted to visit between villages, they blazed paths in the forest like we were doing. Only Saomong and their collaborators used the roads.

Francis was tasked with monitoring transmissions from Command. After two hours he called another conference. "EW's picking up. Saomong is working hard to jam across our frequencies. The software is trying to clean it up, but not much is getting through."

"We expected communication problems," I reminded them.

"Yeah, but what worries me," Francis said, "is we don't have a way to tell if it's a cautionary action because Saomong leadership is about to move, or if they know we're here."

Jesse was all sunshine despite the storm. "Don't worry. We're good. Because if they knew we were here, they'd be after us."

Mason, old and grim and reliable, put a stop to that happy talk. "If they're after us, we won't know until they start shooting."

"Truth," I said. "And nothing we can do about it. We focus on the job. Let's move."

It took us until oh-four-forty to reach the ambush site. "Two hours behind schedule," Mason grumbled. But hell, by that point I was relieved we'd gotten there before our deadline.

The mission planners had picked a point where the road curved like a big smile along the base of a steep slope. "This would have been a good position," Hector whispered, "if not for the damn trees."

He was right. The trees crowded together there just like everywhere else. We could hide easily enough, but we couldn't move quickly and we couldn't get an unobstructed view of the road unless we were almost standing in it. This was a problem, because we were required to collect photographic evidence proving we had targeted the right people. It didn't matter to Command if we collected that evidence before or after the ambush, but dead targets still had to be identifiable, and that's not easy to guarantee when the woods light up.

One more minor point: we wanted to be long gone by the time the CCA's foot soldiers came swarming out of their village barracks.

So, yeah, the trees were a problem, but not enough to stop the mission. We started setting up.

We'd brought with us a weird land-line system that let us wire up a temporary network. It used fine-gauge fiber optic lines. Clumsy. Easy to tangle, easy to break, but while we were sitting still, strung out along the road, it would let us stay in contact without using the radios. Better than nothing.

I reviewed the plan one more time. "We spread out. Take up separate positions. Diego takes point, I follow. We try to scope 'em, get the pictures we need. Once I clear you to shoot, we blow hell out of any vehicle on the road. Incinerate 'em. Then we retreat upslope. Rendezvous on the other side of the hill, where we made our last stream crossing. Clear?"

"Yes, sir."

"Simple and clear."

"Too easy."

Idiots. They liked to play the Hollywood role, that cocky confident attitude. But they were professionals beneath it or they wouldn't have been there with me. Diego, too. He'd been blooded in Kunar. He wasn't a rookie anymore. The mission prep had been thorough, every piece of equipment checked and triple-checked, the geography memorized, and the faces of the targets memorized too.

"Hand me your lead," I told Diego.

I plugged his comm line into an adjunct socket on my audio and handed my own lead to Mason. Francis, Hector, and Jesse hooked up one after the other. "Comm check," I said. "Start with D and move down the line."

"Delgado."

"Walker."

"Abanov."

"Hue."

"Chapin."

"Powers."

"Thumbs-up if you heard everyone."

Gloved hands flashed the gesture. We were all good.

"Mason," I said, "you stay here. Jesse and Francis, spread out down the road."

I gestured to Diego and he set off, weaving silently between the trees in the direction we expected our quarry to come from. The fiber-optic line shimmered behind him, a spider web in night vision, linking us together. I kept close, only a few steps behind, until I'd gone sixty meters. I stopped when I found a place where the trees were a little more open so I could look down between them at the road. "This is my position," I said, testing my angle through the scope.

Diego went on, the cable paying out behind him, laying down across fallen twigs and leaves and catching in the ferns, until he found a vantage another sixty, sixty-five meters along. "Got a good view of the road from here," he said, whispering over comms. "I can see eighty meters or so. Should be able to scope everybody who's not under canvas."

"You do that, you get us a confirmation, and we can burn 'em in a crossfire when they get this far."

"Roger that."

We settled in to wait in the dark and the rain. It wouldn't be long—I hoped. But the road was half flooded, a mud trap. Saomong might cancel their expedition. They might be late. We didn't have a way to know ahead of time. We would only know when Diego got a visual on the vehicle and passed the word that they were coming.

I wasn't used to working like that. None of us were. We were used to Command providing oversight, watching the surrounding region with a UAV, forwarding intel. In a normal operation we'd be told when Saomong got in their vehicles, when the ignition turned over, when they got bogged down in a mudhole and spun their wheels.

None of that was getting through. We were operating off stale intelligence. It was like being hunkered down in the heart of a mystery. All we could be sure about was what we could see, and that was the green-tinted chaos of a wind-tossed forest with rain glittering like flakes in a fucking snow globe. I loved it, I did.

Twenty minutes later, things changed. The rain backed off. The wind retreated. Drops were still falling off the leaves and we could hear the wind above us, but on the forest floor no wind was blowing. A faint mist condensed right out of the night and swarms of mosquitoes started flying—but we didn't have much flesh exposed and our faces were painted. We were okay.

Then Diego spoke in this voice that made my hair stand on end, low and hesitant, like he couldn't believe what he was seeing. "Shaw," he said, "take a look behind you, five o'clock, twelve meters upslope."

I didn't want to give my position away, so I turned slowly, silently. Studied the slope above me, but all I saw were trees. A million fucking trees, spindly trees with moss on their trunks, ferns on the ground between them, and this mist, barely visible, padding the air.

"I don't see anything," I said.

From farther down the line, Francis said, "Fuck. I do."

Then I did too. A thread of light. That's all it was. Shooting between the trees. It lasted a fraction of a second. If I'd blinked, I would have missed it. In the corner of my eye I saw another thread, this one way down the line, close to Francis.

"Laser pulses," Mason said over comms. "The NVG's are picking it up. That's why we're seeing it. It's pitch dark out there without the lenses."

"It ain't the goddamn trees talking to each other with laser comms," Hector whispered. "Who we got on this hill with us?"

"Not who," Diego said. "I've got one only eight meters away. Got to be a device. Some kind of security system. Motion sensor. You know how it is. Saomong's smart. They know we're here."

"What the hell," I said. "You think they got this whole road surveilled? How many point sources you count?"

"I see at least six," Hector answered.

Way too many for it to be fixed surveillance. It was like the mosquitoes. Whatever was making those flashes, we'd brought it here. Our heat, our presence. We were the lure.

"Go check it out, Hector," I said. "Don't get your lines tangled."

"Do my best."

I couldn't see him from where I was. The ground was soft and wet so I couldn't hear him either. We all waited in silence.

"Jesus Christ," he whispered. "It's a fucking—"

Bam!

A short, sharp concussion. Not a gun. An explosive. Not loud either. Just loud in comparison to the silence on either side of it. The flash I saw through the trees was actinic, almost fried my NVG.

Then the forest was buzzing like a nest of wasps had come awake. Far down the line, someone started shooting.

HIRED GUNS

TRUE STANDS, ARMS crossed, one shoulder against the glass. It's cool in the office but her cheeks are flushed with fear, shock. In her mind she's in that forest, surrounded by the green-tinted dark and the endless imprisoning trunks of sapling trees.

It takes her a few seconds to register that Shaw has stopped speaking. When she does, her gaze shifts from the abstract, fixing on him. He is still in the corner where he's taken a defensive position, but it's as if the program he's running on has paused. He's motionless, mesmerized, his attention fixed on something she can't see, something playing out on the screen of his AR visor.

"What do you have?" she asks him.

He lifts his head to look at her through the glittering lens. "You figured out who's following you?"

"No."

That hard half-smile. "Looks like we get a chance to find out."

She reaches into the front pocket of her jacket, sees him tense up, and hesitates. "Easy," she urges, and slowly pulls out her MARC. She toggles the power back on, then uses her fingernail to hold down a tiny recessed button. A purple ready light comes on. "Give me a link in." She holds the visor out to him. "I want to see what you see."

He scowls behind the screen of his own AR visor, then shrugs. "Stand by." He uses his data glove to scroll through menus she can't see. Then, taking his visor off, he holds it close to hers until both devices flash, indicating identities have been exchanged and a link established.

When she puts on the MARC, she sees a livestream. It's an aerial view of the warehouse district taken from a low angle. Their location is noted by a tag, while a caption identifies the source of the video as a high-altitude UAV manufactured by Shin-Farrell. The surrounding streets are empty except for an SUV rounding a corner three blocks away.

Shaw is wearing his lens again, studying the display. All vehicles capable of autonomous navigation have identifying transponders. He says, "The ID links up with a local PMC. Hired guns. Gotta be."

True is impressed. "You've got a link into the city's database?"

"Support your local cops," he says softly. "Background report says they're a new operation. That makes them a pair of amateurs, desperate for business. They were told to follow you, but they probably don't know who you are. For sure, they got no clue who they're gonna find."

The lethal certainty in that statement sends a shiver through her. She finds herself trying to talk him down. "Come on. They might not find us at all. The way they're driving, it's like they think they've got the right neighborhood, but they don't know the exact address."

"You're a nice lady, True."

The truck stops in the middle of a street. A window goes down, two devices take flight. Tags pop up on the video, labeling the objects as Sibolt surveillance drones.

Shaw snorts in contempt. "That didn't work so well the first time, gentlemen. And around here you don't get a second chance."

Fear rises in True's throat, but not fear for herself. She needs to defuse this situation before someone gets hurt. Right action demands it. "Hey, it's just surveillance. No need to start a war." Gentle words, feigned confidence, as she moves toward the door. "It's not like they tried to hurt me before. I'm going to talk to them, ask who hired them. If we keep it civil, maybe we can help each other out."

Better to take the risk herself than to let Shaw take action.

His eyebrows rise above the frame of his visor, and then his scarred mouth wrenches up on one side. "Hold on. If you want to play it that way, you're welcome to it. But don't go unarmed." He palms the lock on the safe. "Take a pistol, at least. Insurance."

Inside the safe is a small collection of firearms. He takes out a pistol, hands it to her. "Nine millimeter, homemade, unmarked."

Printed downstairs, no doubt. It's lightweight with a short barrel, easy to stash in a pocket. She checks the load. She would probably be safer if she went unarmed, but she slides the pistol into her jacket pocket anyway.

"Let's do a voice link," he says. He kills her video feed, leaving her with a clear field of view. Then he puts through a new link. She accepts it. "Comm check."

"Comm check affirmed," she says. She grabs her pack. Shaw is resting hip-cocked on the desk, entranced by his display. "Hey," she says.

"Yeah?" He doesn't look up.

"Don't disappear, okay? I need to hear the rest of that story."

That quirk of his lips as he meets her gaze. "Ma'am, I am not the one you need to worry about. Let's make sure *you* get back, okay?"

"You gonna stick with me, then?"

"Hell, yeah. You're under my wing now, True, and I am your fucking guidance counselor."

Just like that. Adopted.

Her eyes close in relief. She breathes out through pursed lips, bleeding off tension. "Okay, then."

For now, at least, they are on the same side.

"When you get downstairs," he adds, "wait by the door. I'll let you know when you can egress without the Sibolts watching."

It's a brief wait but time enough for True to reflect on what she's seen of Shaw. She realizes now she had thought to find a broken, unstable man, but what she found is more frightening. If asked to describe him, she would use words like *calm, logical, rational.* A man in complete control of himself. He is also the mercenary Miles encountered in the desert, who supervised the execution of innocent men—she doesn't doubt it—because alongside Shaw Walker's calm demeanor is a sense of lethal purpose. It's there, evident in his nature, clear as a cobra's hiss.

Her thoughts turn again to his setup, to Variant Forces. This warehouse is part of his operation. No doubt he has other such places. His Arkinsons are housed somewhere. He has to have staff to help administer things. He has to have soldiers under contract.

Where are they? Do they know where he is?

He doesn't want them to know his business.

Trust no one. That, he said, was the secret to setting up a pirate PMC.

Shaw speaks through comms. "You're clear to exit. Turn right and proceed quickly past this building and the next one."

"Roger that."

Despite the unknowns, and despite his history, his lethality, they are operating in tandem tonight. The agreement has been made, and she can go forth or she can go home.

She's not ready to go home, so she steps outside.

Her slim pack hangs low on her back. Her right hand is tucked into her pocket, fingers resting lightly around the pistol's grip. There are no streetlights and no lights seeping from the nearby buildings, but the moon is bright and through her MARC she can see every detail of the empty street. She can hear a steady low hum of printers. Or maybe she feels it as a faint vibration rising up from the ground. From a few streets away comes the static of tire noise.

She follows Shaw's instructions, walking quickly, staying close to the building. A narrow alley divides it from the next building in the complex. She trots across the open space and keeps going.

"At the end of the warehouse, turn right," Shaw says. "Okay, you see the angled driveway to your left? Take it. You've got twelve seconds to make it to the other end. Go."

She sprints the length of the alley, holding tight to the pistol so it doesn't bounce against her gut. She can see that the alley spills into a wider street ahead. Short of the end, she pulls up. Shaw says, "Good job. They're a block over, but their Sibolt just found you. So they should roll in shortly. If you're still into it, go say hello."

She takes a deep breath, squares her shoulders, and moves ahead until she has a clear view of the cross street. She doesn't move away from the alley. She wants the option to retreat if it comes to that.

She hears the static crackle of the truck's racing tires, then it screeches into sight around the corner, headlights off. Her hand is still in her pocket as she tries to strike a nonchalant pose. *No worries here. I'm just a harmless little girl.* She came out to meet them because she believes their assignment was to watch her, not to kill her. She hopes she's right, but her chest is tight and she's sweating under her arms all the same.

The truck is a four-door SUV, desert brown, tinted glass. She can't see inside. It brakes hard, stopping ten meters away. The front doors open. Two men get out. They step clear. Neither wears an AR visor, relying on moonlight. The driver is an older man, straight-backed, strong-featured, both hair and beard neatly trimmed and shot through with gray. He appears calm and self-assured—in contrast to a partner who is younger, bulkier, more heavily bearded, at least three inches shorter, and who walks with a bully's strut.

It's immediately clear she's misjudged the situation, because both men are carrying assault rifles. They haven't aimed their weapons at her. Not yet. But her working theory, that they are not here to kill her, seems a bit strained at this point.

They yell at her in Arabic, telling her to put her hands in the air. Shaw sounds amused when he asks, "You gonna do it?"

Nope.

Her heart races; she keeps her shaking hands hidden in her pockets. Inappropriate time, but nevertheless she thinks of Alex and how pissed off he's going to be if she gets herself killed even before he has a chance to file for divorce. That would not be fair. Still, she is not going to surrender. Gray and the bully need to know that, first thing.

Her guess is that they both speak some English and if she's wrong, well, maybe they have access to a translation program. The bully, at least, is wearing an earpiece that looks a lot like a TINSL. So, in a voice carefully modulated to sound strong but nonbelligerent, she asks, "Who hired you? I want a name."

The bully doesn't take well to her defiance. A flush darkens his face where it's visible above his beard and he yells at her again, this time in English, "Hands in the air! *Now.*"

Her chest tightens, even as she thinks, *A man should be able to control his temper.*

Gray appears to share this sentiment. He speaks in an undertone, harsh words for his partner. But it's another sound that draws True's attention. A distant, waspish buzzing. She wants to make sure her assailants notice it too, so she lets her gaze drift up into the hazy night sky. She doesn't see anything. She doesn't expect to. But when she looks again at the two soldiers, the dynamic has changed. Gray has realized they're in trouble. He gestures at his partner to move back to the truck and the bully complies. Even he has recognized that this encounter is escalating.

They don't move fast enough.

The waspish buzz ramps up, a dopplered assault of sound as a dark meteorite impacts the hood of the truck, smashing through it into the engine block where it explodes in a confined burst of brilliant light and a harsh concussion that True feels in her chest.

The two soldiers throw themselves clear, diving for the ground. True ducks back into the alley, using the moment to get the pistol out of her pocket. With the weapon secured in a two-handed grip, she peeks out again.

The two men are face down on the street. The engine block of their truck is shattered. "Damn it, Shaw," she whispers. "I came here to circumvent a war, not start one."

"So get on it, ma'am. Best you exert some authority while they're still down on the ground."

Yeah. Good advice. Already the two are looking up, looking around, reassessing the situation. She decides to clarify things.

She steps out of the alley. Determined to remain polite, she keeps the pistol pointed at the asphalt—although it's a section of asphalt right in front of the bully's nose. In a soft voice made gruff by the dryness of her throat, she warns them, "Stay on the ground or the next kamikaze targets you."

Anyway, she hopes Shaw has another projectile or two in reserve.

When she hears his low amused grunt, she decides this was a good bet.

Both men still have a hand on their assault rifles, but they don't try to pick them up and they don't try to get up. True suspects the faint sound of a buzzing wasp is encouraging their cooperation. She says, "I don't want to see you hurt. And I'm sure you don't want to hurt me, right?"

"We don't want to hurt you, ma'am," Gray says in accented English.

The bully says nothing. The look on his face doesn't support his partner's words, but True decides not to comment on that. Instead she tells them, "I'm the nervous type. I get jumpy. So take your hands off your weapons, okay? I've got just a couple of questions and then we can go our separate ways."

"We are not here to hurt you, ma'am," Gray repeats as he slides his hand off his assault rifle. He orders his partner to do the same, but the bully only glares at True, a look that promises a very unpleasant future should she lose control of this encounter. The wasp buzz grows louder. She watches his face as he processes that fact. After a few seconds, he takes his hand off the weapon.

"Make sure they don't touch those guns again," Shaw warns her.

"That's the plan," she whispers.

"Sure. I just want you to understand. It would be bad."

The way he says it, it's as if there is an inevitability to the situation, but she doesn't question him. There isn't time. A new note is playing against the quiet of the night: a faint, faraway siren. Maybe it has nothing to do with the explosion that destroyed the engine block but she doesn't want to wait around to find out, doesn't want to stay any longer than it takes to ask the questions she came to ask.

"What I want to know," she tells them, "is who hired you to follow me. And what were you supposed to do when you caught up?"

To her surprise, the bully volunteers an answer. "We work for your business partner," he says in lilting, contemptuous English. "The one you are here to betray."

Lincoln? She doesn't believe it. Lincoln would not hire uncredentialed thugs. "Damn it, I want a name. What is the name?"

"Chinese name," Gray says nervously. "Li."

"Li what?"

The bully says, "Li Guiying."

True is so surprised, her mind blanks of everything but that name. *Li Guiying.* The roboticist. Tamara's colleague. What does Li Guiying have to do with anything?

"That name mean something to you?" Shaw asks.

She doesn't answer. She questions the thugs instead. "What did Li Guiying want you to do?"

"Follow you," Gray says. "Find out who you are working with. Tag him. That's all. Not hurt anybody."

"Then why the guns?"

Even as she asks the question, she notices the bully's hand moving again to his weapon. "Don't touch it," she tells him, but her warning is smothered by the sharp buzz of a descending wasp.

This time she gets a clear glimpse of the device as it drops. Its fuselage is a flattened, aerodynamic diamond shape, around six inches long and less than three across at its widest point, covered in a dark photovoltaic skin. Its wings are surfaced in PV too. They're long and narrow, mounted on ball joints. Each supports a single rotor. A tiny third rotor sparkles in a vertical mount on the shark-fin tail. Four jointed legs flex to cushion the mech's abrupt landing as it smacks down against the back of the bully's neck. At the same time, the wings sweep back and up. There, revealed on the dorsal surface of the nearest wing, visible for a fraction of a second, a familiar emblem. It's too small, too far away to see in detail, but True knows it anyway. There is one just like it at home, displayed alongside Diego's formal army portrait. Dark star fields flanking a bright sun, angled lightning bolts splitting the sections.

The bully rolls to grab his gun. The mech's legs must have

hooked into his collar or his flesh because it doesn't dislodge. It holds on. As his fingers touch steel, it explodes.

True squeezes her eyes shut against the blast, spinning into the alley, hunkering down against the wall. "Tell me you didn't just do that," she says in a furious whisper.

"I didn't," Shaw assures her. "The swarm is autonomous. It's been assigned to protect you and that's what it's doing."

Every word calm. Utterly rational. A man in control.

It's True whose breathing has gone ragged, whose hands shake.

She looks up from where she's crouched to see the bully's headless corpse feeding an oozing pool of blood. Gray is a couple of meters away, still on the ground, his blood-spattered face staring in shock at the corpse.

She flinches as a third explosion—more distant—booms out of the night sky, echoing off the buildings. "The swarm just took out a surveillance drone," Shaw tells her. "Probably police."

She retreats down the alley at a run.

ICE-COLD

THE WAIL AND stutter of sirens rises in the distance as True flees down the alley. It reminds her of the chorus of howling dogs on the outskirts of Tadmur. That night, they had the legal authority of a bounty behind their actions, but tonight no documentation protects her from the consequences of what just happened, of what should *not* have happened.

"You overreacted," she pants, not knowing if Shaw is still there, still listening. "You didn't have to kill him!"

Two more explosions go off behind her.

"*Fuck! You're a fucking maniac!*"

This time he responds, his voice calm and absurdly soothing despite what he has to say: "You know why autonomous systems make good soldiers, True? It's because they follow the rules of engagement, even in tricky situations. They don't let sentiment or doubt or mercy get in the way." Shifting to a matter-of-fact tone, he adds, "Turn right at the next corner."

She slows almost to a stop. "That's not the way I came."

"Do it, True."

What choice? A wrong move now might make her the next target of the swarm.

All in, then. She jogs to the corner as the sirens are multiplied by echoes resounding off the buildings. "Where am I going?" she asks. She sounds surprisingly calm. Just a slight tremor in her voice.

"Past the next building on the left. There's a small parking lot. You see it?"

"Yes. I see an autonomous cab with the interior lit."

"That's the one. Get inside."

It's a tiny, two-passenger vehicle. She gets in. The light goes out, the windows darken. The wailing of the sirens is muffled. She gets the belt on and the cab slides out of its parking space on a silent electric motor.

"Li Guiying," Shaw says.

"A robotics engineer."

It's an absurdly inadequate answer. He must have searched the name; he knows that much already. But True is distracted. She's thinking about the dead man: her responsibility for what happened to him, and her liability. They are not the same things. She went to meet the two men, thinking it was right action; she was motivated by worry over what Shaw might do if she didn't defuse the situation. But the situation escalated. A man is dead—maybe two men are dead—and she is fleeing the scene.

I let this happen.

"*Damn* it, True." His harsh tone anchors her. "Don't spin out on me. You've seen blood before."

Oh yeah. Roger that. She's seen worse in combat but this wasn't combat. A man—an idiot, yes, but a *man*—got his head blown off on a peaceful street in a peaceful city. And she doesn't want to ask but she's pretty sure the old man is dead too. No witnesses.

Maybe the truck had a dash cam, although that was probably destroyed when the engine block went up.

"I didn't come here to trigger that kind of shit," she tells him.

"I need you to tell me who this Li Guiying is to you."

She shudders, understanding that what happened doesn't mean anything to him. It doesn't deserve so much as a comment or a denial.

He adds, "I've got you as co-author on a paper with her, along with six other names. What else is there?"

"Nothing. Not really."

The car is leaving the warehouse district, joining a light flow of traffic. True leans forward, cycles through the dash display until it shows a map of the cab's planned route: a circuitous path marked in green that runs past the tourist district before turning toward the ocean, doubling back, and ending at a neighborhood less than a kilometer from her hotel.

She leans back again, working her cheeks to get moisture in her mouth. "Am I bait?" she asks. "You trying to see if something's following me?"

"Yes."

"And?"

"Not that I can see. Not so far. Tell me about this Li Guiying. You must know her."

"Sure, I know her. I don't work with her. She's not my business partner."

"Would she like to be?"

True thinks about this, recalling Tamara's teasing words, *She likes you, True. I can't imagine why, but she does. She thinks of you as a friend.*

"I don't know what she wants," True admits. "I only met her once in person but she's friendly to me. Too friendly. It gets awkward. But she's a really good engineer. She's mostly in academia now, but—" True breaks off in midsentence, thinking of the hawk that flew past Daniel's house . . . and the biomimetic deer.

"Say it, True. Whatever the hell you're thinking."

She does: "What kind of surveillance did you have on my house?"

Two seconds of silence. When he answers, there's suspicion in his voice. "Why?"

"What kind of surveillance?" she insists.

"Nothing. You were not on my hit list and I was not running any kind of surveillance on your house."

They had all believed Shaw was behind the ongoing surveillance. They interpreted it as a warning, clear notice that he'd mapped their lives and could hit them at any time.

He asks, "Did Li Guiying have you under surveillance at home, too?"

"Why would she? There's no reason for it. I only know her because we attended a seminar together, six or seven years ago. That paper you found with my name and hers, it's the collected presentations. I remember, at the time, she'd just moved into the private sector. She was networking, making new contacts. Before that, she worked for Kai Yun Strategic."

"Kai Yun?"

His voice is abruptly lower, with that lethal note she heard before. Her own tone softens in response. It's instinct. She speaks innocuously, determined not to trigger his temper. "A Chinese government company. Cutting edge technological development."

"I know what Kai Yun is." That low, ice-cold tone.

A flush prickles in her pores. Her voice sharpens. "What do you want me to tell you, Shaw?"

"Tell me what she did for them."

"As far as I know, the same thing she does now. Autonomous swarms. She's strictly civilian though. I remember she told me she won't work in the defense industry."

"Kai Yun *is* defense industry," he growls.

"Yes, and that's where she got her start. But that was years ago and she's done with it. That's what she told me. She works on humanitarian projects now. She wants to make a positive contribution to the world, and she has. She's done good things."

An alert pops up, telling her the voice link to Shaw has closed.

"*Fuck,*" she whispers in frustration. What did Shaw have to do with Kai Yun? Did he work for them? Was he running from them? "Damn it, Shaw," she says out loud, using her data glove to reestablish the link. "Don't you disappear on me."

The link stays closed.

Frustrated, she drops the MARC on the seat beside her and gets her burner phone out instead. Powers it up and calls him.

No answer.

She berates herself. She should have said nothing about Li

Guiying. Held back the information. Traded for what she needs to know, but she didn't *know*. She didn't know Guiying mattered. Not to her, not to him.

Damn it.

Now he's gone.

FREE WILL

Do what needs to be done.

She checks herself for bloodstains, but she's clean. The pistol is still in her pocket. Logic tells her to get rid of it but instinct's advice is the opposite. She decides to hold on to it.

She puts her visor back on, then instructs the cab to pull over. The navigation screen shows her still a half kilometer from her planned destination. She notes the address, then resets the screen. The cab doesn't ask for payment, so presumably she's been riding on Shaw's credit.

She gets out. As the cab drives off, she starts walking. Not toward her hotel, not yet. She wants to know if he's watching, if she's being followed. She walks past expensive apartment complexes towards the ocean, waiting for him to call.

He doesn't.

After a few minutes she calls him again.

No answer.

It's very late. The streets are lined with parked cars but empty of traffic. She stops in front of the dark display in a clothing store's window. Activating the MARC's sky survey function, she turns in a slow circle, but the program picks up only a single municipal UAV. No private devices at all.

Too bad she's gained the attention of someone on the ground. She takes off her visor, slipping it into her right pocket to obscure the shape of the pistol as a police car glides up beside her. The window goes down. The officer—she is a woman—leans over to speak out the window in stern and heavily accented English: "Are you well, ma'am? Have you lost your way?"

True answers in Arabic phrases: "Shokran, ana kewayisa." *Thank you, I am well.* She shows the officer her passport and her hotel keycard. Tourists should be handled gently and left to their foreign ways whenever possible. So the officer bids her goodnight. True is sure, though, that she has become an object of interest for the municipal UAV on patrol overhead.

She reviews her choices:

Return to the hotel—where she'd be easy to find if anyone is looking. Or head for the airport and hope to get a flight out before she's tied to tonight's incident. By some calculations that would be the smart move. But she walked out on Alex when she came here, she broke the bond of trust between herself and Lincoln, and she wants something back for that.

She wants the truth from Shaw Walker. All of it.

In that context, the watchful eye of the municipal UAV is the least of her concerns. Until the local police can link her to the unwitnessed crime in the warehouse district, she is just another lonely middle-aged tourist.

She walks on, slowly, pondering the question of Li Guiying.

The robotics engineer used to be employed by Kai Yun but she left the technology company years ago. Six years ago? Seven? True is uncertain. It never mattered before. She considers calling Guiying, asking her straight up, *What the fuck?* What the fuck are you doing having me followed? What am I to you?

Before she can decide if this is a bold or a foolish move, her tablet buzzes with an alert. She pulls it out of her thigh pocket. Finds a message from the beetle left on watch back at her hotel. From its hidden perch on the hotel's façade, it's been recording everyone who's gone in or out of the hotel tonight. And it's finally found a set of familiar faces—faces that are absent from most public databases but that exist within the private collection True has compiled, and that are associated with a private military company.

She has just passed under a canopy at the front of a closed café. She backtracks until she's in the canopy's shadow again. She gets out her reading glasses, huddles over the tablet to hide the screen from the view of security cameras, and studies two images. Both were taken from an awkward angle, but it doesn't matter. She doesn't need to read the tags to identify the team filing in through the hotel's front entrance. Lincoln's face is the one she registers first, his scars enhanced by shadows. He's looking up, almost directly at the camera, like he knows it's there, or suspects.

What in hell is he doing here so soon?

He should have gone home, dealt with the aftermath of the bombing. But he didn't go home. He couldn't have. To reach Rabat only hours after her own arrival, he must have booked a seat during the trans-Pacific flight and flown straight out of Los Angeles.

Just to stop me from finding Shaw?

She casts her gaze across the rest of the team and thinks that his presence here could be vendetta, and not an official ReqOps mission. He's brought Rohan with him, and Felice. That's understandable. Both are skilled and aggressive—and single. But he's got Khalid too—a respected soldier of course, but also ReqOps' newest recruit. If Lincoln is planning an operation against Shaw Walker, Khalid should not be part of it, not without months of training.

The fifth face in the picture worries her even more. Miles Dushane. What is *he* doing here? He's an ex-Ranger, sure, but he's no part of ReqOps and he's not to be trusted, not after what he's been through as Hussam's prisoner. True refuses to believe that Lincoln recruited him.

She blanks the screen, straightens up, takes off her glasses. At least there's no indication that Alex came with them. Thank you, God, for that.

She considers going back to the hotel, confronting Lincoln—but dismisses the idea. Like Shaw said, she's not Lincoln's girl anymore. She has her own agenda and she's in deep. Deeper, after tonight, and she's not done yet.

She calls Shaw. Again he doesn't answer. His nonresponse provokes her. She wonders: *Am I being toyed with or betrayed?*

Out of spiteful insistence she tries the call again, whispering, "Answer, damn you. We are *not* done."

He doesn't answer.

She texts: **We have unfinished business. You promised not to disappear.** Nothing.

She reconsiders the address where the cab was meant to take her. She tells herself that in all likelihood it's a random address. Still, it's her only lead. She slips her glasses back on and uses the tablet to find it on a map.

From above, it's a rectangular building, the roof open to a central courtyard. She shifts to street view. From this angle, she sees a private home in the Moroccan style, a riad, with its focus turned inward to the open court. Two enclosed stories are topped by a low-walled terrace on the roof, with no windows facing the street. The riad shares its side walls with the neighbors. All of the houses on the block are riads, looking exactly the same, which tells her this is a modern build. Cars on both sides of the street are parked so as not to block the large, arched doors of each residence.

Is this his home? she wonders. Or a random address?

Is he there?

She puts the tablet away, swapping it for her MARC.

It's not the time to be thinking about free will, but she thinks about it anyway as she sets out on a path projected by her visor, a path she needs to follow. It's not a choice, really. It's the gravity of what happened in Nungsan that has locked her on this course, leaving the concept of free will as nothing more than an abstract academic exercise.

AN INTERVENTION

WE'RE ALREADY TOO late, Lincoln thinks.

It's 0130 in Rabat. He's standing in True's empty hotel room in the company of a foreign liaison officer named Nadim Zaman, who ordered the hotel staff to issue him a key card after True failed to respond to a knock on the door.

"She was here," Zaman proclaims, gesturing at empty air. "The towels and the toiletries have been used. But she has gone out. Perhaps she found another hotel guest with whom to pass the night."

Rohan is in the doorway. He's dressed like a civilian in khaki cargo pants and a brown silk shirt with rolled-up sleeves, but his arms are crossed, muscles showing, and he's got a belligerent look. "That is not what happened," he says.

Nadim's eyes narrow. "When a woman disappears in the night, refusing to answer her phone, this is most often what is happening."

Nadim has made it no secret that he resents their presence here, resents the Warrant of Capture and Rendition that provides legal authority for them to pursue and detain Jon Helm, and resents that he's been assigned as their liaison. He insisted on a full inspection of their equipment and the leased vehicle they picked up at the airport—an exercise that took over an hour—before finally agreeing to look up the hotel name True had entered on her customs document.

Lincoln works to keep his voice low and his temper in check as he explains the obvious to Nadim. "Our concern is that she may be *unable* to answer her phone. She would have begun seeking leads on the location of Jon Helm the moment she arrived. It's possible she asked the wrong questions in the wrong place."

The story he told Nadim was mostly correct. They've come seeking Jon Helm, True arrived before them, they expected to meet up with her. He did not mention that True came on her own or that she may not wish to be found. He did not mention that State granted the warrant only as a least-worst option, to avoid the accusation of prior knowledge of Jon Helm's identity and the truth of what happened at Nungsan.

"You believe she has already encountered this Jon Helm?" Nadim asks.

"I don't know," Lincoln answers.

There's too much that he doesn't know; there's been too little time to prepare.

Only forty-five minutes after they lifted off from Manila, Alex came down the aisle, grim-faced, to tell him what she'd done. There was no outlet for the fury that came boiling up in his throat, not in the packed cabin of a long-haul jet less than an hour into a trans-Pacific crossing, so he clamped his teeth together and he held it down like the worst meal he'd ever eaten. If she sank a knife in his chest, it would have hurt less.

But fuck, he earned it.

He'd learned early who Shaw Walker really was: a self-righteous man, a man of absolutes, a natural leader who possessed a dangerous charisma that made him easy to love and easy to forgive, even when you'd seen his dark side. Shaw demanded everything of his soldiers—but he would do anything for them, too.

True sensed that. She knew Shaw as the last man to stand by Diego, the man who begged to stand in Diego's place. He was a bridge to her son, and maybe she saw some ghost of Diego within him.

Lincoln failed to respect that, blinded by his own sense of responsibility for what he knew Shaw had done since—his alliance with Al-Furat, the atrocities Miles had witnessed, Renata's murder. He allowed those things to happen when he'd failed to make a full report on their last action in Kunar Province. Add True's defection to that list of harmful consequences—but it stops now.

Lincoln engineered this mission, assembling his equipment and his team, from the cramped seats of commercial airliners as he worked his way to North Africa. Chris fought him on the action in a rapid-fire exchange of emails bounced off of satellites.

Chris:

> We cannot undertake another mission now. We don't have the funds, we don't have the staff, and you are needed here. The FBI is here. They're waiting to interview you.

Lincoln:

> You can handle things there. My obligation is to bring Shaw home.

Chris:

> You are not supposed to be operating in the field. By the standards you set for this company, you are not physically qualified.

Lincoln:

> A one-time exception. Shaw is my problem. This is my task.

Chris:

> What's the real goal here? To take down Shaw? Or are you after True?

Lincoln:

> I need to find both of them.

Chris:

> Why don't you give her time to work? She's got her own goal, she can handle herself, and she hasn't asked you to come rescue her.

Lincoln:

> It's not a rescue. It's an intervention. She's never been able to reconcile with what was done to Diego. She wants Shaw to tell her a different story, spin some new meaning out of it. She's

ready to risk her life for that. We already lost Renata. I am not
going to stand aside and lose True too.

Chris:

You actually believe she's going to find him. That's why you're
in such a hurry. You think he'll talk to her. Why? Why would he
do that? Just because she's Diego's mother?

Lincoln:

Yes. Because she's Diego's mother. And because he knew her.
He respected her. He cared about his men. If he's going to talk
to anybody, it'll be her.

Chris:

So you're using her as bait.

Lincoln:

I didn't set it up. I didn't send her after him. But the situation
exists, so I will exploit it. I need to be there if she finds him. I
need to ensure Shaw comes home, because there needs to be
an accounting. It's as simple as that.

Tamara gave them a place to begin their search when she
reported the results of her dust and pollen analysis. Lincoln knew
True would head to Morocco. When his phone logged a missed
call from Dove Barhoum—almost ten hours ago now—he took it
as confirmation that she was in Rabat.

He called Dove after that—several times—but Dove never
picked up, never called back, never tried to contact him again in
all the hours since.

One more thing to worry about.

Now he turns his head slightly so that Nadim Zaman appears
within the full range of color perceived by his natural eye, and
says, "If you could feed her profile to the network of municipal
cameras, we could backtrack, find out where she went after she
left the hotel."

"No." The liaison officer says this in a tone that allows no possibility of negotiation. "I have helped you locate her hotel room as
a gesture of good will but I can go no farther. She is present in this
country legally and she is not named in your warrant. I have no
cause to investigate her activities."

"She may have information material to our search for Jon Helm," Lincoln says.

Nadim turns his hands palm up. "She is a professional soldier, yes? She is on your team. Give her time. If she is passing the night in pleasure, she will be here again in the morning. And if she is hunting this Jon Helm, she will contact you when she has a lead. Until then, I suggest you get some sleep."

The wafer shape of a surveillance beetle clings to the frame of the hotel room window, its camera eye watching the street below and the sky overhead—although at this late hour the city is quiet and no one's about.

Miles watches the street too, even though he knows ReqOps' impromptu surveillance network will issue an alert when True shows up.

If she shows up.

He's here to witness what he hopes will be the last action in the book he's writing. He wants the narrative to end with Shaw Walker being taken down—but True is missing and he worries he'll have to describe one more atrocity before he gets to the end.

"They're coming back," Felice announces. "They just stepped off the elevator."

She's sitting cross-legged on one of the beds, a tablet balanced on her lap as she idly monitors the surveillance feeds. Khalid has been lying beside her, hands behind his head, but he gets up now and goes to the door.

Lincoln booked the team into adjoining rooms with a door open between them, but the three of them gravitated to one side to wait together.

Khalid opens the door, stepping back as Lincoln comes in with Rohan right behind him.

"That Nadim is a real prick," Lincoln announces.

Rohan affirms this with a fervent "*A*-men."

"Did you find anything?" Miles wants to know.

"Nothing in her room," Rohan says, looking worried. "Not even a toothbrush. I don't think she's planning to come back."

"We can't know that," Lincoln counters, irritated. "All she was carrying when she took off was a daypack with a few toys inside. If she went out for any reason, she would have taken that with her. Doesn't mean she's not coming back."

"You want me to launch the copters?" Khalid asks. "Start looking for her?"

They brought four starburst copters with them. Lincoln nods his approval of this suggestion. "Put up two, unarmed, cameras only. Hold the second pair in reserve."

"Hey," Felice says, "looks like our friend Nadim wasn't satisfied with his first inspection of our truck."

Miles sits down beside her so he can look over her shoulder at the tablet. A video feed shows Nadim crouching beside the rear bumper of their leased SUV—a rugged off-road model, desert tan in color. His hand disappears underneath the bumper. Then he walks swiftly to his own vehicle. "Tracking device," Felice says. "Got to be."

"*Prick*," Rohan mutters.

"He's got a job to do," Miles says. "And you can't expect him to be happy about a bunch of foreign assholes showing up in his hometown with a special writ of kickass."

Felice snorts, but Lincoln is somber when he says, "Let's just hope our pal Nadim is not on Jon Helm's payroll."

"Fuck Jon Helm," Rohan says with feeling. "I don't give a shit about Jon Helm. We're not even getting a bounty on him. What I want to know is, where is True?"

It's almost 0200. Too late at night for pleasant assumptions and comforting excuses. "She's with him," Miles says. "Or she's on her way to him. But she's found him. Otherwise she'd be here."

Lincoln's lip curls. It's not what he wants to hear. "Help Khalid get the copters up," he tells Rohan irritably. "And leave the tracker in place for now. We'll get rid of it when we need to go stealth."

TIME ENOUGH

THERE ARE NO sidewalks in this district, so True walks in the streets alongside parked cars tucked up against the buildings. She is cautious as she approaches the address, pausing at the corner to study the block where the riad is located, and to listen.

The neighborhood is quiet.

The street rises uphill, but other than that it's similar to the streets she's just passed—hemmed in by parked cars and high white windowless walls. The conjoined residences can be counted by the number of arched double doors, each pair wide enough to drive a small car through, although all of them are closed. There are four sets of doors on each side of the street. Friendly amber lights illuminate the door of the farthest riad on the left. More lights glow on two of the rooftop terraces on the right-hand side of the street. But the residence True seeks is the second on the left, and like most of its neighbors, it's dark.

She does not want to stay in one place too long so she walks on past the foot of the street to the next block. She lets her MARC run the sky survey and again it detects only city UAVs and private network relays. No unidentified devices. No devices following her.

She walks up the next block, and as she does, she digs a small case out of her daypack. Inside is a soldier from the origami army.

Tamara calls it a sparrow though it doesn't look like one. Its dark-brown avian wings are powered by button batteries packed into an oblong body with a shape that reminds True of a fishing lure, the sort with eyes painted on to make it resemble a fish. A triangular tail serves as a stabilizing third wing. It has a wide-angle camera and radio-frequency sensors, along with software to interpret what it finds, and it's agile enough to fly in tight spaces or securely perch in a hidden niche—so it's useful, despite a limited battery life. She syncs it to the MARC's display and when she reaches the top of the target block, she launches it into the air.

Without guidance, the sparrow spirals upward. True lets it climb until it's higher than the houses. Then she uses her data glove to send it shooting swiftly down the street and over the outer wall of the target house. A circuit of the riad's rooftop terrace shows no one there. One end of the terrace is sheltered beneath an ornate tiled roof held up by graceful white columns. Heavy curtains, tied back by tasseled ropes, hang at the corners. Sheltered beneath are a daybed, upholstered chairs, and a stairway that drops out of sight behind a clean white wall. The rest of the terrace is open to the sky. There are lounge chairs, a patio table with a folded umbrella, and three huge, hip-high terracotta pots presently empty of flowers. At the terrace's center, a well looks down into the interior courtyard.

The sparrow's video feed is distorted, super-wide angle, but True can make out soft garden lights in the courtyard below and a central fountain with four small trees around it.

No one is in sight.

Tipping her hand forward, she directs the sparrow to descend. A balcony overlooking the courtyard surrounds the lightless second floor. Behind the balcony are rooms with uncurtained windows and folding doors all pushed open. She guides the sparrow in a circuit, identifying sitting rooms and bedrooms, but no one is there. The beds are bare mattresses and there is no clutter, nothing personal, even in the bathrooms.

And there are no surveillance devices. None that the sparrow can detect.

She explores the ground floor next, where there are two large salons and a modern kitchen. Again, no one, and no evidence of anyone—no dirty dishes in the kitchen and no ready lights indicating active electronics anywhere—but also no sense of abandonment. The house is clean, the trees and the fountain in the courtyard well tended. She thinks maybe this is a vacation rental being cleaned and prepared for its next booking.

She summons the sparrow back as its battery reserve shades into orange. She considers calling Shaw again, but she has already stood in one place too long, so she descends the steep street until she's outside of the target. Her visor picks out and highlights a tiny camera lens mounted above the arched double doors. She's only a little surprised when the riad's doors start to swing silently open.

If the doors opened all the way, the entry would be wide enough for a small car. But they swing inward only far enough to allow her to enter . . . which she does. On the other side is an arched passageway to the courtyard. It feels like walking into a trap, but her momentum carries her past both fear and good judgment. The doors close behind her, the click of an electronic lock audible past the burbling of the fountain.

She takes out the pistol and walks through all the rooms in the house, repeating the survey she just made with the sparrow, confirming that no one is home. By the time she reaches the rooftop terrace, she has decided that Shaw does not live here, that he never has. It's not right for him. It's too open, subject to surveillance from overhead and, given the open-air rooms, impossible to secure against creeping robotic beetles.

Still, he sent her here. The house recognized her. She is supposed to be here.

She wonders: *Why this place?* and *Will he come?* She could try calling him again, but surely he must know she is here?

Dawn is an hour away. She decides she'll wait that long, and no longer. If he's going to come, he'll come by then.

She changes out the sparrow's batteries. An ornate iron railing tops the low wall enclosing the terrace. She secures the sparrow's perching feet around the rail's lowest rung, positioning the device so that its wide-angle video includes both the street and the sky. The fresh batteries will allow for hours of surveillance if the sparrow is passive and does not fly.

She goes downstairs, stopping in at the kitchen. There's no food, just bottled water in the refrigerator, but her dust-dry mouth and her aching skull make it clear that water is what she needs. She takes two bottles to the courtyard. In a shadowy back corner beneath the shelter of the second-floor balcony there is a cluster of furniture: a padded bench with carved wooden legs, low coffee table in front of it, and on the other side of the table, two cushioned chairs with a porcelain block table between them. The chairs face the courtyard, with a view of the passageway and the front doors, so True chooses one as her base of operations and sits.

Relief floods her body, the gratitude of muscles that are tight and tired. She acknowledges, too, a deep sadness for things lost and broken. She takes off the visor and leaves it on the little block table to hibernate. Opening a bottle of water, she sips it slowly.

After a few minutes of waiting, she flirts with the idea of checking her messages. A fierce anxiety follows. She hasn't checked her regular accounts—voice, email, or text—since she walked off the plane in Manila, knowing there would be an emotional payload and not wanting to be distracted by it. But now the thought is in her head. Nagging at her. She resists for a time, ten or fifteen minutes. Then she slides her tablet out of her thigh pocket.

With the decision made, she doesn't hesitate further. She switches on voice and text messaging, and authorizes her email to download, priority only—priority being determined by Ripley.

There are fewer than she expected. She scans the lists, finding two voice messages from Alex, both date-stamped soon after she sent her last email. She doesn't listen to them. She'll listen to them later, when this is over.

After he got no response to his voice messages, he sent an email with the subject line, **I need you to call me.** Then an hour after that another, pleading, **CALL ME. I need to know you're okay.**

As she reads this, her chest tightens. She squeezes her eyes shut for just a few seconds. But she leaves the emails unread, afraid of the weight they contain.

Nothing from him since. Understandable.

She presses the cool water bottle against her hot cheek and moves on.

Only one message from Lincoln, a voice message, date-stamped ninety minutes after his flight departed Manila. Her breast rises and falls in a deep sigh. No hiding from the content of this one. Lincoln has followed her to Rabat and if he has let drop any hint of his plans or his intentions here, she needs to know it. She plays the message, her anxiety ramping up yet again at the quiet fury in his raspy voice. "*God damn it, True. You need to stop and think what you're doing. Shaw Walker is not a hero, he's not a savior, and he's not a substitute for Diego. He is a dangerous, unstable man . . .*"

Anger flares. "I know," she says aloud through gritted teeth. "I know, I know. Don't tell me what I already know."

She puts the tablet down, drinks water, and evaluates. She's tired and emotionally worn and her temper is short—none of which is an excuse for poorly considered tactics. She's not going to start making excuses. "This is on me," she says. "My choice. My responsibility." But she's never operated in such isolation before.

Time to change that?

She hisses at the thought. No way is she going to call in Lincoln. Do that, and she won't see Shaw again unless there's an open coffin at his second funeral.

A new thought comes: *What about Tamara?*

Tamara might be willing to run a command post. True could link her up to the MARC, and then she'd have someone to shadow her, to watch over her shoulder and witness, and to bring word to Alex if it all goes south—

No.

Tamara is not a soldier. If True is going to connect with anyone, it needs to be someone who's been on the front lines before. And, it occurs to her, it should also be someone Lincoln can't fire when this is done. A cold smile touches her cracked lips. As it happens, she knows someone like that, someone who's got nothing else useful to do.

She picks up her burner phone and puts through a call to Colonel Colt Brighton. It's the middle of the night in the DC area but the old man is a night owl and he's got enough sense of adventure that he'll usually pick up an unknown number.

He must be bored because the phone rings only once and he's on the line: "Tough luck," he says. "She gave you a fake number."

"Don't say anything else, Dad," True warns him. "If you're not alone, end this call, excuse yourself, and call me back."

Two seconds of silence, then a whispered "*Fuck.*"

The call drops.

She waits. Less than a minute later, the screen flashes an incoming call. She picks up.

"What's wrong?" he asks. "Where are you?"

In terse sentences, she tells him. He's not shy with his opinion. "You've gone off the fucking deep end."

"Maybe so, old man, but this is about Diego. You willing to shadow me or not?"

"*Shit.* Yes. Yes, of course."

"Good." Colt is arrogant, abrasive, and domineering—she would never willingly put herself under his command—but he's not shy on the line. He'll back her until this is done.

"Do not tell anyone," she warns him. "Not until this is over."

"Over one way or another?"

"Yeah."

"God damn it, True. You have always been a pain in the ass, but I do not want to see you die."

"Good to hear, because your job is to help me stay alive."

"No matter how stupid you are."

"Nothing ever changes, huh?"

"God help us all. What's the fucking plan?"

"For now I'm going to set you up with two devices, one to watch the street, one to watch this courtyard. But once he's here, you don't talk. You just witness. And if I don't get home, you let Alex know what happened."

———

Forty minutes later, the sound of Colt's low, old-man voice in her ear startles True out of a catnap: "You with me, girl?"

"I'm here," she breathes, straightening in the cushioned chair.

"I've got one armed individual, male, approaching your location from the lower end of the block."

"Roger that."

He's watching the video feed from the sparrow. She reaches for her MARC to confirm what he sees: a lean figure of a man, with an assault rifle slung over his shoulder. The angle is too steep to show his face, the light too dim to be sure of the color of his hair.

"That him?" Colt asks.

"Got to be." She wonders where he's been and what he knows, and why he's carrying the Triple-Y. Does he know Lincoln is here? She swipes with her data glove to clear the MARC's screen. "Quiet now, old man. I'll talk to you on the other side."

She takes off her TINSL before Colt can object, toggles it off, and tosses it into her daypack. Then she's up and moving sideways to the shelter of a column that supports the second-floor balcony. The pistol comes out of her pocket as the front doors swing open, riding on their silent mechanisms.

The passageway amplifies Shaw's soft voice: "You getting jumpy, True?"

"Fair assessment," she admits over the rock-club rhythm of her heart. She peers out from behind the column. Her MARC gathers enough light that she can see he's still dressed as he was earlier in the evening, and he's still wearing his off-brand visor. It's the Triple-Y that's new, and a small daypack on his other shoulder.

"Put the gun away," he says. "I told you before, I got you under my wing."

She steps out from behind the column to stand under the open sky. They face each other across the courtyard. "You went dark on me," she accuses.

"You were taken care of, until you skipped."

"Communications failed. I was not acquainted with a mission plan. Under those circumstances, I felt more secure making my own way." In a more conciliatory tone she adds, "So far as I could tell, I wasn't followed."

"It's quiet out there," he agrees. "Now put the gun away."

She does it, returning the pistol to her pocket.

"Where's your car?" she asks as he crosses the courtyard.

"Down the hill, around the corner." He speaks just loudly enough to be heard over the burbling fountain. "You knew I was coming. You got eyes on the street?"

"Yes." The courtyard too, but she doesn't mention the beetle hidden in plain sight beside a broken tile at the mouth of the passage, where its swiveling camera lens can watch the courtyard and the front door. His narrowed eyes and half-smile tell her he's not fooled.

She hands him a bottle of water. He takes it and drinks half. She's uncomfortable in the open so she returns to her seat beneath the balcony. He eases his pack to the floor, then sits in the second chair, the block table between them, stretching out his long legs, holding the Triple-Y cradled in the crook of his arm. "This Li Guiying," he says. "She has skills."

True takes off the MARC and rubs her aching forehead. "Yes."

He turns to look at her through the clear lens of his visor. "So why did she hire those two amateurs?"

"I don't know. Maybe it wasn't her. Does it make sense that she would use her own name?"

"If she was in a hurry. If she wants you to know."

"Maybe it was just a mistake."

"Not the first."

His focus on Guiying is oddly reassuring. It tells her he doesn't know yet that Lincoln is here. *Good*, because she needs this time.

She says, "Earlier tonight you were surprised that I already knew you and Diego were abandoned, left to die in Nungsan. But you were not abandoned by your country, Shaw. I want you to know that."

"Yeah? I've heard that speech before."

Which, all on its own, is interesting because it implies he's been in contact with some element of the American government. CIA, maybe? It wouldn't surprise her to learn he's done work for them—dark and dirty work—but she doesn't pursue the question. That's not why she's here and maybe she doesn't want to know.

"I haven't talked to anyone else tonight," she assures him. "Except for a police officer, who asked if I was all right."

He takes another sip of water, looking thoughtful.

She tells him, "We had no idea you were alive, until Tadmur."

"How did you work it out?"

"Guesses and gossip and gut instinct." She doesn't want to tell him about Miles. "And if you were alive, that meant the story I'd been told about Nungsan was wrong. I wanted the truth, so I asked a friend in the State Department. A few discreet inquiries were made, whispered answers were given. There's no proof, but there *is* a belief that some faction of Chinese Intelligence knew at the time exactly where you and Diego had been taken. They chose not to share that knowledge, they used disinformation to steer our people away from Nungsan, and in the end they obliterated the village. No one on our side knows why. No one could tell me why, Shaw. But you know why, don't you?"

His answer is gruff, but spoken without hesitation. "Yes."

"Tell me, then." She leans forward to look at the sky above the open courtyard, where a few stars still hide behind the haze. Has the night begun to pale? Dawn can't be far off. She says, "I think there's not much time."

"Time enough."

He says that, not knowing Lincoln has come.

"Did you get a look at the kamikaze drone tonight?" he asks.

It's not a question she expected, not a reminder she likes, but she plays along. "I saw it. The fuselage was flattened, with long wings mounted on ball joints. Tilt rotors, four jointed legs. Rogue Lightning emblem."

"You saw all that?" he muses, sounding impressed. "You've got a good eye." Then he explains, "I copied the basic design of that kamikaze from the mechs that hunted us in the forest that night."

NINETY SECONDS

WE WERE SPREAD out on the slope above the road, at least sixty meters apart—too far to see each other through the mist and past all those sapling trees—and everything had gone to hell. Hector had been silenced by a small, intense explosion. Jesse was the only man beyond him and he'd dropped out of comms, so I knew the line was broken. And there was intermittent shooting down there.

Mason said, "That's Jesse shooting."

Laser pulses, thread-thin, flashed in the mist all up and down our line, and the night was vibrating with a soft, low buzz that made my skin crawl.

"Go to radio," I ordered. Stealth was blown. We might as well try it.

Francis yelled the order down to Jesse. "Go to radio."

I don't know if the software cleaned up the interference or if Saomong just wasn't pissing on our team channel but the radio was clear.

Francis said, "I'm going after Hector."

Jesse reported in. "I hit one of the robots. It's down." Then he added, "*Shit!*" Three quick shots followed.

Mason growled, "I don't have a target."

I didn't have a good target either. With night vision I could pick out fast movement on the slope above, what looked like three small drones. They were coming from the head of the line, somewhere above Diego, weaving between the trees, flashing in and out of sight on evasive paths. I tried to target one, but with the trees so close I couldn't lead with my rifle. They passed, all three going away from me, flying across the slope, moving toward Mason and Francis. A few seconds later something blew up. A small explosion, from way down at the end of the line.

"Jesse, report!"

"I'm here! Still here. One of the fuckers came right at me—" More shooting, swearing. "Fucking killer robots! They've got explosives on them. Don't let them get close."

Fuck me. That's what I thought. Just fuck me. We'd heard talk about this kind of shit. We all knew it was coming. I guess we just assumed it would be our side fielding it first.

No joy. And I couldn't see the three drones anymore. I couldn't see any other movement, no flashes. "Francis!" I couldn't see him either, but I knew he was climbing that slope. He'd be right in their path. "Francis, drop!" I warned him. "The goddamn robot swarm is coming toward you."

His voice came back to me over comms. "Shit. I *can't* drop. No room between these fucking trees." Then, "*Jesus!* Hector's dead. He's fucking dead. He didn't step on a mine either. His fucking head is blown off!"

This triggered Jesse. "Killer bots!" he screamed. "I *told* you. Fucking exploding killer bots. You got that yet? I've dropped three." More shots. "Blown up one. How the fuck many are there?"

"We got nothin' up here!" Mason told him. "They're all on you!"

Mason was right. Jesse was the only one firing, the only one fighting. I could hear the steady, distant concussion of his weapon, and louder, his cursing over comms. "Goddamn, goddamn. Shaw, I need backup!"

"Retreat!" I told him. "Evade! Get the hell out of there." Because help was going to take time. I was moving, but there was no way I could get to him in less than two minutes. It was Hector who'd been in position to back him up but Hector was dead, and Francis was in the path of the approaching swarm. "Mason, we gotta get down there."

"I'm moving, Shaw."

That's when Diego jumped in, lighting up a bogie I couldn't see. "D, what have you got?"

"Nothing." Two more quick shots. "Just want to see if gunfire will draw the swarm off Jesse, bring the bots back up here."

That sounded crazy to me, but Francis said, "Shit, it's working. I got two bots coming back this way. No. *Four*." And I knew Diego was a fucking genius.

I told Francis, "Let 'em get past you. We'll take care of 'em up here. You get down there and help Jesse."

"On it. Jesse—"

He got interrupted by another cracking explosion . . . and Jesse's weapon went silent.

"Ah, shit," Mason whispered.

Francis ignored my order and started shooting. Maybe a mech had survived the assault on Jesse and was coming after him, I don't know. But there was another pop, a scream, whispered cursing.

"I see 'em, boss," Mason said, dead calm. "I'm going to hit the last one in the line."

"Make it count."

I could hear that skin-crawling soft buzzing again and Diego moving, his pack scraping like sandpaper against the tree trunks as he squeezed between them, changing his position. It sounded like he was descending, moving toward the road.

I got my pistol out. It was easier to maneuver between the trees. Mason fired a single shot. "*Shit*."

He'd missed. I couldn't see them yet but I fired a couple shots anyway. Confuse their algorithms. Right?

Mason fired again, again. And I saw one. I led it with my pistol, squeezed off a series of shots, and hit trees. It came at me on a zigzag. Took me three more shots but I got it. It didn't blow up when I hit it. Just spun into a tree branch and crashed. It struck me that they weren't that dangerous, not really, not unless they came at you in numbers. But two, maybe three, had buzzed past me and were after Diego, who was lighting things up in an effort to attract some action.

He got it, all right. The swarm was after him but he was a step ahead of all of us. He'd moved downslope until he was right above the road. Then he pulled a grenade, dropped it where he stood, and sprinted toward me. When that thing went off, it knocked trees into the road, but it made the kamikazes disappear.

"Shaw!" he yelled, trying to find me.

I moved out to where he could see me. He looked okay.

"You hear anymore?" he asked when we met up.

No. I could still hear Francis over comms, soft moans, trying to bite down on the pain, but the forest was quiet. That awful low humming, gone. "I think you got 'em," I said.

The fight had gone on for maybe ninety seconds and I had three men down.

We set off together, moving as quickly as we could. We had to help Francis, and confirm Jesse's status.

"If we see more," Diego whispered, "don't shoot at them unless they're coming straight for us. Don't approach them. I think perceived aggression sets them off."

Perceived aggression. That's how he described it. Hector had tried to touch one and it blew his head off. Jesse had lit up a swarm and then gone silent. A touch, or a fusillade—it was all the same to the machines. But I let Mason know what Diego had said.

We rendezvoused by Francis. His right hand was gone and his face and neck were shredded but he was still alive. We hooked him up to a pack of artificial blood and sprayed dressing on his wounds.

The mission was fucked. We had failed. No way to recover. The CCA would have picked up the explosions, the gunfire. Saomong was aware of us. They would be coming, and we needed to get out. Out from under their radio interference so we could call for a ride.

There was no way we could carry Hector's body with us, not through the maze of that sapling forest. So we took his tags and his electronics and left him where he fell.

I got Francis onto my shoulders and we went to find Jesse.

Diego and Mason broke trees, pulled branches out of the way, tried to make it easier for me. We were getting close to the place where Jesse had to be, when Diego found a broken mech lying in the leaf litter. It must have been one that Jesse shot down. Diego moved in on it.

"Don't touch that thing, D!" I warned him.

"I don't need to touch it." He stopped a couple meters away and scoped it. "Put a light on it, Mason. I need to see the details."

Mason didn't like that idea at all. "We can't use a light," he growled.

Like the CCA didn't already know where we were? I came down on Diego's side. "Get a light on it, tight beam," I ordered. "We need to know what it is, where it came from."

Mason fished in a pocket for his LED. He illuminated the target.

Diego took pictures through his scope. Mason pulled out a smart phone and took a couple more.

I still had Francis draped over my shoulders, so I just asked them, "What have you got?"

Mason came over to show me. We hunched over the screen to hide the light. It showed a clear, magnified picture of the mech. It was lying there, belly up. Its wings and its landing gear were broken but the fuselage was intact. A flattened diamond shape, maybe eight inches, nose to tail. Fucking kamikaze killer mech. First time I ever saw one. Color was light gray. Looked like aluminum or titanium, but it could have been plastic.

"You see those markings?" Diego asked, still studying it through his scope.

I saw them. There was a label with Western-style numerals alongside several columns of Chinese characters. The characters didn't bother me. Those are used in a lot of Asian countries— Japan, Korea, Vietnam. No, it was the logo that burned. Lotus flower, four petals shaped like curved swords. I knew that design. Diego knew it too.

"That's Kai Yun," he said.

Kai Yun. The agency that was supposed to be assisting with oversight on our mission.

"Enough," I said. "Kill the light."

Mason switched off the display. He was still cool. He was always cool. But Diego was winding up. "What the fuck? Kai Yun is supposed to be on our side. And they blew Hector's head off? Blew off Francis's arm? And Jesse?"

"Yeah, and now the CCA knows we're here," Mason reminded us, unnecessarily.

"That too," Diego growled.

Kai Yun had killed us. We all knew it. The question was, on purpose or by accident? That we didn't know—but we had more immediate concerns.

"We gotta get out of here," I told them. "That's the only way we are going to get us some righteous justice. We get out of here, and I promise you I will see to it that someone hangs for this."

They liked that. It settled them down. But we still needed to confirm Jesse's status. We pushed on, leaving the mech where it lay. We couldn't risk recovering it and having it blow up in our hands.

Later, though, I wondered—was it as dead as it looked? Or was it still playing spy bot, recording everything it heard around it? I imagined some technician in a secure facility somewhere in Shanghai hearing those words I'd said—*I will see to it that someone hangs for this.* And I knew we were fucked.

NO UNWINDING IT

THERE IN THE shadows of the courtyard, beneath a distant, dark-blue sky pearlescent with dawn, the past reshapes itself, taking on a new definition, a new truth. Past the filters of her anxiety, her regret, her horror, her exhaustion, True sees at last the process that brought about Diego's tortured death . . . if not yet the reason.

The mission Rogue Lightning was tasked to carry out was an almost-routine action in a war that had been ongoing for decades and whose battles usually passed unspoken. The mission plan was based on cooperative intelligence from both Chinese and American sources. The plan denoted a precise time and place where critical leadership elements of the Saomong Cooperative Cybernetic Army could be found isolated and vulnerable—a precision that implied a spy deep within enemy councils, with ready access to outside communications.

In retrospect such a spy seems unlikely. Far more credible to believe that Kai Yun quietly deployed an autonomous combat swarm to monitor the region, with individual elements situated to eavesdrop on Saomong councils.

The swarm would have been experimental—every ACS was experimental then—but it must have been successful at first. True imagines the little mechs present but unnoticed in the villages and the forest for days ahead of the mission, gathering the intelligence that eventually guides Rogue Lightning to the planned site of the ambush. Then something goes wrong.

"You know what was funny about that mission?" Shaw asks her.

True looks past the fountain, gaze drawn to a point high on the wall at the mouth of the passage where she left a surveillance beetle. Colt will have heard Shaw's story. She's glad for that. He'll follow up on it, if she's not able to. She tells Shaw, "There was nothing funny about the mission."

"No, you're missing the point. The funny part, the laugh-out-loud part, was that none of us needed to be there. Not me, not Diego, not Mason or Francis or Hector or Jesse. None of us were needed because Kai Yun had made us obsolete. They had better fighters in place. More efficient soldiers. Kai Yun could have targeted the CCA leadership with that swarm and done our job for us. I think that's what they meant to do. Show us up, show off what could be done while we were wandering around like bozos lost in the woods. But we fooled them. We were better than they thought. We got there—late, but still in time to execute the mission."

True feels dizzy. *Had* Rogue Lightning been meant to arrive late? The mission plan had woefully underestimated the difficulty of the terrain. Was that on purpose? She summarizes it, needing to understand: "The swarm was there ahead of you, ready to execute the ambush . . . but things went wrong and Rogue Lightning was taken down by friendly fire." It's the conclusion True reached just a couple of days ago, after she'd met Daniel, heard his story.

"So it happens, right?" Shaw works hard to compress his voice into a casual tone, but she's not fooled. She hears the underlying agony. "You gotta expect mistakes with an experimental system. The swarm was operating on its own, doing what it was designed to do. It just picked the wrong enemy. Those algorithms needed a little work." He draws in a deep breath. "But that wasn't the end of it. After Saomong captured us, when they were marching us on this trail to Nungsan, I saw another mech. I saw it twice, following us. Watching. Someone at Kai Yun watching us through its camera eyes."

A shudder runs through him. He stands up abruptly as if to escape it. The rifle falls naturally into the crook of his arm. "That last time I saw the mech, I screamed at it to send help." He touches the scar on his lip. "Saomong knocked a couple of teeth loose for that one." He presses his lips together, shakes his head. "Fuck me, anyway. Fuck them all. Because the truth is that we were abandoned to the enemy to save a black mark showing up on someone's resume. And what happened to D . . . it didn't have to happen. But there's no taking it back. No unwinding it. *Shit*. I'm gonna go make coffee."

True says nothing. He needs time and she doesn't trust herself to talk, not yet. She stares across the courtyard at the bubbling fountain, exhaustion and adrenaline forcing her heart into a frantic, shallow rhythm as she thinks again about Li Guiying, a skilled and highly respected robotics engineer, a specialist in swarming algorithms, who began her career at Kai Yun Strategic Technologies.

Guiying was behind the swarm. True has no hard proof but she believes it. She's sure Shaw believes it too.

Guiying cultivated True's friendship. Why would she do that? Was she a psychopath, wanting to win the trust of those she'd hurt? Or was it a ploy to keep a potential enemy close? Or was it guilt?

True imagines Alex there with her, asking: *So now that you know, what will you do?*

Over the years she's envisioned retribution in a hundred forms—righteous justice—though it was never more than a what-if fantasy, her vengeance denied because no one involved was left alive. She thinks now it was lucky not to have the choice.

Early morning light spills into the courtyard, coloring the limes and tangerines on the little trees. She gets up, follows Shaw to the kitchen—a narrow but modern room with high-end appliances and a quartz countertop. They're out of sight of her surveillance beetle here, probably outside the range of its audio pickups too.

Shaw looks up from his contemplation of the brewing coffee. His AR visor is on the counter. No screen filters his pale gaze.

"I thought they were all dead," she says. "Everyone who had hurt him."

"You were lucky, then. I always knew someone was left. I never thought I would know who it was." Gentle words, wrapped around a cold promise.

True is surprised to discover she wants no part of a murder—if that's what he's thinking. "You need to come home with me," she says, shifting gears, resolving to persuade him. "You are the survivor, Shaw. The only witness. You need to testify, demand an investigation."

"No." He says it casually.

"You don't have a choice," True insists. "You promised them justice. *Righteous* justice. You owe them. It's up to you to shine a light on what happened. That's what she's afraid of. That's why she's been following me."

"No," he says again. "She's not afraid. Not of that. She's had eight years to clean up the mess. There won't be evidence left to find, no proof she had any part in it, or that it ever happened. All you'll hear from officials on both sides is denial and outrage. *If* they respond at all." He surprises True with a slight smile. "She's tried to get close to you because she wants you to take care of it."

This requires a few seconds to sink in, a few seconds for her to grasp his meaning.

When she does, she recoils. "No, you're wrong."

She wants him to be wrong. True wants to imagine Guiying as a psychopath drawn to her because of some twisted fascination at the magnitude of what happened at Nungsan. A psychopath requires no consideration. But if instead she is a secret penitent? Someone haunted by guilt she cannot bring herself to reveal?

True clutches the counter as she is slammed by the weight of a bone-deep exhaustion.

"You going to forgive her?" Shaw asks.

"No." One syllable uttered in soft certainty. *No.*

It isn't possible. It's not possible to escape. In her head the video plays again: Diego's screams, the crucifixion, the flames. The resolute grip of a black hole. Could Shaw be right? Was even Guiying caught in that inexorable orbit?

"I'm putting up a bounty on her," Shaw says as he pours the coffee.

True catches her breath. Her hand goes to her mouth. *Deeper and deeper*, she thinks. She asks, "Don't you want to hear her side?"

He shrugs and hands her a cup that she accepts automatically, only to be startled at the heat against her hands. He says, "Better if you take care of it. That's what she wants. Why don't you call her? Let her know her options. Let her know it's time."

True sips the coffee, a strong brew, perfect, and wonders, *What is right action, in this circumstance, in this time?* She despises the idea of a private bounty. That's retribution. A warlord's justice. Guiying's involvement has not been proven, may never be proven. If Shaw is right, there will be no legal way to make the case.

So don't resist.

Call her. Confront her. Invite her to speak in her own defense. Isn't that right action? It's something close, anyway. Better than a warlord's bounty.

Her gaze returns to Shaw. "You haven't posted the bounty yet?"

"Not yet."

"Don't post it."

"Call her."

True decides instead to compose an email. She keeps it simple, one line:

It's time to tell the truth.

She appends the number of her temporary phone and sends it.

Does she expect a response? Yes and no. The moment feels like a break point between alternate timelines, each branch equally likely. She leans against the kitchen counter, sipping coffee, not thinking too much. Shaw busies himself collecting tangerines from the courtyard trees and peeling them, perfuming the kitchen with citrus oil. After twenty minutes, True says, "She's not going to call."

Seconds later, the burner phone rings.

Shaw meets her gaze, an eager glint in his eyes. She nods, swipes to accept the call, puts it on speaker. She doesn't say anything though, and after a few seconds Guiying's voice speaks into the silence with tentative uncertainty. "True? True, are you there?" Shaw cocks his head, the slant of his eyebrows posing a question. "True," Guiying whispers, "I never wanted any of it to happen."

True hears this as a confession but, if so, it's also a lie. "Yes," she counters. "You did."

"No, I did not *want* it to happen," Guiying says in a soft, confessional voice. "Please, before you say anything, do anything, will you see me?"

Shaw predicted it but True is stunned all the same. "In person?" she asks.

"Yes. I am . . . on my way to Rabat. After last night, I . . . I do not want it all to start again but when I saw that picture of Rogue Lightning, I knew it would."

"The picture?" True asks.

"On the fighter, shot down during your operation in the TEZ."

Shaw looks puzzled but True remembers what Tamara told her about a freelance intelligence agent visiting the crashed Arkinson, taking pictures. Guiying must have had an ongoing search set up for that emblem, maybe for anything to do with Rogue Lightning.

"I hope you are still in Rabat," Guiying says. "I hope you will see me."

True mutes the phone. She tells Shaw, "It could be a trap for you, with Guiying as the bait."

"It's probably a trap for both of us," he says, touching his centipede bracelet, setting it to crawling in slow motion around his wrist and hand. "You willing to take the chance?"

Her smile is bitter. She's been taking chance after crazy chance ever since she returned to the gate in Manila.

She unmutes the call, asks Guiying, "Will you be alone?"

"Yes. I've told no one where I'm going, and I'm flying on a French passport."

So she expects to be followed but not right away. "I am *not* alone," True warns her.

Shaw gives her a sharp look but his expression eases when Guiying says, "I understand."

Do you? True thinks, though she doesn't pursue the question. Instead she asks, "When will you be here?"

"I am scheduled to arrive at the airport in three hours."

"Once you're here, call me again."

The tangerines are sweet and good for a burst of energy but it doesn't last. "I'm going to lie down," True says.

She goes upstairs to one of the bedrooms, lies down on a bare mattress. Stares at the ceiling, thinking. After a few minutes she gets out her burner phone, whispers a text to Colt: "Don't know if you heard all that, but we're waiting on Li Guiying. Going to be quiet for a few hours. Take a break, and don't text me back."

She closes her eyes. She'd like to sleep but Lincoln's presence in the city weighs on her. Using ReqOps' resources, it took only a few days to locate Hussam in the TEZ. If Lincoln fields the same kind of human/machine intelligence here, he might find her in just a few hours. He might find Guiying and follow her here.

True cannot allow that to happen. She can't take the chance that Lincoln will interfere. This drama needs to play out to the end.

So she decides to check in. No more operating in the dark. She gets out her TINSL, knowing that if she wants to contact Lincoln, she has to do it legitimately. No way would he pick up an anonymous number.

"Heads up, Ripley." Her whisper activates her digital assistant. "Text Lincoln. Message to say: Stay out of sight. Don't go about. Don't text me. Don't call. I have an ongoing operation and any competing mission you launch will endanger me. You need to stay clear."

Ripley reads it back.

"Approved," True says. "Send it."

"Text function is turned off," Ripley reminds her.

"Right. So turn it on again. Leave it on this time."

Ripley says, "Message sent."

She closes her eyes and after a time she passes into a fitful sleep that lasts until midmorning.

AT THE RESEARCH DESK

In Rabat the day has just started, but it's late night at ReqOps' headquarters when Tamara's phone chimes a scheduled alarm. She's been asleep two hours on a sofa in the dimly lit lobby—just long enough to leave her feeling disoriented and imbued with dread.

She sits up and dismisses the alarm, then checks her phone for messages. Nothing, of course. Friday would have woken her early if any important updates had come through.

She lets the screen of her phone go dark. The only other light in the lobby comes from the glass exhibit cases. Her gaze rests on them, taking in the flags, the historic weapons, the worn equipment. She's startled to realize that several of the old battlefield photos have fallen over. Knocked down by the concussion wave of the car bomb that killed Renata?

Maybe.

She stands, stiff and sore and disheveled, feeling mildly nauseous from the lingering stink of burning metal that's still present in the building despite the installation of new air-conditioning filters. Or maybe she's imagining the smell. Maybe it's not in the building. Maybe it's in her head.

Maybe it's there to stay.

Getting too old for this, she thinks as she hobbles on swollen feet through the security checkpoint. "How am I doing, Friday?" she asks as she exits the body scanner. "Anything suspicious?"

The AI's voice answers in its consistent, calm tone. "No, Tamara. You are clean."

She washes up, then heads for the break room, where she meets Juliet Holliday coming out. Juliet is on call for any security incursions on the upper campus. She's wearing ReqOps combat fatigues, an armored vest, and a MARC visor that links her to Friday and the security alert system. An assault rifle is slung over her shoulder and a pistol is belted to her hip.

Nasir Peters is on duty at the lower campus.

"Hey," Juliet says. "I just made a fresh pot of coffee."

"Bless you, my child."

Tamara pours a cup, then returns to the mission command post, where she's spent most of the last day and a half. Hayden is asleep on the floor, wrapped up in a blanket beneath the wall monitor. Tamara's assistant, Michelle, is at the research desk. She looks up as Tamara comes in. "Hey, boss."

"Anything?" Tamara asks.

Michelle purses her lips. "Not really. Sun's up. A lot of early-morning traffic. But our copters haven't picked up any sign of True or of Shaw Walker."

In a city of over a million people, this is no surprise. True could be anywhere in it—or she could be gone, traveling on some dusty road, bound for an ungoverned area beyond the Atlas Mountains.

"Thanks Michelle. Why don't you head home, get some sleep? I've got this."

Michelle departs and Tamara takes over the research desk. She sends a text to Lincoln to let him know she's back on duty. His response comes in a few seconds: **Roger that. We need to shake a lead loose today.**

Tamara replies: **Find your friend Dove. He's got to know something.**

Lincoln: **It's on the agenda.** The text doesn't convey gruff irritation but Tamara hears it anyway.

There are other regional PMCs he could call who might be able to provide insight or leads on Jon Helm, but he doesn't want to advertise his presence in Rabat or risk word getting out to Shaw Walker.

Tamara has assigned her digital assistant to search for references to True Brighton, Shaw Walker, Jon Helm, Variant Forces, and to search for murders, kidnappings, assaults, weapons crimes, vehicular crimes, and incidents involving biomimetic robots within the city of Rabat.

She skims the results as she sips her coffee. Several assaults, but none involve anyone of True's description. A double murder in a manufacturing district—gruesome, involving small explosives—but the victims were male.

Her phone beeps with the arrival of a text message. Lincoln, she assumes as she picks it up. But there is no message. The beep repeats. She realizes it's not her phone. It's a cloned phone left on the desk, set up to receive Lincoln's incoming communications so she can filter them, and forward only the mission-centric items to the field phone he's carrying.

The message is from True. Her chest tightens as she reads it. Her heart booms in her ears: **Stay out of sight. Don't go about. Don't text me. Don't call. I have an ongoing operation and any competing mission you launch will endanger me. You need to stay clear.**

"Damn it, True!" she swears, loud enough that Hayden stirs in his sleep. Tamara wants to grab True and shake her—or hug her. Both maybe. The message confirms she's alive because her phone has a biometric lock which means no one else can operate it. And it implies she's still in the city, with the freedom to operate under her own volition and sufficient intelligence resources to know that Lincoln has come. All good signs.

But True does not want Lincoln around. She doesn't want him for backup.

"You've found him, haven't you?" Tamara murmurs. "Now what? What the hell are you up to?"

True isn't saying and she's not entertaining any questions. *Don't text me. Don't call.*

Tamara forwards the message to Lincoln.

It's nearly a minute before he responds and when he does all he says is **Got it.**

"Not good enough, boss," Tamara murmurs, worried over what he might do. She dictates a follow up text. **You need to give her time to work this out.**

You need to find her, he replies.

LI GUIYING

I<small>T'S</small> <small>NOON</small> <small>WHEN</small> the riad's double doors open to admit Li Guiying. She transits the passage in cautious steps, pausing to peer into every corner of the courtyard before she emerges. The sun is witness. It pours a rectangular column of light onto the tiles, the fountain, the citrus trees. The brilliance deepens, by contrast, the shade beneath the balcony—though this late in the year, the air remains cool, not even sixty degrees Fahrenheit.

Shaw has reorganized the courtyard furnishings, moving the chairs and the padded bench close to the fountain, where they're under open sky. True objected to this, but he insisted on it. "Don't worry. I'm watching."

Of course he is. He told her last night he likes to know who his enemies are. He is using Guiying to draw them out. True doesn't like it, but she resists the urge to look up. She's not wearing her visor, so there's nothing she could see anyway against the blinding sunlight.

She sits in one of the chairs as Guiying enters. Shaw stands behind her, stone-faced in his visor, assault rifle held casually in the crook of his arm. Guiying lowers her head in greeting. It is only the second time True has seen her in person.

She is thirty-four years old but still with the same waiflike figure and wispy, layered haircut that True remembers. Like that first time, she is finely dressed, wearing a tailored black business suit and carrying a large shoulder bag, clutching its strap in a white-knuckled grip. There are shadows under her dark eyes, and though her face is round, her cheeks are gaunt and striated with a faint red flush.

True gestures for her to sit on the bench. She does so, setting her bag on the ground beside feet sheathed in graceful black high-heeled shoes. She tries to keep her gaze on True but it drifts up, perhaps inevitably, to Shaw.

True waits, unwilling to direct the conversation. After a few seconds Guiying coughs softly into her hand. Then, in contrast to their first meeting years ago, she looks True in the eye, and her gaze is steady.

Details of that meeting come back to True and it's not pleasant. *All war is risk*, Guiying said. *Advancing technology demands to be used.* Words that might have meant anything, but she clarifies their meaning now, and though her voice is a little hoarse, her English has become polished and her accent refined when she says, "I am responsible for the death of your son, Diego."

At this admission, True feels her heart explode against her ribs. *Eight years late*, she thinks. It angers her, knowing that Guiying sought her friendship, watched her—out of guilt or insecurity, it makes no difference. And *oh!* it hurts to hear it said. But True did not come here for comfort. Only for the truth. At last, the truth.

Shaw, his voice a low growl, reminds them both, "It's not just Diego. It's hard to see past his spectacular exit, but there were more men with me on that mission. Do you know what their names were?"

The red streaks on Guiying's cheeks deepen in color. "Their names were Francis Hue, Jesse Powers, Hector Chapin, Mason Abanov, and Shaw Walker." Beside her the fountain sparkles in the hazy light. "It was a miscalculation," she adds in clipped, determined syllables. "A mistake. I . . . wanted to prove the effectiveness of our autonomous capabilities. I wanted to show that the task given to those men could be done by my swarm instead . . . so that in the future there would be no need to risk the lives of our patriotic soldiers. It was a simple mission. I thought it was a perfect test. But there was an issue with the swarm's instruction set, and . . . we did not have real-time communication to correct the aggressive response."

True leans in, angry now. Guiying calls it a mistake, a miscalculation. Oh, yes. Because what she meant to do was show off her talents. She wanted to beat Shaw's team, hijack their mission, leave them looking slow and ineffective with nothing left to do but quietly withdraw. And when it all went wrong . . . she abandoned them.

"You *had* communication," True says. "You must have, because you instructed the last mech in the swarm *not* to attack, but to follow the survivors, even after they were captured. You knew they were alive." She hears a rising strain in her voice but she presses on. "You *knew* where they were being held. Were you under orders to stay silent?"

"No," Guiying says firmly, insistently. "My superiors did not know what had happened. I made a decision not to report it. Not then. This was *my* decision. I eliminated the data we received and I told them I was forced to destroy the swarm when it lost integrity and the components became scattered in the forest. I did this because I had to put my country first. We could not be seen as the cause of failure. Don't you see? The recriminations that would have followed, the mistrust. Then after the video . . . I was afraid of how it would escalate, of what might happen."

She draws in a sharp breath. "They were *soldiers*. They knew they might be sacrificed for a greater good." She frowns down at the low table between them, composing herself, before returning her gaze to True. "It was your son, and so you think it was the wrong decision, but without cooperation between our countries, how many more would have died?"

"It wasn't your decision to make," True says, forcing the words past her constricted throat. She swallows and tries again. "You're not sorry for what you did?"

"I'm sorry I had to do it."

True presses her fist to her lips while in her mind she hears Lincoln saying, *Someone's got to do the dirty work.*

Shaw picks that moment to step out from behind her. A cobra. Guiying shrinks from him, turning a shoulder to the unforgiving glint in his pale eyes.

"I never did finish the story, True," he says in his calm way. "I didn't tell you about our last stand. It was after Mason got hit. We'd been running for over an hour, and he'd been hit more than once. Then a bullet took him in the knee, shattered the joint. He couldn't walk, but he could still shoot. Diego was all shot up too, hit in the side, the shoulder, the leg. And we still had Francis with us, though he was barely breathing, wasn't gonna last long.

"I was the only one with no wounds, like I had a fucking force field around me. Mason told me, 'I feel sorry for you. God clearly has plans for you and you are going to pay hell for catching the Old Man's attention.'"

Shaw finally moves to sit down in the empty chair. He looks on edge, wound tight. "I told him what I thought of God."

True glances at Guiying, listening with rapt, respectful attention.

Shaw says, "We set up a defensive position. Nothing else to do. And we held that position until we burned through all our ammo. Any UAV in the area should have observed that firefight. Command should have known, no matter what fake intelligence her office was sending them. That fucking Lincoln, he should have known. He was supposed to be shadowing us. He should have sent backup but we got nothing—and we had nothing left."

There *was* a rescue effort. True knows this because Lincoln told her. But the first helicopter had to put down because of mechanical issues and by the time the second bird was on-scene, the forest was quiet and two men were missing.

Shaw doesn't know this, or if he does, he chooses not to believe it. He says, "Francis had passed by that time, and Mason too. He took a final hit right through the eye. Diego was the last of my men. He was in bad shape, running on adrenaline. And me? I wasn't even bleeding. God's a hell of a joker."

His knuckles are white as he grips the Triple-Y.

"Diego didn't want to surrender. He still had fight in him. He got his knife out. Said we were gonna make them kill us. I said okay, that's how it would be—and we tried. There were just too damn many of them, and Saomong knew the propaganda value of taking us alive."

True closes her eyes, tips her head back. *Be still*, she thinks as grief floods in again, a fresh tide, but she is proud, too. So proud. And horrified.

We're gonna make them kill us.

A warrior's resolve, when there's no way out.

Shaw clears his throat. She opens her eyes. He's looking away, looking into the past when he says, "So now you've heard it all, True. I hope it was worth the visit."

She presses her fist over her racing heart, feeling used up, flushed and dizzy. She nods to cover the seconds it takes for her to remember how to speak. Then she tells him, "It was worth it."

Guiying clutches the arms of her chair so tightly her hands look almost skeletal. "I am sorry," she says. "I am sorry for the blood on my hands. I have tried to make up for it in the years since. I've tried to do good things. Then last night two more men died. That wasn't necessary. It needs to *stop*."

Shaw leans forward. "You triggered that when you hired them." His words come at a fast, aggressive pace. "That was an autonomous response. It worked exactly the way it was supposed to. Not like that night in the forest. You fucked up. You fielded your swarm too early. The algorithms weren't reliable. And another mistake—your swarm was too damn small. If you'd had sixty mechs out there, or a hundred, you could have taken care of us with no problem, no questions, no drama. No consequences. No need to be here today."

She stares at him in shock, looking as if her courage has deserted her. Is she on the verge of panic? Will she try to run? No. She recovers herself, retreating into formal academic speech, even as tears swim in her eyes. "I believe you are correct in your evaluations. The swarm had been tested. We believed it to be combat-ready, but it was too small."

"Why did you come here?" True asks her.

Guiying sounds plaintive when she says, "I thought it was over. I am here to ensure it *is* over"—her delicate fingers slide into an angled pocket on the front of her tailored jacket and the hair on the back of True's neck stands up—"for the protection of my government, my country."

True lunges to her feet, sure they've made a fatal mistake, that beneath that stiff, tailored jacket, or maybe in her shoulder bag, Li Guiying carries explosives that she means to detonate, eliminating all of them and burying this tragedy in the past.

Shaw leans in. He has taken off the centipede bracelet. It's quiescent as he lays it on the little table.

Guiying's fingers pull a tissue out of her pocket. She dabs at her eyes with it, even as she casts a wary gaze at the centipede. "A biomimetic. Meant for me?"

Shaw answers, "Your choice."

"*Don't* touch it," True warns her. "It's toxic."

Shaw says, "Painless justice. Doesn't take long. Less time than Diego was screaming."

True's stern self-control breaks in the face of this image. The video restarts in her head. Her breathing picks up and nausea burns in her belly as she sees again the flames licking Diego's wounded body.

Guiying says softly, "I still see it too."

True's anger flares. Her response is a vindictive whisper: "*Good.*"

But a memory rushes up as if in opposition. She finds herself recalling the sense of consolation she felt as Miles walked free from his cell. That moment eased the dark gravity of the past. In contrast *this* . . . this moment . . . the weight of her hostility, the burden of her resentment, is crushing her heart.

Years ago, True used to fantasize revenge . . . but those fantasies never wore the face of this brilliant, remorseful woman—as scarred by war as any of them—who even now reaches for the centipede.

Before Guiying's small fingers can touch it, True is there.

"*No,*" she says. An isolated word, swiftly repeated. "No! Get back! That is *not* how this is going to play."

To ensure it, she stomps the edge of the table. The table flips. Guiying snatches her hand away, scrambles from the bench. The centipede spills to the courtyard's tiled floor, where True crushes it under her boot.

She lifts her chin, turns to face Shaw, and finds herself staring down the barrel of his Triple-Y. He's moved back several steps to get clear of the chairs. His back is to a pillar. A twitch of his finger is all that's needed to end her life and Guiying's, too. True forces herself to look up past the weapon, to meet his eyes, veiled by the screen of his visor. Oh yes, he's pissed off. But he hasn't pulled the trigger yet.

She draws a shaky breath and turns to Guiying. "No deal, no promises. Just get out. Go now."

"That's all?" Shaw demands in a voice vibrant with locked-in rage. "After what she did to Diego?"

Guiying hasn't moved. She stares at Shaw. A mouse caught in the cobra's gaze.

"Her death won't balance his," True says heavily. "And I want no part of a murder. I know Diego would have stepped up. Stopped this. So—"

She interrupts herself as a huge, winged shadow, faint and fast, sweeps the length of the courtyard. "Are they here?" she asks anxiously, looking up, squinting against the sun's blinding light, turning in a dizzying circle to survey the sky.

"I don't know." Shaw sounds worried. "I've got no reports. I don't know what that was. It's got to be stealthed. Get under cover."

Good advice.

True lowers her sun-dazzled gaze to Guiying, who still hasn't moved. "Get out of sight," True tells her. It's not a request. True grabs her daypack and Guiying's arm, hauling her under the shelter of the balcony.

The nearness of death has left Guiying shivering and pale. "What is it?" she whispers. "What's happened? What's going on?"

"You must have known you'd be followed here."

"*Yes.* But I believed I would have time. True, please. I need to make it right."

"You *can't*," True tells her coldly. "Don't ever again look to me for comfort or for absolution. I've got nothing to offer you. Just live with it. Live with what happened. Like I do."

She looks across the corner of the courtyard to Shaw, who stands in shadow, his daypack on his shoulder, his assault rifle in the crook of his arm, his data glove working as he studies the display on his visor, "Shaw, what have you got?"

"Nothing. Streets are quiet."

Something cast that shadow. "We need to move out before ground troops show."

He looks up. "You're holding on to unfinished business."

True's grip on Guiying tightens as he moves through the shade of the balcony, closing the distance between them in his quick silent way. She puts Guiying behind her. The slight shake of his head reads as a judgment on the futility of this move. She argues anyway. "You said this was for me to take care of. I've done that. It's over."

The mission's over. There are no further steps to take, no more mysteries to unravel, no more guilty parties to uncover. It's done. But it's left her hollow. There's no sense of closure, no release. The old scars remain, and they have not faded.

As he looms close, she adds, unsure if she's speaking to herself or to him, "I thought if I knew what happened, if I understood it . . ."

What? What had she expected? Had she hoped to make peace with what had happened? "Nothing has changed," she says, looking up at him. Bitter words.

"Nothing ever changes," he tells her. "It can't. Because we all died in that forest. Even you, True." His gaze shifts to look past her shoulder to Guiying. "Even her. Even if you never set foot in the place."

No raving madman, him. But a killer all the same. Focused and determined. Eight years spent walling himself off from redemption. *Why?*

How did it come to this?

True ponders it, studying him with a tired, unselfconscious gaze, the same way she once gazed into the eyes of her newborns, striving to see into their futures, to glimpse the influence, the effect their souls might have on the world. *For better?* she would ask herself. *For worse?* With Shaw though, she strives to imagine the past. His path circumscribed by the gravity of what happened in Burma and by things that went before.

As if to assure her of his irrevocable fall, he reminds her in his soft dangerous voice, "No qualms."

She feels it coming, the cobra's strike. His gaze shifts. He's a half step past her, faster than she can react. A squeak, a gasp from Guiying as his gloved hand grips her throat, right under her jaw. At the same time, his scarred hand moves to block True from reaching for her pistol.

But she has no intention of pulling a gun on him. She puts her hands up instead, palms out, backpedaling as she screams at him, "Let her go! Shaw, let her *go*."

It's not what he wants to hear. He wants her on his side. Fury contorts his face. Maybe it's hate. He shoves Guiying hard, sending her tumbling to the tiles. "You want her?" he demands, turning to True. "She's yours, then. None of this matters anyway."

"Maybe it doesn't to you." The explosive violence in him is so close to the surface. She should just shut the fuck up. Let him go before she brings it down on herself. But her gaze drifts to Guiying choking on the floor—and she takes the chance. "Maybe it doesn't matter to you, Shaw, but it matters to the rest of us."

"You want to believe that. But there's plenty like me. More all the time, 'cause good men don't last. Diego was a good man and Saomong hated him for it, for daring to be a good man."

"That is *not* why it happened! They didn't know him. They didn't know anything about him. They took him because he was already dying. If you were the one wounded, they would have taken you."

"That's not how God wrote the story, True."

It's his concluding statement. The end of the debate. He walks on, walks away toward the passage. She turns to stare after him, knowing she was wrong before, sure now there is still one more mystery, one more part of the story he hasn't told her. The core of it, maybe. The black heart.

Guiying is curled on the tiles, crying softly. True crouches beside her, a hand on her shoulder. "Stay here," she says. "Your people will come." Then she goes after Shaw, pausing at the mouth of the passage just long enough to retrieve the wafer-shaped beetle from the wall.

Light floods into the passage as the doors swing inward. Shaw slips past them, into the street. She hurries until she's only a step behind. Last chance.

"Shaw—"

He turns. "You don't fucking give up, do you?"

"Nothing changes," she reminds him.

"*Shit.*"

"You need to come home, Shaw."

"You know that's not going to happen. *Can't* happen."

She shifts her attack, a new angle. "You heard about our fighter pilot?"

"Your dead fighter pilot? Yeah, I heard Rihab claimed it."

"Al-Furat," she corrects.

"Al-Furat *is* Rihab now. The kid hates drones. And he's a fuckin' madman. Vicious. Worse than Hussam."

"Come on," True protests. "He's nineteen."

"Sure, but he's lived harder than you and me. He was six when a drone strike killed his mom and two sisters. Burned half his body. Hard to forgive shit like that. You should know how that works."

"Okay. I get it."

"Your pilot was done when she pulled the trigger on those technicals that followed you out of Tadmur. A remote operator, throwing down hellfire to cause the only kills on the mission, no risk at all to herself. No way Rihab could let that go."

"Did you help him?" She steps closer, wanting the truth, even now. "Lincoln thinks you did. He doesn't believe Rihab could have set up the operation on his own. And he will come after you, if you don't come home."

"*Fuck* Lincoln," Shaw says, backing away, backing down the hill. His truck, True remembers, is parked around the corner. "I gave him a peace treaty."

Hope gives a rising inflection to her voice as she asks, "So you didn't help Rihab?"

This is what she wants to believe. She wants confirmation that he had nothing to do with Renata's death. The other things he's done during eight lost years—they're real. No denying it. She's heard Miles's graphic description of his capture and the executions. But she's also heard Shaw pleading for mercy: *Let him live. Take me instead.* She is still striving to reconcile both truths.

"Think about it, True," Shaw says in that low, lethal tone that makes her catch her breath. "I was paid to be protection for Al-Furat, and your operation kicked my ass. You tell Lincoln if he wants to come after me, join the party. Rihab's already gunning for me, but I'll—"

Whatever threat or promise he is about to make is interrupted by a sharp *crack* from overhead, like metal snapping.

KAI YUN

ADRENALINE KICKS HARD. True's heart rate spikes as she drops into a crouch. She looks up and down the street, and overhead. No threat in sight, but also no shelter. The buildings present vertical faces to the street, no eaves and no inset doorways, and the doors to the riad are closed.

She considers a sprint for the corner when a second, more distant *crack* echoes across the city. This time she spots the vertical line of a thin, descending smoke trail in the sky above the rooftops. It marks the swift fall of an object too small to identify.

More pops and cracks and smoke trails follow.

"We need to get back in the house," she warns Shaw as she retreats to the doors, hoping they'll open again before she draws the eye of whatever is out there.

Motion on the periphery of her vision. She looks up to see an object tumbling out of the sky. It slams against the roof of a parked car, skids off, and lands in the street a few feet from where she's standing. It looks like a fragment of a fuselage, maybe from one of the municipal UAVs. And yet she has heard no sound of rockets or any explosions.

Shaw waves her into the riad, where the doors are swinging open. "Get under cover!"

"It's a fucking laser, isn't it?" she demands as she ducks back into the passage.

Shaw is right behind her. "That's my guess. Looks like we've got a clean sweep of the sky underway."

The sight of Guiying, already on her feet and at the inner end of the passage, startles True. The robotics engineer uses one hand to brace herself against the wall; she holds the other raised to her bruised throat. Her eyes flare in fear and surprise at their sudden reappearance. She starts to back away but True tells her, "Stay under cover."

True gets out her MARC, gets it on, listening to the continuing *crack, crack, crack* of shattering machines, now faint, now sharp and near.

She moves up to join Shaw. They crouch in the passage, well back from the street, out of sight of the laser-wielding UAV no matter where it is in the sky. They leave the doors open, pushed back against the walls so they can watch. Shaw is muttering, engaged with his AR visor. True uses her data glove to access the sparrow's video feed—and the colonel is suddenly with her again: "What the fuck have you gotten yourself involved with?"

She studies the sky, looking for the shooter.

"You aren't going to find it," Colt says. "A laser-armed UAV could be a mile up, or miles away."

"It's Kai Yun," she says out loud. She glances over her shoulder at Guiying. "They followed her." True recalls her earlier suspicion. "You did this, Shaw. You asked for this. You picked an open courtyard and baited it with Li Guiying just to see who would come out to play."

Colt swears softly over the MARC's comm.

Shaw says, "Of course it's Kai Yun." Keeping his gaze focused on his visor, he adds, "They think they're invulnerable. They're not even trying to be subtle. I've got nothing left up there. I don't think anybody does, except them."

"They cleared the sky? That's crazy."

"It's gonna get crazier when the Arkinson launches."

"The Arkinson?" she echoes in disbelief.

Colt says, "If you got any kind of exit plan, girl, now would be a good time to execute it."

She ignores him and says, "You can't scramble your air force, Shaw. This is a peaceful country, not a UA. Third-party military actions cannot take place—"

This time he looks at her, a cold gaze from behind his visor. "For God's sake, True, are you quoting legal scripture at me?"

"He's got a point," Colt says. "Think who you're arguing with."

Okay. Right. She sees the absurdity, the pointlessness of protest, but the situation is escalating and she can't help arguing. "Shaw, you cannot engage in an air war above this city."

"I've got a defense contract that says I can."

"*What?*"

"War is my business. It's your business. We are fucking militaries for hire."

"We are *not* the same," she says. "Variant Forces is a black-hat PMC that has not signed the code of conduct and it's run by *you*, a man who does not exist."

"For God's sake, True," Colt rumbles. "Do you want him to shoot you?"

Shaw gives her a dark look that asks the same question—but then admits, "A local PMC is the public face of the operation."

"*Shit*," she says—all she can think to say given the twisted, tangled, dangerous world they live in. Impossible to know who's in charge and who's got military-grade weapons in their back pocket. War can happen anywhere, everywhere, at any moment.

But for now, the *crack*ing has stopped. Doesn't mean it's over.

"Stay put," Shaw warns her. "We're stuck here while that laser owns the sky."

"Yeah, I got that."

To her surprise she hears voices outside, civilian voices. They sound puzzled, worried. She guides the sparrow's camera to look back down at the street. It finds people at the end of the block, looking up at the sky. More people on the roof terrace across the street. They're trying to understand what's going on. They question each other in concern, in disbelief.

"They need to get back inside," True says. She is sure there is a ground game on the way, and really, it's just a question of whether Shaw's Arkinson can eliminate the laser before Kai Yun's foot soldiers show.

That doesn't seem likely.

A civil-defense siren kicks in with an ear-shattering howl.

UNSETTLED TIMES

"I WAS NOT expecting to see you here, Lincoln. I did not know you were in Rabat."

Lincoln sits across a desk from Dove Barhoum, a man he has traded emails with on several occasions but whom he has never before met in person. Dove's weathered face, sun-blackened and set in a deep scowl, suggests he is not at all pleased to be meeting Lincoln in his office now.

"These are unsettled times," Dove goes on. "We all watch one another. We wonder who is an enemy, who is a friend . . . who has a contract for mutual defense. I have no such contract with you. But who will see you here and assume that I do?"

"Only your own staff," Lincoln says. His left elbow is propped on the armrest of his chair, his prosthetic fingers rapidly tapping—a restless motion that draws Dove's gaze and seems to unsettle him. "I didn't announce that I was coming."

Dove's scowl deepens. He's understood the accusation. After so many unreturned phone calls, a surprise visit looked like the only way to find him at his desk.

Lincoln says, "I am not here to put you in danger or to antagonize you. I've lost contact with one of my employees. I need to track her down, for her sake and for mine. I know you talked to her yesterday."

"True Brighton," Dove says. His scowl eases and his gaze grows distant. "She was here, sitting where you are sitting now. We spoke only briefly. She was careful to explain she had not come to me as a representative of Requisite Operations. Her business was of a personal nature. It is not something I can discuss."

"But you called me late yesterday," Lincoln says. "Am I wrong to think you called me to talk about True?"

"You are correct. I was concerned. To see her here on her own so soon after your operation in the TEZ. There are those who would not look on her kindly if they knew. But later, I knew it was a mistake to contact you. My clients need to know I will not discuss their business."

"Is she your client?" Lincoln asks.

Dove smiles, not in a friendly way. "No, she is not my client. She asked only a simple favor. But it's not so simple now."

Lincoln nods. "She asked you to put her in touch with Jon Helm. Did you?"

"No. I told her I could not do that—and that is all I will tell you about what we discussed. I have not seen her or heard from her since her visit yesterday. I do not know where she is."

Later, in the car, as they drive back into the city, Lincoln recounts this short interview.

"Someone threatened him," Miles concludes. He's in the back-seat between Felice and Rohan. Officially, he's an embedded journalist. The terms of their warrant don't allow him to carry a weapon, but he's armed with a phone and wears a protective vest over civilian clothing. "He called you to let you know True had been by. But you didn't pick up, and sometime after that he was told to mind his own damn business."

"That's how I read it," Lincoln agrees. He's turned around in his seat to talk to the crew in back while Khalid does the driving. Lincoln brought Khalid along as an interpreter. He put him behind the wheel because he's the most adept at reading Arabic traffic signs. But like Miles, he's unarmed. He doesn't have a security license yet, and if he did it wouldn't matter. The terms of their warrant are very specific, allowing only three soldiers to enter the country.

"A simple favor," Lincoln says. "That's how Dove put it. I think he got charmed into passing the word that she's here. When the word got to Shaw, he reacted."

"That doesn't tell us jack about where she is now," Rohan says. He's carrying a pistol strapped to his chest, mostly hidden by his protective vest.

Felice is armed the same way. "True's running an op," she says irritably. "When she needs backup, she'll call."

"I don't think we can count on that," Miles says. "You weren't in Manila. She doesn't see him for what he is and she's not looking at bringing him in. He could be gone before—"

"Hey!" Khalid says, leaning over the steering wheel to look up at the blue midday sky. "Lincoln, what is that? You see it? Streaks of smoke, like something's falling in pieces out of the sky."

Lincoln does see it. Thin smoke trails descending over the city. Three or four of them. No. More than that. Everywhere he looks—over the harbor, over suburban neighborhoods, he sees more.

"*Crap!*" Felice swears. "We just lost contact with one of our copters. The channel's showing no signal."

"The other one still sending?" Lincoln asks, feeling his phone buzz. He glances at the screen. A message from Tamara, confirming the dead starburst copter.

"Clear signal on the other one," Felice confirms. "No problem."

Yet, Lincoln thinks. A light wind tears at the first lines of smoke, but more are appearing, trailing out of the sky. "Khalid, pull over. Pull off the road. I want to get a look at this." He turns around. "Rohan, you got binoculars?"

"Yeah, in the back."

The truck bumps and lurches onto the shoulder.

"*Dammit!*" Felice says.

"Second one down?" Lincoln asks as he takes the binoculars from Rohan.

"Yeah, what—?" She looks up from her tablet, looks at the sky, *really* looks, for the first time. "*Uh-oh*," she whispers.

Lincoln does not get out of the car. He stays in his seat, using the binoculars to search the sky, achieving a crisp, clear view by using his right eye only, keeping his imperfect artificial eye closed. But there's nothing to see. Nothing. "Not even a municipal drone," he says out loud. "I think something just knocked down every UAV over the city."

Civil defense sirens begin to wail.

STREET FIGHT

THE WAIL OF the siren claws away the sediment of years, releasing dormant memories of rockets incoming. True crouches in the passage and uses her data glove to direct the sparrow into flight. A quick turn above the street, a survey of a bright blue empty sky. Nothing to note, so she sends it spiraling higher, a sacrificial bird offered up to the laser-armed marauder.

How many seconds will it take for the aircraft's AI to lock on to the tiny target?

As the sparrow climbs, she gains a wider view of the streets. She sees people on the roofs with cameras, children being waved inside from the streets, people rushing to their cars, or from their cars, and more cars jockeying for the right of way at every intersection.

Colt says, "South. Five blocks. SUV. Driving way too aggressively."

"I see it." A tall expeditionary SUV, with grill guards, racks, water containers, and dark tinted windows, bulling its way through an intersection as a smaller sedan accelerates to get out of its—

The video feed winks out of existence. True doesn't even hear the *crack* of the laser strike.

"Bird's gone," Colt says, stating the obvious.

True wonders if it's Lincoln coming in that SUV, but she doesn't think so. She tells Shaw: "We've got possible ground troops. Five blocks out and fighting traffic. Estimating five to six individuals."

"Roger that. The Arkinson is on the runway."

"How long to take off?"

"Too long to help with our new friends." He leans against the passage wall, the Triple-Y balanced in the crook of his arm, no sign of worry yet. He looks at her past the glittering screen of his visor and asks, "You ready for a street fight?"

"*Fuck,* no. How many rounds are in this pistol, anyway?"

He nods. "Good point." He lets his daypack slide to the ground. "I'm kind of busy. Could you dig out an extra magazine for me?"

She scrambles to do it, asking, "You got remote access to your SUV?"

"Won't work. If I move it up here, that laser—"

"Just move it far enough to block the lower end of the street," she says, getting his pack open. "Make them drive around."

"Yeah, I can try that."

She finds the full magazine, pulls it out, and leaves it on the ground where he can get it easily.

A startled squeak from Guiying draws her attention. She turns to see motion in the courtyard. She goes to one knee, drawing her pistol, ready to shoot before she has any idea what's there.

It's a cheap little quadcopter, a toy with a thirty-centimeter diameter. True can't hear its hum over the wailing siren, not even when it accelerates up and out of sight. "We just got our picture taken," she warns Shaw. "And Kai Yun must have mapped the layout."

Guiying has her phone out. She's huddled against the wall. "I will talk to someone," she says in a hoarse, desperate voice. "I will make this stop. I want no one else to die."

A nice thought, but True suspects momentum is against her.

"You got an update on those ground troops?" Shaw asks.

"Negative. Laser took out my flyer."

"Roger that. My truck's moving. Let's see how far it gets."

Colt speaks in her ear: "Any chance that place has a hidden back door?"

"I've been through every room," True whispers to him. "No chance at all."

She hesitates, running through a mental inventory of her equipment. "I can at least get some eyes on the street."

The beetle is in her pocket. She gets it out, uses the data glove to direct it in a quick flight out of the passage. It glides into sunlight—and an explosion shakes the street.

Guiying screams and drops her phone. It skitters across the tiles. True watches it, huddling against the wall, hunched over at the sharp concussion.

The beetle, out in the street, gets taken out by the shock wave. Its video feed goes dead.

The siren continues to wail.

"They hit my truck," Shaw says. "It's reporting damage."

Panicked cries come from surrounding buildings as people realize the danger.

"That wasn't a laser," True says.

"Grenade," he agrees. "You got *any* eyes left out there?"

"Let me try again."

She drops her pack, rummages in it, whispering to Colt at the same time. "You still there?"

"I'm here. Tell me what I can do."

"I'm dumping a new feed into your channel." Her voice covered by the ongoing siren.

She's got one more surveillance beetle, but the little mechs are fragile. She doesn't trust it to survive in the street long enough to be useful. She selects the snake biomimetic instead. It's the size of a standard writing pen, brown camouflage coloration, no flight capabilities, but it can roll on the tiny wheels in its belly, and by rearing up on its segmented body, it can get over curbs and stairs.

She sets it on the ground and, using her data glove, she activates it and links its camera to the channel she's sharing with Colt. Then she guides it out of the passage and under the nearest car. From there she eases it forward just far enough so that, as its camera swivels, it can get a clear view up and down the street.

She tells Shaw, "Your truck's blocking the end of the street."

"So at least it got that far."

"Looks like they decided to finish it with an incendiary."

"Give me a headcount."

"Zero. No one in sight." She swivels the tiny camera to look up the street, but sees only parked cars. "No one up the hill."

She flinches as a small hand squeezes her shoulder. It's Guiying. She speaks quickly in a voice laced with dread. "True, please. No fighting—"

"No choice," True growls, turning the worm's camera to look again toward the burning SUV. In a louder voice she tells Shaw, "Here we go. Three on foot, carrying some kind of submachine gun. The others must be driving around the block. No civilians in sight."

"Got it."

True looks up in time to see his gloved hand slice through air, clearing his AR screen as he moves to the end of the passage.

She gestures impatiently at Guiying. *Move back!* Then a whisper to Colt: "Keep watch. Both sides. Let me know when the rest of them show."

"I'm on it."

True draws her pistol.

"No, True," Guiying pleads. "I will go to them and—"

"You can't stop this," True tells her. "They'll kill you. They'll kill us too. No witnesses."

Staying low, she moves to back up Shaw. He's got his Triple-Y braced against his shoulder. Peering down the sights, he leans out just far enough to fire.

Three seconds, three shots. True's ears are ringing. From the end of the street, a human howl of pain to rival the siren.

"Top of the hill," Colt says.

"Top of the hill!" True shouts. Still bent low, she swivels, pistol ready, and sees the expeditionary SUV rocking on its suspension as it finishes a hard turn into the street. She is in motion and vulnerable when Guiying shoves her, sending her reeling into the smooth wood of the open door.

A thump of impact. A jolt of pain in her shoulder. She draws a sharp breath acrid with the taste of toxic smoke.

Guiying steps past her. Steps out of the passage shouting, "Do not shoot!" The command swiftly repeated in Chinese, and then in Arabic.

True's gaze connects with Shaw. She shares his shock, but only for a fraction of a second, and then he's in motion. It's instinct. His inherent nature. A remembrance of who he used to be. With the Triple-Y in his right hand, he steps after Guiying, hooks his left arm around her waist, and hauls her back toward shelter—a heroic effort interrupted by a blast of heat and steam.

True's eyes squeeze shut against the shock wave. Her brain registers a wet popping noise, easily audible over the wail of the civil defense siren. And Shaw starts screaming.

Fuck, she thinks, smelling a stink of burned flesh even before she opens her eyes. *Fuck, fuck, fuck.* She doesn't need to look to know the laser tagged him. Colt is talking to her but she's not listening.

She grits her teeth and thinks, *Do what needs to be done.*

She hasn't forgotten the expeditionary, charging down between the parked cars. She swivels again toward the street, fires two shots at the windshield to discourage it. To her surprise, white stars of damage appear in the glass. Not bulletproof? The driver brakes hard. He looks as surprised as she is. The assholes probably bought the damn thing thirty minutes ago from a used car lot.

So she's gained a few seconds. She pockets the pistol and goes to her knees, letting the parked cars hide her from the soldiers in the truck. That's when she sees Guiying—and realizes Shaw was not the laser's only victim. The blast must have hit both of them, but Shaw didn't take the worst of it. He's still alive, still screaming.

Shock stops True cold as she stares at what's left of Li Guiying. The roboticist's upper body has been disintegrated by the laser's fierce energy. Her lower torso and legs are all that's recognizable.

Questions crowd True's brain: Did Kai Yun hit her on purpose? Did they mean to erase her existence? Or was Shaw the target and Guiying's death a mistake?

Process it later, True chides herself. No choice.

Praying the laser will need time to recharge, she reaches out over the blasted remains, reaches into the sunlight, far enough to scoop up Shaw's Triple-Y from where it's fallen into the street. She scrambles back and stands up, bringing it to her shoulder. The expeditionary is retreating fast. She hits it anyway with a double burst across the windshield as it reaches the top of the block and backs out of sight.

"What do we got, Dad?" she murmurs as the siren continues to wail.

"Street is clear for the moment. It's not going to last."

"Roger that."

Dreading what she will find, she turns at last to look at Shaw.

He's down and writhing on the threshold. His AR visor is cast aside along with his earpiece. Guiying's body must have shielded him but he's still hit bad.

His left shoulder is burned to the bone. True can see the shoulder joint past a two-inch-diameter gouge where a bite has been taken out of his thin protective vest and the flesh beneath vaporized. But the wound is much bigger than that, much worse, because the surrounding muscle has been cooked by the heat. The damaged tissue is already swelling and weeping fluids. The gouge continues across his chest. It burned through his shirt, leaving it smoldering, and scarred the lightly armored vest underneath. The vest's cloth covering is smoldering too.

She locks down her revulsion, her horror. No time for it. Assess the situation.

He has fallen over the threshold, partway outside, and is surely visible from overhead. Yet the laser hasn't fired again. Possible the UAV is out of position or the laser might still be recharging, gathering power for a direct strike. Or maybe Kai Yun has decided they want to recover him alive, question him on his relation with Li Guiying.

They better hurry up, she thinks.

Already his screams are subsiding into an inarticulate bleating growl. True thinks maybe it's a fatal wound, whether he gets help or not.

Two seconds have gone to observation and assessment. Seconds she regrets, and tries to make up for now.

She slings the Triple-Y, digs her fingers around the waist of his pants, grabs his good arm at the elbow, and drags him back into the shelter of the passage so he can't be hit again. He's got to be at least a hundred eighty pounds, but the smooth floor tiles and her adrenaline let her do it.

He fights her. He claws at the floor with his right hand, kicking, sputtering syllables that might be parts of curses.

Meanwhile, from up the street, competing with Shaw, competing with the siren, competing with the ringing in her ears and the cacophony in her head, a voice shouts in Arabic-accented English that she needs to come out. And another layer of sound beyond that: the fierce roar of a jet engine growing rapidly louder, closer.

The Arkinson? Maybe. She hopes Shaw wasn't piloting it. She hopes it's autonomous.

Shaw goes still—they both do—as a jet streaks in, so close its roaring engine overwhelms the siren and shakes the building's masonry. True drops belly-down beside Shaw as an autocannon hammers the street, kicking up concrete chips that pelt the passageway. Then the jet sweeps away.

True sits up again, shoulders heaving as she catches her breath. Sweat salts her skin. She registers these sensations along with the smell of burned flesh, and the dust-dry odor of broken concrete, and the acrid taste of jet wash. She turns to look at Shaw. He's on his back, eyes half open. His breathing is rapid and shallow. He's not moaning anymore.

Bad signs, she thinks.

"Dad, if you're still there, give me a sitrep. What's out there?"

She reaches for Shaw's pack, thinking she saw a med kit in there when she was getting the extra magazine.

Colt says, "Street's still clear."

"Can you see the Arkinson?"

"I'm a fucking worm on the ground! I'm lucky I can see anything."

She tries to sound soothing. "I know."

She finds the med kit. Pulls out the wound packing. He's not bleeding much, but she'll need to stabilize the joint, cover the injury to keep it clean.

Colt says, "Girl, this might be your only chance to run."

"Not going to happen," she tells him. She makes that promise to Shaw, speaking into his ear to ensure he hears: "You were there for Diego. I'm here for you. I won't leave you."

To her surprise, he speaks, gruff words forced past his pain. "She dead?"

"Yes. I'm sorry. I saw what you did. You tried to save her."

"Fucking stupid," he whispers. "What the fuck was I thinking?"

"You were thinking she was going to die and you needed to help."

"*Shit*," he breathes, closing his eyes. "Fuck me, anyway."

"I'm going to look outside, Shaw. I'll be right back."

At this his eyes open again. He looks at her fearfully. "Give me that pistol before you go."

"No, it's okay. I won't leave you. I'm just going to look outside."

She unslings the Triple-Y and creeps the few steps to the threshold, averting her eyes from Guiying's gruesome remains. Past the body she can see that the street has acquired a beaded centerline stitched by bullet holes.

She straightens up so she can see over the parked cars. Shaw's SUV still burns at the bottom of the street. She looks uphill, but she can't see the expeditionary. The wounded soldier who was moaning just moments ago has gone quiet. Maybe he's been taken away? She can't see any bodies. She sees no one at all.

The civil defense siren continues its rising and falling wail. Her eardrums vibrate with the noise, but it's not loud enough to drown out the Arkinson's distant scream. She listens, wondering if it's hunting Kai Yun's silent UAV, or evading it.

The answer comes in an orange flash: an explosion high up in the atmosphere and far out to sea. She holds her breath as the thunderous noise dissolves. She listens past the blaring siren.

Relief arrives when she hears the jet's roar again, growing louder as it races back toward the coast.

The Arkinson survived. The explosion had to be Kai Yun's laser-armed UAV.

"I need backup," she says aloud.

"You need to get out of there," Colt answers from her TINSL.

"You're right." Her priority is to withdraw from this position, get Shaw out of here, before local law enforcement gears up to penetrate this scene—but she'll need help to do that, and there is only one source of help available to her.

"Heads up, Ripley!"

She shouts the phrase to make sure the tablet's audio picks up her voice over the background noise. "Text Lincoln my location."

"Text sent," Ripley answers in her earpiece.

"Now call him."

Is she betraying Shaw's trust by doing this? Maybe. But she can't leave him here.

GRIDLOCK

ON THE HIGHWAY into the city, traffic has slowed to a crawl. Lincoln sits, tense, in the front passenger seat of ReqOps' leased SUV, caught within a crush of massive trucks and tiny sedans.

Many of the sedans don't have drivers or passengers. They're moving autonomously, at the remote command of distant owners, and they're following all traffic regulations, which puts them at a gross disadvantage to cars with human drivers. Horns honk and brakes slam on every time a manually driven sedan shifts suddenly from one lane to another, shouldering in front of some meek autonomous vehicle, which gives way rather than risking a collision. Human drivers further violate laws by bouncing across the median to turn around and join the lanes leaving Rabat. The exodus is heavy, but traffic out of the city is moving faster than traffic in. Traffic everywhere is red-lined. Not a surprise, given that the city is under attack.

The dashboard radio is on. The volume is low as a man speaks, alternately in Arabic and then in French, advising people to be calm, to stay home, to stay off the roads. That much Lincoln can make out.

Khalid understands more. "Did you get that?" he asks, hands tight on the wheel. "The police have closed some exits into the city center. We're not going to be able to get back to the hotel anytime soon."

"We don't need to go back to the hotel," Lincoln says. "Take the next exit. Let's see how close we can get to the target district."

He has watched an Arkinson fighter buzz a neighborhood of upscale houses, homing in on a column of black smoke unfurling against the noon sky. He's watching the Arkinson now as it returns triumphant after a brief dogfight far out over the ocean.

Rohan leans in from the backseat. "You thinking True's involved in this?" he asks.

Lincoln nods, watching the Arkinson make a wide turn toward the airport. "No way is this a coincidence. She's got to have some part—"

He breaks off as his phone buzzes with a forwarded message. Rohan leans even farther over to get a look at the screen. "It's a text from True," he says over his shoulder, filling in Felice and Miles, who crowd forward too.

Lincoln opens the message to find a map with a marked location.

"*Got it!*" Rohan yells. "That's the target district. What is it, like five klicks? Four? Khalid, you need to get us down there."

Khalid tries to get a look at Lincoln's phone while tailgating the car in front of him. "I'm going to take this next exit and—"

He interrupts himself as the phone rings.

"It's True," Lincoln announces as they join a slow procession of vehicles escaping the highway. He's feeling more bitterness than relief as he accepts the call, putting it on speaker so the others can hear. He says, "You're dead center of this civil disturbance."

"Roger that." Terse words spoken in crisp syllables, no apology in her voice. "You have a vehicle? Because we need a way out of here before the local authorities show."

We. He notes the plural but doesn't question it yet. "Affirmative on the vehicle. We're on the road, heading your way. What's your status?"

"He's wounded. Not ambulatory. When can you get here?"

She doesn't need to say his name.

Lincoln's thoughts flow in layers, his quiet shock confined in the undercurrent: *True found Shaw Walker! Not ambulatory. Not going anywhere.*

From the backseat, Miles speaks in a triumphant murmur, "We've *got* him."

"Ah, shit," Khalid says. "Look at that."

Lincoln lifts his gaze. Ahead is a traffic circle, packed bumper to bumper and barely moving. He wonders if it's going to be like this everywhere, or just close to the belt highway. "We could be dealing with gridlock," he warns True. "If you're in danger—"

He hesitates, stumbling over the irony of what he's about to say. His goal is to take Shaw Walker into custody, but he tells her, "If you're in danger, *leave him.* It doesn't matter. Get out on your own. Walk out, and we'll rendezvous."

"No, Lincoln. Negative. I am not leaving him."

Khalid edges around the traffic circle. The streets beyond look packed for as far as Lincoln can see.

"We're never going to get there in the car," Rohan says. "We need to go on foot. Go in and get him before someone else does."

Khalid says, "I'll put the truck on autopilot."

Lincoln addresses the phone. "True, give me some background. What kind of resistance are we facing?"

"Nothing. The sky's been swept clean. Ground forces neutralized. Right now, there's no one here."

Rohan likes this answer. He grins, turns around in the seat, and starts pulling daypacks from the back of the truck, handing them to Felice and Miles.

"What's your ETA?" True wants to know.

"Unknown."

Khalid continues to edge forward in traffic even as he programs the autopilot. Lincoln holds up a hand in a cease-and-desist gesture and tells him, "You're staying with the truck."

This gets him a dark scowl. He ignores it. He tells True, "We'll come in on foot, secure the area. As long as you feel you're safe, you can stay with him. But do not get yourself hurt and don't get arrested."

"Is Miles with you too?" True asks, suspicion sharp in her voice.

Lincoln reminds himself that her loyalties are divided, that she defected, that they are not on the same side. "Miles is here. He deserved to come."

She says, a little desperately, "He was not behind the car bombing. You need to know that."

Lincoln doesn't want to hear it. "We're coming, True."

He ends the call.

THE BLACK HEART

"WE'RE COMING, TRUE," Lincoln says.

A warning? A promise? True can't tell.

She is on her knees as he ends the call, her chest rising and falling in anxious rhythm as she wonders again if it's right action that brought Lincoln here, or vendetta.

She knows—she agrees—that Shaw must account for more than just Renata's death. There is the threat made against Lincoln and Requisite Operations, the loss of the Hai-Lins, and far worse, the executions Miles witnessed in the desert. No doubt there are many more crimes. God knows what's been done in the name of Variant Forces. And farther away in time, there is Shaw's disappearance, his broken oath, his failure to come home.

Still, True would like to believe Shaw innocent at least of the attack at Requisite Operations.

She turns back to him and as she does, the wailing siren goes mercifully silent. She closes her eyes and whispers a grateful "*Thank you.*" When she opens them again, she finds him watching her. "Hey," she says, kneeling to pull a roll of gauze from the med kit. "I need you to hold on, okay? I'm going to get you out of here."

He surprises her again with the strength of his voice—a hoarse whisper, but coherent, easy to understand. "We done now?" he asks. "You get what you came for?"

He's got a multitool on his belt. "I'm going to borrow this." She takes it and uses the scissors to cut away his ruined shirt, fully exposing the protective vest underneath. It's got flat loops meant to hold gear. She threads the gauze through those loops. "I need to stabilize your arm," she warns him. She doesn't wait for his consent. She takes his ruined arm and folds it across his chest, hearing the catch in his throat, watching his eyes squeeze shut and blood rush to his face. She uses the gauze to tie his arm down, and as she works, she says, "We're not done, Shaw. I want you to tell me one more thing. Tell me why we're here. Why did you take this path? Choose this life? Why didn't you come home?"

"You got my visor?" he asks, voice weaker now.

"It's around somewhere."

"It's under the car," Colt says.

The visor doesn't matter. She pulls both daypacks close and upends them, spilling their contents on the floor.

"Find it," Shaw tells her.

"Answer my question." Working quickly, she inventories the equipment. He's got the extra magazine, a clean shirt, a waterproof sack with battery packs in it, a PV panel, and recharging cables. She's got a small first-aid kit, a few toiletries, one beetle still secure in its capsule, and two tracking discs—"mother's helpers." Not much that's useful, but she slides the beetle and the tracking discs into her jacket pocket. The rest of it she shoves into her pack, leaving his empty. "Why this path, Shaw?" she presses him.

His eyes are closed. A cold smile is on his lips. "Because I survived Nungsan."

An answer that says nothing.

"Get ready," she tells him in gentle warning. "I've got to pack this wound."

At her first touch, he sucks in his breath. His back arches. She's got nothing for the pain and not nearly enough trauma dressing to finish the job, but she does what she can, hiding the exposed bone, talking as she works. "You were angry. I understand that. To go through that, and to be left there, abandoned there. But in the end you won. You rescued yourself."

"*No.*" He growls the word. "*Fuck*, no. God saved me, True. The Old Man set it up, made it work. I cracked two skulls and walked out of there. No one even took a shot at me. Maybe they were all drunk, stoned; it doesn't matter. Whatever the physics, it was a fucking miracle."

She braces for some acerbic comment from Colt, but what she gets is a tired sigh. "Miracles happen," he mutters—a low, reluctant admission.

"A miracle?" she muses. She wants to hear more and she wants to keep him talking too, keep him conscious. His strength amazes her. It makes her want to believe he could survive this after all.

"A *literal* miracle," Shaw insists. "*God*, this hurts. Will you stop?"

"I'm done," she lies. "I just want to tape it all down."

His eyes are open—bloodshot and red-rimmed. His dark tan doesn't hide the mottled pallor of his skin. But his breathing is quiet and though his voice is a whisper, his words are clear as he says again, "A literal miracle. I've thought about it a lot, and I can't explain it any other way than divine intervention."

As he says it, a breeze touches her neck. That's what she tells herself when she feels a chill and hears, faintly, Diego's agonized screams. "Are you a man of faith?" she asks, working a note of skepticism into her voice.

This earns a slight, bitter smile. "You know how it is. We all want to make sense of things. When there's some horror show with only one survivor, people say God meant it to be that way. God was done with the rest of them, but not with that last poor asshole. If you're the survivor, it must be because you've still got something to do, there must be some fucking *reason* for it."

He's right. People do say things like that, and she gets angry every time she hears it, every time she thinks of the life Diego might have had. "Is that what *you* believe?"

"Hell, yeah," he whispers.

"You're lying."

A faint chuckle.

"You know it was just chance," she insists. "Just the way it worked out."

"No, no, no," he says in a mocking singsong. "That's the easy answer. You've got to look deeper. You've got to see down to the black heart. I'm not a good man. Never was. You ask Lincoln. He'll tell you. I've done some shit.

"So when it came down to just me and Diego, it was D who should have lived. A good man. Deserved to get home. But I'm the one who walked away. And after, I wondered, was I supposed to be grateful it wasn't me dying in that fire? Was I supposed to see the fucking light? If that's what the Old Man intended, he miscalculated. I wanted a different deal."

Take me instead.

A sacrifice offered—and rejected. "So you've been feuding with God, Shaw?"

"All is vanity," he whispers. Then in a firmer voice, "What I've learned since Nungsan is that it doesn't matter what we want or who we are or what we do, because our time is over. God's done with us. It's the mechs' turn to be on stage. Li Guiying worked hard making it happen. A million others with her. Mechs build our shit, they run the economy, fight our wars, while we sit on our asses and pretend we're relevant. We're not. *You* know that."

He's not wrong.

What was it Tamara said? *An aggressive, diverse swarm is more dangerous than any traditional soldier, and easy to print up.* True used to pilot helicopters but most are robotic now. AIs fly warplanes, guide missiles, control satellites. They analyze incoming intelligence faster than any human could process it. Artificial intelligence and robotics make it possible for a small outfit like Requisite Operations—or Variant Forces—to operate with formidable force, invade unprotected territory, engage in raids and bombings and dogfights above peaceful cities. To act with the authority of a sovereign nation.

She thinks of Lincoln, in charge of his own small sovereign nation. He's moving on foot through the gridlocked city. She tells herself, *He'll be here soon.* She shrugs on her daypack so she'll be ready to go.

Shaw's eyes are half-closed when he murmurs, "It's the end times, True."

"No," she says in gentle dismissal. "That's nonsense." Her tone is a pose, a false front of confidence, but she is not going to encourage his apocalyptic state of mind. She wipes the sweat and the tears from his eyes with a last clean scrap of gauze. "You know you're fucking crazy?"

"Crazy," he agrees. "Not wrong."

She's almost grateful when Colt interrupts—though there's fear in his gruff voice. "Oh crap," he says. "There's a goddamned armed robot coming down the street."

True is abruptly aware of the ratcheting sound of tracks on the pavement. She grabs the Triple-Y and starts to lever herself up on stiff legs, her head pounding, but Shaw reaches across his body with his good hand and grabs the rifle barrel, pushing it down, unbalancing her.

"Don't try to fight it," he warns her. "You can't win and you're not white-listed."

It comes fast. She hardly has time to look around before it's there: a little armed robotic vehicle, poised on the threshold along-side Guiying's remains. It's got a traditional design, like a minia-ture tank, riding on caterpillar treads. It's only about forty inches long, with a jointed arm supporting a short gun barrel, and behind that, a mast with a 360-degree camera sealed within a spherical transparent housing. Affixed to its armored surface is the Rogue Lightning emblem. Marking another deadly mech. She notes this as the gun swivels, sighting on her.

"*Fuck*," she whispers and perversely her next thought is how tired she feels. But tired or not, she has to do what she can.

"It's my people," Shaw says. "Didn't want to bring them in. Couldn't stop the emergency beacon."

"That's why you needed your visor."

"You'll be okay."

She doesn't believe it. *Don't trust anyone.*

The situation is slipping away. Lincoln is coming but not soon enough. She turns to hide the movement of her hand as she pulls a tracking disc out of her pocket.

"Two armed males just stepped into sight," Colt warns.

She activates the disc, shoves it into a hidden pocket at the waistband of her pants. She gets out the other disc, and under the guise of adjusting the medical tape on Shaw's shoulder, she shoves it between the layers of dressing.

"You got that?" she whispers to Colt.

He responds in a defeated voice, "You think you're going to be a hostage. Roger that."

FRIENDS

FROM THE STREET outside, a youthful male voice with a British accent shouts, "Jon! If you're still breathing, tell your friend to put the gun down and back away."

"Do it," Shaw warns her.

She eyes the ARV, wondering how many shots it would take to damage the thing. "Is it autonomous?" she asks.

"Of *course*."

It would take just one bullet to lay her out, and with no human in the kill chain the shot would come without hesitation.

"Okay," she says, mouthing the word for the benefit of the ARV's camera. But she doesn't put the gun down right away. Still on one knee, she edges back, holding on to the Triple-Y but with her hand nowhere near the trigger. The ARV adjusts the direction of its weapon to track her movement.

"Gun on the ground!" the voice insists. "I won't ask you again."

She's a few feet from Shaw now, so she sets it down at her side, almost behind her. She holds her hands half up, palms out, rising from her crouch. Still moving slowly backward, almost at the mouth of the passage. Just a harmless old lady. The sling of the Triple-Y is only inches from her feet.

"Take the visor off too!"

She does it, folding it, sliding it into her pocket. She's still wearing her TINSL.

Out in the street, two well-muscled, athletic young men come into sight. Both are dressed in neat trousers and button-down shirts, but True is sure that beneath their shirts they're wearing protective vests, and they move with the crisp discipline of highly trained soldiers.

They pause behind the ARV. The shorter one wears a shoulder holster, empty now, because he's holding his pistol in a two-handed grip—muzzle down, for the moment. He has a dark-brown complexion, unruly black hair, and heavy black eyebrows just visible above the nearly opaque screen of an AR visor.

The second man is taller, with deep black skin. Black sunglasses hide his eyes. He too carries a pistol though he's more relaxed, his gun held casually in one hand. "We all friends here?" he asks in that same British voice she heard before.

True would love to think so but it's hard to answer in the affirmative, given that the ARV still has its gun trained on her. So she says nothing. But Shaw speaks, his voice a low, hoarse whisper. "Stop fucking around, Ian. We got to move out now."

The tall man, Ian, makes a show of looking down at Guiying's blasted corpse. "Jesus fuck, Jon," he says, stepping over it to enter the passage. "That's fucking impressive."

True nudges the sling of the Triple-Y with her toe as she eases to one side, a shift that puts Ian between herself and the robotic vehicle. She is very conscious of the weight of the pistol in her pocket. Also of the weight of the second man's gaze as he repositions himself to maintain a clean line of sight.

Ian gives her a casual look-over before frowning down at Shaw, taking in the massive wound dressing already stained with blood and yellow fluids. "Got to say it, brother. It looks like you're having a bad day."

All friends here, huh?

Shaw said these were his people, but True is not sensing the love. "That's what a laser can do," she says cautiously. "One strike. Killed her. Burned him down to the bone."

"*Fucking* shit." He crouches beside Shaw. "No worries, Jon. I'll get you out of here."

"You need to get him to a hospital," True says. She eyes the Triple-Y on the floor, and the ARV . . . and the man in the street, who is eyeing her.

"Fuck that," Shaw growls.

"No," Ian says. "The lady's got it right."

"Don't shit me." To True's astonishment, Shaw manages to roll onto his uninjured arm. He starts to push himself up. But Ian puts a hand on his wounded shoulder and shoves him down. "*God,*" Shaw gasps, back arching in pain.

"Come on, Jon," Ian says. "Don't be an ass. You're in bad shape and that puts me in a bad position. You need to give me access. Give me the keys. Because if you go, Variant Forces goes with you. Money disappears, and I've got nothing."

"You worked that out?" Shaw breathes. "You got to figure, that's on purpose."

"Two years I've had your back. Kept you alive."

"That's your job. Still is. You're paid damn well for it."

Ian looks up, making brief eye contact with his partner. "Farouk predicted you'd do this. That when it came time, you'd leave us on the street. I did not want to believe it, but you've been a stranger since that cock-up with Al-Furat. When you disappeared yesterday, I had concerns. Farouk agreed. We needed an exit plan."

Shaw relaxes a little, he closes his eyes. "So you two been talking to someone? Got a new contract?"

"It's not too late," Ian assures him. "We can put this back together, mate, but I need to be on the inside this time. A trusted partner. Farouk too."

"*Fuck* you," Shaw spits.

The man outside—Farouk—shifts his focus from True to Ian. "We won't get anything from him," he says bitterly, speaking in Arabic-accented English.

True uses the moment to hook the Triple-Y's sling with her toe. She jerks it close, crouches to grab it, and ducks out of the passage and out of sight. In the courtyard now, she sprints to the stairs, climbing them two at a time, pivoting at the turn to the next flight, hearing the whine of the ARV's motor over the concussion of her footfalls and her ragged breathing.

"Heads up, Ripley," she pants. "Text Lincoln. Enemy on the ground. *Send.*"

She reaches the balcony on the second level. From there she can see the ARV, already in the courtyard. Its gun barrel faces away from her, but as soon as she moves, its camera will pick her up. She needs to disable the camera before the gun is in position to shoot.

One quick breath. She bounds to the edge of the balcony, jams the barrel of the Triple-Y over the railing, and squeezes the trigger, hammering at the transparent housing that protects the camera. In the enclosed courtyard the concussions are deafening. Bullets ricochet without penetrating the housing, without breaking it, but white scars blossom across its surface. She's painting it white, blinding the camera. The gun barrel whips around to target her, but partway through its arc, it freezes. A second later, the protective housing gives way and the camera explodes in a spray of glass and plastic.

"Now you got to come find me," she whispers as she shifts her position, moving farther along the balcony.

Through her TINSL, Colt cautions her, "You just stay out of sight."

"Yeah, I'll be okay." She hopes it's true. She pauses at a point where she can watch for movement at the mouth of the passage while she swaps out the partly expended magazine. "They sold him out," she says.

"Nothing you can do about it— Oh, *Christ.* Three more armed males at the top of the street."

"Is it Lincoln?" If he didn't get her text, he could walk right into a firestorm.

"*Shit.* No. According to the identification tag on this display, it's Rihab."

Rihab. Hussam's little brother who inherited control of Al-Furat, who claimed credit for Renata's murder, and who holds

Shaw responsible for the security failure at Tadmur. The two mercs downstairs, Ian and Farouk, they must have sold Shaw to Rihab.

"Rihab's going to kill him," she whispers, just to let Colt know she's still there.

She shoulders the rifle again as the ARV starts up, but all it does is back out of sight through the passage. No one enters the courtyard—not yet.

"Heads up, Ripley," she says, moving back along the balcony to the stairs. "Call Lincoln."

The sun stands high above the confusion in Rabat's packed streets. Vehicles jam the roads. Those with human drivers have started ignoring the traffic lanes; those driven by AIs advance at a snail's pace, constrained by an excess of caution. Police hold command over major intersections, leaving the smaller cross streets as jousting grounds for opposing vehicles. Lincoln has already seen two fistfights break out over fender-benders.

The sidewalks, where they exist, are just as crowded. Where they don't exist, people wade into traffic and make things worse. There's no dominant direction to the movement. It's as if everyone in the city, citizens and tourists alike, just wants to get somewhere else.

At least the nerve-grating civil defense sirens have gone silent.

Lincoln has divided his people, sending them on different routes in case of trouble on the way—and also, so they don't look like a gang. He's got Miles with him. Rohan is partnered with Felice. He left Khalid with the truck, telling him, "I need you here, in place to deploy the last pair of copters if it comes to that. Go ahead and put the truck on autopilot. Then climb in back and get the starbursts armed. Clear?"

The terms detailed in their Warrant of Capture and Rendition place severe restrictions on their weapons and armed robotics. They are allowed to carry only handguns, and lethal robotics may only be deployed in a hostage situation and under the oversight of the Moroccan police.

Or in an emergency situation, on my authority, Lincoln thinks.

He'll deal with the consequences later. With luck they won't have to deploy the armed copters, but it's an option if they need it.

Together, Lincoln and Miles move fast, jogging when they can. Miles is still out of shape from his two-month captivity. He breathes hard, struggling to keep up, but he doesn't complain.

Their only weapon is Lincoln's pistol, which he's carrying in a shoulder holster hidden under his light jacket. His MARC visor links him to the Cloud through the local cell network. Video is impossible, given the emergency load the network is carrying, but he's got a voice link to the mission command post, where Chris is overseeing their movements, with Tamara backing him up.

Lincoln worried at first that the visor would attract unwelcome attention, but it's attracted less attention than his face usually does. Also, he's seen several people narrating the chaos from behind AR screens with active cameras; so far he's heard no one objecting.

He shoulders through yet another knot of people, following a route that displays as a golden path overlaid on the sidewalk. Miles sticks close behind him. He doesn't have a visor, but he's got an audio link.

They shift into a jog as the sidewalk clears. The people they pass look frightened and confused. They're trying to make sense of what's happening, asking questions none can answer, continuously checking the screens of their phones in a hunt for updates.

A green light winks on in his display indicating activity in their ad hoc comm network. Chris speaks in a grim but businesslike tone. "True just sent a text. It reads, 'Enemy on the ground.' That's it. No details."

"Roger that."

He trades a glance with Miles, who nods, acknowledging the gravity of the news.

He says over comms, "Rohan, Felice, find cover as you approach the target address. Stay down and out of sight until we can assess and coordinate."

They respond in low voices:

"*Got it.*"

"*Roger that.*"

He and Miles are crossing a gridlocked intersection, weaving between trapped cars, when Chris says, "I'm forwarding a call from True."

The call icon appears on Lincoln's screen. He uses his data glove to tap the air, accepting it. "Here."

She speaks in a breathless whisper. "It's all gone south. He's badly wounded. Immobile. Helpless. His people have sold him out to Rihab. Rihab is *here*. He's holding Shaw responsible for what we did at Tadmur. He's going to kill him."

Lincoln listens to this, his anger rising. She speaks as if Shaw's safety should be his first concern. It's not. "What's *your* status?"

"I'm alone inside the building. They know I'm here but they haven't come after me. Not yet. Might not be worth it to them. They know I'm armed. I want to take him back, but it's five of them, one of me, and they've got a little ARV."

He comes down hard on this. "You will take *no* action on your own. You will stay out of sight until we get there. Is that understood?"

"It's not that easy. I need to know. Are you here for Shaw? Or are you going to let Rihab have him?"

Lincoln is moving fast. He's not in a mood to negotiate. He's not in a situation amenable to discussion. Even so, if he can keep her talking, that might keep her from pulling another crazy stunt. So, between the shallow breaths that fuel his sprint across the district, he lays out a grudging explanation. "I've got a warrant for him, based on depositions from Miles and from Ryan Rogers. The warrant doesn't pay, but it obligates me to bring him back and deliver him into the hands of American authorities."

"Then what?"

"Not my problem. Not your problem."

"I know he cannot be left to go on the way he's been doing since Nungsan. I know that. But it would be fucking ironic if he ends up in a black-site prison and no one knows he's still alive."

"There's no way to make it right, True."

"You need to get here soon."

"I'm coming."

"I think they're going to take him somewhere."

"I'm *coming*. Stay out of sight. Wait for me. Promise me, True."

She hesitates, but then says, "I'll do what I can."

She ends the call.

"You *will* stay out of sight," Colt orders in his deepest command voice. "They're waiting for you, True. They're expecting you to show."

She has crept downstairs until she's just a few steps from the bottom. Male voices reverberate in the passageway, speaking rapid-fire Arabic that she doesn't have the skill to follow. "Tell me their positions," she whispers to Colt.

"They're positioned to kill you. Put your head around that corner and you're—"

Shaw screams, a drawn-out animal roar of agony.

True's eyes go wide. It's all she can do to hold her position when instinct is telling her to go to him, to help, to do what she can. His scream fades out, and to her horror, nervous laughter follows. "What are they doing to him?"

"Not sure," Colt says. "This goddamn worm! I can't *see*. No, wait. Wait. I think they picked him up. They're moving out. Yeah. One of the new guys has him over his shoulders. Taking him up the street. I think he's fainted. Or he's dead. Either way, they're leaving. The ARV too."

"Are they *all* leaving?"

He hesitates. "I think so. I can't tell for sure. No one's in the passage. Stay where you are. You'll be okay."

That's one option, but is it right action? Here, now, Rihab only has four soldiers with him. There won't be a better time, a better place to confront him, to take Shaw back. But Lincoln is not here, while Rihab and his crew will be gone in just a couple of minutes.

She is the only one who can slow them down.

She makes her decision. She'll do what she can, but she'll do it from the high ground. Colt's protests are loud and virulent in her ear as she turns and sprints up the stairs, back to the second level, then to the roof.

The stairs come out beneath the covered end of the terrace. She arrives, chest heaving, heart thumping hard. The fixed roof casts heavy shade across the upholstered furniture of the sitting area—a sharp contrast to the bright white, sunlit walls out under the open sky.

As she moves from shade to sunlight, her shoulder brushes a curtain tied back against a supporting column, setting it swaying. "*Shit*," she whispers. Extraneous motion is distracting, and it's a giveaway, but at least she's alone.

She holds the Triple-Y at her shoulder as she advances cautiously, moving closer to the edge of the terrace. She needs to get just close enough to look into the street. A glimpse, seen past the gun sight:

Shaw. His body is draped over the shoulders of a man who's moving quickly up the street on the heels of two more men. Another is already at the top of the street. That one, she thinks, is Farouk. He looks back at her. He's got a tablet in his hand.

Ah! The fucking ARV.

Down in the street, on the edge of her vision, something moves. Her brain registers it as a gun barrel rising from behind a parked car and before conscious thought kicks in, she drops to her knees, collapses to her side. A fusillade of heavy-caliber slugs slams into the terrace wall, sending concrete and plaster chips flying over her. She's sure Farouk can't see her anymore but the shots keep coming. It's like he's trying to chew down the wall.

Then it stops.

Colt is swearing: a long low stream of profanities.

"I'm still here," she whispers to him.

Staying low, she rolls to her knees—and motion draws her eye. At first she thinks it's the swaying curtain, but her visor picks out a point deeper in the shadow of the sheltering roof, a point at the top of the stairs, and highlights it.

Her mind flashes on the math: four enemy in the street, one more whose location is unknown. She fires a single shot at the point her visor has marked, then dives to the side and rolls. Concrete chips from the terrace's shattered wall grind into her hip and shoulder and tear at her shirt. She hisses at the pain but doesn't slow down. Scrambling, she gets behind an empty hip-high terracotta planter just as a flash-bang grenade goes off. She hunches, shading her eyes with her arm as a second one follows.

Ian, she thinks, grateful that she's still thinking. Bright sparks dazzle her eyes and her ears are ringing. It could have been so much worse, but she got lucky. The blasts dissipated across the open rooftop and she caught only the edge.

She peers past the terracotta pot. The shade under the roof and the stunned state of her vision make it hard to see, but her visor finds a target for her. It throws a new highlight: Ian, his lanky athletic figure half hidden behind the wall enclosing the stairs. He's leaning out just a little, looking for her, his pistol held in a two-handed grip.

She thinks, *Now he has to gamble*. He has to ask himself if the flash-bang put her on the ground, somewhere out of sight. If so, he has to hurry, because she won't be down for long. If not, when he moves he makes himself a target.

He darts out of the stairwell, crosses to the shelter of a column that holds up the roof. No curtain on this column. He pivots around it, swinging the pistol to cover the span of the rooftop. "Stay down and you won't get hurt!" he shouts.

She bides her time, a half-second, waiting until his chest is exposed. And then she leans out from behind the terracotta pot and fires off two shots that hit over his heart. There's no blood. His vest has caught the slugs, but he goes down anyway. The shock has probably put a temporary stop to his heartbeat.

She runs to secure him. Well, she hobbles really, as her right calf threatens to seize up, but she gets there. She kicks his pistol out of reach. He's groaning, trying to push himself up, so she kicks him in the head. "Stay down and you won't get hurt," she tells him.

She still has Shaw's multitool. Its blade is sharp. She uses it to cut a tasseled rope from the nearest curtain.

"Ian's buddy is coming to check on him," Colt says.

"*Fuck.*" Another kick convinces Ian to be still while she secures his arms behind his back. While he's still woozy, she ties his ankles together. Then she pats him down. The only interesting things she finds are a phone and an electronic car key. She takes them both, but powers down the phone.

"Okay, where's Farouk?" she asks Colt as she moves to the stairs.

"He's coming in through the passage. Alone."

She heads down as quickly and quietly as she can manage. "With or without the ARV?"

"No ARV. He wants his man cred."

"*Man* cred," she scoffs. "That's your generation. He's only coming in because it's too hard to steer the ARV without the camera."

She stops on the second level, peering out from behind the wall that encloses the stairwell. The position allows her to see over the balcony and down the length of the courtyard to the small citrus trees and the fountain, the two chairs and the bench beyond. The overturned table.

How long since Guiying first walked into the courtyard? Thirty minutes? Less?

She turns her gaze to the passage. She can see its mouth, but she can't see into it—and she can't see Farouk. He's probably in the courtyard, hidden beneath the balcony or at the bottom of the stairwell.

Her MARC flashes a red highlight at the top of her visor. She looks up, targeting the highlight with her Triple-Y before recognition sparks: A sparrow. A mechanical sparrow descending from the roof terrace, dropping toward the courtyard in a swift spiral. Not her sparrow—the laser destroyed hers—but the same design.

Lincoln?

Her finger is still floating above the trigger when a shot goes off—it sounds like it's right below her. The sparrow bursts apart as the shot reechoes off the walls.

As the echoes fade, she hears Farouk. He's running, bounding up the stairs. She gives him two seconds, long enough to finish the first half-flight. Then she pivots, aiming the Triple-Y down the stairwell as he comes into sight, his pistol in one hand. He gets off a shot. It cracks past her ear. But she's already hammering him, five slugs to the chest.

He drops like a dead man, sliding down with his back against the wall. She wonders if he *is* dead. It takes him a few seconds to decide—then he starts to wheeze.

"Heads up, Ripley," she says, "call Lincoln."

RUSHING IN AGAIN

LINCOLN WAITS AT the top of the street as True trots up the hill. He's flanked by Rohan, Felice, and Miles.

During her brief call, True warned them to stay out of the target street.

"It's over," she reported, sounding worn and tired. "I couldn't stop them. Shaw is gone. Rihab has him. And this is going to be a crime scene. You do not want to leave any DNA or risk your image being recorded here, so stay away."

He'd seen a photo of the corpse outside the front door so he didn't argue. He told her, "Tamara flew a sparrow over the site."

"I saw it."

"The man on the roof, he's your prisoner?"

"The cops can have him. His partner is here in the stairwell. I've secured him too. They're both Shaw's men, Variant Forces soldiers, and they betrayed him." Bitter disgust in her voice as she said this.

"They came for you next?" he asked.

"Yeah."

And she took them both down. If there was video of that confrontation, he wanted to see it. "Any idea if they've got backup on the way?"

"I don't think so. Those two were out for themselves."

"Tell me about the dismembered body out front. Did that woman betray Shaw too?"

Three or four seconds of dead silence followed this question, then: "You could say that. But he didn't kill her, if that's what you're asking."

Now, as True reaches the top of the hill, he can see her eyes past the screen of her MARC. The fever-bright gaze of a soldier fresh off the battlefront. Wired up tight on stress and adrenaline, and haggard. Her cheeks are gaunt, her skin shining with sweat and oil, her hair escaping from its usual neat braid. She's got a Triple-Y slung over her shoulder, and he's fairly sure there's a pistol in the front pocket of her jacket.

Miles hangs back, but Felice and Rohan aren't shy. "You asshat," Felice says with a grin. And Rohan, his arms wide like he's going to give her a hug. "Mama, what the fuck? You forgot you have friends?"

She startles him by tossing him an electronic key, which he manages to catch in a desperate grab.

"Maybe I did," she admits. "But we got to move. Since you've left your truck behind, see if you can figure out what that belongs to. Maybe we can use it. But don't get close until we check if it's rigged."

Lincoln thought his anger had cooled, but it comes rushing in again as she turns to him. He says, "I'd have you up on charges if we were still in service."

She takes this in with a stonewall expression. "If we were still in service, you'd be right to do so. If you want to, you can still turn me in to the police. They'll probably be here in about thirty seconds."

Felice rolls her eyes. Rohan, who is still standing there with the key in his hand and an uncertain look on his face, turns to Lincoln. "Hey. True fucked up, but we are not turning her over."

"Give me that key," Lincoln says, taking it. He's got no intention of involving the police if he can help it, and no desire to talk to their liaison officer, Nadim Zaman—which means True is right. They need to clear out of here now. He triggers the key. From around the corner, a car beeps in response. They go to find it—and that's when True catches sight of a shot-up expeditionary

SUV blocking the intersection. Traffic is moving on neighboring blocks, but not here.

"*Oh,*" she says softly.

There is blood on the inside of the bullet-riddled windshield. A line of heavier-caliber bullet holes stitches the roof. As they trot past, Lincoln glimpses two bodies inside.

"Your work?" Rohan asks.

She answers in a quiet voice. "It looks like the Arkinson strafed them, finished them off."

Lincoln clicks the key again. A parked SUV responds with flashing lights and a two-tone beep. It's painted in desert camouflage. "Whose car?" he asks.

"I got the key off one of the soldiers at the house. I don't think Rihab had time to wire it, but I want to check anyway."

"No, I'll check," he says.

"I've got a snake." She pulls a little eight-inch serpent out of her pocket. Lincoln recognizes it as one of Tamara's creations. She tosses it under the truck, saying, "Check it out, Dad."

Dad?

She's not using her data glove, she's not controlling it, but the snake moves. It rears up to examine the undercarriage while she circles the truck, looking inside, studying the seams around the doors. He joins her. So do the others. A fifteen-second search for wires and taped explosives. "Looks clean on top," he concludes. "Anything underneath?"

She stoops to pick up the snake. "Nothing."

"Then get in. Everybody in."

Rohan, Felice, and Miles pile into the back. Lincoln slides into the driver's seat. True is opening the front passenger door when he punches the ignition. She flinches, like she's still worried it might blow.

"We're good," he says as the dash lights come on and the air conditioning starts to flow. "Get in."

She dumps her daypack on the floor, but she's still holding the snake and the Triple-Y as Lincoln puts the car into drive. "Who are you working with?" he asks her.

"What?"

"The snake. Who's running the snake?"

"Oh. Colt's shadowing me. He's linked into my MARC too."

In the backseat, Rohan snickers, and Felice sounds incredulous when she demands to know, "You're working with your *dad*?" Lincoln is just as astonished. True has never been able to talk to Colt without butting heads with him. Hell, no one can.

"Desperate times, desperate measures," True says. She gets out her tablet and flips it open, adding, "He says to tell you all he's not senile."

Lincoln says, "I'm going to assume that's not an exact quote."

She shrugs, sliding on her reading glasses. Her fingers tap and glide across the face of the tablet. "I've got a mother's helper planted on Shaw."

Lincoln's scars tighten as this news draws a grudging smile. Rohan is more expressive. "Righteous move, Mama! That's going to make this hunt easier."

And Chris on comms: "Tell True to log in to the QRF. I need that signal."

Lincoln relays the message. She nods and murmurs, "Hey, Dad, I got to log out . . . Yeah, you too. Thanks, old man. I love you. And don't call Alex. I'll talk to him when this is done."

A few seconds later the screen of his MARC shows her logged-in to the unit. Shortly after that Chris says, "Okay, I've got the signal from the mother's helper."

"Good," Lincoln says. "Now tell Khalid to get that tracking device off our truck. And give me a route back to him. I want to dump this vehicle as soon as I can."

"On it. Keep going for now . . . okay, sending you a route."

A route map pops up on Lincoln's AR display. He follows it onto an avenue with heavy traffic, but at least the traffic is moving. "All right," he tells True. "Give us a sitrep. What are we facing?"

She takes her visor off, rubs her eyes, then starts her report by asking, "Tamara, are you listening?"

Chris answers this question from their command post on the other side of the world. "Tamara is here. She can hear you."

True's gaze is fixed on the traffic ahead as she says, "The dismembered woman in the street. That was Li Guiying."

Lincoln grimaces while from the backseat Felice asks, "Who's that?"

Lincoln knows who it is. His prosthetic fingers tap the wheel. He knows enough about Li Guiying's history, her associations, that he's incredulous when he asks, "Was she working with Shaw?"

"No. But she used to work for Kai Yun and they followed her here. That's what we think happened. There's no other explanation."

Kai Yun.

The hairs on Lincoln's arms and on the back of his neck stand on end. Kai Yun is no trivial enemy. "She came to see you?"

"Yes. She came to confess." In spare words True relates what happened in the Burmese forest, describing the swarm, and the surviving mech that followed along as Diego and Shaw were taken to the village of Nungsan.

Lincoln is stunned by this story. Horrified. A fucked-up travesty begun because there was no human in the kill chain . . . not at first.

"So what happened to her?" Felice asks from the backseat. "Because that was a weird fucking mess in the street."

True falls silent, long enough that Lincoln glances at her. She's staring straight ahead, but he doesn't think she sees the traffic when she says, "Guiying didn't want anyone else to die. She thought she could stand in the way, persuade Kai Yun's soldiers to stand down. Shaw knew better. He tried to stop her, get her back under cover." She shakes her head. "They hit her with a laser. The beam clipped him. He's in bad shape."

A laser? That's what took out all the surveillance drones.

It shocks him, the idea of a laser-armed UAV prowling over a peaceful city. He wonders how many there are around the world, masquerading as harmless surveillance platforms—and how often they've been used. A laser is clean and precise, a modern weapon, capable of eliminating a specific target with little to no collateral damage. When True goes on to describe the Arkinson stitching the street, it's a picture of primitive destruction by comparison.

Miles says, "How does it make sense that Kai Yun went after him like that? Their reputation is for subtlety. If they want you dead, you're gone, with no evidence to track it back to them. So why a bolt out of the bright blue sky? It doesn't make sense."

"It's like they panicked," Rohan says.

Lincoln has to agree. The essential problem with a cover up is that over the years the original offense can become an ever-expanding complex of crimes. As each potential witness is removed, there's more reason to remove the next. As more evidence is erased, the incentive grows to suppress questions for fear it might all unravel.

True says, "I think Kai Yun hired local talent for their ground troops. You saw what happened to them. The field's been cleared and that gives us a window of opportunity to go after Rihab and recover Shaw."

Lincoln eases forward into traffic. "Convince me I don't need to worry about Variant Forces stepping in."

"Shaw *is* Variant Forces. The company is vaporware without him. His men knew that. They resented it. They wanted to be on the inside. He said no. That's why they turned."

Rohan says, "Yeah, but he's got to have more people than those two soldiers you left back at the house."

True half turns to look at him. "Sure. But Rabat is not his base of operations." She shifts her focus to Lincoln. "There's no reason to think his crew is here. You got to understand. This mission was personal for him. He told me he didn't want to bring his people in."

"He was quick to bring in that Arkinson," Felice points out. "That something we need to worry about?"

True turns one hand palm up as if to suggest that nothing is certain. "He called it up himself. Ran it fully autonomous, from what I could tell. He said it's subcontracted through a local PMC, but there's no reason to think they know we're here, or what happened. So the field is clear for us to finish this." She checks her tablet, its map displaying the location of the mother's helper. "Rihab is on the belt highway. Moving fast."

"We'll be on the highway soon," Lincoln assures her.

They stop to swap vehicles, rejoining Khalid. "I'm going to drive for now," Lincoln tells him. He puts True into the front seat. The other four squeeze into the back and they get underway, following a route Tamara has plotted. With traffic in the city easing, they make steady progress.

"What's Rihab's game?" Lincoln asks True. "Is he just driving Shaw out into the desert to shoot him?"

To his surprise, it's Khalid who answers. "Rihab's supposed to be an artist, a filmmaker."

True hunches over, hugging the Triple-Y. "*Yes.* If Rihab was just going to shoot him, he would have done it back at the riad. They've got something else in mind. But they aren't going to be able to take him far, because he won't last."

Chris speaks over comms. "In other words, he could be dead before you get there."

"He could be," True says fiercely. "He's dying, if that's what you want to know. I'd say he's as bad off as Diego was when they put him on the cross."

Lincoln glances at her. "Don't go there, True. This is not about Diego."

"It is to *me*. It's starting to feel like Nungsan all over again. We make the assumption he's already dead and we wash our hands."

"Come on," Miles says. "It's a fair question. Is it worth risking your lives to go after him?"

True turns around to look at him. Lincoln takes his good hand off the wheel, reaching out to restrain her. But when she addresses Miles, it's in a surprisingly gentle voice. "You hate him. I don't blame you. You have every right. But he's still one of ours. And you know what they're going to do to him. You know it better than anyone. You've seen it done before. No one deserves to die like that."

A glance in the rearview shows Miles looking askance and uncomfortable. Time to put an end to this debate. "True is right. Shaw's one of ours . . . one of *mine*. If there's any chance he's still alive, we need to get to him. But none of you need to go if you don't think it's the right thing to do. Rohan?"

"I'm in," he says like he thinks it's a stupid question.

"Felice?"

"Yes, sir. We already discussed this. I haven't changed my mind."

"I'm in too," Khalid says.

Rohan tells him, "You should sit this one out, partner. Translator duties are over. We're not going to be talking to these guys. And you're not armed, you're not allowed to carry a weapon."

"Terms of the warrant," Khalid says. "I know that. I don't need to be on point, but I can take over the driving, be the unit medic, deploy the robotics, whatever's needed, whatever I can. I'm part of this outfit now and I'm going."

"I'm going too," Miles says. "If he's still alive, I want to see him. I want to know if he's changed his mind."

WE'LL SAY WE'RE SORRY LATER

EVERY TEN SECONDS the mother's helper pings the cell network. The signal is routed and rerouted until it finds its way to True's tablet, where the position of the mother's helper is updated on a map. As long as the device goes undiscovered, it marks Shaw's location—and with every update his location gets farther and farther away. It's emotionally painful to watch while their pursuit is frustrated and delayed by the chaotic traffic on the outskirts of the city.

True makes herself close the tablet. Chris and Tamara are watching the signal. She does not need to watch it too. The mission is not served by her obsessing over it. It doesn't matter that she is afraid for Shaw. Worry won't help him. It doesn't matter that she's tired. Any energy she has left needs to go toward preparation.

As Lincoln eases their truck into the congestion on the belt highway, she turns to ask, "What kind of gear have we got?"

"Limited. Particularly, firearms. The terms of the warrant were negotiated for us and they don't allow much. One handgun each, for me, Felice, Rohan. No one else is supposed to be armed." He shrugs, deeming this requirement irrelevant going forward. "We've got field uniforms—adaptive camouflage, mixed-use pattern. Extras for you. Rendition supplies—hoods, body wraps, handcuffs. Trauma kit."

Chris breaks in. "I'm leasing a high-altitude aerial surveillance platform. We should have eyes in the sky in . . . another twenty, twenty-five minutes."

"If this isn't over by then," Felice grumbles.

Lincoln meets her gaze in the rearview. "It might be," he allows. "But let's keep in mind that this is not the TEZ. Warlords don't get to operate in the open any more than we do. My guess is, Rihab's going to want to get out into the countryside, away from curious eyes."

"How about robotics?" True asks. "Did the warrant let you bring any shooters? Or is it just surveillance?"

"We've got shooters," Rohan says.

Felice interrupts, sounding disgusted. "We're not supposed to use 'em unless the cops are standing by to give us an okay."

"Don't worry about it," Lincoln says. "We'll use them if we have to and we'll say we're sorry later."

"That's been my strategy," True says softly, a comment that earns a scathing glance from Lincoln. *Point made*, she thinks, before turning to look in back. "What kind of shooters?"

"A pair of starburst drones," Rohan says. "And Roach."

"*Roach?*" She can't believe it. "Roach isn't ready for deployment. It's barely been tested."

"Tamara has run hundreds of simulations on it," Lincoln says irritably, like he's argued the point too many times already. "It's fine. And given the tiny size of this team, I want it along."

"What have *you* got left?" Felice wants to know.

"One more beetle and the snake. You got any explosives? Kamikazes?"

Rohan snorts. "Not on the permitted list. Where'd you pick up the Triple-Y?"

"It's his."

"Huh. Well, that makes you the best-armed soldier here. You got ammo for it?"

"Not much. Just a partial magazine. I've got a pistol too." She pulls it out, hands it to him. "A homegrown model that Shaw printed up. No reloads."

He looks it over, checks the magazine. "Nine millimeter. We're okay."

True pockets the weapon again, wondering if it's possible to pull this off, going in so lightly armed.

They leave the city behind. The signal from the mother's helper leads them west along a good road, smoothly paved, that traverses open countryside. Traffic in both directions is light. Tall trees that might be eucalyptus stand alongside the highway. The pastures beyond look worn out this late in the year, though they're still grazed by dirty brown sheep nuzzling for the last nubs of dry grass.

True has changed into adaptive camouflage trousers and swapped her street boots for the combat pair Lincoln brought along. She's pulled a camouflage jacket on over her shirt, and a protective vest over that, also patterned in mixed-used adaptive camo. She's got her camouflage skullcap ready in her pocket.

Now she's eating a protein bar, watching the scenery slide past. It doesn't seem real to her. The afternoon is so brilliant, so beautiful that it feels wrong, too much of a contrast to what she's seen and done, and what's to come.

Over and over, ugly memories surface in her mind: the centipede bracelet lying on the table, star fractures erupting in the windshield of the expeditionary truck, Guiying's blasted corpse, Shaw's horrific wound, and his agonized screams resounding through the riad.

The Rogue Lightning emblem.

His hired guns hadn't worn it. She'd seen it used only to tag his killer mechs. The soldiers he trusted most.

Don't think on it.

She strives to push away these thoughts and memories. No time for them now. Focus on the next phase of the mission.

But her mind turns to home instead. Not yet dawn there. She wonders if Alex is there, if they'll ever be there together again or if he's gone. After a time she opens her tablet and types a quick message to let him know she's still alive: **I'm with Lincoln now and this is almost over. I'll call you when I can.**

Before long, the land gets steeper. Huge, pale outcroppings of rock rise above the fields, and later, the asphalt road becomes an unpaved track that winds through austere, eroded hills. The dry hillsides support only a scattering of hardy dark-green shrubs. Taller trees grow below the road, marking the paths of trickling creeks.

Here, the signal from the mother's helper becomes inconsistent, disappearing and reappearing as steep valleys shred the cell network, but it doesn't matter too much. Chris is watching now from a high-altitude surveillance platform. There's not much traffic, so he's been able to visually pinpoint the target: a pale-colored SUV moving at a fast clip, a plume of dust trailing behind it.

Lincoln drives quickly too, passing sedans and slower trucks, gradually compressing the distance that separates them from Shaw.

She tells herself that he is still alive. He must be, because if he wasn't, Rihab surely would have stopped somewhere on this lonely road to dump his body.

LIGHT AND SHADOW

CHRIS SPEAKS TO the team over comms: "We've found your destination."

He's shifted QRF communications off the cell network; they're relaying now through the UAV. "About seven klicks out there's a house situated on a flat below the road, close to a stream. Hills are steep on either side, no other structures anywhere near, and we can see a starburst copter patrolling in the ravine. Plus there's a big anti-surveillance canopy rigged beside the house."

True puts out a hand to brace herself against the dash as Lincoln brakes, cutting their speed by two thirds.

Chris says, "The building is a plain rectangular structure. One additional vehicle visible. No people, but we have to assume they're there, under the canopy or in the house. Could be more vehicles too."

So there's no way to know how many enemy they're facing.

He sends a screenshot. True studies it on her tablet. Between the road and the flat where the house sits, there's a rugged, brush-covered slope with an outcropping of rocks in the lower half. A steep lane descends across the slope, angling down to the house, which is roofed with photovoltaic tiles.

Lincoln leans over. Anticipating that he wants to look, she holds the tablet out for him to see. A simple gesture reflecting the smooth way they've worked together in the past, and poignant to her for the broken trust that now lies between them.

Lincoln straightens up. He's driving even more slowly now. "Let's keep in mind," he says, "our goal is to recover Shaw. If we can do that by obtaining a surrender from Al-Furat, all well and good. But our warrant authorizes use of force against armed resistance—and that's how I expect it to go."

True thinks back to the two soldiers she left in restraints at the riad. She got lucky there. It's going to be different this time.

"Movement at the house," Chris says. "Two individuals in sight. Armed with assault rifles, on foot, moving quickly. Okay. They're heading up the access lane to the road, in plain sight."

"They want to make sure Rihab doesn't miss the turn," Felice says.

Rohan snorts in amusement as Chris continues his report. "Confirming that at least one of the assault rifles they're carrying has a grenade launcher. My guess—Rihab knows there's a car on the road behind him. He'll post these two soldiers along the road to watch for it, make sure it's no threat. Lincoln, if you don't want to put them on alert, you're going to have to drive a few klicks past. Then backtrack. Come back down the ravine on foot."

"I don't want to sit here in the backseat while we drive past a fucking grenade launcher," Rohan growls, his humor gone.

True adds her own objection. "It'll take too long, anyway. This could be over for Shaw before we get back."

Lincoln catches her by surprise when he says, "Agreed." Afternoon light lances through the branches of a spindly tree leaning over the road, casting mottled patterns on his scars, making his expression harder than ever to read. "Chris is right, too. Rihab has to be aware someone's behind him."

Chris breaks in with an update. "Here we go, folks . . . Rihab has turned off into the lane that angles down to the house . . . and his vehicle has stopped . . . Okay, we've got a little chat going on with the two on foot . . . and Rihab is now continuing down to the house while the two are heading up. My, these boys are in a hurry."

"So we get to play recon?" Felice asks. "Ambush the ambush?"

"Negative," Lincoln says. "Not right away. They need to see this truck drive past and know it's no threat. Khalid, Miles, that's going to be your task. I want them to believe that no one has followed them out of Rabat, that they're out here alone, that no one is interested in what they're doing. So you two will stay with the truck and keep on driving, like you've got your own destination. The rest of us will exit early. We'll use the ravine to approach the house from this side."

There is a rustle of activity as everyone gets ready. True grabs her pack, shrugs it on. Checks the load on the Triple-Y. Her heart is racing in anticipation and she isn't tired anymore, not deep down where it counts.

Lincoln summarizes the challenge. "Our goal is to take Shaw alive. Our best chance to do that is to get in close, then hit hard and fast, take them out before they can take out Shaw."

"Lethal force?" Rohan wants to know.

"As needed—and I'm anticipating the need. Officially we are obligated to evaluate any offer on their part to surrender, but until we have control, don't waste time on it."

Chris breaks in: "Update on our road warriors. They're in separate positions, about ninety meters to either side of the start of the lane, hiding in weeds above the road."

He sends True a picture with their positions highlighted. She shows it to Lincoln. "There's a spine of rocks running down into the ravine right here," she says, pointing to the feature. "Call it a hundred thirty meters below the house. That'll hide us from the first road warrior as we come up the ravine. But we're going to be vulnerable to the sentinel drone."

"Roger," Lincoln says, returning his gaze to the road. "Chris, register the road warriors as targets and take them out with the copters as soon as the shooting starts."

"Roger that. I've got it on the task list."

"I want a best route, one that will let us exit the truck unobserved, three or four hundred meters from the house, and then drop down toward the stream using available cover."

"Tamara's looking at it."

Lincoln's voice shifts to a more casual tone. "We're still a few kilometers out so I'm going to take a piss break." There's no traffic anywhere behind them, but he pulls half off the road anyway. "Just me and Khalid. Everyone else stay in your seat and out of sight."

He's not wearing his adaptive camo yet, and Khalid too is dressed in civilian clothes. True watches as they walk together to the back of the truck. They really do stop to piss. Then Lincoln opens the back hatch. The starburst copters are already out of their cases, each with a rifle barrel mounted under the central pod. Working quickly, he and Khalid unlock the arms and rotate them so they're parallel, compacting the copters and making them easier to carry.

"Miles, I need you to do a job for me," Lincoln says. "It's not going to involve any direct combat."

Miles is turned half around, his elbow over the seatback. "Let's hear it."

"You get to deploy Roach. But you're going to have to do it fast. No margin for error."

"Yes, sir."

Lincoln details exactly what he wants Miles to do.

No one questions their authority to act. Away from the oversight of the police, it's as if they've become a sovereign agency, making their own rules.

Khalid is behind the wheel when they start again. Lincoln is in the backseat, getting into his camo. Felice and Rohan are already appareled, hoods on and only their eyes showing. True rolls her own hood down, fitting the mask carefully to her face, before putting her MARC visor back on.

Miles rides in the cargo area, holding down the hatch. Tinted windows help hide him from outside observation. Trees and brush, along with a slight bend in the road just before the start of the lane, will take the truck briefly out of view of the watching soldiers. That's when Miles will open the hatch, just far enough to kick Roach out. Ninety pounds of steel, titanium, and ammunition tumbling down onto the dirt road. When the truck drives back into view of the enemy, the hatch will be closed again.

Chris speaks over comms: "Okay, we've got a best route. You'll be able to exit the truck unobserved, six hundred meters below the house. A stand of trees will cover your descent into the ravine."

True studies the route map, overlaid on an aerial photo. She commits terrain details to memory, noting the many curves of the road, the varying cover, and the rugged, rocky slope above the flat. It comes to her that there is a better way to do this.

There's no time for hesitation. Chris will give the order soon to go. So she turns to Lincoln—only to be distracted for a moment by what she sees. Light and shadow flickering across the three figures in the backseat has coaxed complex patterns from the basic dry-forest weave of their adaptive camo. The effect breaks up and blends the outlines of their bodies, even against the solid, artificial background of the seat.

True fixes her gaze on Lincoln's eyes—his good eye and the empty black pupil of his artificial eye—visible past the screen of his MARC visor. She speaks swiftly. "I want to modify the plan, take my own route down so we can come at them from two sides. I can exit after Roach. That puts me on the slope right above the target, midway between the two road warriors. There's good cover in those rocks above the flat. I'll make my way down to them. That'll get me an early look under the canopy. And I'll be in position to use the Triple-Y, offer some crossfire, take out the road warriors if it comes to it, be there for backup if something goes wrong with Roach."

Lincoln's eyes narrow. "You don't have ammunition for that, and I don't want you out there on your own."

"I can go with her," Rohan says.

"Negative. We're going to have a narrow window to deploy the starbursts. It's going to take two to do that, and one for cover fire if the sentinel drone finds us first."

"I won't be on my own," True says. "I'll be behind Roach, and it's capable of a better rate of fire than Rohan's pistol."

"*Hey.*"

"Truth, son. And if Roach works like it's supposed to, the rest of us might not even have to fire a shot."

"Tamara's plotted a viable route for her," Chris says. "If you want to do it."

Lincoln gives her a withering look, but it'll be tactically valuable if she can get in position down among the rocks. "All right," he concedes. "Don't make me regret this."

True nods and turns around.

"Get ready," Chris warns. "We're coming up on the first drop site. Lincoln, Felice, Rohan. Your route will display in your visors once you're on the ground. Khalid, the drop is marked on your visor."

"I see it."

"Ease it down to a crawl. Stop just long enough for the team to clear."

The truck rolls beneath the swaying branches of a small grove of rough-barked trees, the glare on the windshield winks out, and Chris says, "Go now."

Lincoln, Felice, and Rohan bail out the back doors, taking the starburst copters with them. Khalid slowly accelerates and sunlight flashes into the cab again. True looks back, watching as the team enters the trees below the road. Already they're difficult to see as their camo reacts to the hard shadows cast by the afternoon light. The truck rounds a bend and they're out of sight.

Miles is alone in the back now. He's wearing sunglasses, not an AR visor, but hooked over his ear is a TINSL linked into comms.

"You're next, Miles," Chris says. "Get ready to give Roach the boot."

"On your order," he answers.

True looks ahead as sunlight strobes through the branches. She seeks out the place where she thinks the first road warrior is hidden, still a couple hundred meters away. Beyond that, she can see the road winding away along the hillsides, but she can't see the house down in the ravine. She'll see it soon. She's ready to go. Her hand shakes just a little as she holds it poised above the door release.

Chris says, "Khalid, I want you to keep the truck moving slow and steady when it comes time for True to get out. Don't stop or you're going to make yourself a target."

"How well can you see them?" Khalid wants to know. "Can you tell if they're getting ready to take a shot?"

"They're both casual," Chris says in a soothing tone. "Just watching. Not expecting trouble. And the truck is armored."

"Roger that."

Chris continues his instructions. "Once True is out, gradually pick up your speed and continue at least five klicks down the road. Then stand by and wait for further instruction."

"Yes, sir." The sunlight flickers as Khalid looks at True. "Hey, you want to trade places?"

It's a joke, but not a joke. She understands. Khalid is a decoy, a rolling target. Vulnerable, but out of the action. "I won't give you away," she promises him.

"We are going to pull this off," Chris insists. "But timing matters, so let's focus."

True looks ahead, eyeing the slope above the road, the tangle of dry brush and tree shadows, trying to pick out the point where the first road warrior is hidden. Failing. She tells Khalid, "Be ready to drop the back window so I can return fire if it comes to that."

He nods. His hand slides to the control pad on the armrest.

"Only on my word," Chris says.

They all go silent. There's just the noise of the truck as it jounces and rocks on the dust-dry road.

"Okay, you're past road warrior one," Chris says. "Maintain your speed, Khalid. Miles, you ready?"

"Roger that."

They start around the bend in the road that comes just before the lane. "On three," Chris says. "One. Two. Three."

The back hatch opens, restrained by a tether so that it rises less than two feet. The sound of tires on grit, the rustle of a light wind in the trees, the smell of dust. Then a grunt from Miles as he uses his boots to shove the gray, lozenge-shape of the dormant Roach out over the back bumper. It lands with a thud as he pulls the hatch down again.

"Roach is out," Miles says over comms, his voice low, taut with tension.

Tamara too is on edge. Anxious, frightened, and full of doubt.

She's staffing the research desk in the command post at ReqOps headquarters. Naomi is with her. Hayden is at the front desk, managing the video feeds. Chris is pacing. His gaze is fixed on the wall monitor, palms pressed together, fingers tapping his chin in a display of anxious energy. Jameson is in the room too, standing near the door, but he's present as an observer. Tamara is all too conscious of Renata's absence.

She's aware too—exquisitely aware—of the risks that both the team and the company are taking. She tried to talk to Chris about it. "We need to reevaluate," she told him after True was recovered and the team was making its way out of Rabat. "Take a look at the risks, and weigh those against what we are standing to gain. What *is* there to gain, Chris? What? We've got True back. That's what matters. Why go on? There's no innocent to be rescued. No bounty. We are risking the lives of our people to take custody of a mercenary who is probably dying as we speak."

Chris silenced his microphone before he replied. "I don't disagree," he said. "But we're doing the mission. Let's just do it the best we can."

But how do you determine best actions when you don't know what you're facing?

Tamara has no idea what is under the anti-surveillance canopy or inside the target house. She doesn't know how many enemy soldiers there are or how they're armed or if civilians are involved. Children? She doesn't know, because the preliminary work that would have been done on any other mission has not been done. There's been no time.

She's worried too because she has no eyes on Roach; she can't see it deploy. Ideally it will have hit the road flat, with no tumbling or bouncing. Its stout, jointed legs will unfold and activate—three on one side if it needs to right itself, or all six at once if it lands upright. Lens covers will open, giving sight to the tiny cameras that stud its body. The visual data they collect will allow the onboard

AI to map the fine details of its surroundings so it can navigate in stealth, moving quickly and silently, much like its namesake. While this is happening, a whip antenna, a few centimeters tall, will rise from its carapace, and then she will get a signal. The rifle barrel will not deploy. The jointed mast that supports it will remain in its cradle, allowing Roach to maintain a low profile as it scuttles downslope and into position.

Four seconds after Miles reports that Roach has deployed, the robot checks in—

Leg R1 nominal

Leg R2 nominal

Leg R3 nominal . . .

—a long series of reports on each of its components scrolling through a window. She shifts to a navigational view showing a scene in motion: pebbled slope padded with dry leaves and powdered with dust, dry branches slipping past as Roach moves toward its assigned position. She cross-checks its route on a map and announces, "Roach is moving into place. All components nominal."

Rohan is in the lead, advancing quickly and quietly, paralleling a trickling stream as he follows the path projected in his visor. He carries the folded starburst copter balanced on his shoulder, loosely wrapped in camouflage cloth. Lincoln follows a few steps behind, carrying the second copter in the same way, balancing its weight with his right hand, not trusting his artificial hand to do it. Felice is in the rear.

They want to get as close to the house as they can before the enemy's sentinel drone catches sight of them.

A red light winks on in Lincoln's visor. "Sentinel drone about to pass to the south," Chris warns over comms. "Take cover."

His heart booms in slow, powerful beats as he eases deeper into the mottled shade between trees. He goes to his knees, tips the folded copter to the ground, then flattens beside it, pulling his pistol from its holster as he does.

He glances around to make sure Felice and Rohan are also belly-down. Then he looks for the drone.

After a few seconds he sees it gliding past on stealthed propellers. He notes the gun barrel beneath the central pod. It doesn't swivel to target them. It remains fixed, its muzzle pointing backward—a standard practice to reduce the chance of bugs clogging up the barrel. "Roach is awake and moving," Chris reports.

"Roger," Lincoln whispers. He regards Roach as the critical element in a surprise assault on the house, but it's vulnerable to gunfire from the sentinel—so the sentinel is the first element he wants to take out.

Chris waits another twenty seconds. Then: "You're clear to move out."

Felice helps him get the folded copter back on his shoulder. Then they move fast, determined to get as far as they can before the sentinel returns. The soft, slick fabric of their camo doesn't rustle and it rejects the grip of grasping twigs, but it's hot and Lincoln is sweating. It doesn't help that he has to work hard to keep up with Rohan's long strides. He breathes consciously: deep, quiet, steady breaths.

"Roach is in place," Chris reports. A few seconds later: "Okay, you're at the hundred-fifty-meter mark. Prep the copters."

Lincoln kneels. He puts the folded copter down, pulls off the camouflage blanket, pops off the restraints, and pulls the rotor booms into position, locking them in place so that the eight rotors are evenly distributed in a meter-wide circle. Felice stands over him, pistol in hand, watching the sky.

"Copter one ready," Rohan whispers over comms.

Lincoln looks up to check Rohan's work. He's got the rotor booms fully deployed with two of them propped on little rocks to keep the copter level, but he forgot one step. "Get the plug out of the gun barrel," Lincoln reminds him.

"Oops." Rohan pops the plug out and pockets it.

"Cover it with the camo blanket," Lincoln says. "We don't want to launch until True's in place."

True is looking back behind the SUV. She wants to watch Roach transform but by the time she can see it, it's already awake and scuttling off the road.

Miles has climbed over the seatback, out of the cargo compartment. He leans forward to touch her elbow. "Give me your pistol, True. I'm going with you."

She stares at him, incredulous. "Are you serious?"

Khalid glances over his shoulder. "You can't go. You're not here as a soldier."

The mics are on, so Chris is in the conversation too: "Talk to me, people. What is going on?"

True feels a gentle pressure as Miles's fingers close around her arm—not tightly enough to interfere with her imminent exit, but enough to let her know he means what he's saying. He tells her, "I'm going out this door at the same time as you. You might as well give me the pistol."

"You don't have camouflage."

He holds up a camouflage blanket. "I don't need a full uniform. This action is scheduled to start when you're in position and that's going to be ninety seconds after we exit the truck."

Her mind races, seeking options, seeking to fit this new variable into her mental model of the coming battle.

"True?" Chris asks.

"Miles says he's going with me."

"*Shit*," Chris says. "We can't—"

Miles cuts him off. "No time to argue. Just call the mark."

True concedes the truth of this by handing him the pistol. "He's right, Chris. No time left and I've got no way to stop him. He'll go if he wants to go."

"*Damn* it," Chris says.

But what can he do? Tell her to abort her role in the operation? He knows she'd go on her own. So he lets it run. "On three," he says in clipped syllables. He counts down while Khalid gradually slows the truck to a fast walking pace.

The truck is visible to the second road warrior, but he's low on the slope, he's on the driver's side, he's still sixty meters away, and the flash of light and shadow as they pass beneath the trees is a kind of camouflage. True snatches a breath. Again, that soothing eclipse of shade across the windshield. She opens the door, slides out, scrambles hunched over for two paces—time enough to nudge the door gently shut. Then she's over the road bank and into the brush, following the designated route that lights up on her visor, aware of Miles a step behind her, wearing the camo blanket like a hood.

The air is cool despite the sun. It smells of dust and some aromatic leaf. They move quietly but quickly, using the tire noise of the retreating truck to cover any sound they do make as they weave through sparse brush on a path that keeps the rocky outcropping between themselves and the house below.

True hears a man's voice as they enter the rocks. Sudden harsh laughter and water being spilled. She pauses several seconds, waiting as a two-foot-long snake slithers away from her booted foot. *A good sign*, she tells herself. The shy snake's presence confirms no third man is hidden up here.

Over comms Chris says, "Khalid is in the clear and our two warriors are walking back on the road."

True looks upslope, evaluating the terrain, and concludes that the vegetation, the rocks, and her camouflage will combine to keep her hidden even if one of the soldiers is standing on the road's edge, looking directly down at her position. She creeps forward again.

Now she can see two SUVs, below and to the right. They're backed up almost to the shade of the anti-surveillance canopy as if poised for a getaway. One of them—not the one Rihab drove, but the other—has plastic crates and cardboard boxes lashed to a roof rack, and twenty-liter plastic jugs in a rack on the back bumper. The blue jug is labeled *water* in Arabic characters. The other is red-orange. There's room for a third.

She works her way around a boulder. When she can see the roof of the house and the anti-surveillance canopy on the flat below, she gets down on her hands and knees and crawls.

Ten meters separate the bottom of the slope from the canopy. Close enough that she can hear the pulsing tone of an alert. She pauses to look up at the span of sky framed by the ravine's walls, searching for the enemy's sentinel drone, but she doesn't see it.

The tone cuts off. A man speaks in Arabic, his voice carrying easily across the quiet afternoon. He sounds annoyed, not alarmed. Something about goats . . . in the ravine? If they've been dealing with false alarms, it will make them less wary.

"I'm in position," she whispers to Chris.

"I see you."

Miles is a few feet away, crouched under the camo blanket.

True tips her head sideways to peer over the rock. She's come down the slope far enough that she can see into the shaded area beneath the canopy. She looks for only a moment. Then she ducks down again, whispering, "*Oh God.*" Her hand goes to her face. She pushes her visor up, using the pressure of her fingers to fight the pressure in her eyes.

No one deserves to die like that.

HELL BREAKS LOOSE

LINCOLN STANDS IN the shadows under the trees, back to a tree trunk, perfectly still, his pistol in his right hand, watching the sentinel as it returns up the ravine, passing over their position. He's impatient, eager to move on. But he holds his position. They all do. No one moves—but the sentinel must have detected something because it circles back.

"*Shit*," Rohan whispers over comms.

"Alarm's going off up top," Chris says.

"Don't move," Lincoln breathes. "The gun barrel is still locked. It hasn't got a target yet."

It's possible the onboard AI issued an alert when it noted a change in the terrain caused by the camo blankets.

Chris says, "The enemy has decided that was a false alarm. True is in position."

"Roger."

The sentinel moves away, but instead of heading up the ravine, it goes back down again.

Chris adds, "Be aware that Miles is with True."

"*What?*" Lincoln demands in a whisper. "*What the everlasting fuck?*"

"Save it," Chris says. "We've got aberrant behavior in the senti-

nel. It's circling, coming back for another pass. We need to launch.
Clear those copters so I can get them in the air."

Nothing to do but do it. "Let's go, Rohan."

They both move. Lincoln steps into the open, then stoops to
carefully lift away the camo blanket. As soon as it clears, the rotors
hum, each set winding up into a circle of blurred motion. The starburst takes off straight up and, as it does, its gun barrel swivels.
Behind him, Felice starts shooting. She's not the only one.

Tamara has preloaded both Roach and the starburst drones with
multiple instruction sets. One of these sets uses map locations and
biometrics in a two-factor confirmation to delineate human targets. The team is white-listed and so is Shaw Walker. There are
also instructions for distinguishing children and noncombatants.

The drawback of this instruction set is that running the biometric identification procedure before every shot is slow, even on
a human scale. In the frantic chaos of battle, the enemy can pull
a trigger before an AI achieves a kill decision. It's a parallel to
the situation in traffic, where aggressive human behavior puts a
properly schooled AI at a disadvantage. Tamara is unwilling to
let that happen. She has seen what is under the anti-surveillance
canopy—the cameras on True's MARC visor captured it. She is
certain there are no women and children present. There are only
torturers.

Her breathing is ragged but her hands are steady as she revises
the instructions so that Roach and the two copters can operate at
a faster rate. The new rule requires only an initial biometric identification. Known elements to be tracked on an active battle map.

Lincoln draws his pistol as the starburst rises into the air. It's dart-
ing and rocking in an evasive behavior as it immediately takes
enemy fire. A bullet impacts one rotor. The parts shower down
around Lincoln, but the controlling AI compensates for the damage, rebalancing the load on the seven rotors that remain, even as
it shifts the gun barrel to target the sentinel.

The two machines trade shots as they rise higher and higher

into the air, whirling and dancing and dodging around one another in a manic duel that shares the frantic grace of a flight of mating insects. They're moving too fast for Lincoln to get off even a single shot at the sentinel, but if they're doing any damage to each other, he can't see it. The buzz and whine and crackle of stray bullets tears across the ravine in every direction.

He's peripherally aware that their second copter has darted away, up the ravine and toward the house, to join Roach in the first wave of the attack—the machine wave.

Eight seconds, maybe nine have elapsed since launch. He turns to check on Felice, remembering the sound of her pistol going off. He finds her hunched over, one arm pressed against her breast and her hand coiled into a fist as she staggers toward him, still carrying her pistol in her other hand.

"Hey! Are you okay?" He grabs her shoulder with his artificial hand, just as a flurry of shooting erupts from the direction of the house.

She straightens up, looking that way. Past teeth clenched in pain, she says, "Bruised ribs, I think. Not broken." Her arm lowers to reveal two spent bullets embedded in the left shoulder of her vest.

"*Jesus*," he whispers. "Sit down."

"Never mind that. You go. I'll follow. Don't leave True up there alone."

He hears the firefight at the house intensify, punctuated now by the screams of maddened men.

True is on her knees, bent almost to the ground, gloved hand pressed to her forehead, fighting back against the dark gravity of Nungsan and the certainty that she has been here before, seen all this before, lived it and relived it so many times in dreams and not once able to make a difference.

Ah, Diego!

This time, it's not a dream.

In her glimpse beneath the canopy she counted eight Al-Furat soldiers. Rihab was one. He wasn't carrying a weapon that she could see. Two of the men were armed with video cameras. All the others held assault rifles either slung over their shoulders or casually in the crook of an arm. There might be more soldiers in the house. She doesn't care.

She eases up to look again.

The canopy shades a nearly level, unpaved pad strewn with grit and pebbles. Three dirty white goats are lying down beneath it, close to the house. Shaw is staked on the ground at the center of the pad, face up. A U-shaped steel rod has been pounded into the ground over his ankles to hold his feet in place. A second rod arches over his neck, and a spike has been driven through the palm of his right hand, pinning his arm at an angle to his body. His left hand, the hand crippled in Burma, is still tied to his vest the way she left it, to stabilize his wounded shoulder.

His face and shoulders and the surrounding ground are wet. *It's just water*, she tells herself. She wants to believe that. Water poured in his face to frighten him, to get him to talk. But she smells the reek of gasoline. A red-orange container, identical to the one in the bumper rack, is stowed beside the house. She hears a conversation, strangely clear to her mind despite her rudimentary Arabic:

Someone will see the smoke.

Let them see it. We were never here.

Shaw must be listening, too. She feels sure he understands them, that he is aware of what is about to happen. Impossibly aware, given his condition, but the knowledge is apparent in the taut arch of his back, the quick sharp breaths that make his chest rise and fall, the fixed, maddened stare of his eyes focused on the brilliant perforations in the canopy.

She remembers Daniel speaking of Nungsan and the syringe used to inject Diego with a stimulant to ensure he was awake for his execution, and to make him seem stronger than he was.

Shaw's strength is not in doubt. He is a fortress, locked up tight. He makes no plea, no threat. He asks no favors. He allows not even a groan of pain. Waiting.

At this point no one even needs to strike a match. Gasoline is highly volatile. Its fumes are heavier than air. They hug the ground and spread. All it will take is a crackle of static electricity or a spark thrown by a ricocheting bullet to ignite a flash fire.

It is surely too late to change the outcome.

Right?

She sees that one of the Al-Furat men—she realizes it is nineteen-year-old Rihab—has a fireplace lighter in his hand, the kind with a trigger and a long tube to direct the flame. He walks toward Shaw, barking instructions at the camera crew, but it seems to True that his fierceness is an act. As she aims the Triple-Y, centering its sight on Rihab's skull, she understands that he is afraid of what's coming. He doesn't really want to do it. But for him, as for all of them, there is no backing out.

A breeze flows beneath the canopy. It flutters Rihab's shirt and lifts ghosts out of the dust. She prays for it to carry some of the fumes away, and she squeezes the trigger.

Simultaneously, there is a flurry of gunshots in the ravine.

A second later, all hell breaks loose.

Miles is taken by surprise when the assault starts. He didn't hear Chris initiate it. He only knows it's on when True fires the first shot and Rihab crumples. The air reeks of gasoline fumes so he's surprised when the shot doesn't ignite a flash fire. God help Shaw Walker if that happens.

One of the armed Al-Furat soldiers yells. Miles picks him for a target, squeezing off rounds from his pistol. A streamer of blood on the man's shoulder suggests he's been hit but he doesn't go down. The two with the cameras try to retreat to the house, while the armed men, including the one Miles wounded, turn their guns on the slope. They don't know exactly where their enemy is hidden, but they start laying down suppressing fire.

Miles ducks behind the rocks. True goes belly-down too. Rock chips and lead fragments pepper them.

Another gun opens up from a position off to the side and lower on the slope. Rapid shots a half-second apart. A rhythm so precise, it's got to be Roach.

From below, a drawn-out, agonized scream and, simultaneously, a roar of raw, guttural rage. Someone holds down the trigger on an assault rifle, chewing through the magazine, sending dust and broken twigs fountaining around Roach's position.

True chooses that moment to stand up. She brings her weapon to her shoulder—but she doesn't fire. There's no return fire. Even Roach stops shooting.

A pastoral silence spreads across the slope: a breeze rustling through the brush, the muttering stream, the faraway bleating of a goat. Miles is acutely conscious of his rapid breathing. He asks himself: *Is it over?*

He lifts his head to look cautiously past the rocks. Under the canopy, everyone is down. Pools of red blending with dust in the filtered light. He counts six Al-Furat soldiers, plus Shaw.

There should be two more.

Behind him on the slope, the faint distant crack of a stick. Still on his knees, he wheels around, pistol raised. Motion just below the road. An electric charge erupts across his skin and he reacts before his conscious mind understands what he has seen. He dives at True, knowing it's already too late. One of the road warriors carried an assault rifle outfitted with a grenade launcher. What Miles saw, what he reacted to, was the black mouth of that weapon aimed in their direction.

But as True's knees buckle, as he drags her to the ground, he hears the soft hum of a starburst copter and four quick shots. Then a withering explosion as the grenade blows up somewhere high in the air above them. Miles ducks his head, hunches his shoulders against the concussion. A double punch is delivered against his ears. A blast of searing heat. He feels the pummel of fragments impacting his vest and a sharp pain in his skull.

For a few seconds after that he hears nothing but the ringing of his ears. Then Chris's voice, sounding muffled: "Miles. True. Report."

"I'm good," True says, voice husky. "Miles, get off me!"

He realizes he has her pinned and rolls aside. In a moment she's up on her knees, doffing her visor, peeling off her camouflage hood. Her face is flushed, her eyes frantic, sweeping past him to look downslope. She puts her visor back on and picks up the Triple-Y. Then she's away, boosting herself over the rocks to charge at an angle toward the bottom of the slope.

Miles starts to follow, but Chris shouts over comms, "*Stay put! Stay put!* We've got enemy still in the house!"

True keeps moving, stumbling and sliding, dry brush bursting apart as she hits it.

True is trusting Roach and the starburst copter to cover her. They've owned this battle so far. She's pretty sure the copter took out the two road warriors on the high ground, hitting one just as he pulled the trigger on his grenade launcher, sending the explosive on a wild arc.

She reaches the bottom of the slope. Cuts right to angle across the flat. As she does, Roach emerges from the brush in front of her. It's a meter-long monster, moving with swift, revolting grace on its stout insect legs, gun-barrel head supported on a jointed mast as it snaps around to target her. She is so startled, she cuts sideways and almost screams. The barrel shifts again, upslope, where she left Miles.

It doesn't shoot. Both of them are white-listed. True imagines a database table updated with her current position, a description of her that reads "potential obstacle," and the instruction "do not harm."

Roach moves on, skittering with frightening speed toward the house just as the copter buzzes into sight, appearing around a corner of the building and flying low. The copter banks around the SUVs, then cuts under the canopy, a half-second behind Roach.

Two soldiers are still in the house. With the mechs pressing the assault, True knows the firefight could erupt again at any second—but the way to the SUVs is clear.

She sprints for the one with the twenty-liter jugs. Her hands are slick with sweat beneath the fabric of her gloves as she grasps the cap of the blue jug and wrenches it open. She smells it to be sure. *Water.* Hauls it out of the bumper rack without bothering to cap it again and runs with it beneath the canopy, the forty-pound mass banging against the outside of her knee and water sloshing out. She runs to where Shaw is pinned against the ground.

Gunfire again. A single shot. So close and so loud, every muscle in her body tenses. A glance shows her it's Roach, shooting into the house through the open door. The mech skitters inside. The starburst copter swoops away, out from under the canopy and out of sight.

Leaving the conclusion of the battle to Chris and Tamara, True sets the water jug down. She drops to her knees. The stench of gasoline that's rising from Shaw is almost overwhelming. His eyes are open but he doesn't seem to see her. She tips the jug, spilling water over his face. His eyes squeeze shut. She drenches his face, his scalp, his neck, his shoulders. She wets the ground around him and he starts shivering. He turns his head to retch, then whispers something. She leans over him to hear him better. He says it twice more before she understands: "*No way back.*"

She is crying. She takes off her MARC visor and drops it beside the Triple-Y, using her sleeve to swipe at her eyes. Then she grabs the steel loop around Shaw's neck that's helping to pin him to the ground. There's hardly enough room to get her gloved fingers around it, but she does. She tugs at it. It's solid, so she rocks it a little, back and forth, careful not to hurt him as she loosens it. After a minute she's able to pull it out. She pitches it away.

Only then does she notice Miles standing a few feet away, bright red blood staining his collar as he watches her with what looks like simmering anger.

RIGHTEOUS JUSTICE

WHEN THE SHOOTING stops only a handful of seconds after it started, Lincoln wonders, *Is it done?*

He and Rohan are still charging toward the house, scrambling around boulders, not trying to be quiet anymore. More shots fired. "Chris!" he pants. "Report!"

"True and Miles are ambulatory, we have secured Shaw Walker, and Roach has two combatants pinned down in the house. I need you up there, Lincoln. Someone's got to accept a surrender."

"Surrender?" Rohan demands, scrambling up a final slope. "You mean that's it? The mechs took the fight and we're just the cleanup squad?"

"That's it," Chris tells him.

"What happened to the road warriors?"

"The copter took them. Welcome to the new world order."

"*Fuck.* What the hell are we even doing here?"

Lincoln's wondering the same thing. Chris answers the question for both of them. "You're accepting a surrender. *Move.*"

They never stopped. They climb fast, up to the flat where the house is situated. "What's Shaw's status?" Lincoln pants.

"Not good, but he's alive. True is with him."

Lincoln holds up a hand, signaling Rohan to pause as they

reach the edge of the brush. From here he can look across the flat
to see the back of the house and the two parked SUVs. Khalid is
bringing their truck bouncing down the lane from the road. No
one's in sight.

He struggles to pull off his camouflage mask with his prosthetic
hand, gives it up, holsters the gun, and uses both hands to get the
mask off. Sweat trickles down his cheeks. He looks back, and spots
Felice a hundred meters behind, following slowly. Somewhere
below her, goats are complaining in a chorus of bleats.

Chris says, "I need you inside the house, Lincoln."

"Yeah." They need to close things out, pack up, and go. So why
the fuck is he hesitating to take the next step?

Rohan peels his mask off too. Gives Lincoln a quizzical look.
"Now you get to see him again after all these years. That's got to
be a hell of a thing, given the history."

"That's about it," Lincoln agrees. "Come on. Let's go."

They trot together across the flat, meeting Khalid just outside
the house. The area under the canopy is a reeking charnel floor.

"*Jesus*," Lincoln says, taking in the scene.

The six dead men have all fallen to precision headshots, brought
down by Roach in a rough half-circle around Shaw. The starburst
copter hovers in a stationary position just beyond them, gun barrel
trained on the dead—an eerie sentry, standing guard . . . in case
they have not quite crossed over to the other side?

Miles has a weapon too. He's bleeding from the back of his
scalp, red seepage soaking into his collar as he holds a pistol in one
hand, looking like he wants to use it.

"You're wounded, Miles."

"It's nothing," he growls.

True crouches at Shaw's feet, wrestling to loosen a bent steel
rod that pins his ankles to the ground. She's weeping.

Lincoln is glad that someone can.

Shaw's eyes are open, aware, but he hasn't noticed Lincoln yet.
His head is turned as if to contemplate the smooth steel spike
that's been pounded into the ground through his right hand.
Blood pools in his palm before trickling to the wet ground. This

man, once a friend, a brother. *What have you brought us to?* A bitter thought. Lincoln's anger rises, a subsurface flame that burns off both pity and guilt, and hardens his sense of duty. Finish the job.

He turns to Rohan. Voice low, businesslike: "I need you to secure the two men in the house. Take Khalid with you."

"You got it, boss."

He tells True, "Let me help."

She looks up, eyes defiant behind her tears. Whatever she sees, it reassures her. She makes room for him. He uses his good hand and together they work the U-shaped rod out of the hard ground. He gets out his med kit, telling True, "I'm going to put a tourniquet on that arm before we try to get the spike out."

His work is interrupted by a hoarse whisper from Shaw: "*Fucking* Lincoln. At least you showed up this time."

Lincoln stops what he's doing, the tourniquet only half on. "I thought you were out of it," he says, meeting those familiar pale eyes. "I'd tell you to go to hell but you're already well on your way."

"No argument," Shaw whispers as his eyes drift closed. "Rihab's a fuckin' artist, just like the Saomong. Or he was, anyway." Cocky still, but his whisper is getting weaker.

True kneels on his other side. She strokes his forehead as if he were a sick child. "You're going home," she promises him.

His words are slurred when he says, "One way or another."

Miles steps closer, the pistol still in his hand, his tone belligerent: "I don't know. Maybe we should just leave him here."

"Maybe we should just leave him here," Miles says, remembering the pain of gravel grinding into his knees and the desert sand soaked with the blood of innocent men on that day when he said nothing. The smell of blood is making him sick.

He has stood here and watched True weep, but he refuses to believe these tears are for Shaw. She cannot be crying for him. Her tears must be for Diego.

"He's dying," Lincoln says tiredly, tying off the tourniquet. "You can see that. Let him die in peace."

Miles checks the chamber on the pistol he's holding. He only remembers firing three or four shots, so he should still be good. *Roger that!* There's another cartridge in the chamber. "Why?" he asks, looking at Lincoln, honestly perplexed. "He doesn't deserve it."

"No, he doesn't. We're going to give it to him anyway."

Shaw's eyes are open again, turned in his direction. Miles feels himself caught in their fierce focus. He waits to hear some smart-ass remark harking back to that day—*you shouldn't have come here, Dushane*—but Shaw's brow only wrinkles in puzzlement as he whispers, "Who the fuck are you?"

True is looking up at him too, wide-eyed, fearful. Only then does Miles realize he has the pistol aimed at Shaw's head.

"No, Miles," she says.

Lincoln rises to his feet, gaze locked on the pistol. He speaks softly, "Give me the gun."

Miles shakes his head in disbelief. "He doesn't even remember that day. It's just one more forgotten atrocity for him, one more day of banal carnage. Not so different from today."

"Don't make it worse," Lincoln says.

And True: "What he did to you . . . there's no reason for it. No reason for any of it. Nungsan destroyed him. Don't let it destroy you, too."

Shaw is the calmest among them. He gives up on the puzzle of who Miles might be. Gives in to the situation. "Hell, you need some righteous justice, brother? Go ahead. Do it."

Miles is tempted, but disgust chokes off the impulse. Shaw is only playing with words. Miles knows there is nothing righteous here. Not in himself—it doesn't take a brave man to speak up from behind a gun—and not in Shaw. Miles tells him, "To forget a day like that—it's pathetic."

But that's how it goes. Atrocities, one after another, spinning off from the storm front of violent conflict, so many even the perpetrators don't remember them all. It's a reminder to Miles of the idealism that sent him into journalism post-army. It had felt necessary to tell the stories of those affected . . . both the victims and the aggressors.

It still does.

He lowers the pistol, takes out the magazine, ejects the cartridge.

"I'm writing a book," he tells Shaw. "You're going to be in it." He hands the gun and the ammunition over to Lincoln. "That's my righteous justice."

Turning back to Lincoln, he indicates with a nod the spike piercing Shaw's hand. "You want me to try to find a saw to cut that?"

"*Fuck*," Shaw says in disgust. "Just pull it out."

BITTER PHILOSOPHIES

THEY'VE LOWERED ONE side of their SUV's split backseat. Shaw is laid out there, wrapped up in an emergency blanket, with a nest of camouflage blankets padding his head against the bounce and vibration of the road. Still breathing. A bag of artificial blood sways from a hook. He's drifted in and out of sleep since a morphine injection. True watches as his eyes blink open again.

She sits cross-legged beside him, crammed into the cargo area, her shoulder against the back hatch. Rohan shares the cramped space. He's sitting with his long legs bent, an elbow over the seatback, turned so that he can watch the road ahead. Felice and Miles are squeezed into the half-seat. Lincoln is up front, with Khalid driving.

They are rushing to make a rendezvous arranged by Lincoln's State Department contact. A bulk transport helicopter has been hired to ferry them out of the country. They should be aboard in another twenty minutes.

Shaw's eyes turn to look for her. He seems uncertain. True isn't sure how well he can see. His corneas look a little cloudy. Scarring from the gasoline, maybe. She leans closer, touches his bearded cheek. "Almost there."

He surprises her with a faint smile. The scar on his upper lip—a souvenir of Nungsan—is bloodless and pale. He fainted when they lifted him from the wet ground under the anti-surveillance canopy to move him into the car, and he's said nothing since. But he speaks now, a whisper barely audible over the road noise: "*Eight years late.*"

Raw truth. It'll all be over soon and they both know it.

Before they moved him, Khalid had bandaged his hand and replaced the outer layers of the dressing on his shoulder. Shaw had spoken through that process, revisiting his bitter philosophies in a manic episode discharged in an angry, panting whisper—his last chance to get it all out there: "We're done. Done. Our time's over. The human race is getting phased out and we deserve it. Diego saw it coming. I laughed. I laughed at him when he talked about robots taking over our job. But he was right. Mechs make better soldiers. Easy to print, easy to train, ruthless. And no one gives a fuck if they're shot down, blown apart, burned up. So what are we for, True? You ask Lincoln that, okay? What's left? What's left when you're a species running on an outdated operating system? What's left to do but rage, rage."

Eight years squandered on rage. What a fucking waste. But he gave some comfort to Diego in those last hours, and even knowing what he's done since, it's a consolation for her to do the same for him. It eases the bitter ache. She braces herself against the hatch door and leans over until her lips are close to his ear. "Thank you for taking care of him. I know you would have saved him if you could."

She sits up again, swaying with the motion of the truck. He watches her in silence for another minute, maybe two. Then his eyes drift, until a final stillness comes over them.

What's left? Lincoln asks himself. He's got the air conditioning running full blast, countering the heat of too many bodies in the truck, and the stink of sweat and of blood and the faint lingering reek of gasoline . . . though that last might be his imagination.

He did what he could to secure the battle site before he left.

With Rohan and Miles helping, he searched the house and inspected the two SUVs. All the weapons they found—assault rifles, handguns, grenades—they stacked in one vehicle, setting it on fire before they left. The electronics—tablets, laptops, phones, cameras—he confiscated. Tamara might find something useful in them.

He left the second SUV to the two surviving Al-Furat soldiers, along with the task of dealing with their dead comrades. Maybe they've left the bodies to rot, but Lincoln was hoping they would take them somewhere and bury them, out of sight. What he was certain about was that they would not risk arrest by going to any police or other authority to report what had happened.

The starburst copter that had dueled with the sentinel was a loss. Tamara lost contact with it, concluding that the two battling machines likely collided, or if there was a victor, it probably ran out of battery power before it could return. Their second copter and Roach are back in their shipping containers, secured to the roof racks along with the rest of the team's equipment. There's no room anymore for the gear inside the packed SUV.

He turns to check on the team. Miles gazes out the window, lost in thought. Next to him, Felice is nodding. Rohan, who's leaning on the seatback, notices his gaze. He turns to nudge True, who looks up, red-rimmed eyes bright and fierce and bitter. When she sees Lincoln, her lips part as if she's about to speak, but she changes her mind and instead she draws her fingers across her throat. And it hits him, a sharp blow, more painful than he thought it'd be. He nods brusquely and turns back to face the road ahead.

What's left?

Shaw said a lot when Khalid and True were working on him, getting him ready to move. Lincoln heard most of it, words that might be easy to dismiss as the ravings of a dying man, except that more and more lately, Lincoln has been thinking the same things.

When autonomous fighters command the air space, self-driving tanks control the ground, and agile robotic vehicles scout and secure cramped urban areas, what need will there be for soldiers on the front lines?

Times change. War grows ever more impersonal. Anyone who dares to look can see it coming. Combat duty will be limited to a control room half a world away from the front line. That's where Lincoln is supposed to be now.

His prosthetic hand runs through the tapping sequence. He regards it, admiring its functionality but resenting the limitations it puts on him. And he is conscious of the blindside deficit in his vision that makes him see Khalid as an indistinct figure behind the wheel, cast in shades of gray.

He is not qualified for field duty. He knows this time he's going home for good. That shouldn't feel like a tragedy—God knows he's experienced his share of battles—but it does anyway. *What's left?* He's acutely conscious of a sense of loss, of dislocation, not just for himself, but for a profession that reaches back to the days of the American Revolution. Soldiers, always ready to step up when they were needed, ready to serve, to trade their lives for the defense of the country.

It'll be robots instead in the years to come, because, like Shaw said, who gives a fuck if they're shot down, blown apart, or burned up? Better to lose machines than sons and daughters, right?

Yes!

Lincoln has been shot, blown apart, and burned. He doesn't ever need to experience any of those things again, doesn't need to see others suffer them.

He asks himself again: *What's left?*

This time he has an answer. Claire is at home. She might still be willing to try to patch their broken marriage. Unlike his father, he might get to see his children grow up. He's grateful for that chance.

Even so, it provokes him to think that his profession will become the exclusive province of programmers, mechanics, engineers, and the autonomous systems they design.

Autonomous warfare will not be bloodless. War by machine proxy is still war, with the sacrifice pushed out of sight, the burden unloaded on distant people. The repercussions, inevitable.

It's not hard for him to imagine an armed Arkinson—or something worse—engaging above an American city.

The tragedy of the world is that for all the clever minds and brave hearts that have ever been, no one has figured out yet how to forge a lasting peace. Lincoln is confident that armed conflict will not be going away. If he keeps Requisite Operations on the cutting edge of battlefield technology, he could be in business for a long, long time.

Alex sits on the wide ground-level deck behind the house, boots propped up on a stool, gazing at the trees across the lawn, watching their shapes slowly emerge from the grip of an early-morning fog. He hasn't slept all night. Yesterday he went home from work early after messing up on a call. He let them know he wouldn't be back—not until he knew if she was alive, if she was coming home, if he could ever forgive her.

He's read her last message a hundred times. *I'm with Lincoln now, and this is almost over.*

The deck heater kicks on, humming quietly as it struggles against the cold. His phone is on the table beside him. Jameson called thirty minutes ago to say the team had recovered Shaw Walker and were on their way to a pickup point, but since then the phone has been maddeningly silent.

When it finally does ring in its standard-issue corporate chime, he doesn't reach for it right away. He lets the tune play for several seconds before he leans over to see who's calling. If it's Jameson, it's probably another update. If it's Chris . . . well, that would be bad news.

The call is from her.

He picks up. Waits.

"Hey," she says after a few seconds. Her voice sad, hoarse. He thinks she's been crying.

"You all right?" he asks gruffly.

"I'm not hurt."

"Jameson said you're bringing Shaw home."

"Yeah."

"Was it worth it, True?"

She takes a few seconds. When she does answer, she speaks

slowly, trying to find the right words. "You told me that Nungsan was like a black hole that we'll always be circling around. You were right. It'll always be there. But we don't have to look at it all the time. I don't have to. Not anymore. Alex, are you going to be there when I get home?"

He thinks about this, thinks about his options, and tells her the truth: "Where the hell else would I be?"

"Okay, then. I'm on my way."

Acknowledgments

I want to thank those who helped with *The Last Good Man*. First and most essential, my freelance editor, Judith Tarr, who read an early and incomplete version of the manuscript. Her feedback helped me to move ahead with the story and, when I had a complete draft, Judy went over the manuscript again, providing insightful suggestions throughout.

Early beta readers were Larry Clough, Mark English, and Nancy Jane Moore. My agent, Howard Morhaim, provided additional suggestions, as did Andy Baguio. After I completed another round of revisions, Alex von der Linden took on the heroic task of reading the manuscript during the holiday season. Vonda N. McIntyre provided detailed feedback on a near-final draft, and Cat Rambo did an incredibly helpful line edit.

I also want to acknowledge those who helped with research questions: Yasser Bahjatt, Nyan Aung, Aung Phone Myint, Ramez Naam, and Ken Liu.

Everyone mentioned here has my thanks and my gratitude. They tried to steer me in the right direction. All remaining errors and deficiencies are my own.

I'm grateful as well for all those who share their knowledge via the Internet. Without you, this novel could not have been written.

And last, but certainly not least, thank you to my readers. I'm so deeply grateful for your continuing support and encouragement.

Linda Nagata
February 20, 2017